SPIRIT'S TETHER

a novel by

John C. McLucas

SPIRIT'S TETHER

Editor: Clarinda Harriss
Graphic Design: Ace Kieffer
Cover Photo: John C. McLucas
Author Photo: L. Hewitt Photography

BrickHouse Books, Inc. / Stonewall 2020
306 Suffolk Road
Baltimore, MD 21218

Distributor: Itasca Books, Inc.

ISBN: 978-1-938144-72-1

Printed in the United States of America

For my students,
my teachers,
my colleagues,
my neighbors,
my family and friends,
and
(with lightness)
Italo Calvino:

"Thou art in the midst of them."

TABLE OF CONTENTS

Chapter 1 9

Chapter 2 24

Chapter 3 40

Chapter 4 61

Chapter 5 82

Chapter 6 97

Chapter 7 115

Chapter 8 133

Chapter 9 160

Chapter 10 179

Chapter 11 206

Chapter 12 229

Chapter 13 261

Chapter 1
July 2015
[flashback: earlier that month]

After Joe's sudden death in the summer of 2015, the subtle and gracious Rachel did something she virtually never did: she gave direct orders to people she loved.

"Jimmy," she told her only child, "you will move into Godfather Jim's house. He needs you. You'll keep him grounded as he adjusts to life without Uncle Joe."

I learned only later that she had said this to Jimmy. At the time, to me, she said,

"Jim, your godson needs you. He can help you around the house, and you'll keep him grounded as he starts graduate school."

Jacob Fleischer-Neuberg was named after his paternal grandfather Josiah Neuberg, but from before he was born he was called "Jimmy" by everyone who knew him, in my honor. Technically, it was just a fond fiction that I was his godfather. His parents were Jewish, and Joe and I thought they were increasingly observant after his birth, but really his birth had allowed us to understand how privately observant they had always been. It was a point of pride with them to adopt the term "godfather," to make public their reliance on a Christian gay friend in the raising of their only child. On the "godfather" issue, it was almost pointless for me to observe that, as a Presbyterian, I didn't really have any particular notion of what a godfather was or did.

Jimmy's father Tony was my best friend from college; well, to be honest, I was in love with him for many years. Rachel and I had spent decades negotiating whatever tensions lingered from my adolescent passion for her husband. Joe, however, had come along just in time, shortly before Jimmy's birth, my mismatched and perfectly adored lover, life companion, "husband." (I was too old ever to get used to that word. Even calling him my "partner" early on had felt mercantile and assimilationist to me, but in time, legally as well as emotionally, we were married.) For twenty-some years we four lived our lives as couples in tandem, parallel, proving to the world that gay and straight friends could share values and commitment.

Watching Jimmy grow had been one of the deepest and most bewildering joys of my life with Joe. We never had children of our own, and Jimmy was not the son we could by any stretch of the imagination have had. His bris in April of 1994 was one of the first public acts of our life together. This was just before Joe actually moved to Baltimore to live with me; he was still wrapping up the strands of his life in LA. We met at O'Hare and went to stay in the most lavish of the guest suites at Tony and Rachel's sprawling Prairie Style house in Glencoe. We firmly said "Mazel tov" to the few skeptical relatives who found it hard to understand what we were doing there or even that we were there together. We helped Tony and Rachel tend the ugly little bundle who lodged occasional mewing protests against his private truncation. Two or three times, in the first days after the ceremony, it fell to us to change the dressing on what the rabbi, to dispel drama at a critical liturgical moment, had called "a nice-sized penis."

My relationship with Jimmy was always uniquely intimate. The first time I cradled him, I thought that I had never seen a funnier-looking baby: purple in strange places, raisin-faced, his large head asymmetrically crowned with thick black hair. It was one of life's oddities that two parents so extremely handsome could have produced such a bizarre little monkey. Yet in my arms, that very first time, he compassed a seduction as complete as if an infant Barrymore had set out on purpose to make me his vassal forever. Within half an hour there was nothing left of my freedom. I was afraid that someone would try to take him away from me, and part of my mind was calculating how I could hide him in my overcoat and escape the house before the police were called. Rachel, perhaps relieved to have him off her for a bit after an exhausting labor, and preparing for the frenzy of a large house party and ceremony, looked up from the couch, smiling guiltily, and asked,

"Aren't you sick of holding him?"

"I'm sick of being manipulated, if that's what you mean."

Joe convinced himself, and most of the public, that he was the one who understood babies. On his side was the fact that Jimmy quieted and cooed as if on cue any time he was swept up into Joe's muscular embrace. Joe radiated physical centeredness at a cellular level. Jimmy felt it, and always leaned into him as though nestling against a brick wall wreathed in soft ivy tendrils and warmed by a summer sun. With me he was often fretful and fussy, tetchy, as a famous nurse might have said; yet I clearly fascinated him. He would stare into my eyes with his remote, azure enchanters, and, though I couldn't be sure that he liked me, I had an electric awareness of a sentient creature, not mine and not myself, who was sizing me up and making critical decisions about my reliability and discretion.

Once that first weekend, Tony looked at us and said, "I think he knows your name already."

"He knows he'll be able to hit me up for money when he learns to talk," I said. I hugged him a little closer and kissed the top of his chaotic head possessively. He complained with choking little cries, and Joe took him from me. As his puppy voice was stilled and he melted into the contentment of Uncle Joe's enveloping affection, he continued to look at me, not with reproach, but with curiosity and perhaps a very mild disillusionment, as though he'd tried to tell me something important and I hadn't understood him.

As Jimmy grew, he became a distinctly odd child. Of course he was terribly smart, but he was owlish and stand-offish as a toddler. He was a sturdy kid, and in repose he might have been described as athletic, but in action he was cautious, tentative, and solemn. He might whine over nothing. He seemed to have inherited none of his parents' good looks: from Tony, he took his penetrating blue eyes and firm, determined gait, but with none of Tony's prowling energy. Rachel's thick, curly black hair – on her, a magnificent frame to her proud Mediterranean features – on Jimmy was just a disorderly mop. He had also inherited her aquiline profile, and for several preadolescent years he seemed all nose.

He always liked things to be orderly and hierarchic. He looked up from his high chair once at breakfast to announce, "I'm the boss of my orange juice." Another time, when the family cat jumped onto the top of a kitchen cabinet, he looked at her disapprovingly and then, turning to me, said, "S'posed to be down."

Early on, I noticed that he was extremely musical. Rachel loved music; she played piano decently and had a fair grasp of canonical classical repertoire. Tony notoriously could barely carry a tune and responded only to jungle beats for dancing, when he danced at all. The main artistic result of his undergraduate experiments with playing the guitar had been a drawing I did of him practicing once in our dorm room. Though I was not a particularly gifted draftsman, the picture documented, and would have clearly communicated to a space alien, my unspoken, closeted devotion and desire. He put the guitar aside forever shortly after.

Somehow, these two had produced a little boy whose native language seemed to be music. Jimmy would toddle to the piano and pick out little tunes, often in exactly the same key and/or tempo as something we'd just heard on the radio. He was also an uncanny mimic, and at three years old could already repeat simple songs from memory after hearing them twice. His voice was charming and true. When Joe and I visited, or when the Fleischer-Neubergs came to us in Baltimore, it quickly became a tradition that we would tuck him in. He loved "Golden Slumbers," which I often sang to him, but it was almost counterproductive at bedtime because he would devise descants instead of letting himself be lulled. The first time I told his parents that I thought he was unusual was when I realized that his improvisation was actually a standard bass part transposed up into his fluty treble octave.

Any time he complained over the next couple of decades about practicing the piano or studying theory, Tony or Rachel would say, "Blame Godfather Jim. He told us you were a little Mozart." By the time he was ten or eleven, he could accompany any song Joe or I wanted to sing, once we sketched out the tune for him. I didn't even have to remember the key for familiar songs; I'd just say, "It goes up to an F" and he would take it from there. He was a rising virtuoso on the keyboard, knocking out serious classical piano repertory with mechanical precision and also picking up the basics of other instruments. He was writing his own music by nine or ten, primitive and rhythmic, and glacially dissonant.

He also was almost incapable of making eye contact with strangers. He interacted as little as possible with classmates, and looked furtive and unhappy at gatherings of more than four or five people.

Jimmy adored Joe...followed him around wordlessly, sat in his lap, turned big quiet inquiring eyes up at him during adult conversations which he couldn't follow. But with me, Jimmy seemed to be ashamed of not having more to say. Any piano was a sanctuary for him. If he entered a room with people and a piano, he would always turn to the keyboard as if it were the only sane person present, and if he could get away from the people and sit before the piano he would look relieved and calmed. Often when we were together and his verbal shyness became uncomfortable for either of us, I would just ask him to play. He knew that I loved Schumann's *"Traümerei"* because my mother had often played it on our family heirloom Victorian square-grand piano. He would find a way to modulate and segue into variations on the piece when he felt me approaching. I would wordlessly put my hand on his shoulder as soon as I recognized the tune. When he reached adolescence, I came to associate this gesture with the slightly sour smell of his clothes. He had very vague views of personal hygiene, and Rachel sometimes had trouble wrestling him out of his favorite shirts or underwear.

Around ten or twelve, he became much less reticent in speaking, and took on a preachy, stilted, otherworldly courtliness of diction, with occasional lapses into babyish repetitious speech patterns from a few years before. What would seem pompous or arrogant in other kids sounded like just part of Jimmy's quirky angular personality. Once when he was in junior high, he gave me the scribbled score of a song he'd just written which started with the voice unaccompanied. He nodded, a bit condescendingly, to indicate that I could begin, and when nothing happened he looked at me to see why I wasn't singing.

"Uh – could you give me the starting note?" I asked. He smiled genially... a boy whom I had held in my arms at his bris.

"Oh, that's right; I forget not everyone has perfect pitch," he said.

Through his teen years, he dealt with some social deficits. His laser intelligence and perfect retention of content made him off-putting to his peers. He did have a few friends, with whom he plunged into shared obsessions and intense colloquies in private dialects. The rest of his classmates held little interest for him, and Rachel worried he was lonely at school. In his mid-teens, he grew, suddenly and a lot. He was suddenly towering over his parents, gawkish and slouching, with hands out of all proportion and a tendency to knock over furniture from several feet away. It was as though a shy skittish moose colt has invaded their house. His voice also plummeted to an insecure bass, but in moments of excitement he could span three octaves within a few seconds, hitting shrieky heights at times, even after puberty had settled.

Jacob, "Jimmy" (I eventually took to calling him "Jimmy Jack" and, in time, "J.J.") was a complicated presence in my world. I was nervous about his future, though Joe waved away my worries and exasperations, implying that all of Jimmy's oddities would adjust themselves in time. He was shy and awkward; he was dreamy, detached, self-consulting, inward-turning, and childish, and brilliant in ways which didn't make life easier for him. I accepted his homeliness and all the strange edginess of his social interactions, but I withheld certain kinds of approval because I hoped to signal him, without words, that his speech or silences or behaviors were unconventional and perhaps hard for others to understand. My constant worry made me a bit irritable with him sometimes. Even so, he kept his dazed, inarticulate focus on me from his infancy, and he always seemed to know that, beneath my austerities, I fiercely believed in him.

Though I knew that Joe loved Jimmy deeply and saw him, as he saw everything, realistically and in three dimensions, I always felt that I knew him better, because I was more neurotic than Joe, and I understood strangeness from the inside out. I also believed, though I never dared to say it out loud, that I *loved* Jimmy Jack more than Joe did, perhaps more than even Tony and Rachel did. I loved him quite literally as though he were my own child, and every eyelash and cuticle of him was perfect to me.

He repaid me a thousand-fold. He always had ways of showing, oh so oddly, that I was his favorite. He would shoot me looks of complicit, naked amusement; he took my hand without warning as toddler and teenager; he lagged behind or ran ahead to walk with me in group outings. When he was six or seven, he once asked Rachel's mother if she could guess whom he loved most in the whole world. Of course she knew he would name her, and was starting to make a modest grandmotherly moue. When he was sure he had everyone's attention, he squeaked, "Godfather Jim." I would not have embarrassed Mrs. Fleischer for anything on earth, and I could feel her surprise and mild, mortified disappointment from across the room. She recovered instantly and said, "That's sweet, honey; you *know* how he loves you." I gave her a grateful look. No one in the room wanted to reprimand the little guy for his faulty diplomacy, but we all felt that she had taken a bullet for civility and domestic harmony. Nevertheless, it was and remained one of the most purely gratifying moments of my life, one which I treasured privately and never mentioned again to anyone. In my mind and heart, there was absolutely nothing wrong with Jimmy Fleischer-Neuberg.

Starting around sixteen, he had a girlfriend named Lyric. She was willowy and poetic, pretty and vapid, with long blond hair and an affected hippyish gentle speech pattern. She was a source of great relief to Rachel especially, who had been afraid that her little Ferdinand the Bull would never find a mate. She became a fixture at the Glencoe house, locked with J.J. into shared sensitivities no mere grown-up could comprehend. Lyric sang in a voice I found gratingly sweet and childlike, and Jimmy wrote songs for her to poems of his own composition, largely about evanescence and diaphanous sublimity. Joe once suggested in private that Jimmy might want to write about his own life and feelings. Jimmy looked at him with genuine compassion.

"I write for Lyric," he said. "Her voice is from another universe. She's in touch with things you don't think about yet."

Joe was seven years younger than me. Once or twice he had suggested to me that I didn't understand his generation. He looked to me for sympathy when Jimmy pontificated in this way, and received none.

When Jimmy went to college at Northeastern, majoring in piano but taking and acing just about every course in the catalog, Lyric went to Berklee to study voice. Joe and I hoped that their being on the East Coast would bring them more closely into our world, but of course Boston and Baltimore weren't all that close, and we considered ourselves lucky if they came down for Thanksgiving or for a couple of days of Spring Break. They would huddle in the guest room talking in their private code, and then emerge for meals, hand in hand, exchanging looks of soulful reciprocity.

Lyric sometimes explained Jimmy to me.

"He's learning so much," she said once during their freshman year, "that I'm afraid he'll lose his simplicity."

"You think he's simple?" I asked, hoping to sound civil.

"He's got a perfect woodland spirit," she said, a straight-tone Pythia. "His teachers are trying to civilize him."

Rachel almost never mentioned Lyric without the adjective "lovely." She seemed to delight in saying "My son's lovely young lady." I hadn't ever really taken to Lyric, and as she and Jimmy reached young adulthood, that didn't change. As a senior college professor, I felt I could claim to know something about the young. Once or twice over the years I came close to criticizing Lyric to Rachel. On the phone after the exchange about the perfection of Jimmy's spirit, I said something cranky to her about it.

"Lyric is a bit earnest and she means to be wise," Rachel said. "She thinks she really loves Jimmy, and we should never make light of people's attempts to love. Time will tell. They're young yet." The Presbyterian elder in me agreed with her, but my allergy to Lyric was unassuaged and I had a feeling of traps being laid for Jimmy. He might drift, or be herded, into marriage with her. I was afraid that he would discover fifteen years later that he really wanted to transgress, to make awful juvenile mistakes, to stand on eminences in thunderstorms and be lashed with Wagnerian passions which would probably take disruptive forms. In bed that night, I tried complaining about Lyric to Joe. He always seemed perfectly at ease with her, and treated her with the same off-hand politeness and good humor he directed at everyone he didn't actively dislike. In response to my grouchy comment about Lyric, he hummed, as he always did when thinking, and then said,

"Yeah, she can be a bit much." He thought for a second. "No one's good enough for your Jimmy Jack."

"Can you actually picture them together in the long run?" I asked sullenly.

"Not our call, Tiger," he said, and rolled over away from me. I put an arm around him, spooning gently, and said,

"She makes him weird."

"Uh – he's fairly weird to begin with."

"Right," I said; "that's why she bugs me. I wish he'd meet some nice brassy girl who would make him mad sometimes and goad him out of his goofy cage... make him a little more..."

"Jim," Joe said, starting to sound sleepy and tired of the topic, a tone in his voice which was often the prelude to a bead-read, "you know our boy is kind of spectrum-y, don't you?"

I'd never heard that term. I had always resisted pathologizing Jimmy's otherness, but the diminutive "–y" was fond and undramatic, and I found it helpful and funny.

"He'll be fine," Joe continued. "Everyone loves him, did you ever notice that? For his weird goofy self. No one takes offense when he's strange. You need to relax about him. If he and Lyric are meant to be together, they'll be together."

"I think you're a very good uncle," I said, hugging him tighter.

They came to stay again in the fall of 2014 when Jimmy was interviewing for a Master's program in composition at Peabody. A few years earlier, Joe and I had moved into an old brick townhouse in Bolton Hill, a twenty-minute walk from the Peabody campus. I had to suppress my eagerness for Jimmy to choose Peabody (I had essentially no doubt he would get in) because I knew he was considering most of the other top conservatories in the country. Lyric was applying too, for a graduate program in voice, though I was less sanguine about her chances. They ran through a couple of her audition pieces for Joe and me the night before she was to sing for the faculty.

With her Berklee training, her voice had become even more tediously pure. She sang Servilia's *"Se altro che lacrime,"* with Jimmy coiled at the keyboard of my late mother's piano like an obedient trained chimp. She sang perfectly in tune and had a silvery shimmer in her sustained upper notes that vaguely reminded me of Lucia Popp. Though I loved the aria and though she sang it intelligently, something about the performance made me want to throw them both through the front parlor windows. It wasn't just that her Mozart was gutless; it was that she made Jimmy's Mozart gutless, and he let her do it. While Joe and I applauded politely, the two kids simpered and awarded themselves the Nobel Prize for Exquisiteness of Execution, and I felt sterile and angry.

That may have been the first time that I ever consciously wished Jimmy were gay.

In the event, Jimmy did choose Peabody. He and Lyric found an apartment across Mount Vernon Place from the school, and would be moving to town in late August, even though she had not been accepted into the graduate voice program.

Then Joe died.

I staggered through Joe's funeral by force of will and habits of public decorum. There was a deep, unaddressable wrongness in the universe for which I held the Most High directly responsible. My historic downtown church, which boasted the wackiest lefty congregation and the most magnificent Victorian Gothic sanctuary in the city, had been my home for over thirty years, one in which Joe had gradually found his own place and where he was universally loved. I was used to finding comfort there. Through this ordeal, though, there was none. There was good will, there were the kindest friends, and yet I remained numb and unreachable. Perhaps the worst part was that no one seemed to notice anything strange about my behavior. Everyone was gentle, solicitous, two steps ahead of me in my tiniest unspoken wish. I wondered if maybe my normal personality were so repressed and robotic that people couldn't tell the difference between me before and me after this stunning bereavement.

My widowed mother-in-law, Constanzia "Connie" Piatelli Andreoli, came down from Brooklyn with one of Joe's sisters and two of his brothers and an assortment of grandchildren. All of them were dear and kind, immersed in shocked mourning of their own which they shared with me in tenderness and respect. They all acknowledged without words that my loss was the greatest. Connie threw her arms around me with deep tenor-clef sobs when she first arrived, and called me "my other boy" and sat right next to me every chance she got, holding my hand as though we were posing for a picture.

At the service itself, she clung to my arm as we hobbled down the center aisle to take our places as chief mourners in the front pew. She had visited the church many times, and had a vague awareness that Presbyterians did certain things differently. Still, she always referred to any church service anywhere as "Mass," and the Communion table was always the "altar" to her. For Joe's funeral, she wore the deepest mourning – the Queen Dowager of Spain processing into the chapel of the Escorial – with a black veil that seemed to fill the visual field from front door to pulpit.

This provided perhaps the closest thing to comfort my frozen lacerated heart got that day: a visible sign that things were bleak, barren, changed, abnormal, awful. As we reached the front of the church, she stopped in front of the Communion table where the urn with Joe's ashes sat among red and white roses, in front of a Celtic cross. She crossed herself and genuflected deeply, to a sacrament which was not present in any part of the building. I could feel a shiver of respectful surprise ripple through the congregation; probably no member or friend there had ever seen a mourner dressed like that for a funeral, and her heartbroken bending of the knee showed a Catholic piety which they found exotic. Yet even that felt right to me for that moment. Joe wasn't there, and there was no holiness left in the world, and her faltering, elderly curtsey was an acknowledgement of absence, and an unspoken, near-insolent reproach to authorities which had badly mismanaged things.

By the next afternoon, Joe's family had all left. I would be seeing them at Christmas if not before. No one was left at my house but Tony, Rachel, and Jimmy Jack. Knowing that these out-of-towners would stay another night, even my sister and her son had left, and Walter and Ricardo and Marie had gone back to Washington after the reception. Neighbors had brought food; there was really nothing that needed doing. Tony was by me on the sofa. Time had become imprecise, and conversation seemed disjointed and pointless.

Suddenly I had to tell Tony something.

"He knew it was happening," I said.

"What, buddy?"

"He knew he was dying. He said I could handle it. He said I was brave." These words had just come back to me from the incredibly few days earlier when Joe had died in my arms. Everyone by then had heard the medical details – the freak infarction, the undiagnosed, asymptomatic underlying heart disease, the almost painless collapse, the sweet lucidity up to and through the very last moments. But these words of Joe's had gone into a file seared shut in my mind in those surreal instants. Tony's being there apparently unlocked something in my memory. "But I'm not brave. Not at all."

A great bleak vista spread out before me, filled with alarms and affrights which I had never needed to name. There was something appalling about them and, to my own complete astonishment, a sob of pure fear and grief came up out of me. No other words could follow. I felt all three of them freeze in sympathy. By long habit, I expected Rachel to find the right words to get us through this seizure. But Tony was next to me.

He had always been such a rock of common sense, such a dependable regular guy, that even after forty-plus years of intimate friendship I wasn't always prepared for his wisdom and emotional courage – what I sometimes called his beautiful Jewish soul. As a Presbyterian elder floundered and decompensated in a dark wood beside him, he knew exactly how to hold me. Tony was physically strong in a way that reminded me of Joe, and I sagged into that refuge. I was doing something I had absolutely no memory of ever having done in my life: sobbing openly. It felt horrible, dangerous, and marrow-deep painful, as though jagged broken bones might start breaking the skin and protruding all over my body. I thought Tony would be embarrassed by my display, but instead he just crooned and cradled a bit, saying quietly,

"Of course you're brave. Of course you're brave. The only person who knows you as well as Joe did is me, and we both agree. You're a brave, brave guy." I continued to cry, sorry that I was probably drooling on Tony's crisp blue shirt.

Jimmy came and perched nervously behind me. It was not easy for him to approach me: he had never written an atonal song or neo-Symbolist poem about feelings like these. He leaned his curly head forward onto my shoulder and just breathed softly while his father held me. It took a moment for him to find words in his inexperienced, devoted young heart.

"It's amazing that Uncle Joe had that clarity as he was dying," he said. His voice was so soft that it stayed in his lowest bass register; there were no sudden falsetto yelps. "Only a great soul can face that. He was taking care of you when he said you were brave. He was *making* you brave."

A moment later, I stopped crying, almost as suddenly as I'd started. Maybe I was "cried out," as I'd heard people sometimes say. Jimmy's odd words had brought me some balm. I straightened up and Tony said, "Aw" and they both hugged me. I had one arm around the firm Doric shaft that was Tony, one around Jimmy's willow-sapling waist. No one laughed with relief; no one said "Jim Sandwich" or "Group hug"; but for the first time, I started to imagine that there might be comfort in the world.

When I had recovered enough to look over at Rachel, I saw her eyes brimming… with love and compassion, yes, but also with deep pride in what Jimmy had just done.

"Tiger, come here. I need you."

Joe's voice had an abnormal distinctness and I jumped up from my desk chair and ran into the bathroom. He was standing at the sink, holding on to its edge, oddly hunched on his bare legs. He looked at me, smiled a little shyly, and said,

"Help me sit down."

Joe was always a strong man: a strict gym regimen in support of his acting/modeling career, and a naturally robust Italian constitution. He was almost never sick, and never expressed physical vulnerabilities. Startled into efficiency and operating strictly on muscle memories of impersonal politeness, I put my arms around him. I felt an odd momentary physical detachment from this man with whom I had shared twenty-two years of embraces. Together we sat, a bit awkwardly, on the bathroom floor.

"You feel woozy?" I asked.

"A little," he said, apologetically. "It's better sitting down." He was slightly disoriented by his own sudden faintness. He gave me one of his cagey flirty smiles, the ones he always used to manage his cranky older lover. "It's better with you here."

He felt warm and muscular in my arms, like a thick flexible tree with the resin running in hot sun. Joe was always my link to normality and vitality. I didn't know what to make of this unsteadiness, totally out of character.

"Shall I call someone? Do you want some water or something?"

"I just want my Tiger, and he's right here." He looked up from my shoulder and his gaze shot directly into mine. His beautiful green eyes were one of the dependable joys of my life. I felt reassured; he needed a little time for the spell to pass, and then we'd get him up and maybe make a doctor's appointment.

"I know you," he went on. "You're not afraid of anything. You can do this."

"Do what?" I asked. He had just said I was unafraid, yet in a nanosecond I was nothing but fear. An awful premonition singed my follicles. My Presbyterian brain stem still kicked in and I continued falsely poised, unfazed. I smiled at him, as though he were being silly.

"This," he said, closing his eyes as though he were tired. "You're my love." He had said that many years before, soon after quoting Auden to end our first terrible quarrel.

"We'll just take a minute and then stand you up and make you some chicken soup," I said. I heard how practical and maiden-auntish that sounded, even as some part of me felt an existential abyss opening below us. Some gentle angel prompted me now and, without seeming alarmed, I squeezed him, quite hard, and said, my voice catching a little, "You're *my* love… always." Just in time.

"Yeah," he said, giving a contented soft snuggle into my shoulder. His curls had lots of grey by now, but there was no wiriness or bristle; they had never been anything but silky, and their tickle along my throat now was a caress.

He made a sudden little grunting, humming sound, as though suppressing the almost pleasurable strain of a slight physical effort. He threw his head back a little and opened his eyes just enough to give me a yearning, serene, disembodied small smile. It was a look I had often seen on his face when we reached shared climaxes in bed. Then his jade pine emerald seaweed clover eyes closed and his weight seemed to double against my chest.

I knew instantly that he was dead. I hoped he would forgive me my first thought: that the "little death" and the great one had been, for him, identical. My life as a professor of Italian language and literature made that thought self-evident and inevitable. Joe knew me well enough not to be insulted.

He was still in the room and I had to stay with him, to protect him from whatever fear or confusion he now faced at negotiating the next steps. Simultaneously I knew that he was trying to come back, or at least to save me from what I would soon feel. We worried for each other, as we always had, but after all I was older and I had to take the lead. I was a thousand years old and Joe was a child, a precious prattling young explorer in uncharted territory. We had never been so close.

'Divo,' I thought, 'you just go forward now. You and I will always be together. I'll be fine.'

These were automatic thoughts, things I'd sometimes actually said out loud to friends dying of AIDS years before, to my mother as she faded into her cancer. I cradled Joe for a moment, willing to hope for a miracle.

After a moment I laid him down on the floor. His supple big body needed very little arranging. The experienced model had naturally lapsed into a dignified handsomeness, like a mediaeval Celtic tomb slab in a "Lord of the Rings" movie. I saw him entire: his reliable sexiness and the homey press of his arms, his companionable masculine presence, his voice, his scent, his smiles, his contours, the absolute rightness of the fit as he accepted my love and offered his. All were sweetly familiar. He was hovering, perhaps admiring his own good looks, dispassionately, professionally, as he often did, with absolutely no vanity. I thought he might also be trying to slip back into that well known, expertly used body. In a moment he would open his eyes and we could discuss what had just happened.

'Come back if you can, Joe,' I thought, a rote thought bordered by a rising panic. 'But I think you may need to look for light somewhere; I think there's someone who comes for you.' I knew that Joe's body would soon grow colder. If he was coming back, it needed to be now.

Joe looked down at me and smiled gently. With his usual cool kindness, practicality, modesty, he opened a door and walked through it. He glanced back at me almost impersonally, but with a shadow of sympathy and regret, and then he turned away and the door closed behind him. I looked at what was now just his body, every inch of it familiar, lovely, wanted, known, dear. It was empty now.

With a sudden shudder I scuttled backwards on the floor, scrabbling with hands and feet till I was stopped by the side of the bathtub. Wedged miserably against it, I looked at Joe's body with mixed horror and sorrow. Something dreadful happened in my throat, and from a great distance I heard an old man make a squeaky, howling cry, Lear on the heath in the opera Verdi never quite wrote... mercifully, because its grief would have driven the world mad.

"Joe!" I called.

No one and nothing answered.

Chapter 2
August 2015
[flashback: July]

Tony and Rachel and Jimmy were heading back to Chicago two days after the funeral. As the coffee was steeping in the kitchen before breakfast that morning, Rachel told me that they had decided Jimmy was to live at my house come Fall. She said it was something I could do for him during what might be an awkward time of transition. I would be doing her son a favor by sheltering him for a time. She also told me that Lyric would not be moving in, though Jimmy didn't know this yet.

Tony was upstairs packing. When Jimmy came down and the three of us were seated in the dining room, I asked him if he was OK with the idea of moving in. He already knew the guest room that was meant for him. It was private and had its own bath. His new friends would always be welcome. He would have no official Jim-sitting or housekeeping responsibilities, I said, and should plan on coming and going as he pleased.

"No rules," he said; "no promises needed. This is where I belong, G.J." This was his new solution to what to call me: "Godfather Jim" had made sense for years, but it would be too cumbersome for daily use and perhaps embarrassingly juvenile in front of his future grad student friends. "Plus I love your piano." That had the ring of truth. Almost no one else could coax tones so lovely from my plunky, muted, introverted old instrument. Its parlor timbre made his chilly compositions sound gentle, and when he called on it for power, he knew exactly the indirect, insistent encouragements that brought it to whatever crests and peaks it was capable of. "And… Lyric and I don't know anyone in Baltimore."

I looked at Rachel. She turned him and said,

"Jimmy, play something for us while we talk." He was obviously used to obeying her. He got up from the table without complaint or counter-offer, and ambled to the piano in the front room, where he hunched ungracefully over the keyboard. The music of Jimmy finding his way into an idea started to fill the house.

I took a moment to look at Rachel, almost as though I'd never seen her before. In our mid-sixties, she did not look a single moment younger than she was, though she was still, as she had been for decades, the most beautiful woman I knew. She was far too proud to resort to any expedients. She had never cut her hair short, and she virtually never wore it down; it fell easily past her waist when she did. She still had the aristocratic tilt of the head which came from the heavy chignon at the nape of her neck. When we were younger, I had imagined that someday her hair would be a lustrous white, like that of commanding old-money Yankee matriarchs. Instead, it had simply quieted over the decades from the lustrous black of our youth to a rich Deco interlacing of greys and silvers. Her face was lined, tightly laid over noble bones, and lit by wise, incisive black eyes. Years before, her eyes had been deeply kind. Time and life had added flashes of irony and freedom from illusion. It was a sibyl's face, taut and worn, fine, deeply-etched, unimpressed yet not jaded, interested in life, expecting nothing, ready for beauty and goodness when they happened along. While I believed her marriage had remained strong, her high-profile career as a children's rights activist had meant a roller-coaster ride through shifting political seasons, and had summoned forcefulness and toughness which I hadn't initially suspected in her.

Most of all, Jimmy was not the easiest child she might have had. She had been almost forty-two when he was born, and we had all assumed that, being Rachel, she would have the perfect child and raise him effortlessly. Well, perfect or no, Jimmy through the years had been at times demanding, dysregulated, timorous, blustering, pompous, and inappropriate. Rachel did her best to guide him through the shoals of his unusual giftedness and awkwardness. She was a rock against which he could always lean, but she also loaded him with strictures, hints, and micro-disapprovals, to help him learn what people expected. In particular, she had always shown a detectable disappointment when he fled company, and she summoned a beaming smile when he overcame his reluctance for social engagement.

"My son is a born schmoozer," or "No one works a room like my son," she would say complacently at such moments, loudly enough for him to hear her, to the stifled smiles of her closest friends.

"Yes he is!" or "You got that right!" we would murmur, furtively catching each other's eyes; "Yessiree!"

Now, while Jimmy meandered through chord progressions which made perfect sense to him, she leaned over her cooling coffee and spoke to me directly.

"I'll talk to Lyric and her parents," she said, "sometime in the next few days. They'll understand. Well, I mean I'll *make* them understand." She gave a little apologetic smile of self-irony. I couldn't recall a single time I had heard Rachel raise her voice to get her way, but I knew that Lyric would never move into any of my guest rooms and that I would never be required to discuss the subject again. "Then I'll tell Jimmy. I don't think he'll mind. He may secretly be glad to have you all to himself. He idolizes you. Maybe even more than he did his Uncle Joe. Joe was so kind, so much fun, so casually approving. Jimmy has always been a little in awe of you, though."

I must have looked quizzical; this was certainly a new idea for me.

"Your doctorate, Jim," she explained flatly. "Your five languages; your swarms of adoring former students. Your publications; the way in your spare time you know more about music than some of his teachers. He's smart and nerdy enough to care about those things. And your vast network of friends; your conversation… Most of all, your reserve. You've never suffered fools gladly and you can almost not *force* yourself to give praise where you don't think it's due." This was a mild shock to me. I had always prided myself on how convincing my false smiles and gritted-teeth compliments were. "Jimmy is very attuned to that. He lives for the moments when he can tell you honestly think he's wonderful –" here I must have made a face of protest, because she filled in quickly: "No, Jim, that is *not* always. When he disappoints or confuses you, your body temperature drops. He can feel it across the room."

"He is arguably my favorite person on earth… now," I said. "I think he is perfect in every single way." She gave the smile a mother sphinx might give.

"I know that, and so does he. So has he always. Still, I think it will be affirming and flattering to him to have your full attention."

"He's had my full attention since he was two days old. And of course Lyric is welcome here any time," I lied. "That apartment is a fifteen-minute walk away. They can be together almost as much as they have been in Boston. Thanks for handling her."

Rachel smiled: 'Oh it's nothing…'

Suddenly her face contorted and before she made a sound there were tears on her cheeks.

"The only reason we're discussing this at all is that someone irreplaceable is gone. Joe should be here. Dear wise loving complicated *beautiful* man. Jim, this breaks my heart. *I* miss him so much that I can't even let myself think about what you must be feeling." She finished her lovely words before she allowed her voice to break.

Somehow I was around the table and had my arms around her. I was crying too.

"You're giving me everything you have to give," I said. "The only thing that could help right now."

Jimmy must have heard the acoustic shift in our conversation, even though it had been too soft for him to catch our words. The piano music faltered and stopped, and a moment later I looked up and saw him come through the door into the dining room. Perhaps because my eyes were clouded with tears, it was as though I were seeing him too for the first time. There was an adult energy in his gait: he sensed that he was needed. He looked lanky and lean and strong rather than clumsy and disjointed. His brows were down in worry, shaded by his inky curls which today seemed to have fallen for the first time into photogenic Michelangiolesque order. The proportions of his features were coming into harmony, I noticed; his Roman nose was starting to be balanced by the jut of his small round chin, which sealed the new strong arc of his jaw. His eyes were a startling icy blue in his olive face, and they showed a plain kindness and empathy which I didn't recognize... none of the cagey calculations and self-interrogations I was used to in his expressions. I wondered how often, if ever, he had seen his mother cry. He knelt by her chair and looked up at her imploringly, as though he wished he could be a child again, if only to make her the strong and happy young mother he remembered.

I distinctly heard Joe's voice in my head, saying (an actor/model's cool professional appraisal, and a doting uncle's pride), 'He will be a very, very handsome young man, someday... soon.'

A few hours later, they were gone and I was a widower in a large, silent, empty house.

There were agonizing days when I was practically alone. Friends were kind; neighbors were attentive. Nevertheless the house was an echoing shell in which, as I had always been the principal caretaker and provisioner,

I found myself worrying pointlessly over whether there was enough soap for the guest baths or how recently the garden had been watered.

Dressing every morning was an ordeal. Joe had at times been ironic about my life-long preference for vivid jewel tones. He fancied me in WASPy tweeds with suede elbow patches, and Oxford cloth button-down dress shirts. My weekend tendency to reach for a bright red canvas shirt or a purple cotton sweater struck him as quaint. He would sometimes say,

"Yes – intense colors; good for your eyes, your high skin tones." But I knew he thought I looked better in grey and blue. He might have been satisfied now, when my hand seemed incapable of choosing anything that wasn't grey or white or black. Nothing else drew my eye. I talked about it with Connie on the phone one day.

"When it's time for colors again, Jim," she said, "you'll know. Joey will let you know."

"What are you wearing?" I asked.

"Head-to-toe black," she said. "For a full year. Not to be dramatic; it's just our way. Joe loved me in bright colors, but I just don't *feel* that way yet. It just won't feel right to me for a year. It won't feel right inside. My boy is gone." She cried audibly for maybe twenty seconds while I made ineffectual humming noises, meant to be consoling. My heart genuinely went out to her, but my own grief was selfish and narrow. I felt that all the sympathy should have been flowing towards me, even though she was the one who had carried and borne him, nursed him, weaned him, bandaged his scraped toddler knee, tended him through mumps and measles, and defended him unconditionally when he came out in college. I wanted her to mother *me*. She was too old, too experienced, and too wise to make any such attempt.

"Jim," she said, "we'll talk in a couple of days." A couple of days later was Joe's birthday, and we had already promised each other to speak then, knowing it would be awful. "Nothing can fix this but time – no, not even time. It's unbearable but we have to bear it. Wear mourning for now. This is where we are. *Te vojo bene.*"

Nights were hideous. I would lie in bed looking at the ceiling, my throat constricted, my eyes dry, until the tension in my body extruded tears that hurt my eyes and cheeks. I would make pathetic puling squeals which I tried to stifle, even though there was no one to hear, and I could hear myself trying to say Joe's name. I never for an instant imagined him in the bed, where he belonged; I never tried to speak to him or pretended that the pillow was my vanished love. Fitful sleep would come, eventually, with no dreams I could remember. My mind just became numb enough to the pervasive desolation that my exhausted limbs and organs would lapse into an hour or two of subhuman regeneration, with a kind of recovery-room psychosis just below the surface. A dark, miserable unease and disorientation filled even these brief respites from consciousness, creeping into the cracks where dreams should have been. Several times a night, I would wake up just enough to remember that Joe had died, and my skin would crawl with loathing of this new reality. My body registered a mitochondrial-level rejection of a life too bitter and stark for belief.

Three weeks after the funeral, Tony and Jimmy were back to move J.J. into my second guest room. It was an informal back garret on the third floor, down the hall from my own room, with a double bed and a small full bath. Putting Jimmy there would bring life to an eerily quiet part of the house, and it would leave the more glamorous guest suite on the second floor for grown-up visitors.

Almost a month into bereavement, I was a functional automaton. Preparing for their arrival had been something to focus on. I had taken down most of the pictures in Jimmy's room in case he wanted to hang posters of Webern and Ravel over his bed and desk. The winter linens and clothing which normally filled the closet in that room had found a new home in the basement, to make way for Jimmy's meager wardrobe. Jimmy had brought a high-quality electronic keyboard, programmable in to-me unimaginable ways, capable of synthesizing the sounds of marimbas, Bach's organ in Leipzig, a Klingon trombone-harpsichord… I was awestruck. At first, I was hurt that he didn't want to use my piano, and told him he was always welcome to do so. He bowed slightly, almost nervous. He had prepared his response.

"Your piano," he said: "performing, '*Traümerei*,' improvising, therapy. This box: composing, practicing, pounding."

"OK," I said; "we'll treat the square grand as the genteel Victorian lady she is."

After dinner that night, Jimmy went upstairs to unpack his fourteen belongings and to call Lyric on Skype.

"Give her my best," I said, feeling and probably sounding false. Tony and I took snifters of brandy and went to sit in the parlor.

"Four weeks," he said sadly, and shook his head. He was looking around the house, and I was sure he was going to say he missed Joe. First, though, he said something very Tony-like.

"Remember your first house?"

I knew what he meant. When Joe and I started our life together, I had been living in a very small, plain old row house in East Baltimore. It had been renovated down to the slab in the 1970s, and once one crossed the threshold it might have been a modern two-story, two-bedroom apartment. Joe and I had enjoyed sharing it for a couple of cramped years, and Tony had been very attached to it. He thought of it as a manly love-nest, in contrast to his own increasingly bourgeois existence.

He and Rachel were by then already very prosperous, thanks to his eye-popping compensation as a corporate attorney and the respectable second income brought in by her consultancies and grants. They had lived since long before Jimmy's birth in a big Prairie Style house in Glencoe, amply terraced, cantilevered, and balustraded. I knew for a fact that Rachel could throw a dazzling black-tie reception in it for two hundred people without breaking a nail. Her superb, cool taste filled it with big modern furniture, striking massive canvases not always rectangular, antiques from several countries, and profusions of houseplants. Visually it was a perfect amalgam of opulence and sobriety. The only small things in the house were Rachel's shifting collections of curios and found objects, showing her atavistic attraction to bits of mosaic, copper wire, *cloisonné*. She also collected the kinds of colored sticks, stones, and shells that children might gather on walks. She enjoyed arranging them on railings or shelves in all but the most formal sectors of the house. It was a very masculine house, with its boldly-proportioned public rooms, aerodynamic contours, and natural materials in grand striations, but it spoke much more of Rachel than of her husband. His presence was most apparent in the house's visible expensiveness. One step into the clerestoried foyer and one knew that a devoted husband and father of very substantial means took pride in keeping this particular show running out of love for his family.

The contrast with my little low-maintenance back-alley row house in Baltimore had always seemed to fill Tony with a sense of roads not taken. When Joe and I moved into a larger place near the main campus of Hopkins, and lived there for fifteen years or more, Tony said more than once that he missed our little starter-house.

The house where Joe died had been a shared folly... mostly mine, really, because Joe saw how much I loved it at first sight. We had lived there for only a few years before his death. It was a beautiful brick row house of the 1850s on a quiet street in Bolton Hill. The look of the house was different from our earlier homes: grander spaces, greater formality, boxwood hedges, and so better antiques, linens, and flatware.

Tony's question, "Remember your first house?" was thus a little like asking, 'Do you remember when we were young and had no idea any of this would happen?'

"I remember thinking that a thirty-two inch waist would take care of itself forever," I said, coolly, meaning to sound brave and detached from recent tragedy. If I sneezed or broke into sudden spasmodic sobs, I might crush the big round fragile snifter in my hand, certainly slashing my palm, and I'd bleed to death; I had been taking anticoagulants for several years. "And I remember thinking that life-long happiness was possible."

Tony nodded and met my eye for an instant, taking my meaning and aware of the poverty of words. Then he looked down. I was grateful that he wouldn't say anything until he had thought of something interesting. I had reached the point where I planned to murder the next person who said to me, 'I'm sorry for your loss,' or 'You're in my thoughts and prayers.' I could stand anything from Tony but a cliché. Tony had been the great unattainable love of my life for decades before Joe showed up. I had never doubted Tony's constitutional straightness: he had been happily coupled with Rachel for two or three years before I met and fell in love with him in college. Nevertheless, without ever actually hoping for carnalities, I had known in the depths of my heart that he was meant for me, somehow. There had been shy confidences, bungled attempted intimacies, soul-blanching disappointments, and also the world's easiest, dearest, most bracing and sustaining companionship. He and I had said every possible embarrassing thing to each other, both in conflict and in affection. I waited to see what he would say now.

He looked up, his blue eyes pale and candid in his ruddy face. Perhaps a little as he missed my first house, I missed the soft corn-silk curls he had kept well into our forties. For years now, he had kept his hair quite short, and it had become wiry and spiky as it faded to grey. He was lucky to have kept most of it; the bald spot where his cowlick had been was as neat as a tonsure. His face was still as familiar to me as the one in my mirror, but the sunny handsomeness of our youth had given way to something craggier, distinguished and sometimes weary-looking. He could still have been a model, perhaps for the classy, dashingly mature gentleman tossing the keys of his Maserati to a valet or lifting, with a knowing smile, a martini glass filled with an élite gin.

"Jimbo," he said, "life-long happiness *is* possible. You have about the best chance of anyone I know of experiencing it. Right now is a tragedy, but you can handle it. Joe said so, and I say so. You've had something most people never have: a genuine, close, honest marriage. This hurts because you miss Joe like hell. That won't last forever…" Suddenly his eyes flickered down, and he smiled modestly, as though he'd caught himself being pretentious or glib. "Listen to me, right? I can't imagine how you feel. I haven't had your loss. I have no idea what would happen if I lost Rachel or Jimmy. But I know how I feel about losing Joe. Not how *you* feel, but how *I* feel." I noticed that Rachel had said something similar: how much she missed Joe, and how she couldn't imagine how I felt. Their years together, approaching fifty by now, had brought them into a unity of feeling that touched me.

"How do you feel?" I asked quietly.

"Remember how I didn't like Joe at first?" Yes, I remembered. For the first few days after I met Joe while on vacation with Tony and Rachel at Rehoboth Beach in 1993 (or more precisely, re-met him, because we had been slightly acquainted at Yale years earlier), Tony had found him unimpressive. Joe at that time was a madly attractive, defensive, self-doubting, semi-successful actor-model(-waiter) in LA, but Tony, impervious to his sex appeal and perhaps even resentful of his increasing hold on me, had said he looked like a hedgehog. This was his shorthand for scruffy, untutored, and intent on unimportant achievements in tawdry industries. Twenty-odd years later, it was almost funny to recall this two- or three-day reticence on Tony's part, because it had been so quickly made moot by his friendly surrender to the love he saw I actually was falling into with Joe. I nodded.

"Maybe that's why I got to love him so much," Tony continued. "I've never known anyone like him and I doubt I ever will again. He leaves a big hole in my heart."

"Describe him in one word," I said. This may have been the first time I had smiled thinking of Joe since his death. It was a very pallid smile, but I felt and noticed it from the inside. Tony rocked his head back and studied the plaster medallion on the ceiling. Then he looked straight at me.

"Kind," he said. I nodded. I was sure he was referring to Joe's generosity in dealing with others. Joe was always wonderful with working people, the elderly, children, waiters, my brilliant and often under-socialized colleagues, his students and mine. I had always noticed Joe's kindness in how he treated those in need, the vulnerable, those less powerful than himself. "He was so kind to *you*. Proud of you, loyal to you, yes, all of that. But most of all, kind."

Tony's sense of Joe's kindness focused on me, apparently, and at first I didn't understand that. I was as strong as Joe, wasn't I? Yet clearly Tony felt that I had required kindness from my lover, and looking back, I realized he was right. Joe had rescued me from the wasteland of gay dating, in which, probably through no one's fault but my own, I had been frustrated and wounded for years despite my attempts to be tough and resilient about it. My *recherché* intellectual vaporings and cultural posturings and crashing snobberies, and my over-analytic and often uncharitable second-guessing of people's feelings or motives, never seemed to bother Joe for long. He had a way of shrugging his shoulders, telling me to relax, and calling me "Tiger" with a patient smile. I must have been a drag at times, an overwrought killjoy, and Joe found good-natured ways to help me be less suspicious and negative. More amazing, he found ways of loving me nevertheless. *Kind.*

"And he was kind to me, too, you know." That frankly astonished me. Tony surely didn't need kindness; Tony was a rock. "He could have hated me. At first it was obvious that he was jealous of me. But he got to love me for your sake." That was true. Joe had initially found Tony smug and superior, and keenly felt his disapproval, in those earliest days when Joe too wondered if he and I could be a couple, let alone over the objections of this oh-so-handsome, oh-so-smart, oh-so-successful best friend of mine.

Yet Tony was right that Joe had learned to love him, because I did. "How many people have that kind of class? of... originality? Joe worked things out in his mind and heart that make most people just mean and resentful. Joe was a *mensch*." I felt the tears rising in my eyes.

"He wasn't mean, you're right," I said. "Never, to anyone... no, not mean. And never to me, even when he had every right. Maddening and stubborn and even kind of dumb about some things, but never, never mean. He didn't know how." The tears were on my face now, and my voice was shaking, but I wasn't afraid of breaking down. Tony just reached forward enough to pat my knee. He didn't try to hug me or move to sit next to me.

"You are a lucky person," he said. "You've had that. Being sad for Joe's death is very different from not ever having known him. You know how to be happy now. That's Joe's gift to you. Who knows if you'll ever meet anyone or get involved again? The point is that you'll be fine. You'll be happy again. Trust me, Jimbo. This is Doro speaking." "Doro" had been my pet name for Tony from the first moment I knew I loved him in college; the lamplight in his blond curls had drawn from me an entranced murmur of *"capelli d'oro,"* "golden hair," and for years the name stuck. It lapsed when Joe and I became a couple. By invoking it now, Tony was teleporting us back to Eden. For an instant I glimpsed an image of my future self: a solitary sage, gaunt and prophetic, sexless, smiling wanly at young lovers, blessing them silently, offering them majestic counsel when asked. Maybe that was what "fine" would look like.

Tony sighed suddenly and changed the topic.

"You don't know how grateful we are that you're taking Jimmy in," he said. I waved my hand dismissively.

"That's a huge gift to me," I said. He looked at me steadily to be sure I meant it.

"Win-win, then, I guess," he smiled. "He's a special kid. I know he's kind of an oddball, but it will be good for you to have someone in the house. And I think he'll grow a lot here. We should set up a Skype schedule; maybe do a group check-in every week or so."

A few minutes later Jimmy Jack came downstairs. As he entered the room, I felt a lift in my spirits; I was glad he was there, and I was interested in whatever he might have to say.

"Lyric says Hi," he said before sitting next to me on the sofa.

I nodded as though in appreciation, and asked if he wanted a drink.

"Do you have any… Chardonnay?" he said, as though he had just learned a word in a new language. I told him I could find some Pinot Grigio, virtually positive that he wouldn't know the difference. As I was about to stand, he said,

"She just broke up with me."

A few weeks before his death, Joe came home from the gym one afternoon and was standing in the front hall looking at the day's mail as I was coming down the stairs. He smiled up at me and waited for my quick kiss before saying,

"Rachel is so old-fashioned. I love how she writes us letters like it's 1903." He was holding a torn envelope on which I recognized her bold Italic script, and a museum card with an oddly erotic 19th century neo-Pompeiian image of a chastely clad young woman seated coquettishly in the lap of a muscular, dark-skinned, almost nude young man. "'Wishing you an idyllic time in sultry summer Baltimore,'" he read. "Huh?" I took the card and glanced at the back.

"Oh," I said, "*ça s'explique*: Bouguereau, '*L'Idylle.*'"

"She's hilarious. Anyway, you should read this." She had folded a page-long printed letter inside the card; he was reading from it. "She's getting organized about Jimmy Jack and Lyric moving to Baltimore. '*Le jeune ménage,*' she calls them." Joe smiled tolerantly. He had put a lot of time and effort into learning Italian in our first years together. He had a head-start: two years of Italian at Yale, and parents, both children of immigrants to Brooklyn from Fascist-era Rome, who often chatted in their own brand of Americanized *romanesco*. Joe and his siblings could have simple conversations in their parents' mixed dialect, but to keep up with me, he had committed to bringing at least his spoken Italian up to modern national standards. He was justifiably proud of being able to fend for himself during our frequent trips to Italy, and even to converse comfortably with all my Italian friends and colleagues. He pretended to be irritated by the fact that Rachel often peppered her letters with little tags of French, though he knew snippets of it himself and had acquired a decent pronunciation from his voice teacher at Yale. He had worshiped

Rachel since their first meeting, and had to dig this deep to identify even an alleged flaw in her.

Rachel's letter included some ideas for the apartment Jimmy and Lyric were going to live in. She mentioned that it had two bedrooms, and that the two kids had agreed to set it up as though they slept separately, to allay the mediaeval scruples of her parents. (I had somehow never thought about her parents. She might have been hatched from a milkweed pod or beamed to earth in astral form on the ray of a cosmic vibration; either of these would have accounted for her core vocal tone.) Rachel thought that perhaps Joe and I could help make the two-bedroom arrangement look natural.

I said that we should try to get into the place soon to reconnoiter. The current tenants were sure to be Peabody students and probably wouldn't mind the meddling gay uncles' paying an exploratory visit. Both Joe and I had guest-taught courses at Peabody more than once, I in Italian vocal repertoire, and he in stage movement, and it wouldn't be hard for us to get the occupants' numbers and arrange a time to drop by.

Joe looked up from the letter and asked,

"Do you think they actually have sex?"

I was genuinely flabbergasted by the question, but his asking it pleased me.

"Well, we know they sleep together. And at their age, wouldn't it be automatic?"

"They're both pretty disembodied," he said.

"Maybe they've found their way, groping innocently, like a couple in an Arcadian-porn Hellenistic novel," I suggested. I had always avoided speculating on any details of Jimmy's sexuality. It wasn't what he was about in my mind. I would have loved to love his girlfriend, his wife (the right one), but my fond thoughts would always have stopped at the bedroom door. Now that Joe had raised the curtain, it seemed to me that the only way Jimmy and Lyric could have had sex would have been that he wondered why his "nice-sized penis" was changing profile and suffusing him with sensations, and Lyric would have gently and indirectly guided him into port, clasped him, managed him, and rewarded him with anemic approval which they would both have mistaken for passion. If none of that had occurred, it was indeed just possible that these self-etherealizing juvenile ninnies were in fact still virgins.

"Or…" Joe said, smiling a bit lewdly, "let's not forget the magic of morning wood." That magic had saved our marriage more than once in the past few years, as we were at times less ready to spring to attention than we had been in our thirties and forties.

"I never forget that magic," I said; "it's my favorite magic. Part of me wishes it were morning right now." He chuckled and kissed me lightly.

One of the first blessings I always counted was that Joe had never ceased to smell and taste good to me. Though I still had my eye for handsome young men, I had found it relatively easy to remain faithful to Joe through the years, because, though the good looks of his thirties shifted into something more leathery and weather-beaten, he kept his soft curly hair, his glowing green eyes, and his close-to-the-ground hunkiness. He was like an Italo Cagney, a Roman Caan. Touching him was always exciting: he was still vigorous and shapely and responsive, and his kiss was youthful and fresh. I had no idea what he saw in me, as I settled into a florid, podgy academic portliness, but I had better sense than to question it. Part of Joe's deepest erotic was his pride in the non-sexual aspects of our closeness. If we went a week without sex, I always accused him of bragging about it to his friends. To him, that was proof that there was more to our relationship than sex. Before we got together, while I was trying and largely failing to score, he had a long run as one of the hottest young men in LA. He had banked whatever thrills were to be gotten from constant tricking and a string of successful seductions, but worried that he would never find someone who could love him for other reasons. Our symmetrical deficits had made us a perfect match.

I also always felt lucky that becoming my lover did not, in fact, ruin Joe's career. Leaving his well-trodden LA circuits of clubs, modeling agencies, open-mic nights, and soap opera casting calls to move in with a Baltimore professor had been a real leap of faith for him. He had always loyally insisted that I brought him good luck. This was because coincidentally, during our first two weeks together at the beach, an ad campaign for a new cologne had been launched, featuring a full-face close-up of Joe taken a few months earlier. In it, he looked implausibly glossy, up-market, and desirable. Against all statistical odds, that cologne had sold very well for several years, and the company used Joe for a series of ads which made his face familiar to many millions. Some of his professional bios actually started with a reference to his having come to prominence as "the Pennington Man." On that basis, he had maintained a thriving career as a model and actor in commercials, being hired, as he matured, less for high fashion campaigns and more as the likable, easy-going guy with a dependable testosterone count: the trusted good-natured mechanic; the gruff, affable father; the working stiff with the twinkle in his eye.

Living in Baltimore made New York auditions and gigs feasible, and his big break came about five years into our relationship when he was cast in a secondary role in a hit prime-time soap opera. I was disappointed that the TV series made so little call on his understated, perhaps under-developed abilities as an actor. However, it was extremely well-paid, and it made him something like a star. His main job was to smolder and threaten. He played the working-class, apparently Latino ex-husband of a spoiled rich girl whose family saga furnished the show's main plot, if it could be called that. Everyone hoped that, after the shipwreck of this bad first marriage, she would accede to the courtship of a country club youth with a perfect profile and raven hair; his deep nobility of character was stipulated, though the only evidence of it was that he occasionally said something polite to a servant. Joe lurked in the background as her guilty secret, a potential blot on her record, threatening to reveal all to her swanky friends. The wretched girl might have moved forward with her life had this ex- of hers (a known boozer, womanizer, and swindler) not been so dreadfully attractive. Any time she incautiously stepped alone onto a terrace during a cotillion, Joe would emerge from the shrubbery, grab her upper arm, and lean murmuring into her cleavage, usually after having broken something in an outburst of unspecified ethnic rage. All America felt the undertow, the invitation to madness, the danger of relapse.

From this role, Joe had leap-frogged into a very steady stream of regional theatre work. He had shown actual courage and vulnerability in just the right roles in standard repertory: his Biff in a summer stock *Death of a Salesman*, for instance, was a cherished memory for me. He landed several recurring roles on TV and even a few parts in movies, most often as one of the guys who stood there reacting while the star said or did something at a party or funeral.

With these credentials he had been able to earn a contract as an adjunct instructor, and in time Lecturer, in the Theatre Department at my university. This was perhaps his greatest role. He was practical, honest, supportive, and challenging with his students, and over time he became one of the most beloved members of that faculty. He was starting to talk about forming his own studio for young working actors. The large, unfinished basement of our house could easily be turned into a suitable space. I was planning on retiring sometime in my mid-sixties and perhaps coaching young classical singers on a more regular basis. Joe's career had never involved a set calendar or schedule, so we were starting to envisage a time within a few years when we would both be working at home with interesting, talented young people.

Now as we looked together at Rachel's letter, Joe said,

"I still think it's possible they've never gotten it on. Lyric could probably step up, but our boy is… not totally in touch with himself about certain things." I smiled at his very gentle way of saying that Jimmy Jack was an abstracted dope.

"The lesbian in you, however," I said, "will probably agree that it's good he's gotten used to sharing a bed with someone he trusts and cares about, with or without fornication." Joe was on record as having said about a million times that the most important part of a relationship was just sleeping next to each other; this implied something about trust and mutual knowledge. On that basis I had often said he was secretly lesbian.

Joe punched my arm.

"I'm sure everyone feels very sorry for you because I never put out," he said. "You live in a sex-starved desert and it's all my fault." He put his arms around me and I suddenly didn't care if we never had sex again; being that close to him was all that mattered. Mad at myself, I realized that, after twenty-two years, he had won me over to his way of thinking. Then I remembered with a Lothario thrill that in fact we were the envy of many other long-term couples for the subtle shared eroticism we still shared. Joe could sense both these thoughts of mine. "It will be good for these two kids to see us together. They'll want to be as sexy as we are when they're our age."

The happiness I felt in that little hug contained no warning of any kind that it might not last forever.

Chapter 3
August-September 2015
[flashback: June-July]

Preparing for the start of the Fall semester helped structure my days and get me out of my rut of mourning. Jimmy's presence in the house also distracted me from my grey repetitious thoughts. Every time I heard him let himself in the front door, every time he loped into the room, I could feel my blank, featureless grief lighten just a bit... not any form of joy or excitement, but a detached, fond curiosity as to what might be on his mind.

He reacted to Lyric's sudden stark announcement in stages. With Tony and me the first night, he had seemed unaffected. Tony wasn't convinced by his glib, almost jokey display of stoicism; he looked at his only child with apprehension, as though J.J. might break down from minute to minute. Of course we both asked what Lyric had said, and Jimmy replied,

"She said she's decided to stay in Boston to keep studying privately with her teacher there." He offered this explanation in a calm, reasonable tone of voice, as though we grown-ups couldn't be expected to understand that this was a perfectly normal transactional conversation between young people. "She said that since we weren't going to be living together anyway, it didn't make sense for her to uproot herself just to be near me."

I could see in Tony's face that he was both sorry for Jimmy and angry at Lyric, as was I. Even though I was relieved that Jimmy Jack was at least starting the process of disentanglement, I thought Lyric sounded very cold. She must have known she was getting off easy if she could end a several-year relationship in a ten-minute phone talk with a boy who had always let her take the emotional lead. Normal break-ups required protracted negotiations, recriminations, apologies, and pleas. Perhaps Lyric had wanted Jimmy to push back, or to cry and beg her to stay, all reactions of which I was sure she knew him to be incapable. Tony met my eye for an instant. He was catching a plane home early the next morning. I would be the on-site adult in Jimmy's life now.

When Tony's Uber came at six the following morning, J.J. and I said good-bye to him on the marble front steps.

"We'll talk tonight, champ," he said to his son. "Keep smiling, OK? Mommy will want to see you smiling." Jimmy still called his parents Mommy and Daddy. Tony gave him a bear hug and kissed him hard on the cheek. Back in our college years, my only male friends whose fathers ever kissed them were Jewish. Tony was in that group, though the custom had now swept the hipster universe. Likewise the paternal "I love you" which had made my face prickle with embarrassment decades earlier had since become the absolutely obligatory sign-off between all men and their children. Tony's embrace of his son still struck me as both tender and modern.

Jimmy looked shifty and unsure, like a little boy left at the threshold of kindergarten on the first day of school who knows he's expected to be brave but who deeply wishes he could run home and hide.

Suddenly he took my hand, turned to Tony, and said,

"Don't worry, Daddy. I know I have a job to do here": he would look after me on Tony's and Rachel's behalf. Absurd and almost presumptuous as that was, it touched some unshielded spot in the exact center of my grieving heart. I found it beautiful that in his emotional confusion he had decided it was his job to protect me. Tony and I looked at each other, and I nodded slightly.

Tony reached forward and hugged me. I didn't remember his ever having hugged me so hard or so long. I heard his breath catch slightly, and I sensed his feelings: worry for Jimmy, sorrow for me, gratitude.

"Take good care, Jimbo," he said, his voice shaking a little. "I love you."

Late that night as I went upstairs to bed, I knocked on Jimmy's door to ask if he needed anything.

"I'm OK," he said, and opened the door. He looked calm, freeze-dried.

"Really?" I asked.

"Totally. Yes."

"We can talk about Lyric whenever you want to," I offered. "There's plenty of time. This is a major change for you."

"I don't see how someone who's going through what you are could care about two kids breaking up," he said.

It was a little stilted for us to be having this talk leaning against the door-frame of his room, but it would have to do.

"I do care," I said. "Not about Lyric, to tell you the truth, but about you. But you don't have to talk about it if you don't want to. It's your business and your feelings. Just so you know I'm here."

"I know that." He mustered a bluff business-like smile. "I guess I have to cheer you up too. I think my youthful energy is supposed to keep you connected with life."

"Well," I said, "you can start by being honest. I don't need a therapist or a nanny, but I am really glad to have my godson in the house." His eyes became furtive and clouded for a moment, wondering what honesty consisted of, and hurt at my implied accusation.

"I always mean to be honest. I'm just weird, I guess." My crabby response had nicked him a little, and something stirred inside me that I hadn't felt in weeks: concern for another creature. I paused before responding and managed a very pale smile.

"No," I said, "'weird' is too strong. Just keep being Jimmy Jack. I'm deeply grateful that you're here. Good night."

I hugged him, a bit awkwardly, as any approach came up against his extremely private physicality. I hugged him because I had to, because his presence *was* important and healing for me. Despite the very slight, detectable rigidity which had always passed through him at any bodily contact, it occurred to me for the first time in his life that he tolerated, and always had tolerated, such approaches better from me than from virtually any other adult. The reticence he expressed with me was fear of not getting hugged right, of being judged, of not knowing how to share his feelings. I didn't care. A stiff, nervous embrace from Jimmy was better than the practiced surrender of the average millennial scatterer of 'I love you's.

"Good night, G.J.," he said, and ducked back into his room.

The next night, I heard him crying softly when I walked past his closed door. 'Thank God,' I said to myself.

"Need anything, J.J.?" I called quietly.

"No, I'm fine," he said, his voice surprisingly steady. "Good night."

The following night, we talked at dinner about his day of orientation at Peabody. He marshalled a series of smart, not very engaged comments on other students in his program. There was one he referred to as "crazy-smart," named Kevin.

"Also a composer?" I asked.

"Music theory, actually," he said. "But there's some overlap in the programs, I guess. He said something about Schenker that only the professors understood. He's a little guy."

I blinked. Kevin's size had nothing to do with what Jimmy was saying about him. Then he changed the subject and talked about how he would be assigned a faculty mentor.

At two or three in the morning, I was awakened by the creak of my bedroom door opening. My face prickling for a fight-or-flight instant, I made out Jimmy's tall frame silhouetted against the dim moon-glow coming through the skylight in the hall.

He shuffled in diffidently and stood next to my bed. The street lamps outside gave just enough light that I could see he was wearing baggy pajamas with dinosaurs on them. I didn't know such things came in adult sizes.

"I can't sleep," he said. "Can I climb in here with you for a while?"

"Of course," I said, glad that the room was too dark for him to see the furious lobster blush which I could feel scorching my face. He clambered across me to Joe's old spot and flopped into place, lying on his back and looking at the ceiling. As he flicked the top sheet to cover his chest, there was a slight lack of freshness coming off his PJs.

"I'm used to having Lyric next to me when I sleep," he explained. "It feels weird being alone at night. And I thought maybe you feel that way without Uncle Joe here."

"Not exactly," I said. "I just feel that the world is sick and wrong." He took quite a long time to speak, and his reply was a question.

"Who's the one person you love most in the world?"

Not for the first time, he had taken my breath away. I flashed back to the time he'd told his grandmother that he loved me most. I thought hard for a moment of my sister and nephew, of Tony and Rachel, of Walter and Ricardo, of Marie; of dozens of friends in Italy who competed in spoiling me on my yearly visits; of cherished colleagues, of neighbors, of fellow activists and volunteers and artists; of Joe's gifted, loyal, and hilarious tribe of actors, models, and pop singers, and of his roiling devoted Italian-American clan. All of these people enriched every day of my extraordinarily lucky life. Yet I knew the answer to Jimmy Jack's question.

"Since Joe died," I said, "you are, funny J.J."

"And I guess you're mine. After Mommy and Daddy. Since Lyric dumped me. So in a way it could make sense for me to sleep here sometimes. On Uncle Joe's side of the bed."

In my freaked-out bones, suddenly as snap-fragile as the chicken wish bones my mother put to dry on the kitchen windowsill when I was a child, I could tell that there was no possibility of my feeling an ambiguous attraction to J.J. For me, he would always be a kid, and I would have been as likely to get an erection for a newborn, for a pet cat, for Eleanor Roosevelt.

At the same time, I knew that any time he spent in my bed would have to be a secret. It was simply too strange, too private. I knew that he was immune to the idea that outside observers would find his presence perverse. In his extraterrestrial innocence, he was proposing a bold experimental therapy, for both of us. I felt like someone secretly experimenting with hallucinogens in psychiatric labs in the late 1940s. Perhaps someday it would be normal to send a bereaved person's most beloved young friend to his or her bed as an antidote to sorrow, as a human teddy bear or comfort animal.

"You may be right," I said. "Night time gets very lonely for me. If you ever hear me crying, please don't feel like you have to fix it. It will pass. Just having you in the house is a big help."

"I'm happy being here." He thought a minute. Jimmy's difficult thoughts had always been almost audible to me. I'd never heard him say 'Hmm' or 'Soo....' but I could always feel the rise and crest of his pondering and predict when a sentence would finally pop out. This one, though, surprised me. "I didn't really love Lyric. She was my friend and she got me in some ways, and I knew everyone thought she was very pretty. We never ran out of things to talk about. I was thinking I'd get hot for her eventually, but I never did."

"You were so close," I said. "Everyone could see it. Kindred spirits."

"Kind of, I guess… but I feel like sooner or later you should want to…" He was embarrassed by what he meant to say. "You and Uncle Joe always had sex, right? I think Mommy and Daddy still do, too. I never wanted that with Lyric. But I know it's considered normal, even though the idea of sex to me is kind of…" He shivered. "But that's weird."

"So in other words, you're OK breaking up with Lyric because you think you and she should have been more physically intimate, but you also don't like the idea of physical intimacy in the first place. *That* I find hard to understand."

"I know," he said, sounding confused and discouraged.

"There's a lot more to love than sex," I said. That sounded like something Joe would have said. I agreed with Jimmy that his apparent lack of physical attraction was proof that he had not really loved Lyric. I didn't think it was possible for an adolescent boy not to get raging hard-ons from the mere thought of someone he loved, whether or not he was able or inclined to act on them. I recalled my own earliest erections, which were always associated with thoughts of boys in my middle-school classes or with accounts in books I read of devotion or attachment between men. This was years before I fully understood what erections were for or where they might be aimed and placed. Surely J.J. must have had such thoughts and reactions, and if they weren't for Lyric then he couldn't have been in love with her.

Jimmy didn't say anything in response to my bromide.

"Do you get… hot… for anyone else?" I asked him after a pause. It should have been a more embarrassing question that it was, but I felt quite sure no adult had ever spoken with him about such things, and he must be confused or worried.

"Yes, well… for ideas, I guess. Some music, or when ideas for music pop into my head. Sometimes playing the piano." A few beats of silence went by; he was thinking. "Sometimes just because my pants feel tight." He was too goofy to realize he was funny. "But thinking of people that way is just like…"

"You never imagine making love to someone? Being that close, touching, connected…?" He gave a weird little shudder and a noise in his throat like a child who sees something gross, as though the notion of physical closeness made his skin crawl. For several slow breaths he said nothing.

"I heard you crying last night," I finally said. "If you didn't love Lyric, why were you so sad?"

"She was the only girl who ever liked me. I was thinking that now there will never be anyone else. It made me sad. But I don't get the whole sex-thing, so…" I wanted to tell Joe that he had been right about J.J. and Lyric being virgins, but he was gone. "But I also don't like feeling lonely. Maybe I always will be. I know I'm the least cool person in the world. I know I've never even been normal."

"Being normal is overrated," I said. "But for what it's worth, fear of loneliness is the *most* normal thing in the world. You're fine. You're just sad right now." He actually squirmed a bit; he was about to ask something he found embarrassing.

"How important *is* sex? Or why is it so important to everyone but me? I don't get that. It's like my body ends here and other people's bodies start way over there. I don't totally want people touching me. Or to touch them."

"It's different for everyone. There's a 99% chance you'll feel differently someday, when the right… person comes along. It's an initiation: grief, frustration, exaltation, wanting. All the books and songs and operas and movies suddenly make sense, like you speak the same language as humanity."

"I've never really spoken human," he said after a moment.

"Jimmy," I said, "you will. You're the most remarkable boy in the world. Someone will notice and want to be with you, and you'll learn to talk human for that person's sake. And meanwhile, you've got people who learn to talk Jimmy because they love you. You've got your little fan-base. It's not you against the world."

By now I was quite awake, comfortable with chatting in the semi-darkness. I felt like a kid in college sharing secrets with a new friend on the hill outside the dorm late at night. His father and I had actually done exactly that in the fall of 1970. As then, I felt now that there was no reason to stop talking, every reason to let this closeness follow its own unpressured rhythms. Daybreak might find us still lying side by side, looking straight up and tossing deep new ideas back and forth.

"I've got my parents and you, anyway," Jimmy said; I heard a shy smile in his voice. He thought for another few moments. "I think I can sleep now. I'll go back to my room."

I felt the way I'd felt when he was an infant and someone reached to take him from my arms. I had always been happier when Jimmy was right next to me than when he was anywhere else – two feet away, across the room, down the hall, or across the country. He must have heard my thoughts.

"Do you want me next to you?" he asked.

'Yes,' I thought.

"No, no," I said… "go. It's been nice to talk."

"I'm just down the hall, G.J.," he said, comforting me in what he sensed was another separation in my lonely universe. He was right: part of me didn't want him to leave, ever, in any sense. "I'm never far away." He was standing now. He came around to my side of the bed and reached down to give me an elbowy hug; again, a faint trace of mildew came off him, and it was OK with me when the hug ended. "Good night."

"Thanks. You're my boy." He hadn't minded touching me or letting me touch him, I reflected. Mine was not one of those menacing, over-there bodies. I realized that I belonged to a rather small category in his world. He didn't feel or communicate any bodily rejoicing in our hug, but he was willing to initiate or accept it.

After he padded back down the hall, I reviewed our little scene for only a few moments and then slept very well till morning. At breakfast, though, I spoke briefly to him about laundry and deodorant. I even offered to take him on a guided tour of my cologne collection. He listened with eyes down, then smiled up at me and said,

"Did Mommy tell you to say that?"

When classes started, I found myself a deft actor after all, snapping by habit into my cheerful, energetic teaching persona. Several colleagues were close friends and had attended Joe's funeral and been to visit since. The others now struck a range of right notes: "I hope it helps to be back where you're needed and loved," said one, and another, "I can imagine that the routine will be a comfort." My department had a tradition of collecting funds to plant trees in memory of colleagues' loved ones, and someone had found a way to plant an umbrella pine tree in a Baltimore park in tribute to Joe's Roman ancestors.

Many students in my second-year Italian class had been with me through the two preceding semesters, and when I walked into the room the first day, I found a beautiful hand-made card propped against the monitor: *"Ci dispiace tanto,"* "We are so sorry," signed by all of them and with personal notes (a few of them actually grammatical) in Italian. I learned later that my junior colleague Renzo had sent them a group e-mail to notify them of what had happened. I grasped the podium hard for a moment, knowing I wouldn't be able to speak. Glancing out at their faces, I saw they were very moved, unsure what to say or do. Chris "Cristoforo," the best student in the class, broke the silence by saying,

"Le vogliamo bene, professore." They loved me: I smiled and shook my head a little, aware that I couldn't phonate yet and conscious of a few actual tears coming down my face. After several seconds I was able to take a deep breath and say,

"Anch'io a voi. Siete molto cari." That was no more than the truth: I *did* love them, and they *were* very dear. Then I asked what each of them had done over the summer; it was my longstanding way to start each new semester's review. Several of them lingered to speak and to hug me at the end of class. None of this was exactly comforting, but I could feel myself becoming more alert, less listless, almost natural.

I studied all my students that week, the ones I was just meeting and the ones I'd known for a year or two. I noticed that none of them stirred me the way Jimmy did. Part of the energy flowing through each day on campus was my anticipation of seeing him later at home and hearing how his explorations at Peabody were going. I had taught at my university, a large public diploma mill, for over thirty years, and had always loved the upward mobility of my students. They were respectful, funny, wide-eyed, smart, resourceful, diverse, ambitious, and eager. It was extremely rare, though, for one of them to express an idea about course content that had never occurred to me. True, for many years I had learned from them about tech, pop culture, local eateries, and shifting political sensitivities. They had quite recently, for instance, started to raise my consciousness about trans issues, and I had also had small, unwelcome intimations of a rising nationalism among some of their communities of origin. I loved and respected them, but Jimmy was intriguing in ways they weren't.

I was lucky that both Joe and I had kept our wills updated. Our attorney and executor, George, had the logistics of Joe's estate very well in hand. I had learned when my mother died years earlier that mourning was largely a season of putting aside deep personal grief to talk to total strangers about money. George mercifully took much of that burden from me, and gave me clear instructions on the conversations that only I could conduct. As he predicted, within little over a month, by opening all the bills and notifications addressed to Joe, I got a decent grasp on the overall picture of his private finances. I was able to refer most things to George without emotion and to follow his recommendations in a brisk businesslike low-affect way.

One evening after dinner, a week or two into the semester, it occurred to me for some reason to look at Joe's calendar. Like me, and in part for my easy reference, he had continued to keep a paper desk calendar, though unlike me he relied mostly on the one on his iPhone. The phone itself had harrowed my feelings during the lead-up to his funeral, when I consulted it for the names and phone numbers of his friends, read through some recent carefree texts between us, and choked myself up by noticing in detail, for the first time, which pictures he stored there to show people in conversation: pictures of our house, his family, and, to my surprise, many, many pictures of me through the years, dating all the way back to our courtship days in 1993, plus a couple of my childhood and baby pictures he had apparently scanned and saved there. Of course I knew that Joe loved me, rightly or wrongly, but this little iPhone album came close to breaking my heart, perhaps because I knew how close to his own he had carried it.

I opened Joe's desk calendar really for no logical reason. Everyone who might be on it had heard of his death; there was no one who would be surprised if he didn't show up for an appointment. The sight of his handwriting was painful to me, but I had been dealing with enough of his documents that I was almost inured to that. By this time I had made arrangements for the disposal of many of his belongings. Most of his clothes, for instance, would be of use to a homeless shelter. A few of his shirts and jackets were too dear for me to let them leave the house. Perhaps someday I would have the heart to wear them, to live that *Brokeback* moment of handling them and feeling him close. Illogically, I found that I wanted some of his other very favorite clothes out of the house as soon as possible; the sight of them paralyzed and leveled me. There was a moment of dumb recognition when I found, at the bottom of one of his drawers, a faded blue T-shirt from the Lyric Opera of Chicago. It had been a gift to me from Tony and Rachel in the late 1980s and was already old when I loaned it to Joe on our first day together at Rehoboth in 1993. It became almost a fetish for him during those early weeks, a way of staking territory by wearing something that reminded me of Tony and that represented my high-class cultural interests, which he knew I didn't think he fully grasped. Here it was, still in his keeping decades later, though I didn't recall having seen him wear it in many years. Pressed to my face, it still brought back his scent and raked my nerves sideways. It could not be discarded, or worn, or looked at… but I stowed it at the bottom of my own drawer as a pledge of love, a middle finger raised to death.

The calendar, though… I flipped at first through the pages of his last few weeks. Things we'd done together, conversations he'd told me about at dinner, catch-up sessions with friends of his whom I barely knew, professional appointments, notes to call the Coast (with neat check marks when the call was completed and the business handled)… then I noticed that he'd had an appointment with his doctor for a physical the day after he died. How did that get handled? Perhaps a neighbor or my sister or Rachel had taken the call when the doctor's office called to see why he hadn't shown up; they had probably told me and I hadn't really heard. Then an appointment with the architect who might have had ideas about renovating the basement for his studio; then one of his brothers in Brooklyn, visiting on his way to DC, was to have stopped for lunch (but of course he knew everything by now). Some plans of ours: dinners with friends, some of which Joe would have cooked for; movies; plays; a long weekend in New York in early October for a friend's début at the Met (note three weeks earlier on booking a hotel if Danny couldn't put us up). Shut-ins to visit and flowers to deliver (Joe was a church deacon by the time he died); former students coming by to chat about their careers; reminders about his nieces' and nephews' birthdays, and any number of appointments with photographers, his agent, our lawyer George. All moot now.

In mid-October, there was a simple note: "Call Netflix ab't series." Of course there was no check after this note.

I was Joe for a minute, standing at the sink in our bathroom. Something clutched in my chest and I took a deep, slow breath to relax it. For a moment I was dizzy, fuzzy-headed... I had to blink a few times to see clearly. My legs felt shaky underneath me and I reached to hold the sink with both hands. My calendar flashed before my eyes – doctor, lawyer, nieces and nephews, agent, old church ladies... NETFLIX... I knew I might be dying. Something felt unreal, something was too strange, something couldn't be postponed or fixed or handled. I didn't have the strength to call all these people and cancel. Many of the appointments were routine or annoying, but many were things to look forward to, things to laugh about, things I'd hate to miss.

The part of me that wasn't Joe was in a rage that he had had to face that chaotic list of cancellations so quickly and with so little warning. Vicarious disappointment and separation-terror swept through me. There were dozens of things which only he could really do, which would go undone or done wrong if he died; joys and successes he deserved but would now never have. The compassion I felt for him in those moments was horrific; it cut into me; it broke me. I wanted to brandish something at heaven, to protest the whole wrong-headed, childish, petulant experiment of human mortality. I would have taken to myself ten times the grief and confusion I could feel, as Joe, if I could have taken them *from* Joe. My entire soul rebelled in disgust and hatred against the system which had made him go through that.

I noticed that, as Joe, I felt no fear. Joe could die without dread, but not without hassle...a calendar cut short, things he had said 'Yes' to and on which he would now be delinquent... and not without the deep grief of good-byes unspoken. Connie and her obstreperous brood flashed before my eyes; our friends, people who needed him or loved him, professionals who were counting on him. I could sense the besieged pressure he must have felt, impossible triage, disorienting conflicts of obligation, till one idea rose up with almost consoling simplicity and from the inside I called, 'Tiger, come here...'

Suddenly I was hunched on the floor weeping. I had been sitting at the secretary in the parlor, and the spasm of sorrow that had just gone through me had knocked me off my chair. I heard the loud thump as I hit the floor, unhurt. Within a few seconds there was a disorderly tumult on the back stairs from the third floor. Moments later, Jimmy materialized next to me, kneeling and reaching to put one long arm around the shifting target I presented. He must have seen Joe's open calendar on the desk.

"So much to say good-bye to," I cried, "and he had no time. He must have been so sad… so scared and hurried. He should have had time, to plan, to arrange things. God owed him that." I was over-inflating, theatrical by the standards of a justly-superseded theatre, and the theologizing struck even me as unfair. It wasn't Jimmy's language and he shouldn't be asked to respond to it. The few seconds it took him to figure out how to get both arms around my awkwardly folded-in body exactly matched the time he needed to find his words.

"No," he said. "The only thing or person he really *needed* to say good-bye to was you, and he had time to do that." He paused. "God gave him just enough time for that."

I knew that the last phrase was acutely difficult for him to say. He could much more easily have said something about the cosmos or reincarnation or souls transmuting through the time-space continuum to come back as dandelions and chameleons and moonbeams. But whatever it cost him, he hit the bull's-eye. There was some kind of genial smile reaching me from the ceiling, or above it, and I let Jimmy Jack hold me for a minute or two while I stopped crying. When he heard that I was done, he propped me up a bit so that we were seated cross-legged, facing each other, his hands on my shoulders, our foreheads touching.

"Are you OK – I mean, for now?" he asked. "Not like forever… I mean, I know this will take a long time." It was almost as though he knew this from reading a book about human emotions.

"I am, strangely," I said. "You take after your mother in some ways. She always knows exactly what to do and say."

A few days later, Gene dropped by after dinner. Patrick was with him. Gene, the Handsomest Man in Baltimore, had lived for decades in Bolton Hill. Joe and I, by a strange chance, had bought a house just around the corner from his brilliantly lit, lavishly bedecked townhouse, where we had attended God only knew how many parties of shrieking, glamor, WASP socialite pearl-clutching, and rampant gay hilarity, always overlapping at every party. His friend and role model Patrick, whom I had likewise known for over thirty years, was somehow, and quite suddenly as it seemed to me, looking eighty in the mirror, defiantly, with elegance undiminished. It vaguely registered with me that if Patrick was eighty, I was myself no longer thirty-two. Gene, now settling majestically into his late fifties, had taken gracious responsibility for Patrick's social life. This often entailed driving out to the suburbs to pick Patrick up before parties and cashing in on the countless social favors he was owed to get Patrick a ride home.

"Dearest lamb," Gene said. "We saw the lights on and made bold to knock."

Jimmy was hovering over my shoulder; I could feel his nervous sense of duty as co-host.

"Dear Jimmy," Gene continued, extending a hand almost as though Jimmy might kiss it. He pulled him in just enough for a quick air-kiss to right and left. "Baltimore thanks you. You are looking after someone irreplaceably precious." He then turned to me and leaned in to hug me, and with his lips hot against my ear, he murmured, "*PRE*-cious!" in a high husky exhalation. I realized that I was no longer the only one to have noticed that Jimmy had suddenly become handsome.

Patrick went to the piano just inside the parlor and sat on the small stool.

"Jimmy, hon," he said, "show me some chords. I *love* to hear you play. *Teach* me!" He sounded like Cole Porter entreating a stevedore, disarming helplessness and rock-solid élite entitlement in equal measure. He smiled archly at me, as though he knew I wasn't expecting such tact. He had met Jimmy at Joe's funeral. Indeed, over the years, he had met him several times, though he didn't recall them. Jimmy's new height and chiseled profile had made him snap into three dimensions for Patrick. With his old man's wisdom, Patrick also saw Jimmy's unique vulnerability and tentativeness, and he had picked up, somehow, on how the piano was a social lubricant for him. Something in his eye allowed me to see that he was also picturing, in detail, how Jimmy might look naked. I made a mental note about how I hoped to be at eighty.

Jimmy went and stood gravely to Patrick's right at the keyboard. He leaned over Patrick's shoulders to sketch out some rather avant garde harmonies for Patrick, who added some suggestive jazz below.

"Beer?" I asked Gene. He nodded and we walked back to the kitchen. After I'd popped Gene's Natty Boh, I over-filled a highball glass with ice and poured bourbon into the interstices, spanking a sprig of mint to dress the lip. This was Patrick's summer beverage. For J.J., there was a glass of Chardonnay, which I now stocked, and with a quick nod to Gene, I delivered these to the parlor.

"This is my new friend Kevin," I heard Jimmy saying. I glanced around, wondering if someone had actually come in without my hearing. Then I realized that the harmonies he was exploring represented Kevin for him; Patrick must have heard enough on this subject already to understand what Jimmy meant. His lynx eyebrows shot up as he turned to me – 'A-*hah!*' He was trying to telegraph to me that J.J. was sweet on this boy Kevin, whom I hadn't yet met or even heard more than a sentence or two about. I shook my head, a silent 'Just *stop!*' I put the two glasses on coasters on the piano, and withdrew to the kitchen. Gene was seated on a stool at the counter, and pulled out the one next to him for me.

"Joe should be here," he said, clinking his beer can against the glass in which the last of my martini had long since turned warm. He was right. More than once, Gene and I had sat on those stools while Joe stood on the other side of the kitchen island, mixing or pouring for us as though he were our bartender. "How are you tracking?"

I was afraid to admit how barren and lonely I felt inside. Gene firmly believed in the stiff upper lip; grief was something one managed and moved on from. His reign as gay Baltimore's *jeune premier* and, in time, mature benevolent tyrant had begun more or less in synch with the start of the AIDS epidemic, and he had presided over a community which might have collapsed into self-pity and despair. He had done a great deal to preserve our collective morale, hosting fundraisers and negotiating alliances among agencies while handling his own awful losses, smiling through tears and keeping up a determined façade of unflagging courage. The primal-scream side of me had often thought his coping was a bit wooden, even dishonest, but the years had taught me the value of his squared shoulders, iron self-control, and resilient optimism, what might almost be called faith.

He had forms of wisdom and strength all his own, and I valued them. Now I was quite sure I could meet his stoic expectations. With my inner iciness just barely starting to thaw, too, my break-downs so far had been confined to the immediate family.

"'Still in life,' I guess," I said. "As an old lady from Russia told me once, when I asked her how she was doing after her husband's death. Baby steps, really. Devastated; resigned; toddling forward by inches." He nodded, with genuine sympathy.

"That's my strong baby," he said. Sudden shift in tone: "Speaking of *babies*… how old is your Jimmy?"

"Twenty-one," I said.

"Piss me *off*…!" He tossed his head in mock-fury, perhaps in his mind also flicking raven curls off his forehead. "*When* did he get so handsome?"

"About five minutes ago," I said. "I've loved him devotedly since his second day on this planet, but God knows he was no beauty till recently."

"It's our Baltimore water," Gene suggested.

"It's living in my gracious home," I replied. He nodded.

"Now could this be a prospect for soothing your grief?"

"Dear God, no," I said. "I don't think of him that way. He's my little angel boy."

"He may be an angel boy, but I'm willing to bet money he isn't *little*," he said, his eyes slightly hooded.

"Now now – that's not decent," I said. Secretly I was happy that Gene and Patrick had noticed J.J.'s dawning good looks. That was their way of noticing his importance. I also still liked it when the public thought scandal of my association with any attractive young man.

"I have other plans for you, in any case," Gene said. "You remember Paul?" I shook my head. "Yes, you do. Paul and Charlie." Oh yes – a couple, a few years younger than me: Paul a handsome banker, quite fervently Catholic, with a high, pinched, brittle laugh though otherwise insistently masculine; Charlie rather fey, funny, passing for sweet, lofty-coiffed, slim, agitated, and exhausting. When I nodded, Gene said, "Well, there's to be no Charlie anymore. After almost twenty years, he has just waltzed off with some Delaware queen they met at Rehoboth this summer, leaving Paul miserable, broken, *ravaged;* ripe for the plucking. Oh, and you know he's always thought you were the hottest professor in all Baltimore."

I wished for a moment that I had followed Connie's lead and swathed myself in black *crêpe.* At least then I wouldn't have to remind dear old friends that the love of my life had dropped dead scarcely six weeks before. Part of me wanted to draw myself up to my full height and tell Gene with cold grandeur that even speaking of such things was in appallingly bad taste. But I looked at his kind hazel eyes and understood that he was offering me the best consolation he could imagine. He was right that embracing life was my next project. I didn't believe in indulging a broken heart with displays and laments, gloom and despondency. I was also flattered by Paul's purported long-standing interest in me, which I had never suspected. Though Gene had assured me in the years before Joe that any number of men found me fascinating, he had usually been speaking of guys I found lackluster: plain, earnest men who would be described by their references as conscientious, dependable, or hard-working. Worse yet were the clones of myself: professor/curator/tutor of X, elder/vestryman in church/synagogue Y, devoted to cultural activity Z [symphony/Broadway/contra-dancing]. Paul, by contrast, had always struck me as unexpectedly sexy, as long as he didn't laugh. Before I answered Gene, I surveyed my inner landscape, still blasted, lunar… there was simply no possibility of a flirtation, let alone a love. All of that was Joe, and Joe was elsewhere.

"Darling," I said, "I cherish you for thinking of that. I am just not nearly there yet." Despite his quick comprehending nod, he looked only temporarily put off. I knew he would return to the topic soon and often in the weeks to come.

"Paul does *not* enjoy the single life," he said. "He is going to marry *some*one in the next six months, and you can make up your mind about whether or not it should be you. But I know what you're saying. I just need to know that your soul is mending and that you'll gladden the populace again with your sweet smile. In the very near future."

"You should be a poet, dear," I said. "In fact, you already are."

"And meanwhile I am going to lay ruthless siege to your *beautiful* Jimmy Jack." I had literally never known Gene to fail in any seduction to which he put his mind.

"Don't *make* me brandish my meat-cleaver," I said. We stood and went back to the parlor.

Earlier that year, maybe April, someone at Netflix contacted Joe about building a new series around his teaching. Joe had spent a fair amount of time over the years explaining evolutions in the media and technology worlds to me. I had barely gotten used to the idea that people streamed movies on line and paid a subscription for the right to do so, and I had no clear understanding of how the company that handled that market could also produce its own content. Joe managed to walk me through this new landscape without once rolling his eyes at me.

He was normally allergic to reality TV. He and I had often had that conversation ('What "reality" do these people inhabit?' and 'Who says nasty and spiteful = "reality"?'), but Netflix pitched this concept to him in a way he found intriguing and flattering. The idea was that a minor star whose career had peaked or plateaued would provide positive, common-sense, real-world guidance for young people pursuing careers as performers. Joe would be a combination of teacher, mentor, and life coach for students or young professionals, helping them prepare for auditions, negotiate contracts, find agents, identify their own look and niche, develop personal and professional networks, and generally manage their lives as working artists. Netflix would recruit, with his help, the young people he would work with; this process would fill the first couple of episodes. Clips of his own career over the years would occasionally be used to demonstrate points he wanted to make, positive or negative, and he would have frequent chances to show off his own chops, as acting teacher and vocal coach, and in role-play, when he would take the part of the prospective agent, the audition committee or panel of judges, the co-star in sample dialogue or duets.

With his department's permission, some scouts in expensive jackets and sunglasses, wearing espadrilles without socks, came to observe a few of his acting classes at the university. The whole project, which he would discuss excitedly with me after each new meeting and phone call, was a great boost to the ego of the man I had nicknamed Divo during our very first days together. It was deeply gratifying to me that he was receiving this kind of recognition. He was in fact the ideal person for this concept: quite well-known, a familiar face but not a major star, universally liked and respected in his professional circuits as actor, model, and singer, and known as a creative, engaged instructor.

One night at dinner he surprised me.

"They asked me about you today," he said.

"What about me?"

"If you want to be in the series. Or I guess I should say if you'd be willing. They like the diversity angle; they like that we're married."

"So do I. So… so what's their thinking?" I could already tell that I liked the idea that Joe's life-partner would occasionally kiss him on his way out the door, or show up for a workshop performance; that Joe would sometimes say, 'I'll have to talk to Jim about this' when a scheduling issue arose. Maybe we would tie each other's ties before a fancy dinner, or host celebrations of cast-members' successes at our house.

Joe had never been closeted about me. In the first years of our relationship, that involved his threading a lot of needles. His most famous evening soap-opera role had been menacingly hetero, and in those years he had shown up every now and then on the cover of "People" or "TV Guide" in a ripped t-shirt or with his tux jacket thrown over one shoulder, an alluring glimpse of chest hair showing, always as an icon of hunky straightness. There had been some pressure on him then to date starlets or attend awards banquets with some female sauciness on his arm; friends of his told me more about this after his death than he had ever mentioned to me. At first, he had found ways, when pressed, either to go to public functions alone or, very occasionally, to take me. I had gotten flutters of star-struck excitement at a few of these, meeting Drew Barrymore (next to whom Joe had stood in two scenes of "Riding in Cars with Boys") and Gregory Harrison (the patriarch-star of Joe's evening soap) and some others. All of these colleagues were clearly very fond of Joe, and faultlessly gracious to me. Gradually, as the profession matured, it became an open secret that he was gay and lived with me. In time, one or two magazine profiles – not that he was the subject of many – referred to me as his "companion" rather than as his "roommate." In recent years we had gotten a minor kick out of the fact that our marriage actually got a mention, with a picture of us in church, in a major entertainment rag and on its website. Gay Baltimore, of course, thrived smugly on Joe's near-fame, thanks to which I was often pointed out to newcomers as a community celebrity.

"They'd want to shoot here sometimes," Joe said. "Like you and me at home; maybe have us discuss my classes, ideas… stuff like that."

"Would it be scripted? Would they tell me what to say? You know I'd choke on 'I think she needs to *hone* her *craft*,' or 'He hasn't found his *voice* yet.'" He laughed out loud. He had almost no tolerance for academic jargon, and knew that I had even less for show-biz twaddle.

"No; I think they'd actually want us just to talk. Like you'd be my reality-check."

"Or fan club," I said. "You know me. Most of the time I'd just be saying, 'Oh, that sounds amazing,' or 'Those kids are so lucky to have the benefit of your experience.' I could provide really very little of the arms-akimbo head-wagging trailer park first-cousins'-divorce stuff. Quite unlikely I'd ever scream 'Girl-FREN' you better watch yer fuckin' *mouth!*' at you and hurl my cocktail in your face. 'Reality TV' *so-called!*' I shuddered ostentatiously. It would have been a brilliant reality-TV moment.

"I know, right?" he said.

"Every single person on reality TV apparently went to the same academy of bad acting. They literally *all* have the same trashy vocal inflections and pseudo-jive mannerisms…" I was off on a favorite rant of mine.

"… 'and they don't think anything is "real" until it's hideous and obscene.' I know, Tiger. Relax," Joe said. "They want me to teach *good* acting. And they'd just want you to be you. That uptight incredibly polite classy professor I married."

"What would they say if we were talking like this and I suddenly lunged across the table and showered your face with burning kisses because you were just so adorable?" He laughed.

"Our ratings would *soar*." He looked down at his plate. "I don't get the impression this would be a big part of the series. I don't want you to think they'll be traipsing through the house constantly or bothering you or messing with your schedule." I looked across at him and was still surprised, after all these years, to see that he was modestly nervous, worried that I would think this project was a low-class imposition. In fact, I was finding myself more and more attracted to the general concept, and extremely flattered that I might have a small part in it. Joe, whose name and face were known to a vast public, had for decades played a supporting role in my social life. He had been my stalwart loyal consort at church, in Baltimore's clannish gay community, among classical musicians, in the tweedy circles of linguists and Renaissance scholars who made up my professional life. He was now offering me a chance, unsought and un-auditioned-for, to sample his life of semi-notoriety… a chance, even, for a kind of fame.

"So you're saying this isn't going to catapult me into stardom?" I asked.

"*This* won't," he said, smiling. "But you never know about the next show…"

"I actually think it's a cool idea. It would be fun for me to see your world from the inside. I might give an outsider's perspective on your work."

"That's what I meant about the reality-check," he nodded. The circling-back was so neat that something suddenly clicked in my head.

"Was this their idea or yours?" He didn't look up.

"Totally theirs. Like I said, it's the gay angle. They like it. They think it's now." Objectively, and not just for my vanity, I agreed. I was also absolutely sure that Joe had floated the idea to them and then pitched it, argued for it… and that he would never admit it.

"I love it," I said. I counted to ten in my mind; then he looked up. It had taken him that long to trust that I'd fallen for his version of the story. When our eyes were locked, I said, "And I love *you*, Divo."

"Hopelessly/madly?"

"Madly/hopelessly."

We lifted our wineglasses and touched their rims together across the table. They made a lovely deep *ching*. An hour later we were side by side in bed, in a loose wet embrace, and occasionally whispering each other's names seemed one of the sweetest and deepest conversations we'd ever had.

Chapter 4
October 2015
[flashback: April 2015]

Walter and Ricardo came up from Washington for a weekend in October. Plan A had been that Marie would come with them. Clare had left her barely a year earlier, after more than twenty years of sharing a home on Capitol Hill, for the only woman in Washington with less humor or style than Clare herself. Her departure left me largely indifferent, but Marie was devastated. Her ebullience and dash, which had overflowed enough to make Clare seem almost fun at times, now sloshed unchecked around the large empty house, creating manic whirlwinds one moment and echoing voids the next. Clare's children, whom Marie had co-mothered from their early childhood, were grown now, smart and funny and deeply fond of Marie, but both settled in distant places. Though Marie never admitted to being lonely, Joe and I worried about her quite a bit. She had certainly been kind and attentive after Joe's death. Nevertheless I could tell that it was still hard for her to enter completely into another's bereavement, as I think it would have been for me in her place: her own, of a different kind, was too raw. She was still at the height of her profession as a DC attorney. The press of work was always a good explanation when she needed time to herself, and this was one of those times. We had a long talk on the phone, something that had become very rare in my life since e-mail and texting and smart phones. I had a sense of us calling to each other across the broad canyon of widowhood, missing a word or phrase here and there, and filling the occasional void with vague gesticulations of good will. We made a date for lunch in Washington a week or two later.

Since July, Ricardo's every conversation with me had begun with crying. As he got out of the driver's seat at my front door, he glanced up at the façade of the house as though it were draped in black. His face fell and he looked across the car at me and suddenly tears started streaming down his cheeks. He swatted his hand in the air and turned aside for a moment as though he could banish some sight or thought, then came around the car in silence, with his arms out to embrace me. Only then did the quiet sobs begin, interspersed with the word, "Darling." In my peripheral vision,

Jimmy trailed through the door and hopped down the stairs, and Walter put his hand on his shoulder.

"Jacob," he said, with his usual gravity.

"Hey, Uncle Walter," J.J. said. Walter and Ricardo had been intermittent features of Jimmy's whole life. Tony and Walter were both classmates and sometime roommates of mine in college, and saw each other any time the Fleischer-Neubergs came east to see Joe and me. Walter had also stayed once or twice at the Glencoe house when museum business took him to Chicago. Walter had always been "Uncle Walter" to Jimmy; Ricardo was simply "Tio."

J.J. was quite efficient in hefting bags up the front stairs for them. Doing was always easier for him than chatting; he still spoke of this as his difficulty with "people-ing." He enjoyed showing his familiarity with the house.

"We find it's easier to come up this way even though the back stairs are closer to your room," he explained. "The back stairs have too many turns for luggage."

"Honey you're so re-*spon*-sible," said Ricardo.

Walter and I went down the back stairs while J.J. lingered to help Ricardo place and open the bags. Walter glanced at me with one eyebrow arched.

"'We'?" he murmured. "A tad officious, perhaps?"

"He's actually a big help," I said. "You should see him unpack groceries and empty the dishwasher." Walter smiled.

"If he can decode your Byzantine systems for tasks like *those*, he's earned his OCD Badge fair and square." He was right that Jimmy's quirks made him the perfect co-denizen for me in an elderly house. Things I was usually embarrassed to explain to guests (doors that opened only when slapped at the top, or toilets whose handles had to be jiggled just so) appealed to his love of arbitrary, rigid order. I had gotten used to the sight of his desk through his door at the end of the third-floor hall, with his laptop perfectly centered and his pens and books placed at exact right angles to its corners. In the kitchen now, Walter smiled wryly as I reached into five or six cupboards and drawers to assemble the ingredients and glasses for the Negronis I intended to mix. As he had implied, my kitchen was organized according to criteria and distinctions which would be difficult to explain. By now, Jimmy Jack knew just where to look for everything.

Like me, Walter had thickened a bit about the waist over the years, and his coloring was more florid now, which gave an intenser sparkle to his pale blue eyes. Unlike me, he had kept his full head of hair, still baby-fine as it had always been, and he wore it at more or less the preppy length of our college years. By now, most of the yellow had faded and his hair might almost be described as snowy. He was an accomplished scholar, a gentleman to his finger-tips, and a wicked wit. Once the four of us were strolling the Mall in DC when a magnificent young man jogged by, glistening and exhaling an aphrodisiac scent of cologne and clean sweat, clad only in expensive running shoes and silky shorts with a Union Jack pattern. In his wake, an enraptured gay silence had fallen over the group, into which after a moment dropped Walter's quiet, courteous suggestion: "Shall we offer to lower his standard?" His ability to read me like a New England Primer had never faltered.

As he and I took our first sips, Ricardo and J.J. came down the stairs. J.J.'s descent always sounded like a delivery of coal. Ricardo had the innate poise and carriage of one of nature's great beauties, and he took the last step like a panther landing silently from an outcrop of rock. His shock of thick straight hair, streaked with grey on top and white at the temples, threw into relief his falcon face. The lines framing his mouth and eyes seemed to come only from smiles; some generous ancestor had let him keep much of the fullness of his cheeks and the tautness of his chin. His eyes had aged into wisdom but were still candid, optimistic, and at times child-like. He had lived for decades now with HIV, and was incapable of anything as crass as innocence or denial.

"Honey," he had said to me more than once, "when my time comes, I'm just GO-ing. The world owes me absolutely nothing." What the world owed him, I often thought, was everything: no one in my life modeled such consistent dignity and sweetness. But he believed himself extremely lucky, he said... Walter, Joe and me, his shop, his friends, all the fun he'd had, his faith, even his health.

He grabbed Jimmy from behind now, his head resting on the back of Jimmy's left shoulder, and squeezed him hard.

"Jimmy's my new boyfriend," he said. "The perfect host. He showed me everything upstairs – the closet, the dresser, the towels… And look at how big and grown-up and *hand*-some our little boy is! Baby" (this to Walter), "you can sleep on the couch tonight." J.J. positively blushed; Ricardo's brand of eros-free flirtation was too rich in subtext and irony for him.

"Tio," he said, "behave." Ricardo released him.

"Oh honey," he said. Those two words from Ricardo always meant that everything was right with the world. "I'm too *young* for you."

Jimmy and I gave Tony and Rachel a video call after dinner that night, sitting close together on the Victorian loveseat in the parlor with his laptop propped in front of us. Rachel and Tony sat side by side in one of the broad grey and tan spaces of their house; some prompting from J.J. helped me to recognize it as Tony's office.

"How is my son behaving?" Rachel asked.

"He's my lifeline," I said.

"Still smiling, champ?" Tony asked his son, a gentle allusion to Lyric.

"I'm not the smartest kid in class here," Jimmy said. "I told you about Kevin, right?"

From a thousand miles away, I saw Rachel stiffen very slightly.

"The music theory boy?" she asked. "He sounds like a potential kindred spirit. I'm glad he's keeping you in awe."

"I think he's gay," J.J. said.

There was never any logic to the way Jimmy talked about Kevin. This particular non sequitur hit a nerve in me. I felt slightly embarrassed by Jimmy's even mentioning gayness in his parents' presence. Of course they were loyal friends and allies, but I had always gone to great lengths of diplomacy and euphemism to make my homosexuality as unobtrusive to them as possible. The once-in-a-lifetime miracle of meeting Joe and making a shared home with him had made it feasible for me to present my lifestyle as relatively similar to theirs. Moments alone with internet porn, bumps in the fidelity-road for Joe and me, my private political doubts about gay marriage… none of those had ever come up. I never mentioned that I lived in daily dread of the time when Joe no longer struck me as

64

desirable. He seemed able to love, even want soft-waisted, shiny-pated me, but I had no such confidence about myself. Perhaps the most *outrées* things Tony and Rachel knew about my gayness were that I nurtured a celebrity crush on Prince Harry and hoped that Colin Firth would play me in any biopic that might one day be made about me. For Jimmy to raise the topic to his parents, especially when he was living under my roof, made me feel exposed and indicted as a bad influence or incompetent chaperon.

Both Tony and Rachel showed, and quickly covered, a slight reaction to this update about the admirable Kevin, and then J.J. burbled on to the next subject.

With our nightcap brandy snifters in hand, Walter and Ricardo and I sat in the parlor while Jimmy drifted up and down the keyboard. Walter had taken a large wing chair, while Ricardo perched next to me on the old loveseat, which we had turned, auditorium style, to face the piano. We looked prim and attentive, mostly because the little sofa required sitting up straight. Jimmy was playing beautifully. His lifelong attraction to harsh Martian harmonies seemed to have abated for the evening, and there was something almost Windham Hill about his gentle, introspective New Age meanderings. Suddenly he looked back over his shoulder and said,

"G.J., I wrote this for you. I'm not improvising; I've memorized it."

We all gave some version of our 'Oh, how nice!' smiles and settled in for a few minutes of incoherent tinkling and hammering.

Instead, Jimmy started with something gentle, shimmering, and, to my ear, slightly generic… a bit *Clair de lune,* quite vanilla by his standards. After a few moments, something jazzy and jangly started to break in, quietly at first, and the two atmospheres mingled before the more forthright melody started to overwhelm the iridescent background. And it *was* a melody, faintly traced, and then subjected to some inventive variations and inversions, but gradually recognizable as "Broadway." I remembered having recently told Jimmy that this was one of Joe's signature songs, something he had brilliantly and memorably belted at a party when we were first a couple and then, many times over the years, brought out for auditions, Karaoke, open mic nights, galas. Something in J.J.'s playing became brash and brassy, and I could almost hear Joe's voice for a note or two at a time, vaulting skyward, challenging fate, claiming territory, declaring *'I am!'* I couldn't recall any occasion when Jimmy would actually have heard Joe sing the song, but if he hadn't, he was certainly channeling something elemental about Joe's personality and charisma. I had almost adjusted to the nostalgic tug of remembering when something tender but peremptory started to intrude. Jimmy brought into the bumptious upward-modulating song a very gentle subtext, a melody soft and too subtle to name, but which refused to be drowned out by the syncopations of the main theme. Within several seconds I realized that self-effacing traces of *"Traümerei"* were asserting themselves, rising in volume to match "Broadway." Somehow the two tunes merged; the rising triads of one and the descending lines of the other danced together on the tips of J.J.'s fingers, bounced off the pre-Civil War soundboard of the piano and across the parlor floor, up my pants-legs, into my heart. Jimmy Jack had distilled the intertwining of my life with Joe's into a completely unexpected duet of opposites.

Ricardo had been holding my hand. Like the clownish victim of a 19th century hypnotist, I rose slowly and silently from the sofa. Ricardo stirred as if he might rise with me, but then cut some invisible string to free me. Very dimly, I felt Walter's eyes following me. I had to put my hand on J.J.'s shoulder, to signal that I had heard *"Traümerei."* That tradition was too sacred to omit simply because my heart was breaking. Like a sleepwalker I came up behind him, and when my hand touched him I could feel him relax. He was moving into some final stage of his composition. The melodies blurred and grew gentler, and then the swaggering "Broadway" tags quite suddenly stopped. For a few more measures, faint echoes of the Schumann continued to peek out, until they too disappeared into an anonymous progression of paler chords, sending, bidding, releasing. Someone or something had rustled out of the room, leaving a fragrant hush and peace. As the absence spread through the parlor after this gracious departure, I knew that my face was wet. The house seemed vast and empty, filled with missing, yet also charged with memory and with the presence of friends. The fact that one of us was irretrievably gone was palpable in the chords that sank, subsided, and bade farewell.

After an entranced silence, I asked,

"What do you call it, Jimmy Jack? It's… perfect."

He reached up to pat my hand on his shoulder.

"I call it, 'Good-bye Uncle Joe,'" he said. "It's for you."

The next night J.J. texted me from Peabody to ask if he could bring Kevin to dinner. They showed up half an hour later, just as Walter, Ricardo, and I were finishing our hurried exchange of speculations about him.

"Do you think Jimmy might be gay?" Walter had asked.

"I realized last year that I hoped so," I said. "I didn't even tell Joe; it seemed too *cliché*. I was in one of my snits about Lyric, so I thought maybe I was just wishing he weren't with her. And for a gay gentleman of a certain age to think too much about his godson's sexuality just sounds creepy."

"Honey you've already touched his penis," Ricardo laughed; "more than once as I recall."

"And as all the world knows, it's a *nice* size," I answered. The bris story and its immediate hygienic aftermath had become parts of fond family lore. I wanted to laugh Ricardo's joke off, to avoid any appearance of being embarrassed to discuss the topic. Since Jimmy began his occasional wee-hours visits to my bed, I had tried to pass my attachment to him through my attraction-to-students filter. For decades, I had said that the whole pedagogical project was erotic by definition, that professors taught by enticing their students to admire, trust, and follow them. I maintained that healthy teacher-student relationships required the teacher at least inwardly to acknowledge when he or she found a given student physically attractive. When I noticed that kind of magnetism between me and a student, as happened every couple of years at least, I had a battery of strategies to deploy. These young men surely knew that I liked them; I liked almost all my students, as I hoped they could all tell. Because I was so careful to show no preference, the actual objects of my special interest risked becoming the ones I most often corrected in class. My firm belief was still that teachers who indignantly said, 'Oh, I would *never...!*' were, like homophobic Republican politicians, the ones most likely to end up on the evening news, up to their shifty self-righteous eyes in degrading scandal. Perhaps I was becoming one of those self-deluding hypocrites. I didn't let myself insist to Ricardo that J.J.'s member, whatever its size, was of no practical or libidinous interest to me.

I noticed that Walter looked at me rather closely.

"So you hoped he was gay... why?" he asked.

"I guess I wanted him not to be cornered into something too conventional. He and Lyric were like all those dreary hippies in college…" (a population Walter and I had been ragging on since 1970) "… pretending to be avant-garde but always *so* sensitive and *so* in touch and *so* in love, and I thought she was leading him to some bourgeois hetero-normative slaughter."

"Well," Ricardo said, "I think Jimmy has a crush on Kevin, whether he's gay or not. He's kind of intimidated by him, and that's hot."

"Have you glimpsed the boy yet?" Walter asked.

"No. I've heard that he's little. And scary-smart. That's all I know."

"I'll bet he's darling," Ricardo said.

As usual, Ricardo was right. A minute or two later, we heard Jimmy let himself in the front door, escorting a boy who came up about to his waist. Kevin was a tiny fireball of a kid, ginger in tone, lithe and muscular, with the upright swaggering posture of people short since toddlerhood. His pale Irish eyes darted around the room and his wavy auburn hair gave a kind of Kennedy cachet to his sharp regular features. He was very good-looking. If one absolutely needed to find a flaw, apart from his size, one might have critiqued his jutting little mug-handle ears, but in fact they were an ornament, one adorability the more. He was naturally winning and energizing. I wanted to wrestle him onto my lap and pat his little hiney and invite him to confide his tiny problems to me, for hours, forever. His affect, however, made it pretty clear that he had virtually no idea what a problem was.

"He's told me all about his *fabulous* gay godfather," he said, hand out to me in an instant. Just hearing him say "He" and "his" seemed to make Jimmy almost squirm with pleasure, as though Kevin had familiarly jerked a newsboy thumb at him and called him '*This* guy…'

"I've heard you're up for this year's Nobel Prize in Smartness," I said. "Jimmy also mentioned that you were no giant." There seemed to be no reason to avoid that subject. He was probably something like five-five, and every other man in the room would have found it easy to bend down and kiss the top of his head; at least the three older of us certainly considered it.

"Oh," he said off-handedly, "I don't mind that. Just put a bucket over the tall ones' heads and swing from the handle… It's worked so far!"

I didn't think Walter would fall for all this breeziness, but during dinner Kevin completely charmed him with a brilliant, dumbed-down-for-laypersons Schenkerian analysis of Susanna's fainting scene in *Nozze di Figaro*, showing how she would come in on the same pitches as other characters but use them as different *solfège* values in related keys, as though to reframe reality for them in her intentional deception.

"He knows opera ten times better than I do," Jimmy explained. "That's one of like a million things I can learn from him."

"May I call you Barbarina?" Walter asked, turning back to Kevin.

A few minutes later, a swift incomprehensible exchange between the two music students made reference to the "Scriabin mystical chord."

"The what?" I asked, knowing I was meant to. Jimmy said,

"He used it in a lot of his pieces." We were done eating, and I rose and walked into the parlor to stand at the piano. Jimmy called in from the dining room:

"Start with the lowest note and work up. Left hand, C below middle C, then F#, B-flat; right hand, E, A, D." I plunked the notes out one by one as he dictated, and then struck the chord. An eerie cold serenity wafted through the house.

I liked it, and sketched it out and struck it several more times. I noticed something, and did some silent counting to be sure I wasn't about to expose myself as an idiot.

"Wait… if the A were a B-flat, wouldn't the two hands be the same chord in two keys?" I asked.

Jimmy, not needing a keyboard to be sure, said, "Yes, I guess so." But Kevin completed his thought.

"But I think of it as a quartal voicing of a C13#11 chord." I looked over my shoulder into the dining room and saw Jimmy shining at Kevin something like the private adoring glances he had sometimes aimed at Lyric in the past. The difference was that I did not find it irritating now.

"Of course you do," I said. "Of course you both do. You're known lunatics."

Walter caught my eye, brows lifted, and Ricardo, knowing that neither of the boys could see him, silently put his hand on his heart and smiled like a Puerto Rican grandmother.

Several hours after lights-out, Jimmy crawled wordlessly into my bed. This no longer caused me any shock; I had learned to wake gently and to wait for whatever idea he wanted to ventilate. He gave off a faint whiff of patchouli. He had found most of my and Joe's colognes too modern and worldly, and dabbed oily drops of this ancient harem-scent here and there instead. It was like having a small spicy brush-fire lying next to me. He had gotten control of any noisome odors that might have bothered me in the past, and this incongruous small touch of exotic seduction in his chaste, clueless self-presentation was endearing. He wriggled a little into Joe's old spot before he spoke.

"Can you see why I like him so much?" he asked.

"He's a delight," I said.

"I knew you'd like him. He thinks you're adorable. That's what he said."

"So is he officially a gay boy?" I asked.

"Yeah, he told me while we were playing." The two boys had sat at the keyboard and improvised for a bit while the adults talked after dinner.

"Do you think he's sweet on you?" I asked. Jimmy thought for a minute.

"I think we like each other equally."

My turn to pause and choose my words.

"So are you maybe a little sweet on him?"

"How would I know? How do humans know? "

I understood that simply telling Jimmy, 'Oh, you'll *know* when it's right!' would be no help at all.

"Do you think about him? Can you describe those thoughts?"

"Yeah," he said, "I think about him all the time. I wonder what he's going to say." He thought for a minute. "Then I wonder what he's going to be wearing." After a short beat, he asked with a funny urgency, "Do you think he's hairy? He's got this crazy-fine copper hair on his arms and legs but I wonder about his chest." It was dark enough that he couldn't see me smile. I had a funny idea that Joe could, and sensing that he might be perching somewhere nearby was not at all painful, perhaps for the first time.

"Would it be good or bad if he were hairy?" I asked.

"No, it's fine for Kevin just to be Kevin." Though Jimmy was a bit underdeveloped socially, he was incapable of splitting an infinitive. "I just wonder."

"Maybe you can ask him how he's feeling," I said. "He probably knows you well enough already to understand that you get places by different routes than some people."

"Than *most* people," he said, shyly.

"He obviously likes you, and if you're right that you like each other equally, maybe he can explain what that means… to him, at least. Then you can see if that rings true for you, too."

"How can you tell he likes me?" He was too curious to be cool or coy.

"Everyone who knows you likes you." He waved a hand.

"Oh, that," he said. "Everyone thinks I'm goofy and maybe sweet. That doesn't count."

"Well then, I can tell he thinks your musical mind is fascinating. You complete each other's sentences when you talk about music. Also I liked the way he passed you the bread without looking at you. He knew you wanted it."

I could feel his smile in the dark.

"He did, didn't he?"

A minute or two later, I could tell from his breathing that he'd fallen asleep. This was a new barrier of intimacy breached. It felt cozy, and a bit annoying. Perhaps I was obliged to watch over him in some way, to tuck something around his neck, to remain alert and on guard while this Candide dreamed his way into some unimaginable new garden. But it was probably only ten minutes before he stirred and hunched himself upright.

"OK," he said over his shoulder. "Good night. I love you."

Very cool air poured in under the sheets which had been tucked around us just a moment before.

"You too," I said.

"I think I just decided I'm gay."

Inwardly I bellowed out Cavaradossi's *"Vittoria! Vittoria!"* in such a voice as to make the shades of Gigli and Björling turn pale with envy. There in my room, however, to Jimmy, I just smiled and said,

"Just be J.J. That's all you need to do. You know I think you're perfect." I could feel him waiting for something else. "And I do think Kevin is lovely."

He half-fell, half-lunged over to my side of the bed and wrapped his long sinewy arms around me. I reached up to pat his back, which felt strong, fragile, and resonant, like a great cello or double bass. Something was thudding inside him: I could feel his pulse in the slim springy muscles of his back. The waft of patchouli was clear now. I wondered if he put it in his hair before retiring.

"Yeah, he is."

"Sleep tight, honey," I said, and he lurched to his feet and went back to his room.

After he left, I dreamed of Joe, the first such dream that I could remember. We were in a small convertible, speeding along a two-lane highway, straight across a vast flat desert, under bright sunlight. It wasn't clear which of us was driving; sometimes the car seemed to move of its own accord. Really it was more a membrane than a machine: Joe and I sat side by side in a tight, comfortable open cocoon which somehow had wheels and industrial, sporty lines. Occasionally we were in two small cars and we were moving closely in parallel, neither edging more than a few inches ahead or behind. The air was bracing despite the hot landscape. We passed a tiny gas station with antique pumps; on top of each pump you could see the fuel in a large glass jug before it drained into your tank by gravity. We didn't stop. Jimmy was standing at one of the pumps in blue overalls. Apparently he had some sort of summer job there. He waved and smiled as we sped by, and the pressure of Joe's shoulder against mine in our narrow vehicle seemed part of the same joy we felt in seeing this dear awkward young friend. Then Joe's little pod seemed to speed up. He was ahead of me, then far ahead, then suddenly just a tiny point on an incredibly distant horizon. Somehow the sight of Jimmy had enlivened him, made him oblivious for a few moments to my elderly slowness, and he was carelessly but irrevocably expanding the gap between us. I was angry at myself, incompetent and helpless because I couldn't catch up with him. Perhaps if I kept up my labored, slogging pace, by nightfall I would find that he had noticed my absence and stopped by the roadside to wait for me. From far behind me now, I could hear J.J.'s voice in a cracking treble, calling after me, "Don't worry. I'm right here."

When I woke up, I had an instant of feeling warm about having been with Joe; the next instant came the stab of remembering that he was gone. Nevertheless, after a few short minutes of sadness, I knew that we *had* been together, that in some way we would continue to have these shared moments. I was grateful that Joe had found a way to get that across to me, grateful that he had been allowed to… that this broken system had some retrofits or work-arounds built imperfectly into it. I pulled on a dark grey corduroy shirt and headed downstairs to make coffee for our guests.

A few minutes later, Walter stood next to me at the kitchen counter, sleepily filling his cup. We were the only ones stirring yet.

"Did I hear you and Jimmy talking in your room in the middle of the night?" he asked, practically his first words to me. The fact that he was barely functional made the question marginally less startling, but I was still mortified. Though the room where Walter and Ricardo were settled was rather far from mine, a floor below and at the back of the house, he would have been able to tell that our voices were coming from my room, not from Jimmy's directly above them. That Ricardo had heard nothing was unsurprising; he always slept like an Elgin marble.

I was enough of a hypocrite that, while sure there was nothing to be ashamed of in J.J.'s nighttime visits, I extremely disliked the way they looked. I shot a sideways guilty glance at Walter, and saw that he was looking at me steadily through his grogginess. His eyes, always canny and intelligent, in this moment were also very understanding.

"Yes," I said. "Jimmy Jack apparently sometimes still climbs into bed with his parents when he's at home. He's transferred that to me. He gets lonely or disoriented sometimes, especially when something is preying on his mind. He's dropped by my room at night maybe four or five times since he moved in."

"Your room in the sense of your bed, right?" Walter asked, puzzled. Then he smiled. "I won't call Protective Services. Knowing Jimmy, I am quite sure this is an all-male *Sonnambula* of irreproachable purity. But is there – do you think… should I be worried about this? You know how odd it looks?"

"I don't think you should be worried; I'm not. At least not now."

"So you know it might be seen as very strange?"

"I do," I said. I was feeling relieved. Walter was being honest, but he wasn't horrified; he trusted me. "Almost everything about Jimmy is strange. I love him and it's not possible for me to scold him for being needy at times." My coffee needed a few seconds' zap in the microwave, and this gave me an excuse to step away from Walter. Over my shoulder, I said quietly, "He would have absolutely no comprehension if I tried to explain what people might think of his coming to my room that way. It would appall him; it would gross him out completely."

"I understand that," Walter said. I turned back to face him. He waited, then said, "I'm worried about *you*. You're old enough to know about love… how complicated it is, how there are no names for so many forms of it. Jimmy is one of the great loves of your life, and you notoriously have no immunity to the charms of young men you like. And what to make of this new precious Barbarina? Your eyes were like searchlights at dinner last night; I'm sure you already have detailed theories about Kevin's potential as a bum-boy. Now, perhaps thanks to this entrancing Irish boylet, Jimmy suddenly shows dim signs of erotic awakening, and has suddenly and coincidentally… shall we say?… grown into his nose. To the immense surprise of all who know him, he has become a beautiful boy, a kind of knobby pin-up, a strapping clueless brilliant yokel by Parmigianino. And here *you* are in the depths of mourning, sharing your home with this one person on earth with whom your relationship absolutely *must* remain perfectly platonic, and he worships you from the core of his pre-lapsarian otherworldliness, *and* he betakes himself to your bed with a kind of benighted innocence which none of us knew still existed… *This* worries me."

"It worries me too. I think it will be OK. I honestly have no such feelings for J.J., and he's decades short of any kind of perversity."

"Innocence is the most perverse thing in the world," Walter said. He smiled again, though, and I knew, as we sipped our coffee and waited for the toaster's *ping*, that he was satisfied with this topic for now. "Do you think he might be in love with Kevin?"

This seemed like too fresh a secret of Jimmy's to be shared even with Walter.

"I'll keep you posted. If he is, it won't be long before he tells me."

Joe and I had moved to Bolton Hill in late October, and our first real introduction to the neighborhood's rituals was Hallowe'en a few days later. The house was still stacked to the ceiling with boxes. Framed pictures, some still wrapped in padded brown paper, leaned against the walls in parlor and dining room. Our new next-door neighbor Carl had intimated that we might want to buy some candy, and suggested we meet him around 5:30 on the front stoop to greet the children. During our years in our previous house, it had been our unchanging Hallowe'en practice to close all indoor shutters and turn out all lights in the front rooms. The occasional rings of the bell there were due to drunken Hopkins undergraduates, sometimes disguised to the extent of a smear or two of face paint (savage? avatar? punk rocker?). Joe and I had learned simply to huddle in back and play dead. After years of this, we had mostly forgotten that there were children in the world or that they might frolic by to demand sugar on October 31.

At 5:30, Joe in an Indiana Jones hat and leather bomber jacket, and I in a Renaissance robe, sheepishly appeared on the front steps with a small bowl of M&Ms, expectations somewhere down around our ankles. We were astonished to find the street jammed with children in costume, with hovering watchful parents a few steps behind them. Neighbor Carl was already holding court in full witch costume, surrounded by hordes of small dragons, pirates, princesses, and Spider Men; adult voices would prompt from a few feet away, "What do you say?" and "Just take *one!*"

Carl laced one witchy, lecherous arm around Joe's waist and suggested that "an adult beverage" might come in handy for the next two hours. I fled shrieking to the kitchen and returned with two stiff Manhattans in plastic cups. Carl was right: until nearly eight, we greeted urban urchins, accepted their shy 'Thank you's, exchanged pleasantries with their parents, and sipped furtively on our cups. Others of our new neighbors cruised by every so often, with many introductions on the fly, and begged candy from the inexhaustible Carl, who happily shared mini-Snickers from a huge bag indoors.

The children and their parents were almost all people of color, from less than a mile away, a neighborhood where we almost never set foot and which was known nationally as the setting for *The Wire*. I vaguely knew that it was a Habitat for Humanity destination for several activist members of our church. These parents showed a quiet, stiff vigilance and watchful determination. They met our eyes unapologetically, wary and poised. They knew that in a functioning republic, parents on our social rung would share and respect their intentions for their children. It dawned on me, after the first shock at the mob scene, that they must feel safer bringing their bedizened kids to our block than to their own. Our alien neighborhood, sharing their ZIP code, was a resource for sheltered after-dark festivities, for the programmatic flirt with danger which children hope for on Hallowe'en.

Joe and I pretty much drained Carl's candy reserve before the crowds started to dwindle, and we asked him over for a nightcap. His pointed hat came off; his green face became even more grotesque with the removal of his pointed putty nose. After a moment of trying to be polite, I had to ask him to wash his face. Settled, raw-faced, on a box in the unassembled parlor a few minutes later, feet up, glass in hand, he reacted to my question:

"Isn't this all a little... plantation-y?"

"I think it's fun," he replied.

Shendra, a sometime colleague of Joe's, was occasionally in Baltimore for her part-time role on *House of Cards*. She prided herself on being a force of nature, and wore her forty-something years very lightly. Her glowing skin and curvy body projected an embodied common sense which was starting to earn her a certain kind of success in the profession. She was pretty and sexy enough for leading-lady roles, but her vividly lived years on the planet were steering her towards parts, larger and larger as time went by, as the wise-cracking sidekick, the seen-it-all beautician speaking her truth, the disenchanted laser-eyed judge, the mamma bear springing to the defense of her cub. Her current role was as a fast-talking political operative, perhaps a nod of some kind to Donna Brasile; she was entirely complicit in the star's ruthlessness, but managed somehow to find a way, in every episode in which she appeared, to dress him down and to put his Borgia wife in her place. Though the show paid her a small fortune and was prepared to lodge her at some gilded plastic high-rise hotel downtown, she usually preferred our guest room. Much of the filming took place in our immediate neighborhood and she claimed it saved her time to crash with us. I knew it was really that she loved Joe.

Shendra was staying with us one evening in April of 2015 when the smell of smoke drew us from our parlor. Sirens were starting to blare, and from the middle of our street we could see that the sky a few blocks north and west of us had become lurid. We knew that those streets, the home of many of our trick-or-treaters, were in various stages of uproar since Freddie Gray had died in police custody and been buried just a day or two before. Baltimore, which was by now enshrined in the American pop-psyche as an epicenter of criminality ('Oh, you're from Baltimore? We love *The Wire!*'), had been contending for generations with its heritage of systemic racism.

My AIDS activism had taken me, in the 1980s and -90s, to speak at a number of historically black Presbyterian churches. These congregations had a complex, proud, painful history: several had been founded by slave-holding Scotch-Irish Presbyterians before the Civil War for their "people," the domestic staff who, in their view, should be taught accurate Calvinist theology. Some early members, too, had been among the thriving free black middle class of antebellum Baltimore. They produced the vast majority of Baltimore's sixth- and seventh-generation Presbyterians, whereas majority-white congregations, especially lefty ones like ours, were often full of refugees from other denominations. One historically black church had hosted a community dialogue during the Rodney King riots, at which, in an atmosphere of perfect hospitality and among people with whom we had often worshiped on Martin Luther King, Jr. Day, we learned that attorneys and doctors my age and older were often stopped by the police to see if they owned the cars they were driving.

I had always known that Baltimore was a majority-black city, but encounters like that one brought me face to face with the fact that my personal Baltimore was barely integrated. Still I resented the fact that our city was considered the most benighted and dangerous in the United States, when the entire country was a powder keg of injustice and simmering, justified rage. Baltimore, for all its compromised past and present challenges, had sometimes seemed to me to find some kind of gracious equilibrium around issues of race.

Joe had been after me about this for years.

"You think you're slightly cooler about all this stuff than you are," he would say. Joe worked with many artists of color: Shendra, of course, but lots of others too, especially in his pop-music life. I learned, gradually, that he also had gotten the numbers of some of the parents on Hallowe'en – contractors, satellite-TV technicians, owners of coffee shops and specialty stationery stores – and touched base with them from time to time on business. They would drop by the house sometimes and they seemed to know him rather well.

He called me out on a story he heard one of my Southern cousins tell during a visit to town. It was part of our family lore, a tale dating back to Jim Crow days, which had been repeated, as funny, in my presence as far back as I could remember. My great-grandfather had allegedly delegated to the local black Presbyterian pastor the task of beating a sharecropper who had been caught stealing. The implication of the story was always that my ancestor would have given the offender a few symbolic taps on the back, but that the pastor, to enforce morality among his flock, beat him much harder. Any time the man cried out, his pastor would yell, "BEAR your CROS-ses, SIR!" My Southern kin found this story diverting, perhaps because the black pastor incarnated the values of the white congregation more rigorously than they did themselves, and this in and of itself was seen as vaguely comical, bumptious, uppity. As a child, I wondered if my great-grandfather (whom I had never known, but who was the revered grandfather of my father) hadn't secretly known in advance that the pastor would feel himself expected or pressured to be crueler than the white gentleman would have been. If so, didn't he bear moral responsibility for the beating? I had never asked my father what he thought of the story. Dad had had his entire career in the North and, more importantly, had an innate sense of equity and fairness. He could not abide any kind of racial slur and intensely disliked being called "sir" by men of color, whatever their social status or relation to him. Still, sitting next to him during any telling of this anecdote, I had noticed that he smiled at the punchline. This was what we smiled at; smiling at this was how we cemented our family bonds. There had been no passionate abolitionists or civil rights activists among the Southern branch of my family.

In the car coming home from the reunion dinner at which my cousin had resurrected this story, Joe said,

"You realize how completely fucked up that story is?" I was instantly defensive.

"Of course I do," I said, clucking, checking the rear-view mirror and glancing over my shoulder before changing lanes, hoping to change the subject.

"I wish you'd said so," he said.

"It's just a story about 1875," I said.

"It's one tiny example of what minorities go through. It's baked in now, to them and to us."

We continued into an actually quite smart and interesting conversation about prejudice and systems of injustice, about whether the real victim was the man accused of theft or the pastor, sublimating his own suppressed rage and outraged integrity by wounding his fellow in oppression. Joe even implied that my great-grandfather might have been injured from childhood by his inherited, unjustifiable privilege. All that was fine. Then he said,

"Next time I think you should say all of this to your cousins. This crap has got to stop."

I looked over at him. I was very irritated, because I had always flattered myself on my lefty consciousness, but this conversation struck at the core of things I had considered normal since infancy.

"They're your cousins too, now," I said. "We're married, remember?" That wasn't one bit fair.

"Yeah, I remember," he said, reaching over to cover my hand with his as I rested it on the gearshift. "Families are hard."

The night we smelled smoke, Shendra and Joe and I ran down to McMechen Street and saw that crowds were looting the Save-a-Lot grocery and Ride Aid pharmacy. Grocery carts had been commandeered and merchandise was flowing west from Bolton Hill to the neighborhood where a pharmacy was already on fire. One of my white neighbors was walking his two enormous dogs on leashes; they were thrilled with the chaos and barked obstreperously at some teenagers who were carrying six-packs of soda to their cart through the shattered window of a store. The kids almost dropped their armloads, startled by the dogs, and their mother looked at my neighbor, harassed, and said,

"You need to control those dogs!" He looked at her blandly and said,

"You need to control those kids!"

A small cordon of neighbors was ranged in front of an independent hardware store in the same strip mall. The looters respected that. The removal of staple groceries and medicines from the chain stores continued with almost a sense of order. There was no feeling of personal danger as we watched this surreal scene. The flames were several blocks to our west, and most of the sirens were concentrated there. After a while, Joe and Shendra and I drifted home.

Seated on our front steps were a couple of young men with two overloaded grocery carts. They were doing triage: they intended to transfer the really valuable things (meat, Band-Aids, aspirin, canned soups) to one cart, and put the things they could do without or procure easily elsewhere on the sidewalk for others to gather.

I didn't recognize either of them; neither, apparently, did Joe. As we approached, I jingled my keys.

"Mind if we step inside?" I asked. Joe's hand was on my elbow.

They slid to one side of the steps.

"No problem. Good evening, sir," one of them said.

"Evening, sister," the other said to Shendra.

"Hey friends," Joe said; "the grocery cart you don't use – could you take it back to the store? They'll probably want it tomorrow for clean-up."

"You got it, boss," one of the young men said. I knew he would return the cart before he headed home.

We stepped back into the house and locked the door.

The following day on campus, I got an e-mail from a student.

"Dear Professor," it read, "I live in Sandtown. My church has organized a clean-up crew for today and I'd like to be part of it. With your permission, I will miss class today. I will get the assignment off Blackboard. Thank you for your understanding."

"Dear Brynna," I wrote back, "thank you for your note. I am extremely proud of you. I will see you in class next week. All my best wishes to you and to all the members of your congregation and community."

I mentioned this exchange to Joe at dinner that night. Shendra hadn't gotten home yet from her day of filming. He gave me a nod, smiling gently, almost proudly.

"That was a great response," he said. After a pause: "Everyone bears crosses, I guess."

Chapter 5
November 2015
[flashback: January 2013]

Tony and Rachel took a cab from the airport on Wednesday afternoon for their Thanksgiving visit. They wouldn't need a rental car this time; their only agenda in town was to check in on Jimmy in his new setting.

By then, I knew that Jimmy and Kevin were boyfriends, but I didn't know if J.J. had told his parents yet. He had "spoken" to Kevin the day after our talk in bed that night in October, and Kevin had accepted his virginal, infatuated suit. As for physical intimacy, I wasn't sure. Kevin did not strike me as the type to wait long for the first tumble. On the other hand, I could see that he actually cared for Jimmy, and perhaps he realized that rushing him or putting sexual pressure on him might backfire. As often as he teased Jimmy, his raillery was always tender. Most of his teasing was actually a form of bragging.

"Oh my God," he said one day, "I'm going to have to start packing a Taser. I mean, these smart Peabody queens just relentlessly hitting on our boy here..." Another time, it was, "No, honestly, I thought the prof would drop his upper rack when he asked who the most influential composer in Hollywood history was and Maestro Jacob here waited till everyone had said something stupid like 'Mozart' or 'Korngold,' and then he leans back and says, like *Oh* so cool, 'Who *gives* a fuck?', 'Ravel.'" Jimmy virtually giggled with gratification at this story, running one hand through his curls. I was sure that his affect in class had actually been guarded and defensive; he was waiting to see how the conversation tended, hoping to fit in; but then, when there was no time left for anything but honesty, he had blurted out his minority truth and won the professor's unexpected approval. Kevin leaned over and grabbed J.J. by the neck, pulling him till their faces were very close for a moment and then giving a low, growly "You..." I saw a light in Jimmy's eyes which was new to me: alert attraction, wondering whether or not to make a leap.

Jimmy seemed stronger, older, and handsomer when Kevin was darting around him. He took on a kind of mild benevolence that reminded me of the way Tony acted when someone he loved was being quicker, funnier, or less conventional than himself. By the time Tony and Rachel arrived for the weekend, Jimmy had spent several nights at Kevin's apartment near Peabody, putting up with the gentle shade of Kevin's roommates, which I knew embarrassed him. When the two infant prodigies wanted "an oasis of quiet," as J.J. called it, Kevin stayed with J.J. in his room at my house. The sounds emanating from it were as chaste and chatty as when he and Lyric had visited.

Kevin was not at dinner the night Tony and Rachel arrived; he had already left to spend the holiday with his own family in New Jersey. The four of us had a relatively normal supper. J.J. answered a long string of questions from his parents about his classes and new friends. Several times he found ways to drop Kevin's name into his replies. Tony and Rachel exchanged a private glance the second or third time. I said that I had enjoyed getting to know Kevin a little that he was the funniest and nicest of Jimmy's friends I had met so far. This comment earned me a grateful smile from Jimmy.

After dinner we sat in the library upstairs. The senior Fleischer-Neubergs looked a little tired from their flight, and I thought we were all set to retire early. There would be plenty of cooking the next day to justify an early rising. Walter, Ricardo, and Marie were going to join us, and Shendra, and Carl from next door; Gene, his hectic madcap social calendar permitting, would come by for dessert. None of these people were used to inattentive or bungled catering.

Just as I was about to say 'Look at the time,' Jimmy cleared his throat and gave a portentous "Umm." He was making nervous little spider-on-the-mirror gestures with his fingertips touching, and unconsciously rocking in his seat, as I hadn't seen him do since he was a little boy. He harrumphed again as if he were about to bring a shareholders' meeting to order.

"Mommy, Daddy," he said, "I suppose it's obvious by now that I'm in love with Kevin." A brief congealed silence fell over the room. Tony broke it, inexpertly attempting levity.

"Did Godfather Jim convert you?" he asked. I was too surprised to react. The coincidence was in fact striking enough that for an instant I wondered if he might not be right.

"Oh Anton, hush," said Rachel, sounding for once genuinely exasperated. He looked abashed for a moment, but then said to Jimmy,

"It's so soon since Lyric left you. Give yourself time. I think you're still processing."

"I can process and love Kevin at the same time, Daddy," J.J. said, cross and childish.

Rachel looked a bit chilly and non-committal. She was too sophisticated to be regretting the chuppah, the grandchildren. Nevertheless, in her eyes I saw her bone-deep preference for a hetero outcome to her only child's meandering emergence into adulthood. She had spent the past two decades bracing for the time when she would have to relinquish this boy to another woman's keeping; she had memorized her "lovely" to describe her, and the smile that went with it. She was ready to be practical and experienced, a maternal model and ally to her daughter-in-law, grateful to her for taking on the confusing bit of manhood they would manage together, ready to guide from afar Jimmy's fumbling lurches towards fatherhood. She was far too wise and realistic to nurture fantasies in the face of evident facts. Surely something in J.J.'s brusque declaration made sense to her, answered old questions, knitted together some dangling threads. I thought I could see in her face a shadow of 'Of course, now I understand.' She needed time to adjust her inner landscape. I felt sorry for her. I remembered the explosion of joy which had broken out in my cramped heart when Jimmy told me he was gay. She was having the opposite experience.

"I'm so glad you have shared this truth with us, sweet son," she said, after a moment. "And so glad you have found someone you can really love. I just wish we could meet him this weekend. We will very soon, I hope."

"How did you know?" Tony asked. "How did you know for sure? You've been meeting a lot of new people, right? Girls and boys?"

"I guess I was sure when I asked G.J. if he thought Kevin was hairy," he said. He had already snapped into the cheerful dollhouse babble he used when talking to me about his wee boyfriend. "Saying out loud that I was speculating about his body was revelatory."

"Our boy J.J. uses the word 'revelatory' in everyday conversation," I commented. I didn't really like Tony and Rachel hearing that he and I talked about things like Kevin's body hair. Some things that made perfect sense between gay people sounded inappropriate outside the tribe.

"Do you have any pictures of him?" Tony asked.

"A bunch," Jimmy replied. He pulled out his iPhone, and provided a quick slideshow of the Many Moods of Kevin: whimsical, intellectual, soulful, gluttonous, and sensual. Among the pictures there was one of Kevin sleeping, shirtless, on Jimmy's bed upstairs… a dear little Irish angel, his manic charm switched off, captured in a moment of supreme, undefended kissability. The picture answered Jimmy Jack's initial question. Kevin's chest and belly bore a perfect dusting of silky, springy red hair, which the light behind his head lit as if from below. There was no possible question that the person taking those pictures was in love with Kevin; it radiated off the little screen. Jimmy's face as he showed these pictures was meltingly shy and devout. He was too naive to make any attempt at coolness as he explained to us his boyfriend's quirks, preferences, beauties, and virtues.

He must have shown us ten or fifteen of these shots. Tony nodded sympathetically and smiled at his son's commentary, trying to enter into his enthusiasm. He made a few passing remarks of his own: "Cute!" or "Huh, he looks very smart." It was obvious that one or two pictures would have been enough for him, that night at least. Rachel was better at faking it: "What a great picture! Oh, he looks *so* nice… !" The shirtless sleeping picture was the hardest for her because it was impossible to see it without speculating on their sexual intimacy.

At some point we all made our way upstairs. At the second floor landing, Jimmy lingered with his parents. I completed my climb to the third floor alone. Maybe an hour later, as I got up to turn out the lights in the back stair, I heard their voices in the guest room below. The lights were still on because Jimmy hadn't yet come up to our floor. Tony and Rachel's door was still open, so that their gentle words carried clearly in the quiet house.

"No, of course not," Rachel was saying. "All we care about is that you be a kind, honorable person, and that you be happy… that you find someone to be happy *with*." I heard Tony's hum of assent, and a sheepish "So I'm still your boy?" from Jimmy. There was some kind of blush in his voice, and a squeak of the mattress that suggested a wordless family hug. I tiptoed back to my room, leaving the light on.

Rolling over a while later without checking the clock, I noticed that the back stair lights were out, and probably had been for some time. I closed my eyes but was surprised, after only a moment or two, to sense

Jimmy quietly ghosting into the room. He lay down beside me and pulled the covers up around his neck.

"I love Mommy and Daddy. Good night," he said, and promptly fell asleep.

I wanted to wake him up and make him go back to his own room. Knowing that his parents were barely a hundred steps away was acutely embarrassing to me. The godfather in me, though, was reluctant to disturb a child's slumber, and his steady breathing was touching. After a few minutes, I began to relax as well, and eventually fell asleep.

I awoke several hours later to the sight of his unruly black curls on Joe's pillow. His back was to me; his pajamas bore some comical graphic of crabs and the odd heraldic Maryland flag. He must have felt me wake up, because he stretched suddenly, smiled over his shoulder, and said,

"Rise and shine!" He bounded up with barely a glance in my direction, and dashed towards his bathroom down the hall. A minute later I heard the water running.

I was in the kitchen soon after, my own shower finished. Jimmy must have gone to his room to study or listen to music after washing up. I was wearing my tatty old terrycloth robe, which hung shapelessly on me. In the past, when Joe hugged me through this robe, it had felt warm and cozy; sometimes the hug even led to unrehearsed sensualities. Now I was aware mostly of looking like someone who would never have sex again. It didn't matter anymore.

Tony was the first to join me. By then, with the coffee maker steadily dripping and filling the room with its happy morning scent, I had already wrestled the turkey out of its wrappings and was rinsing it in the sink. When I saw Tony come in, I propped the turkey upright in the main sink to drain; then I washed my hands in the smaller adjacent sink and slipped a few slices of bread into the toaster. Tony took a seat at the counter. I pushed the milk carton and sugar bowl closer to him.

Tony was capable of blunt honesty, though in our youth he had also been willing to string me along for decades at a time about his reactions to my passion for him.

"Is it my imagination," he asked, gesticulating with his spoon as he doctored his coffee, "or did Jimmy go to your room after he left us last night?"

We were past sixty now, and a direct question like this was actually a relief to me.

"Yes, he did," I said. "He occasionally drops in late at night to talk to me. He tells me he does the same with you." I met Tony's eye. He registered that I wasn't afraid or ashamed. Perhaps some ancient model had suggested to him that I would cower, that my gayness might feel to me like something to apologize for. He had never played that card, because he was generous and we loved each other, but it was part of the political air we both breathed. There was not a shred of that diffidence left in me now. A few times I had tried to calculate how often, before Joe came along, I had masturbated to fantasies of Tony. With my young randiness at rip tide, it might have been as often as four or five hundred times a year for as many as twenty years. Looking at him now, I saw that he was still someone a man might imagine humping like a dog.

"So... what do you talk about?"

"He asks me about life, about his feelings, about his break-up with Lyric, about Kevin. These are things he finds it hard to put into words. Apparently he feels safe asking me about them."

"Of course he does," Tony said kindly. "He knows he can trust you. He knows you care." He looked at his coffee; he did not look up. "Do you completely trust yourself?"

"Jimmy is sacred to me," I said, hearing my own voice break slightly. The toaster had pinged by now, and I fished the hot slices out and put them on little plates, offering one to Tony and placing the butter and jam between us on the counter.

"I know that," he said. "I don't for a minute think anything... improper, or..." I made a gagging, hissing sound of some kind, and Tony rushed to continue. "Nothing like that. Of course not. For God's sake, Jim; we all adore you." He slurped his coffee and I stirred mine. "Is there some part of you that's happy, or gratified, or... ?" He paused. "Was there any time when you think you might have tipped some kind of balance in his mind, or something?"

"Is there some part of you that wishes he weren't gay?" I countered. "Is this a disappointment to you? Millions of parents would agree with you if so; it's nothing to be ashamed of. I'm sure if I were straight I'd want my son to be straight too."

"But you know Jimmy almost as well as I do. He's a mystery to himself; he's not always in touch with his body, his mind. Who even knows if he's gay or straight or bi or what? He may change his mind by lunch time. I just don't want him to sign any documents or seal off any options."

"You didn't worry about sealing off his options when he was with Lyric," I said.

"Give me some credit!" he said, a bit hotly. "I wasn't all that crazy about Lyric either. I just…" He left his sentence unfinished. He looked as confused as I felt. I wanted to hit him with some hot political zingers, but he didn't deserve them.

"OK," I said; "to be totally honest, I've been a little sorry he wasn't gay. I thought Lyric was some kind of phony neurasthenic succubus who would sap all his goofy vitality. I could probably have liked the *right* girlfriend, for Jimmy's sake, but there was never anyone but this awful contrived wisp of a girl, and I couldn't force myself to like her. And when they broke up, and when he started to drop odd comments about Kevin, I'll admit it made me hope he was building up his courage for this. When he told me he loved Kevin, I was glad."

"Because… what? You have him in your tribe now? Or he's a mini-you for the future?" He looked at me and smiled a bit tightly. "I even… *we* even named him for you. I guess we should have seen this coming."

"You-singular named him for me. Rachel told me when she was first pregnant that you wanted to call him Jim if he was a boy, that it was your idea." I could see in his eyes that he remembered and knew I was right.

"It's so long ago now," he said, vaguely; "was it my idea? Did she really say that?"

"She did," I said, with a quick bureaucratic click of competence in my voice. I felt like an Austrian functionary citing facts and figures to shut down an evasive confused inquiry from a petitioner. "And naming him after me or not naming him after me would have had nothing to do with determining his sexuality." He looked unhappy.

"Why are we arguing?" he asked. "Are we arguing?"

"Well I think you just *almost* accused me of enticing your son to be... homo-*sex*-ual." The last word was one he would never have used, and I was a bit ashamed of myself. "Anyway, no documents have been signed as of today. There is no permanent gay contract that I'm aware of. Jimmy is his own confusing self, today and tomorrow and probably forever. If he thinks today that he may be gay, I personally am not going to pretend I'm sorry."

After a moment's silence, Tony put one arm out, gesturing me from around the counter.

"Come here, buddy," he said. I walked around to his side and he put the dangling arm around my waist. "I'm grateful for everything you're doing for our boy, especially when you've got more than enough on your mind already. On your heart."

Whatever heart I had left softened at these words. For an instant I missed Joe so much that I thought I might wail out loud. Tony had identified one truth which I hadn't quite put into words before: there was an enormous void at the center of my life, where Joe had spread a permeating, clarifying light, and perhaps I was unconsciously trying to fill it with J.J. Certainly there had been no partings of my grey clouds since Joe's death, except when Jimmy said or did or even just *was* something. Tony continued.

"I'm just trying to understand something new in the life of someone I've known since... well, since before he was born. I've never thought of Jimmy as gay before. I'll have to get used to this, I guess."

"I've never thought of him as a sexual being before," I said. "He's always been... what did you say? an oddball? To me he's seemed way beyond all *that*..."

"... not *ready* for all that," Tony nodded. "Just our weird little go-it-alone wild child. I used to think he'd meet some bossy girl in engineering or biomedical research, and she'd mold him, I guess... order him around, whip him into shape, wake him up." I smiled. I'd thought, even tried altruistically to hope, the same thing.

"I think he's waking up now," I said. "Wait till you meet Kevin. He's a live wire. J.J. may never sleep again." Tony laughed in spite of himself. "Who knows how Jimmy will end up? He's definitely a little one-man emerging nation. But I can guarantee you he genuinely loves Kevin –

'loves' in Jimmy terms, I mean. Something is happening. There's electricity when they look at each other. Kevin is worldly and canny, and J.J. is a smitten puppy, but…"

The polite, open-minded look on Tony's face showed me that he preferred not to think of his son as smitten with a small copper-flecked Hibernian who oozed homoeroticism even in recumbent photos. After a moment he took a last slug of coffee and said,

"Hey, let me help you stuff that turkey. Where did you put the stuffing? I can hold the turkey open and you can pack it."

"First we towel it out and salt and pepper the cavity," I said. Before getting my hands buttery, I turned on NPR and was glad to hear the strains of a symphonic "We Gather Together." It seemed the right accompaniment to counting some Thanksgiving blessings, like togetherness and maybe-gay godsons and even memories of my happy marriage, ended too soon. Before long we were wrist-deep in what promised to be a beautiful bird.

I sat facing Rachel, who took Joe's place opposite me at the far end of the dinner table. Walter, Ricardo, Marie, and neighbor Carl felt Joe's absence as I did; they had been at our two-daddy Thanksgivings in years past. I had placed Marie to my right and Jimmy Jack to my left. Tony was next to his son; Walter, Ricardo, and Shendra filled in the other sides.

Shendra had bustled in on her first entrance and thrown her arms around me, quietly sobbing for a moment and then reeling back to grab me by both shoulders and say, blinking back real tears,

"You know what we say, sh'ree: the show must go ON."

Her glib theatrical tag was something I had learned to value in the immediate aftermath of Joe's death. No one had been kinder, busier, more frank, more intuitively wise than his theatre friends, quick to pack things and greet visitors. They knew when to stop and embrace and weep, and when to rear back and yell, "This fucking *sucks!*" before getting back to their tasks. Shendra had organized those brigades, and when she said the show must go on, she was speaking a hoary existential truth.

Marie… well, she was there. She still grieved Clare's departure; it showed in her slower movements. Though she still swam her relentless miles at every lunch break, and still slipped easily into her oldest jeans, she seemed almost hunched at times, her shoulders stiff, her neck curved, her nods less emphatic.

Dinner was perfect. Rachel let me take total responsibility for the turkey, stuffing, gravy, and cranberry sauce, intervening only to wave some kind of magic wand over the gravy when it threatened to lump. She produced the mashed potatoes, some brilliant roast pumpkin served with a garlic and yogurt sauce, a plain green salad with a vinaigrette of pure wizardry, and, in her spare time, a latticed pecan pie which could have graced the cover of *Southern Home*. While we whirled in the kitchen, everyone else had the sense to stay in the parlor or on the far side of the kitchen island, out from under foot. Jimmy Jack glowed with self-importance as he set the table to my exact specifications. Throughout dinner, conversation didn't flag.

In a brief kitchen intermission before dessert, I trickled some Drambuie into the cream as I whipped it for the pie, and was gratified when Rachel withdrew her gilding-the-lily warning after tasting it on her finger tip. Back in the dining room, we passed the Drambuie bottle along with the magisterial pie. Ricardo, a veteran of many Thanksgivings with me, knew the drill.

"So – what are we all thankful for?" He was saving me from seeming dictatorial, because he knew I was about to ask that question. "I'll start! I'm grateful for our lovely *host,* and for this big wonderful *godson* of his who is suddenly so *gor*-geous and grown *up*. And I'm grateful for years and years with… with the *right* people on Thanksgiving. And if I say another word, we'll all cry." I smiled tightly and nodded. He was referring to Joe's absence. I would have given the floor to Shendra, who was next to Ricardo, but he instead turned to Jimmy. "Your turn, honey."

J.J. straightened in his chair, slightly pompous as he faced another rite of adulthood. I could tell that he had prepared his answer.

"I'm thankful for Mommy and Daddy, who are amazing. I'm thankful for Godfather Jim… who is my best friend." I was very surprised and touched by that comment, and I reached to put my hand over his on the table.

"God only knows how often you've saved my life in the past few months, J.J.," I said; "I'll love you forever for that." He gave me a funny look. I had interrupted the little homily he had memorized. I withdrew my hand, and he picked up his train of thought.

"And I'm thankful for Kevin, who has taught me what love is."

Shendra beamed at him across the table.

"Sh'ree," she said, "if you were any sweeter I'd eat you with this spoon." She lifted her glass and said, "Let's toast this Kevin. I can't wait to meet the child."

As the clinks subsided, Rachel did something with the tilt of her chin which let us all understand that she would speak next. After a moment, she said,

"I'm grateful... Anton, don't you agree with me?... that our son has such honesty and such courage. I'm grateful for the new closeness that comes from your telling us about Kevin. Jacob, since the moment you first kicked inside me, you've taught *me* what love is." As always, she spoke with the words almost of another age; in her mouth they sounded candid and natural. Now she looked directly at me, and said, "And dear Jim, what's in your heart this evening?"

I knew perfectly well what I would say. I had seen this moment coming for weeks, and I was ready, unafraid. I gave a rueful little smile and twirled my glass by the stem. I looked up and opened my mouth.

Absolutely no sound came out. It was as though a sudden acute laryngitis had gripped me. The two or three seconds of my unplanned silence, filled to the brim with my obvious intention of speaking, brought a hushed, concerned expression to every face around the table. Still stammering soundlessly, I looked down the long table at Rachel, whose eyes locked on mine, strong and generous. I could see her count to three in her mind; then, when she could see I genuinely would not be able to speak,

"May I?" she asked. I nodded several times, fast, the flustered nod of a Miss America contestant about to weep at children's hunger. "You're thankful for Joe. For dear, kind, gifted, lovely and loving Joe. Years together, devotion that can never be taken away. Love is never wasted, even when it breaks our hearts."

"He's right here, you know," said Ricardo, his eyes shining.

"Always," said Walter.

"To Joe," said Shendra. We all lifted our glasses. I didn't cry; I didn't smile. The wine I'd chosen was a bold acid Berardenga, and it tasted exactly right for my feelings: it warmed, and it cut. Joe was gone; he was still there.

I loved him and missed him in the same precise moment, two solid objects occupying the same space, overlapping, consoling, desolating.

Marie and I were alone in the kitchen, dealing with turkey scraps and plastic containers while the others started to stack dishes in the dining room. She was brisk, efficient, and tactful. I passed her a sealed box full of left-overs to stack in the refrigerator, and our eyes met. I was surprised at the depth of sorrow in them. She was not normally voluble about her feelings, but there was urgency in her eyes. It was obvious that our moment alone would end very soon; the ferrying of dishes from the dining room might start any second.

"I think I envy you tonight, BooBoo," she said. "I know how heart-broken you are, and that breaks my heart too; you know that. But it's so much cleaner to have your lover die than to have her leave you. I'm sorry. I know how awful that sounds. There was something perfect about you and Joe, and that can't be taken away, now or ever."

I found her words a bit chilling. More than a year after Clare's ridiculous desertion, I thought she might have moved on and entered into the griefs of others a bit more warmly. Yet I also realized that she was absolutely right. I knew that I couldn't have borne it if Joe had left me. Our love was somehow sealed and safe now; no risk forthcoming from sultry male starlets or the creeping ruthless be-ringed and frosted gay *roués* who always seemed to circle ostentatiously happy couples like us, sniffing for trouble. I had to respect Marie's honesty. I had learned that perhaps nothing in adult life was more self-centered than grief. My mourning had made me intolerant of bunk and humbug in any form, and even the most egotistical truth-telling now seemed refreshing to me, almost comforting. I put down my plastic container and put my arms around her.

I did not expect her to cry, but she did; instantly, in my arms, she shuddered and let out a series of silent, gasping sobs.

"I just *miss* her," she said, several times. "Damn it! She doesn't deserve for me to *miss* her."

"No," I said, "she doesn't. But you miss her because you're an honest person with a big open heart, and you let her in. You loved her; you still love her. Someday you'll let her go. You'll be happy again."

She stopped crying, almost as quickly as she'd started. My own ability to spout robotic comforting catch-phrases to an old friend whose grief I didn't entirely respect disappointed me privately. I still thought that she was being a bit selfish, self-pitying, wallowing. Yet objectively it felt good to hug her, and something of the release I felt in her slim shoulders helped even me. Perhaps perfect honesty was overrated.

She pulled back from me and placed her fine small hands on my shoulders. Her eyes were still wet but she blinked hard and smiled.

"*We'll* be happy again," she said.

Joe and I were married in mid-January, 2013, the first month it was legal in Maryland. The legislative outcome was clear long enough in advance for us to plan the ceremony before we were technically eligible. Marriage seemed redundant to me in a way, because we had had a very public, very festive Holy Union years earlier.

The wedding itself was private, a religious ceremony only for immediate family and closest friends, and marked by multiple absences. Our pastor Hal had died, and our church had an interim minister who barely knew Joe and me. Joe's father Dominic was gone; my sister was a widow.

It had been Joe's wish that we marry. I had a number of bloviating political reservations. It was a paradox of our union that I, who had dreamed for years of a monogamous relationship, had strong enough memories of early Gay Lib talking points to think that gay people might point the way to less bourgeois, patriarchal, possessive models of life partnership. I both believed in monogamy and thought that marriage was for self-deceiving assimilationists. Though I was actually terrified of the kind of freedom practiced by jaded singles and swinging couples, I had a theoretical loyalty to the ideals of the Sexual Revolution of my youth. Meanwhile Joe, having years before screwed his way indefatigably through California's gay A-list, deeply wanted the public legitimacy of marriage.

The inveterate, obsessive hatefulness of the political right eventually wore me down.

"God damn Rick Santorum," I said to Joe one night, throwing down the paper; "he's going to talk me into gay marriage."

94

"Be honest," Joe said. "It's not his politics you hate; it's his sweater vests." He smiled and came to kneel in front of me.

"Will you marry me?" he asked, taking my hand.

"Just to spite Rick Santorum, yes," I said. He laughed, but I knew he was serious.

"Let's send him an announcement," he said.

"Get up. This is silly." I didn't want him to move, really. His eyes were hypnotically green just then, as he looked up at me with patient, steady fondness. He was offering me the heart's desire of millions of gay people who had lived and died without this option, but he knew he would be met with the rag-tail phalanx of my political bugbears and hobby-horses.

"No," he said. "Not till you say 'Yes' and mean it."

"Divo," I answered, "we're already married in every important sense. God already knows what we are to each other; so does everyone we care about."

"Tiger," he said: "insurance; estates; powers of attorney... let's just do this."

"Let's not do it for that," I said, with a sudden sentimental scruple. In my mind I was already saying 'Yes.' "Insurance and estates have bugger-all to do with you and me getting married." Now he did get up and sat next to me on the sofa, slipping one arm around my shoulder.

"You're my love," he murmured. "I'm your love. Our Holy Union blessed that, and that's all that really matters. But it's also why we have to get married, now that we can. It's the final thing we can do to say, 'This is real.' We don't need it, but the world needs it, needs for *us* to do it. We can afford it, we can risk it, our friends and families will support us. We can do this for gay kids and for old dykes who live in small towns and have no one in their corner."

"It's a piece of paper," I said.

"It's a piece of very powerful paper," he said. "Plus you know what? I want it. We're more married than most married people. Your buddy Rick Santorum thinks he's more married than we are. Fuck him."

"No," I said; "ick. The sweater-vest..."

He waited a moment, as I scanned his shady-forest eyes. He meant every word he had just said. Even more, though, he was a Nice Italian Boy from Brooklyn and he wanted to be on the right side of matrimonial law.

He wanted our gold bands to mean exactly what they appeared to mean. Deep down inside, he still carried the fear that I didn't quite respect him, I with my steady career and family heirlooms, he with his racy past and professional life stitched together of irregular gigs. The idea that a man so sensible and kind could ever for an instant have such a doubt, and the knowledge that my own airy, speculative detachment could be one cause, drew a sudden surge of protective compassion from me. His arm around my shoulder was a reminder that he was much stronger than me physically, and probably emotionally as well.

"You're my love," I said. "I'm your love. Yes. Yes. Yes…"

Everything after that was easy.

Chapter 6
December, 2015
[flashback: ca. 2012]

I drove Jimmy to the airport on my way to Brooklyn. He was flying home to Chicago, and I was to spend Christmas with Joe's family. Jimmy was acutely disappointed that Kevin had elected to spend the holiday with his own family. There had been a week or ten days when it seemed quite possible he would go with Jimmy to the Glencoe manor for the full-on fiancé state visit. Though I thought it was a bit premature after barely six weeks as a couple, Jimmy had set his heart on it. He went around the house in a moon-calf cloud of romance, speculating on what Rachel would do or say or cook or plan to entertain Kevin and make him feel part of the family. Knowing her, I was almost afraid for Kevin. I had absolutely no doubt that Rachel would be the ideal hostess and even, in time, mother-in-law, but her dazzling arrangements might intimidate a young first-time visitor. Kevin might also detect pretension or condescension in whatever symbolic gestures Rachel devised. I was almost relieved when his visit was called off.

We pulled up to the departures gate and I popped the trunk. When Jimmy leapt out of the car without saying anything, I turned on the blinkers and got out too, to hug him good-bye. He had already slung his big duffel bag over his shoulder when I got to the back of the car, and he was looking abstractedly at the lobby. If I hadn't caught him, he might have sprinted into the terminal without a word. As it was, he gave me a lugubrious look and uncoiled his spare arm to hug me.

"Give my love to your parents," I said.

"Of course; I have to give them Kevin's, too, since neither of you will be there," he replied. I was sorry he was taking this so personally. I was quite sure that Kevin liked him, but this wasn't the time or the place for that conversation. He needed to catch his plane and then greet his parents with a smile at O'Hare.

"Every minute with your parents is time well spent," I said. "They made you, Jimmy. They'll be there for you always. You and Kevin will have a million happy moments to share in the future."

He wasn't at all consoled. He would spend every second of his time at home missing Kevin and wishing they were together.

"I'm going to miss my little boy," I hazarded. "The house is going to seem big and empty." His face turned mellow and old and wise.

"You'll be in Brooklyn most of the time I'm gone," he said. "You won't have time to miss me. I'll be home just a couple of days after you get back." Home = my house; I heard and noticed. "How often should I text Kevin, do you think?" he suddenly asked. But before I could answer, his expression changed again. He took my face in his two hands and looked straight at me.

"Don't miss me, G.J.," he said. "I'm never away. I'm always here – wherever you are; and you're always there – wherever I am."

Yes, he was his mother's son: at times and out of nowhere, he commanded her fearless other-worldly emotional eloquence. His frequent inconsequent swerves likewise no longer surprised me. I leaned towards him just enough for our foreheads to touch briefly.

"Do you remember the other night, at City Café?" he asked. "The waitress said I was your boy." I did remember: when we were considering dessert, she had asked me archly if he'd 'been a good boy.' I'd thought her innuendo went over his head. "I loved that."

"You're always my boy, Jimmy Jack," I said. "I'll call you tonight when we're both settled. Ask your parents if they can Skype with us."

He pulled away from me, stood to attention, and saluted. Then, like a child playing soldier, he turned about smartly and marched into the terminal. I waited long enough to see that he didn't turn at the door to wave.

"When's the last time you saw Dario?" Connie asked me, two days after Christmas. We were sitting in the parlor of her Carroll Gardens row house. She had taken on a settled handsome stateliness in her old age. Mourning certainly became her. Her grey hair was neatly pinned up in a retro Pompadour which framed her austere Roman face beautifully. The late-19th century room where we sat made me almost visualize jewelry of jet and woven hair, but in fact she wore no ornaments except her wedding ring. Most of her various children and grandchildren had been in and out of the house throughout the Christmas holiday, and it had been a great bathtub of kindness and embraces, tears and laughter. Joe's siblings had been dear in-laws to me, without exception, for decades, and their kids saw me and treated me as their widowed uncle, a man perhaps different in some way from their blood relations, but an honored and well-loved presence in the world as long as most of them could remember.

Amid the several-day swirl of family meals and visits, Connie and I had had little time to catch up privately. Today, the last before my return to Baltimore, we caught our breath and smiled at each other, perhaps a touch grimly, like fellow-veterans of a bitter war, survivors coming back to the edge of some crater where a beloved comrade had died and on which grass had just started to grow again. I was grateful for our friendship. The sound of her voice always reminded me of the first time I heard it, when Joe and she spoke on the phone in my Rehoboth studio during the first days of our relationship and I, eavesdropping avidly, pretended to nap. Then in her late fifties, she had a firm diaphragmatic push and a clarion placement which projected out of the receiver and reached me across the room. She was practical, grounded, proud of her matriarchal authority and shameless in asserting it. She had reputedly been a bit of a tigress in Joe's defense during the initial crisis of his coming out in college. She was cautiously good to me from the beginning, and more reliably as she came to trust my affection for her boy.

Today we were waiting for Bobby, Joe's youngest brother, and his family. They lived in California, and had spent Christmas with his wife's parents there. They were making their annual pilgrimage to Brooklyn now and would stay with Connie through New Year's. Though Joe and Bobby spoke on the phone quite often, they saw each other mostly when Joe was on the West Coast. I hadn't seen Bobby in person in several years. I remembered his son Dario as a very dashing, funny little boy… impish grin, wicked darting eyes, and a propensity to swing from things or toss them across rooms. Connie told me he was now sixteen, and after a moment's incredulity I told her I probably hadn't seen him in ten years.

"Then brace yourself, *caro,*" she said, with an inscrutable smile that would have done credit to the aged Empress Livia. A few minutes later the doorbell rang.

Bobby and his wife Lisa were the first through the door and the first to hug me. They were probably the Andreolis I knew least well. Even so, their sympathy and their own grief were touching to me. Their college-aged daughter Maria, who was at Rutgers and had represented her branch of the family when Joe died, was her usual brassy, affectionate self. Dario came in last, carrying bags from the car. As I saw him, I felt Connie's hand on my shoulder in a hard grip of solidarity, as though she expected me literally to stagger.

At sixteen, Dario was almost incredibly like the undergraduate Joe I remembered from Yale. I had nursed a brief, frustrated infatuation with Joe then; memories of it gave piquancy to the earliest phase of our actual love affair when we met again thirteen years later. Bobby, a compact, humpy Italian-looking guy, seemed only loosely related to Joe, but there had evidently been a genetic leap from some forgotten ancestor and through Bobby to this adolescent avatar.

"Hey, Uncle Jim," he said, and clapped me into a one-arm embrace as he put the bags down. "I am so sorry for your loss." He clearly had the dependable, correct politeness that flowed from Connie down through her entire gene pool. There would have been no point in Dario and me pretending that we were close. That was what my mind was telling me, as my nerves reacted less rationally to the scent which came off of him: precisely the same mix of clean, rich topsoil and spicy apples which always rose from Joe's skin. I had not responded erotically to anyone in several months, but part of me might have had sex with Dario that very instant.

"I can't believe how tall you are!" Dario laughed and squatted down enough to look up at me from a six year-old's height.

"Does this help?" he asked. His pale jade eyes were piercing my heart... no source of laughter there. He wasn't exactly handsome; neither had Joe been. He was exuberantly embodied, exhilarating to see and hear and stand next to. He clearly thought of himself as attractive, a self-image which for Joe had come mostly from decades of external affirmation and which he had carried modestly and self-critically, without the breeziness that Dario projected. Though Joe had lived his adolescence publicly as a popular straight boy with serial girlfriends and a fair amount of sexual experience, he had carried the claustrophobic burden, familiar to me and millions, of his secret attractions to other boys. Dario had none of that self-monitoring and self-doubt. His cockiness probably reflected a long string of easy conquests among the Courtneys, Kaitlyns, and Madisons of his Santa Barbara high school.

Never strong at math, I took a silent moment to calculate that, if by some miracle Dario came out and we fell in love but chose to postpone our marriage till he was the age Joe had been when we fell in love, I would be eighty-one. As Dario hugged his grandmother, she gave me a look over his shoulder: a look of deep, objective compassion, as though she had read every single thought of mine in the past two minutes.

Before bed that night I called Tony and Rachel for a Skype chat. They were both already in their bathrobes and our conversation was sleepy and hunkered down, as though sleet were lashing our windows. Rachel was cupping a mug of some exotic tisane, almost hunched over it so that the steam rising from it seemed to be her breath in freezing night air. Tony sat with his hands under his arms as though huddled under a snow bank. Within a few minutes, J.J. came bumbling into the room and wedged himself between his parents so that his face was centered on my screen. He was wearing a yellow t-shirt, and although I had seen him only a few days before, I was surprised at the muscularity of his shoulders and bare arms. He looked strong and ready to pounce. He seemed to be painted with brighter colors than either of his parents. Their wintry faces, in the reflected blue glow of the laptop's screen, looked wan and bleached, dimly basking in the sunrise of his energy. Striking as they would always be, they were eclipsed by the inky blackness of Jimmy's mobile hair, which flooded radiance from Glencoe to Brooklyn.

"Kevin says 'Hi,'" he said to me. "We were just doing FaceTime."

"How is the tiny genius?" I asked.

"Pretty sure he's missing me."

"Of course he is," I said. "Have you been chatting every day?"

"Almost," said Jimmy. I knew that, if it had been up to him, it would have been much oftener.

"Get a sweater or something, buddy," Tony said to Jimmy. "It makes me cold just to look at you." Rachel said nothing, but rubbed Jimmy's shoulder as if to transfer the heat of her tisane to him.

I told them all about Dario. Tony and Rachel had wise, gentle smiles for the story; J.J. was a bit brisker.

"You seem restless," he said to me. "The holidays are a vulnerable time. Being with Uncle Joe's people these past few days... I don't think you need to be looking at boys right now."

"He's not 'looking at boys,'" Tony objected; "he's remembering Joe."

"I'm your boy," J.J. said, undeterred. "And I'm coming home soon."

Rachel cuffed him.

"This is your home," she said. "And you're Jim's godson, not his 'boy.' Good grief, what a bizarre thing to say." Jimmy looked at me sentimentally, protectively. He completely ignored his parents.

"I miss you," he said. "Kevin and I are going to make a big fuss over you when we're all back." I couldn't help smiling.

"OK, Jimmy Jack," I said. The preceding thirty seconds had shown their family life in its most condensed comic light and I savored their slightly prickly interactions. "I'll hold you to that."

I was home two days before J.J.'s return. It took all the first day for the house to warm up, as the furnace caught up with the chill which had settled into the walls and floors. My brush with memories of Joe was still haunting me. Dario, with a hetero self-assurance and entitlement rare even among the quick-breeding Andreolis, had somehow cottoned on to my infatuated focus. He had come to sit by me a couple of times and lavished on me the shifting shades of his green eyes. He had even asked me once point-blank if it weirded me out that people said he looked just like Uncle Joe at his age. He babbled cheerfully on about his California life, his girlfriends, his surfing, his taste in music, his vague plans and hopes. He kneaded my shoulder or knee at times for emphasis, punching my upper arm affectionately, smiling suddenly with a slight upward jerk of his chin which was uncannily like Joe's.

I had packed my car to leave and said my good-bye to a weeping Connie, who reminded me twice to call her when I was safely home. Then Dario walked me out, carrying my last bag. Shivering on the sidewalk, he suddenly pulled his hands out of his pockets and gave me a big teenager hug. He was the last Andreoli to see me off; perhaps some family council had assigned him this duty, on the theory that evocations of Joe would be comforting to me. To my relief, he was too slim and lithe and juvenile to feel at all like Joe in my arms, but I still felt an obscure ambiguous charge coming off him.

"Happy New Year, Uncle Jim" he said as I got into my car. "We'll be thinking about you" (the Andreoli 'we'). Then, "Don't be a stranger! I'll add you on FaceBook." As I drove away, I saw him in my rearview mirror, watching and waving and then turning resolutely to walk up the brownstone stoop and into the house. It was always a firm superstition of Connie's and Dominic's, faithfully preserved by Joe, that it brought bad luck to watch departing loved ones out of sight. It gave me a nostalgic twinge, not unpleasant, to see that it had been passed on to the third generation.

With these memories fresh, I felt the need to bundle up in the slowly warming house. On a sudden whim I went into the dressing room and put on one of Joe's very favorite blazers over my sweater. It was among his clothes which I had been unable to give away, a soft nubby grey and black Italian tweed that might almost have been made out of an old horse blanket, but by Zegna. Joe wore it sometimes several times a week in cold weather, and I loved it and couldn't imagine giving it away, but it had never occurred to me to try it on. Though Joe was thickly muscled and hunkier than I was, we were roughly the same size, and an unstructured, Raglan-shouldered garment of his, like this one, could fit me well enough. I caught just a tiny whiff of him as the jacket billowed when I put it on. It gave me a glimpse of a gentle, undemanding, resigned, consolable widower-hood into which I might someday grow. I glanced in the mirror on the armoire and said, "You're my love."

Putting my hands in the patch pockets, I found a piece of old paper in one of them, soft and frayed with age, folded in quarters. Absent-mindedly, I pulled it out and smoothed it. I didn't recognize the handwriting.

"Just bit a green apple and thought of you – juice on my chin. Yummm…! Can't wait till tomorrow night. Barry xoxo" There was a stupid smiley-face next to the 'Yummm…!' The name Barry meant nothing to me.

Instantly I understood that Joe had had an affair with some dull, conventionally sexy Barry, at some point in the past. My immediate reaction was unimpassioned. It took my deadened mind only a couple of seconds to remember a time several years earlier when Joe had called from California to say he would be coming home a day later than planned. I had been mildly put out at the time, because I was chafing at the enforced chastity of a week's separation. When he was back, there was something shifty about him at first, a slight avoidance of eye contact, some illogical fatigue, a laugh too hearty at some fond comment of mine. I asked him about the trace of an unfamiliar cologne I caught when he pulled his shirt off and tossed it into the hamper, and he gave me an actor's quick frank look and said, "A sales guy sprayed me in one of those vendor stands in the airport." I shrugged and forgot it, but I remembered now that there had been a series of such moments for a while… less than a year, probably, but spaced over a long enough time to register. Before I became actively worried, they ceased. It took me a few weeks or months to notice that whatever had been nagging at me was no longer happening. Now, reading this tattered old note, it probably took me less than two minutes to reconstruct that sequence of distant events, and I looked with affectless clarity at this infidelity of Joe's which, one way or another, had ended, without his ever having felt he had to speak with me about it. After all this time, it didn't matter.

It bothered me, though, that Joe had kept this note in his pocket. I might have found it there at any time. Also, if I was right about the approximate time of the affair, he would have had to take this note from the pocket more than once when the jacket went to the cleaners, and then to replace it. It was a relic or fetish of some kind. True, the risk of my finding it was low. I loved seeing the blazer on him but would never have thought to put it on. He wore it especially around the house and for informal parties and nights out, and the idea that he must have touched the note literally thousands of times was hurtful.

I went to the shelf in Joe's tiny office off the dressing room, where his old calendars were stacked. Within half an hour I had found a "drinks with Barry" during a California trip in mid-summer 2003. Skimming through the next several months, I found a few appointments with B, mostly in California but once in New York: "dinner w/ B," "mt B at studio," "Oyster Bar w/ B." In April 2004, back in Los Angeles, I saw "B for drinks, hotel – last!" The word 'last' was added in a different ink, and underlined so hard it made a groove in the page; the exasperation was clear. Three days later, "dinner City Café w/ J" – me. I went to my desk in our bedroom and, reaching to the shelf above it, consulted my own calendar from that year, and found a matching "dinner at City with J" – Joe. I had put a heart next to it, again in a different ink, clearly after the dinner occurred. It came back to me now that that had been a deeply romantic outing, as though we'd been apart for months, not days. We took a high-top in the bar, secluded but with a nice view of other tables. Joe had a sudden impulse to order a bottle of Champagne instead of cocktails. Friends dropped by, glasses in hand, teasing us about being "love-birds" when Joe, in a slightly out-of-character move, grabbed my hand under the table. As I gently pulled on this thread of memory, I found us back at home later that night, with the quilt tossed to the bedroom floor, not all of our clothes completely off, and a mad, hungry rush to foolish awkward love.

"The neighbors, Tiger!" Joe had whispered when it hit both of us that the curtains were open and that we were making a fair amount of noise. Then we both exploded into laughter which we tried, imperfectly, to stifle. It was exactly the reunion I might have dreamed of during my nights of frustrated desire while Joe was away. If the façade had blown off the house that instant, we would have continued doing just what we were doing, leaving the neighbors to cope as they might.

Now at last, at this memory, seated at my desk in our new house, with both old calendars open in front of me, I cried.

Only ten or fifteen minutes later, I went to my computer. I didn't feel ravaged, betrayed, or miserable. I missed Joe terribly, but it wasn't his love I missed; it was his physical presence, it was having a lover, it was having sex with him. I felt aggrieved by his absence. I was mad at him for having been unfaithful, and for having died – the ultimate, unanswerable infidelity.

Absent-mindedly I went to FaceBook and found a friend request from Dario waiting for me. I clicked on "Accept" and glanced quickly through his pictures, most of which showed some girl or other twined around him, and all of which made him look so young I was ashamed of myself.

In the right-hand margin of the FB page, I saw that some algorithm thought I might want to look at pictures of extremely handsome young men in shockingly brief briefs made of Space Age fibers. In one of the models, I recognized a porn star I had seen on sites I sporadically visited. Since Joe's death, I hadn't been to any of those sites, and the memory of the porn star's name came back to me from a dusty corner of my mind. His name, at least in the industry, was Andy Ferrara. The underwear ad showed him very sleek, oiled all over, with a gentle crooked smile, quite unlike the aggressive sneering top he usually played in videos. The ad also predated the scattered tattoos (tribal bands around biceps, tramp-stamp of a fleur-de-lys, a martini glass and some woman's name on one glistening geometric pec) that were part of his porn look. He had the kind of manly face that looked equally attractive scruffy or fine-polished.

On impulse, I checked to see if he had a profile on FaceBook. The site suggested "Andy Ferrara, Entertainer." Clicking on it, I went to a fan page which showed chastely cropped versions of several pictures of him I had seen before. The underwear ad I had just admired was also there, with others from the same shoot, none of them cropped because they were at least technically decent. One of these shots showed him from the back, wearing the same tiny briefs and showcasing a pair of powerfully curved buttocks.

I looked to see how many 'likes' he had, how many 'friends.' The numbers were well into four or five figures each. Knowing that he probably never checked this page, I sent him a friend request and message: "Dear Mr. Ferrara, I think you're quite magnificent. Do you ever come to Baltimore? I know a distinguished, recently-widowed professor of Italian who would love to buy you a drink if so." I got up to wash my face as soon as I sent it.

Within less than fifteen minutes, I heard a ping from the computer and, drifting back to it curiously, saw that Andy Ferrara had answered me. He suggested we chat on yahoo messenger and asked for my name there. A few seconds later he paged me:

> *Ciao prof!* ur hot
> *Oh Andrea!*
> Funny timing Ima be in DC first week in Jan – see some clients

'Clients'… the universe suggested I check something on line. I did a quick Google search of "andy ferrara escort" and immediately got directed to *www.Callboy.com*: "top only, friendly, clean, fun; out $350/hr; overnight $2,000."

> Not sure I can get down to DC.
> Awww… cum on!!
> We'll see. Anyway we're both tops.

No prob. We can still have alot of fun. Good 4 me 2 save my loads.
I like my ass played with – no fuck tho
We'll see. You're a nice guy.
Lemme kno prof! u r sexy

I closed yahoo and FB abruptly, as embarrassed as if the entire church
Choir had been reading over my shoulder. Checking my slim inbox on aol,
I answered a few e-mails and then glanced back at FB and yahoo. Andy
had left me a last message with a link to his site, *www.andyferraramuscle.*
com, and his cell phone number. Several of the pictures on the site, I knew,
would be on my mind as I tried to fall asleep that night. I sent him an
answer, asking him to let me know his schedule in Washington.

The next morning, the day before I was to meet Jimmy Jack at the
airport, I got a text from Kevin. "Can I ride along tomorrow to meet Boy
Wonder at BWI?" he was asking. "Most definitely," I answered; "be here
at 2 pm." I texted him a P.S. that he would have to sit sideways in the tiny
back seat of my convertible on the way home, but he was game for that and
in fact was probably the only adult I knew who would exactly fit.
The next day he showed up right on time.
"Oh flawless godfather," he crooned when I opened the door for
him.
"How long have you been back?"
"Couple of days." He made an affectionate lunge for my neck, as
though I were the dearest and most harmless codger in town. His small
body was absolute electricity in my reticent arms and I would have liked
to show him, there on the floor of the hallway if necessary, that I was
in fact a very wicked and dangerous old man. I reached down with one
hand to pat his butt, because his tight pants always flattered him. I was
lucky not to have yielded to the same impulse with Dario. Kevin's hiney
was rock-hard, perfect complementary hemispheres which only the hand
could appreciate. My hand had gone so much faster than my intentions
that it was already too late to apologize. My hand lingered a few shameless
nanoseconds longer.
Kevin released my neck.

"You should give lessons to that godson of yours," he said. His eyes showed no tinge of outrage or offense. I looked at my watch.

"We'll be fine if we leave in ten minutes," I said. "Do you mind if we sit briefly?"

Bracing one hand on the back of the velvet loveseat, he vaulted over its back and landed in its exact center. It was closing in on two hundred years old, but it took his slim weight as though it had been waiting since the reign of Louis Philippe for exactly this humpy boy to flit onto it, and had borne with patience the intervening generations of prim Presbyterian ladies and repressed academics. I went around and sat in the wingchair.

"So have you missed our Jimmy?" I asked. Obviously he had, because riding with me to the airport had been his idea.

"Well, mad about the boy, you know," he said, winking at me. "How well do you know Montclair?" I shook my head. "Husband central. Major eye-candy the past ten days… I guess those preppy guys still catch my eye." If this was his answer to my question about his missing Jimmy, it was not promising.

"Dalliances?" I was guarded, trying not to sound too shocked or disapproving if that was his point.

"No, of course not. I'm with Jacob. But I'll stop noticing other guys when I'm dead and not before. Jus' gotta do *me*, right?" His 'gotta do *me*' was rattled off in a jokey jazz cadence; his normal speech patterns were elegant, a junior Noel Coward minus the cigarette holder.

"I need to ask you one extremely rude question, and I'm asking only because J.J. is one of the great loves of my life and I was put on earth to defend him, with my bare hands if need be," I said. Kevin was unfazed by this preamble.

"I know what you're going to ask."

"Then tell me," I said. I felt that he did know, and that I was speaking with a kindred spirit, at once an incorruptible old sage and a millennial Priapulo.

"You're wondering if I boink our boy," he said, one arm up on the back of the loveseat, pointing a forefinger at me like the barrel of a child's cap gun. "Or vice versa. You think he may still be a virgin and you're wondering how I handle that."

"So?" I asked, after about two beats of silence. I was suddenly afraid of seeming to take a prurient interest in the question. "I worry about him. He's not always... in his body, you know. He doesn't know himself in that way."

He looked at me from the great height of his twenty-some years, with comprehension and generosity.

"The way you two love each other is sweet." I had always felt about the word 'sweet' the way some people felt about 'moist,' but Kevin went on before I could comment. "I know he goes to sleep with you sometimes, and I know it's totally innocent. Not just because he's a baby, but because *you* are. You're in mourning, of course... plus he's too Jimmy-whatever for that in your mind. And *he's* got less than one clue about any of that stuff. I doubt he's ever imagined you having sex with anyone."

"Or himself with anyone, for that matter," I added. "Except, recently, with you."

"Right." He looked down, then raised his eyes candidly again to mine. "The quick answer to your question, is... yes." For a second I'd forgotten what the question was. "Jacob is not what I'd call a major bobcat in the sack, but he's launched." I thought I might blush, but I felt no heat in my face. "Part of him might be content just to hold hands, and talk till dawn about cycles of fifths, but we've gotten past that. One from Column A, one from Column B... he's done some experimenting."

"He feels safe with you," I said. Kevin suddenly grinned in a way that made him seem twenty years older than Jimmy Jack.

"He's a fox," he said. "Sometimes I can't believe how lucky I am." I was beginning to love the way this conversation was going. Kevin was like a one-man stand-in for the entire world of gay dating and romance, and from what he was telling me I could see that J.J. was getting his shy ignorant start with someone who liked him, could show him some options, and found him beautiful. Kevin had said nothing so far about his own emotions.

"I suppose it's obvious that he loves you," I said. He looked down again for a moment; as he looked back up, his eyelashes actually fluttered, yet another small flirtation dispensed from his endless store. He smiled.

"I know he does." There was a long pause, which he could easily have interrupted by saying he loved J.J. too. I counted to ten. To my mental list of Kevin's virtues, I added honesty.

"We should get going," I said, breaking the silence and glancing at the grandfather clock behind him. "Enjoy the front seat while you can, before we toss you back into that cramped little rumble seat…"

"Honey," he said, "if you only *knew* the places I've been tossed."

As I opened the garage and let him walk ahead of me towards the car, he stopped on the threshold and looked back over his shoulder.

"Don't *tell* me you're not going to pat my ass again," he said, so I did.

Jimmy greeted Kevin with melting languid calf-eyes, and clearly wanted to hug him, hard and perhaps forever, right there in the Arrivals lane at BWI. Images of nurses and sailors and Times Square on VE Day came back to me in their first quick all-elbows embrace. The look Jimmy gave me, by contrast, was unsentimental, but there was a deep taking-for-granted sense of home in it which warmed me. He hugged me absent-mindedly and handed me his bigger duffel bag to toss in the trunk. While I was occupied, he entwined himself again around his dapper beloved. I came around the back fender of the car to see them breaking a quick hug, for my benefit or for that of the not entirely charmed passers-by.

The Boys chose to spend their nights at my house, despite having free range of Kevin's apartment. It was Jimmy's home, after all, and there was free food. A total stranger would have understood from across the room that J.J. and Kevin were lovers. It wasn't just that they exchanged tender glances; those had been the stock in trade of Jimmy's unconsummated relationship with Lyric. Kevin's and J.J.'s glances led to short stares, often sealed by sudden touches and clasps. Sometimes in my presence there were even urgent retreats upstairs. There were times I heard without trying to. I was happy to hear that, after any culminating moment that filtered down the stairs, there was always laughter, silly, wordless, and private.

Kevin must have been considered adorable since infancy. Awkward, floundering Jimmy, on the other hand, was growing from day to day into a kind of manly beauty for which decades of loving him had not prepared me. His first love had given him a new stature, noble height, breadth of shoulder. I did experience a regret that Jimmy didn't drift down the hall to my room on nights when Kevin was with him. I noticed my mind going tenderly to them, though, to their togetherness, to the fact of touch and embrace and entry. The thought was vicariously happy for me, but paired with an elderly loneliness, a sense that certain doors were closing for me, forever and much too soon.

Three days into the Boys' Bolton Hill idyll, I got an e-mail from Andy Ferrara, and we arranged to meet at his hotel in DC early in January.

Was Joe a good actor? I had often asked myself this over the years. I was an impenetrable liar about certain things, and I knew that I had kept Joe from suspecting the worst of my doubts. It almost didn't matter if Joe was a real artist, because much of his living always came from his modeling work. He had a practical mechanical confidence about his ability to look good on film. Still, his heart was in his acting and singing, his ability to move the public by something more than his appearance. This was where my reserve sometimes seemed to disappoint him.

I *had* always been fascinated by Joe's abilities as a performer. He had real brass in his singing voice, and there was always something genuinely exciting to me about his ability to spin certain high notes out like a braying trumpet. That quality, to me, was different from the actual telling of a story through the song. The only story his singing ever told was that of a boy from Brooklyn who became famous and admired because of his pluck, determination, steely vocal cords, and freedom from fear. He was in fact one of the very few singers in any genre for whom I never felt any apprehension as they approached a high note. Joe seemed physically incapable of missing a leap into his galvanizing, almost terrifying top. When his voice slammed into that belting register, it gave the listener some of his brazen certainty. Artistry and finesse were pettifogging and moot; one was forced to take heart and believe.

As an actor, too, he could touch the viewer's feelings, not just because he was attractive, but because he cared. He was skillful and hard-working, and he always hit his marks. He wanted very much to be good. That yearning in him was a form of charisma and I could usually feel it radiating off the screen... could almost warm my hands at it as at a

111

campfire. I missed in him what I called the gift of hysterics. I was impressed by actors who could freak out, go off, explode in terror or lust or laughter. Joe wasn't one of those.

He got enough fan mail to make it clear that a certain largish number of people, many of whom obviously nursed fan-crushes on him, flogged their infatuations into thinking of him as a powerful and courageous actor. As a Leo and as the object of the desires of millions, he got enough of a kick out of his own successes that he could accept whatever reservations he sensed from me about his talents. He knew that I didn't think he was a great artist. It was a grief to me, because I was truly proud of him, and I loved yielding to his magnetism when he was on stage or screen. He was absolutely a star to me, someone who could make me shy backstage when strangers came up to him. Dazzled and stammering and star-struck, I felt almost not worthy to be going home with him. After almost every performance, though, there was a moment when my affirmations tapered off and I could tell that he missed the things I hadn't said. The few times that I felt he really did approach greatness, I could see in the very back of his eyes the awareness that I was coming closer, but not quite all the way, to a kind of praise I'd never yet quite voiced. Lying next to him on countless nights, I'd been able to say with complete sincerity how much the public had loved him; how well he had pulled off certain moments I knew he was aiming for; how everyone had envied me for leaving with him; how grateful I was to be the love of someone so dynamic and hard-driving. The discretion and humility with which he settled for that slightly less-than support always touched me.

One night soon after we moved to Bolton Hill, we were watching TV together, and unexpectedly an ad for the Red Cross came on which he had filmed a few months earlier and which I hadn't seen yet. He recognized it immediately, and I heard a tiny hum of surprised satisfaction from him. "Oh, hey," he said modestly. I recognized his tone, stopped whatever gabbling I had launched into when the commercial break began, and turned my attention to the screen. Joe had talked about this commercial during the filming; it had been physically strenuous and emotionally challenging. I instantly knew this was it, released and aired at last, and I reached to take his hand. It was only half a minute long. Joe was a father whose house was flooded, and the ad began with him swimming out through an attic window with one of his small children in the crook of an arm. He passed the child to his wife, who was huddling safe in a rescue boat with the rest of their young family. The emergency workers were pulling him onto the boat, when they all heard a cry. A small, dark child was screaming, alone on the roof of a house a hundred yards away, with a torrent rushing between it and the boat. Another boat could now be seen, bearing the appalled immigrant family of this child implacably downstream. Joe and his wife exchanged a quick look. He released the gunwale of the rescue boat and hurled himself back into the cataract.

The look on his face as he took this plunge lasted barely a second. It was a look of pure heroic courage. For that instant, this man didn't care about his own gene pool; he cared only for the child of strangers, people with no claim on him but their shared undefended humanity. He flailed through the raging water until he was close enough for the terrorized child to jump into his arms; then, holding the child above the water, he let the current sweep them back to the waiting boats. The rescuers fished the child first, and then him from the stream, and he collapsed, exhausted, onto the floor of the boat where the new Americans embraced their rescued toddler and reached beseeching hands to their spent savior. His wife in the other boat, her face streaming with the rain and with tears of pride, mouthed a silent prayer and cradled their children as the two boats raced for high ground. The slogan which flashed on the screen at the end, "We're all heroes," was completely unnecessary.

That one fleeting look on Joe's face... no, on the brave father's face... completely undid me. Nature's rage could not quench the goodness of that man. He turned and saw a need, and from the depths of his heart, unsummoned, rose an unvanquishable, self-forgetting strength and generosity. For a moment, it seemed possible that humanity was good and kind and true. I was exalted by a surge of optimism and trust coursing through me. And Joe, the actor who had done this, was my lover, was next to me, was the sustaining force and presence in my life, someone whose daily kindness I ran the daily risk of taking for granted.

I intended to bestow some deep, heartfelt praise that would make up for my years of reticence. I turned to him with my eyes brimming, meaning to say, 'Divo, how beautiful,' and I burst out crying. He looked at me amazed. He laughed and caught me in his arms, and I cried into his neck and hugged him. "Thank you," I finally was able to choke out. "Thank you."

He cradled me as if I were a child he'd rescued from a flood, his own child or another's; it didn't matter to the vastness of his goodness and kindness. He hummed a little, as he often did when he didn't have the words yet. I could tell how deeply gratified he was, how he savored this one moment when his acting had landed an effect far beyond any of my critical criteria. One of the most spontaneous and unrehearsed prayers of my life went up: a prayer of thanks that he existed, that I knew him, that he loved me, and that he finally knew I could, false as I was, and at least sometimes, admire and adore him without reservation.

"No," he whispered, suddenly shy, "thank *you*."

Chapter 7
January, 2016
[flashback: 1999]

I walked into the lobby of Andy Ferrara's hotel in Washington, just off Embassy Row in North West, and looked around a bit guiltily. I was self-conscious about my squalid errand, and wondered if any of the hotel staff could tell why I was there. No one seemed interested, though, apart from an affable bellhop with a luggage trolley who said, "Good afternoon, sir" and smiled broadly in case I had any steamer trunks for him to take. I counted the seconds in reverse as I got on the elevator, assuming it would be about sixty till I met Andy face to face. I was right on time and knocked discreetly at the door number he had given me, with eleven seconds to spare. As I waited for him to open, it occurred to me that I hadn't had sex with anyone but Joe in twenty-three and a half years.

He came to the door dressed only in some white nylon briefs. To my surprise, he was much better-looking that most of his photos, in which, God knew, he was good-looking enough. He had a friendly, candid smile and seemed unassuming and good-natured. His face lit up when he saw me, as though we were old friends, and he said,

"Hey, you're so much sexier than I was expecting!" As soon as the door closed behind me, he wrapped his arms around me, and a scent came up from his skin which was both soap and salt, erogenous, clean, and fleshly. His body glistened; he was naturally almost hairless. Touching him was like caressing a doll made of silk laid over the firmest, most resilient upholstery.

He drew me in to kiss him and my arms seemed to find their own way around his responsive waist and back. I hadn't expected such a comfortable fit, considering that we knew each other not at all. Though it was clear he was much stronger than me, I could feel his willingness to surrender. He had a practiced sensitivity to another's leading, and I instantly felt capable and commanding. After a few seconds, with a very genteel murmur, he pulled away just long enough to say, "Did you bring the tip?"

'Of course,' I thought: 'he doesn't know me, and for all he knows I might be trying to get something for nothing.' I released him and pulled a small, pre-folded wad of bills out of my wallet, laying it on the nightstand. The outermost bill was a hundred. Andy barely glanced at it, but his eye was probably practiced enough to assess the thickness of the wad.

He led me to the huge bed which took up most of the room and lay down, and I shed a couple of layers to join him. He had lost his only garment by then. His cock was large and cylindrical, and though there was no reason he should be expected to respond to my own fading charms, it was optimistically alert. He kissed me quite warmly, and my right hand strayed down to his crotch, wrapping itself admiringly around his generous erection. To be clear, I reached gently behind it and reminded him with a fingertip that I might hope for something else. As I did so, I remembered that I had read on line that he was engaged in legal wrangling with his wife, who claimed he either had been abusive or had lied to her about his immigration status, or both. From his on-screen career as an unimaginative top, it was not surprising to think that he might be a dominant, over-entitled straight man, yet he was showing no outrage or revulsion at my suggestion. He did, however, stop kissing me to say,

"I almost never do that. I did it in one video, and they had to stop every minute or two to give me more of that aspirin lube. You'll have to be very gentle and it still maybe won't work."

"But you did that video," I said. I hadn't seen it.

"Yes," he nodded, "but that guy wasn't huge like you."

Whatever he knew about my size was only from touching through my pants, and in any case I knew he was simply doing his job, delivering the cajoling flattery any competent escort would. The man he had bottomed for on film (he named him, and I recognized the name) was certainly of another class than me. Yet Andy was mouthing these courtesan clichés in a natural easy-going way. I was enjoying having this splendid young man all to myself for an hour.

"If I do fuck you," I asked, incredulous at my own shamelessness, "do you think you'll come?"

"I doubt it," he said. "It's not all that hot for me to think about."

"I don't like the idea that you wouldn't enjoy it," I said. It was important for me to think of myself as a nice guy, even while negotiating unfeeling intimacies.

"I know you won't hurt me," he said. "I can tell you're a gentleman. I'm comfortable with you. I'll do my best." Good; I was still a nice guy in his mind, as, with absolutely no emotional engagement, I planned how I might enjoy the touch of his famous body. "And like I wrote you," he went on, "the guy who's coming at three is going to want to see me shoot. If I save a load with you, so much the better."

"What's it like for you?" I suddenly asked. I might never be able to ask again. "You're so good-looking. If you wanted to date guys, you could have your pick. How can you have sex with any man who walks through that door?"

He didn't seem to think I was prying or wasting his time. In fact, he had just more or less admitted that it might simplify his day to burn through part of our hour in conversation.

"Well, there's something cute about almost anybody," he said. "I can almost always find something about a guy that turns me on." That, I thought to myself, was why I could never be an escort, not that there had been any particular public clamor for me to do so. "A couple of times in my life I've had to tell some man it wasn't possible."

I found this reply very endearing. Andy Ferrara was some kind of self-image healer. As my shirts came off and I showed him all of the bulges and sags which no one but Joe had had to evaluate in decades, he smiled at me in encouragement. He rolled over onto his stomach, hiding a magnificent set of abs but lifting for admiration an ass of marbly perfection. Seated next to him, I started to rub his back, and he hummed companionably.

"I read recently that you're married," I said. There was some blog about famous porn actors which had mentioned an arrest in connection with those allegations of abuse by his wife or ex-. "Does your wife know about your work?"

"She and I got married when I was seventeen," he said, "back in Czech Republic. We have a son who's almost that age now. She knows I do this work. He doesn't."

"Did you ever hit her?"

"No; she thought she would get a visa or green card through me, but we hadn't seen each other in a couple years when she applied. The abuse thing was her best angle." That actually sounded plausible.

"Are you close with your son?" He smiled.

"Yes; he's my boy. All he cares about is girls and soccer, but he loves me. His big famous father in America. He knows I'm a model; nothing more. I don't see him very often. But he calls me and we Skype. His mother tells him I don't send any money, which isn't true. I think she spends it on drugs or gives it to her new boyfriend."

"That all sounds complicated," I said.

"She's a bitch. She thinks I should bring her to America. She's not really my wife now, though. We haven't had sex in ten years or more. Hell with her."

"Would you say you're a gay guy now?"

"No, I have a girlfriend. But I like sex with men, and it's a living."

"I didn't realize you were Czech," I said like a dullard. "I assumed you were Italian-American." I had never heard him speak enough dialogue to detect the slight Slavic accent which was detectable, and completely charming, in person.

"I picked the name because I like Ferraris," he grinned over his shoulder. "Mmm... that feels so good." I had just started rubbing his shoulders with both my hands.

I found this conversation very credentialing. He seemed like a sincere, unprejudiced man who took life as it came. It was a huge pleasure to caress his body. There was no part of him which it wasn't a joy to touch. Soon my pants were off and I was lying on top of him, and by rising and flexing he was able to create some helpful friction for me almost without penetration. Reaching below him at one point, I noticed that his own erection had subsided; he was in no danger of wasting an orgasm on me. The experience of holding and caressing him was more connoisseurship than passion. Any objective observer would have had to admit he was beautiful. It was a privilege to be so close to him, to have his refined contours at my disposal, to be the beneficiary of his courteous, calculating availability.

"You're so big," he murmured, with his eyes closed dreamily; "I only wish... maybe next time... I need to get used to you, to trust you..." I admired his masterful delivery of these lines, as if I were listening to Charles Ribera sing *"Ich baue ganz."* I fell into the spell he was casting as willingly as I often had, in opera houses and theatres around the world, when a gifted and handsome actor or singer performed.

Fifty-eight minutes after my arrival, we had finished a short, fond shower together and agreed to meet again the next time he came east. Perhaps he could even find a way to come to Baltimore; he had other friends there. I was dressed again, in my Oxford cloth and tweeds and corduroys, and got to watch Andy towel off and stretch and yawn and preen in his glorious nakedness. Already sporting a renewed hard-on (good news for the friend he was expecting), he slipped into a fresh pair of shiny white briefs.

The minute I walked in the kitchen door from the garage, J.J. came galumphing down the back stairs. His eyes were ablaze with a mix of worry and disapproval.

"Where's the teeny one?" I asked, hoping to deflect.

"At the library working on a *paper*," he said, as though to underscore that at least one man he knew was engaged in the quest for academic truth and not mere philandering.

I hung up my keys, glancing at the clock. It was barely 4:15.

"It's five o-clock somewhere in the world," I said. "I've been working hard. I think I've earned a cocktail."

"By what?" came the hot answer. "By banging a porn star? That's your big accomplishment for the day?"

I devoutly wished I hadn't ever mentioned this whole escapade to him. I had let myself assume that, with his virginity behind him, he had become worldlier than he really had. On that basis I had told him that I was tired of celibacy and upset by news of Joe's passing infidelity, and that I felt entitled to a tumble with Andy. I had a half-baked theory that honesty about my own sexual and emotional life would provide a template for him and show him that gay life didn't have to follow the Rick Santorum playbook.

"Well…" I temporized. "'Banging' might be an overstatement. There was a timid approach to banging. No profound banging was accomplished. Future options for banging were cursorily discussed." Jimmy was slouching back against the kitchen counter, hands in pockets, with his ebony curls like Medusa's snakes hissing suspiciously, clustered around his lowering forehead. His face was almost a tragic mask: he was offended youth, disillusioned with his elder idols, their bunioned feet mired in clay.

One godfather had gone on a booty call, in an attempt at mitigating his grief, and the whole adult world was proven to be a sham, a hoax, a lie. He was a gargoyle of glum judgement. In a sitcom, he would have been hilarious.

"Show me his picture," he said. It was a surprising turn of thought. I pulled out my iPhone and clicked through a few of Andy's on-line publicity shots. One of them, which showed him face down on the floor, looking up at the camera while his burnished naked back filled the top of the frame, struck me as unbelievably erotic, though I had just seen him and knew that he was at least that good-looking in person.

"He looks really interesting," he said, with leaden sarcasm. I was stung.

"He is not uninteresting," I answered. "He's oddly sincere and good-natured. He made me smile, and he made me feel good about myself for an hour, in some weird weak pathetic way."

"An hour by the clock, I'm sure. That's his *job*, G.J." He was right that it had been precisely an hour, by the clock, and that Andy had had the smooth expertise to make that feel natural.

"I know that. That's the whole point. Don't make it sound like he's dirty or stupid or cynical and depraved. I was the consumer here; blame me. Or better yet, don't. We're not talking about romance here. We're talking about two decent people making decisions that benefit them both and that they both have every right to make."

I fumbled to find some of Andy's texts to me on Facebook, and showed them to Jimmy like a child showing a parent his report card. I was hoping he would think they were sweet and honest.

"He's practically illiterate," he said, rolling his eyes in exasperation after a glance lasting perhaps as long as five seconds. I snatched my phone back.

"I'm going to see him again," I said. "I'm not ashamed of this. He's a nice person, doing excellent work in an industry in which grown-ups can agree to participate."

"You're defending him to defend yourself." His accusing glare was too heavy for me, and I turned away. I opened the liquor cabinet and pulled down the bourbon and sweet vermouth. I could feel him glaring at my back.

After a long moment, he went to the refrigerator and got out the bitters, and took the Luxardo cherries from another cabinet. Then he handed me my favorite silver julep cup and fished a small spoon out of the dish drainer. As I started mixing my Manhattan, I could feel myself cringing slightly under his gimlet eye.

"I'm old, Jacob. I don't know if I'll ever have a lover again." I was astonished to feel my voice almost shaking, and my grief and self-pity for once were not for Joe's death, but for my own selfish bodily loneliness. "I'm also not old enough to give up on sex. This may be how it works for me now."

As I faced the counter, he leaned backwards against it next to me and put one long arm across my chest and around my shoulder. It was an awkward embrace; he was pinning my arms so that I couldn't finish mixing. He leaned down to kiss the top of my head. I heard him sigh and I turned so that I too had my back to the counter.

"You're such a romantic," he said.

Joe had said those exact words to me the first time we talked at Rehoboth. For an instant I wondered if I had ever told Jimmy that story. He said the words without irony or sarcasm, but as if I were a perplexing child he was worried about. It was the way I was used to thinking about Jimmy himself, and it was almost the same tone Joe had used in talking to me so many years before. Only later had I realized that Joe was already starting to fall in love with me when he called me a romantic. Jimmy was not in danger of that. I put my free arm around his waist and gave him a quick squeeze; then I stepped away.

"Is the munchkin coming to dinner?" I asked. "Should we start cooking?"

"Not tonight. Just us. Make me your carbonara." He had never asked me to cook any particular dish for him and generally didn't really seem to care what he ate.

"Who are you?" I asked. He smiled self-deprecatingly. "That won't take long. Let's just sit and talk for a while. Do you want anything in a glass?"

"Is there any Frascati open?"

"Yes, on the top shelf of the fridge," I said, starting for the parlor; "pick your own glass." Then I paused in the doorway and said, over my shoulder, "You're the world's very best godson."

Kevin did come for dinner the following night. The three of us sat in the upstairs parlor after dinner. The Boys monopolized the long Morocco leather sofa while I lounged back in an old club chair sipping a clear grappa.

Kevin was sitting in J.J.'s lap at one point, and then at another J.J. had his long legs stretched out so that Kevin could rub his feet; occasionally they were perched primly at opposite ends of the long sofa, and from time to time they were entwined in the center in geometrically implausible ways. They managed to sustain this level of smoldering eroticism on almost no alcohol: their glasses of Drambuie went largely untouched, but the conversation never lagged.

Kevin was never less than cocky and ebullient. Boys who knew they were attractive had always struck me as an alien species; their swaggering little ways made them seem childish and clueless. Almost everything Kevin said on topics of actual interest, like music theory or LGBTQ rights, was intriguing and original. His way with Jimmy was especially endearing: respectful and affirming. His rote little gay witticisms, on the other hand, often made him seem like just a glib stylish kid.

Jimmy, by contrast, seemed that evening like the man in the couple. As he sat apart from Kevin, he beamed at him a solid, grounded approval and fascination, as if ready at any moment to turn to me and brag about Kevin's wit and culture. When they did embrace, Kevin seemed almost to disappear into the shelter of Jimmy's arms. Jimmy glowed with competence and benign maturity.

At some point in their intermittent spooling and unwinding, Kevin turned to me and said,

"So be honest… what's it like working surrounded by all those hot young guys? And don't tell me they don't hit on you sometimes, and don't tell me you don't notice they're hot."

"I notice everything," I said, staring into my little grappa glass.

"He notices everything," J.J. said, nodding to signal that I had vast experience and intuition.

"Joe used to tease me," I said. "He said I seduced all the straight boys at school. Any time we'd have a party for my classes, the cute hunky jocks would cluster around me, vying for my attention, and he'd give me endless grief about it later."

"Kevin says all straight boys secretly want to put out," Jimmy told me. He sounded slightly awestruck at this opinion of Kevin's, like a country boy visiting his city-slicker cousin, amazed that he could decipher the subway map and knew what to order in an Ethiopian restaurant.

"Well," I smiled, "I don't think I've ever seriously been interested in one of my students. I've always said that a former teacher and student can make a good couple about one out of every thousand times, if they wait till after... But, conveniently enough, it never materialized."

"But you always had favorites, didn't you?" Kevin asked.

"Of course he does; how could he not?" J.J. said, as if defending me from some lewd implication.

"But I have always had a pretty strong internal prohibition against mixing worlds." I looked across at Jimmy. I was getting used to the fact that his face had by now taken on some of the striking geometry of his mother's twenty years earlier, a quality that could only be called beauty, though he was still on the geeky side of that spectrum. There were prohibitions there, too. "I mean, I enjoy my students' good looks and I absolutely love the fact that they idolize me. I think a lot of butch young straight guys are intrigued by male mentors who are refined and sensitive and lefty and classy. Usually they have decent fathers in their lives, but maybe I'm a different model of what men can be."

"Has a gay student ever fallen in love with you?" Kevin asked with a knowing look.

"Yes, a few times." Something unpleasant about myself occurred to me. "Never one who led me into temptation." I didn't like the fact that the nervous, high-strung, oddly over-groomed, un-athletic boys had never attracted me. I gave myself partial credit for the fact that I had been a decent mentor for many gay boys. "A few of them have come to me for serious advice, about coming out to their parents or dating, or even for AIDS counseling back in the day. But there's never been any fascination or flirtation on my part."

"I think that may be a stroke of luck," Kevin said. "Between the hot straight boys who love you and the gay boys who aren't your type, you've gotten through thirty years without a breath of scandal."

"I'm proud of you," J.J. said, laughing. Suddenly, he remembered a conversation a few weeks earlier. "Tell me more about Dino. I got some kind of vibe from what you said about him."

Suddenly I was tired of this topic. It was making me feel not only old, but like a foolish old goat. Dino was a former student, perhaps the most beloved, and our tenuous friendship, surviving over the twenty-plus years since his graduation, through his marriage and the births of his two children, still cost me a restless, disappointed little ache.

"Let's leave that lurid interlude for another evening, if you don't mind," I said. Jimmy might have pursued it, but Kevin gave me a comprehending look and changed the subject.

"Jacob tells me you know Charles Ribera," he said. "You know he's coming to town, don't you? He's got some gig in DC and he'll be doing a master class at Peabody." This snapped me right out of my grim little reminiscences.

"No, I didn't know that. You didn't mention it," I said to J.J., maybe just a bit reproachfully. "Of course, I'm perfectly capable of forgetting my own middle name these days, but I wouldn't have forgotten that Charles Ribera is coming to Baltimore."

"I'm pretty sure I told you," he said. He looked vague for a second and then gave a curt nod. "Yeah – I just decided I *did* tell you. You said, 'Oh, good' or something like that." 'Oh, good' was something I virtually never said. "Besides, his gig is in DC. The Early Music Consort at the Peab somehow talked him into doing this master class."

"How long have you known him?" Kevin asked. "And for that matter, *how* do you know him? He's kind of a big deal."

"Well…" I said, drifting off into an attempt at math. "Joe and I had only been together a few years, I think. I was the first opera queen I knew to become obsessed with Charles, and I'm not saying I didn't craft a poetically adulatory fan letter or something… it's all a bit vague to me now. Then when Joe saw that I'd bought one of Charles' CDs, he mentioned that he'd known him slightly in LA, which struck me as an incredible coincidence. We got in touch. He crashed with us occasionally when he was singing in this area. His career was kind of taking off in those years. Original instruments, A = 405, a fair amount of straight-tone Mozart ensembles, but with Charles singing his heart out like a plangent demigod… he did an *Idomeneo* at Wolf Trap that remains one of my most sacred memories. Sixteenth notes in torrents, of course." The Boys seemed surprised at how substantial the connection turned out to have been.

"So…" Kevin asked after a longish silence; "what was he like – or what *is* he like? It almost sounds like you're friends."

I gave Jimmy Jack a quiet, pointed look: I couldn't possibly have forgotten that he had told me Charles was to be in town. "No, we're not friends now, really. I remember him as a bit difficult socially… defensive and ambitious, ironic, suspicious, and harshly judgmental… of others, yes, but mostly of himself. I gathered he'd had a more or less terrifying upbringing in LA, with anti-Latino discrimination and one of those menacing homophobic Mexican fathers. He had wary glittering eyes, and he always seemed to recognize something in me, not especially flattering: maybe a kindred cynicism, a disenchanted intelligence. He *was* like me in some ways. He always seemed on the verge of thinking everyone was a jerk or an idiot." Jimmy shook his head.

"I don't get that part of your self-image," he said. "No one else sees you that way."

"Oh," said Kevin, "don't sell your godfather short; he is a wicked, wicked man." I loved that he'd said that. Jimmy looked genuinely shocked, worried that Kevin was blaspheming, or harrowing my fragile nerves. I just smiled.

"He was a laryngeal divinity when he sang. From the beginning I was fascinated with his voice; it was all core, all heart; no quarter given or asked… brilliant."

"That actually sounds like Uncle Joe's singing," Jimmy said. I nodded. Joe in pop and Charles in classical had shared that quality of complete certainty in the athletic aspects of their vocalism. I heard Joe's voice for a quick moment.

"I wish I could have met Joe," Kevin suddenly said, flipping unexpectedly into an unguarded simplicity. J.J. gave him a quick, worshipful look, as though he had just spoken the most perfectly tactful syllables ever uttered. It was hard for me sometimes to remember that Jimmy Jack had loved Joe independent of our marriage. Joe had been his beloved uncle, much less complicated than his touchy godfather, dependable and patient, as he was with everyone he loved. My face had turned a blazing red at Kevin's words. I knew that I might cry.

"So do I," I said, shaking my head for a second. My throat was very tight. 'It's been seven months,' I thought wearily. 'I can't cry every time.'

Kevin leaned far forward from his seat on the sofa and barely reached to put one hand on my knee. His sweet little face was still, his moues and pouts laid aside. It was perhaps the handsomest he had ever looked to me, and I could imagine how he looked to Jimmy in private moments.

"He's still in this house in some ways," he said to me, "and I can feel what a welcome he could make. You and he made a home. And you practically raised our boy." He jerked his head back towards Jimmy, who reached and patted his shoulder, but he didn't break his eye contact with me. "No more tears," he said kindly. And in fact, as our eyes remained locked for one more second, I knew that I would not cry this time… that I would cry less and less often as time passed. The constriction in my throat which had seemed so menacing just a moment before eased. I felt the color drain from my face, and the crisis passed. I was sure that I could trust my voice not to waver.

"So… was Charles Ribera hot?" Kevin asked. He settled back into the crook of Jimmy's arm.

"Scorching," I said. "Diffident, self-questioning, guarded and proud, like a brave child; olive skin, the blackest eyes ever seen, and a face like a sleek shiny seal's. He knew that I genuinely admired his singing, and that I liked him and sympathized with some of his past struggles… But I'm maundering."

"Don't leave out one syllable," said Kevin, laughing.

"We met during a time of heart-break for him," I said. I felt a hardening around this whole nexus of not-joyful memories. "He had just been badly broken up with by this guy Tory, whom Joe actually knew fairly well, who had been a flight attendant but then enjoyed brief notoriety as a… well, a minor – porn star – but…" Here Jimmy of course fizzled or coughed, and I hastened to cut him off. "Oh, *much* too long a story! And it was a time of… I don't remember exactly: repressed tensions between Joe and me. We were still newish, and he always worried that I didn't respect him. This unspoken kinship between Charles and me at a certain point felt dangerously like an attraction; Joe and I had a spat. I'll spare you the details, but I decided we should stop hanging out with Charles. And Charles never raised the topic, didn't make any effort to keep in touch. I was afraid that it might have hurt him. He tended to think of himself as badly used; he had a history of feeling rejected or told 'No.'" Jimmy looked sad, maybe at the idea that Joe and I had hit another rough patch. "I did see Charles occasionally over the years, usually just to shake his hand backstage after some triumph of his. I think Joe may have gone once or twice with me as well, to prove it was OK; *'per sdrammatizzare,'* as he put it. Perfunctory Hellos, the blessed air-kiss, etc." I paused. "Charles sent me a very kind note when Joe died; some show-biz mutual friend must have let him know. I will be glad to see him again."

Joe and I had been together several years. Charles stayed with us for a couple of nights, doing a memorable "Acis and Galatea" with a local early music ensemble. As usual, he brought a full-throated passion to his part, with brilliant execution and metallic, masculine tone. Because he was the most distinguished individual artist in the group, having a respectable discography and a flourishing local fan club, the maestro had allowed him an encore if the public called for one. It did. He favored us with *"Il mio tesoro,"* the band sawing away conscientiously and the conductor waving a rigid yet listless hand from the keyboard. Charles' Mozart sounded almost vulgar after the refinements we had just endured. His voice came pouring out of him as though he were going to murder Don Giovanni there in front of us with his bare hands, and when he came to his long *roulades,* his typewriter-perfect delivery of the rapid passage work sounded dangerously macho after the lilting, ardent legato phrases. This was a Don Ottavio to worship, to fear, to wait a year for, to trust with your assailed honor. I leapt to my feet before the silence had quite settled after the orchestral coda, shrieking an embarrassing *"Bravo!"* Joe looked at me with bemused irritation, even though an instant later the entire audience was echoing my cry, with shufflings of Birkenstocked feet.

Walter and Ricardo had come up from DC for the performance, and stayed to dinner the following evening, Charles' last in Baltimore. Walter mentioned that he remembered Charles' Pedrillo fondly, but had always hoped to hear him as Belmonte. Charles, while acknowledging Walter's sincere praise of his time-stands-still "Serenade," had done a wicked chimpanzee version of Pedrillo's first line in the quartet, *"Also, Blondchen, hast's verstanden?"* with savage *staccato* quackings which showed better than words how mortifying it was for a lyric artist to sing such lines. After dessert, Walter volunteered to drive Charles to the airport. He might apologize to Charles for my display after the Mozart, or he might admit that he too had found Charles' ornamentation, including one of his signature immaculate trills on the entire last whole note before the flourish on *"Cer-CA-te...,"* absolutely riveting.

As I closed the front door behind them, I turned back into the house and said, in what I meant as a comic confession of smitten fandom, "Charles is just *so* dreamy."

"And *so* neurotic," said Ricardo, smiling at my infatuation. He and Charles often chattered in Spanish, and I suspected that Ricardo actually knew him better than I did. "But oh my *God,* can he sing!" Joe said nothing, making a fair amount of clatter as he finished clearing the table. I got just the whiff of something dark from him. Once we'd loaded the dishwasher and polished some silver serving pieces, we all went into the living room to talk while we waited for Walter to stop back to pick up Ricardo for their drive home. It wasn't really exactly a conversation; I had a few more opinions to share about what had been particularly glorious in Charles' performance, and after about the seventeenth of these, Joe gave a grumpy, rebellious look and said,

"I don't know; there's something a little showy about his singing. He kind of wears me out sometimes: like he's singing because he's mad about something." This was quite on point: Charles' vocal confidence might strike some as over-aggressive. But I wasn't entertaining any critical *aperçus* that night. I fancied myself an expert in finding ways to seem not to talk down to Joe about classical music, so I felt safe in saying,

"Well, he has to find new interpretations each time a phrase of text is repeated. If he sings, *'cercate di asciugar'* eight times, sometimes he's mad;

sometimes he's serene; sometimes he's romantic... And he counts on the audience's knowing the tune, too, which helps us enjoy his variations."

"I know all the tunes he sang last night," Joe said, a fair response to my pompous little lecture.

"I know you do, Divo," I said. It sounded glib and condescending even to me, once it was out in the room. Joe looked more and more resentful. Ricardo stepped in.

"Well he's a great singer," he said. "And a very mixed-up man."

"But so handsome, don't you think?" I asked, predestinated. "There's something so *young* about him when he sings, so easily hurt but so courageous and hopeful... And that *skin* of his...! And those eyes!"

"Oh for fuck's sake," Joe said, shifting in his seat, a storm-cloud gathering.

"Don't mind Jim," Ricardo said, trying to laugh it off. "He can't help himself. And we're all just as bad. Charles is a mess, but I *do* think he is hot." It didn't quite work; there was still a charged, unpleasant silence for a long moment.

"He's a pathetic sneak, is what he is," Joe finally said. There was a deathly serious undertone in his voice. "He waltzes into town and talks about damn vibrato and stuff with you all, and he cries about Tory to Jim and he maybe kinda *sorta* thinks he can break us up..." His words were angry, but his face looked sad. I knew exactly what he was saying: he had noticed my flirting with Charles and it had hurt him. I was also weak enough to be glad that anyone could even for an instant take seriously the idea that Charles might be attracted to me. I was sorry and ashamed, perhaps too much to admit it, so I blustered forward, claiming an outraged innocence which I knew I didn't deserve.

"That is perhaps the single stupidest thing I have ever heard you say," I said, for all the world as though those words proved how incapable I was of caring about another man. I could hear Ricardo suck in his breath very quietly.

"Because I say so many stupid things," Joe said, on the brink of crying. He had never seemed so weak to me. In most of our arguments, I was the squishy wounded one. I didn't have the skills to manage the argument we were suddenly having now, in which apparently I was cruel and impervious and neglectful. "I know I didn't get beaten up by my father, and I know I have no class. So why should anyone care about me? I get that."

None of this made any logical sense. I was so at sea that I couldn't think of a word to utter in reply. Maybe if I just sat there he would snap out of it. He looked at me for a moment with pure desolation and terror in his eyes. He truly thought that I might not respect him, and that I might love someone else more. He was fidgeting with the gold band on his left ring finger, and suddenly it slipped off and was naked and hollow there in the fingertips of his right hand. This seemed to surprise him. He stared at it with grief and self-pity. It looked thin and defenseless off his thick strong finger.

Then he suddenly jumped to his feet and flung his ring at me, very hard. It hit me in the chest and rolled away on the carpet. I flinched; it actually hurt, and it shocked me. His face was beet red.

"And I know I don't sing *Mozart!*" he yelled, and ran out of the room and through the dining room to the kitchen, slamming the door behind him. The silence that came through the door was agonizing.

Frightened and humiliated, trying to restore normality with a fake worldly shrug, I turned to Ricardo and asked,

"What the hell just happened?"

Ricardo, the beautiful and tender, the youngest and most fragile person on earth, looked at me with loving, wise, disappointed pity. He whispered,

"I think Joe just reminded you that he loves you… very, very much." He came close enough to pat my shoulder, as though I were a much younger and extremely maladroit friend who had just conspicuously blundered into a catastrophic gaffe, but whom he nevertheless still cared for and hadn't quite despaired of. "I would guess you have about ten seconds to get into that kitchen." I didn't even nod or try to pat his hand; I just bolted for the door.

Joe was standing at the sink, hunched over it with tears streaming down his face. I could actually see two or three of them drop from his cheeks and splash on the rim of the sink. His shoulders were shaking but he made no sound. He was just a human being; he was made up of all kinds of amino acids and enzymes and God only knew what. I had a second of watching a primordial ooze separate, galactic ages before, moments after some precipitating collision with an asteroid, into some strain which would one day become a Roman gene pool. From it – after ages of single-cell organisms, primitive amphibians, screaming velociraptors, flat-faced tool-making monkeys, hulking saber-tooth tiger fodder – came a long line of curly-haired, annoying, instinctual, green-eyed people, conquering the world, then wasting their lives for Cola di Rienzo, rioting over forgotten candidates for the corrupt papacy, rutting in the ruins, posing on broken Corinthian capitals for cheesy academic German painters, eating *porchetta* with their fingers and doubling the -b- in *sabato*. In time, one of them, Joe's grandfather, looked at what the Duce was up to and said to himself (I had heard the story from Joe's parents many times), "So you know, *basta*," and stowed away on an Italian merchant marine vessel in the mid-1920s and jumped ship in New York; met an Italian girl, made a son named Dominic who bought a house in Carroll Gardens and married Constanzia Piatelli (which she always insisted was spelled with one -t- in Rome… she even claimed that "Constanzia" was a real Italian name). At literally any stage in this series of evolutionary accidents, the merest divergence would have kept my Joe from existing. That split in the protozoa billennia before had inexorably and providentially led to the creation of this good, scared, shuddering, strong, completely desired, painfully dear man who was weeping over our kitchen sink because of my stupidity and superficiality.

Because I hated scenes, I wanted to be dignified and to approach him slowly and calmly. However, he didn't look up when I came in; he made no appeal to me. A sudden vacuum of need… his, mine… sucked me to him, and I threw my arms around him passionately. I had no pride and no dignity. I had to be with Joe. I was crying too without having noticed when it began.

"I don't give a fucking *fuck* about any of that," I cried. "About anyone else on earth. You're my Joey. I'm your Jimmy. That is literally *all* I care about. Please tell me it's OK."

He turned convulsively to me. He had heard something primitive and Roman in my hoarse voice. He didn't say a word. We rubbed our wet faces together, and slowly, in our formless embrace, we sank to the floor. After a minute or two he was comforting me. His lips brushed my face and neck and he was murmuring something incomprehensible. There might have been syllables resembling my name, or the words 'Love' and 'Yes' and

'OK.' I was shaking, horrified, grateful, shattered, harbored in and nestling someone both powerful and helpless.

About five minutes later we were recovered enough to stand up, rinse and dry each other's faces, and go back into the living room. We were smiling like abashed, guilty children. Ricardo was sitting there. Though he was not literally seated in a rocking chair, he was the image of the aged parent who would rock on the front porch till all the wayward children of the world found their tortured way home. I was shy of looking at him. When I did catch his eye, he looked at me as though everything that had just happened were entirely my fault. He reached out one hand to Joe, without breaking his gaze on me. Joe and I were holding hands, but his left hand was free and he placed it in Ricardo's beckoning right. Ricardo took Joe's hand very firmly, looking up at him with a quiet smile which baked away every cloud in a thousand-mile radius.

"I found this under the sofa," he said, opening his left hand to show us Joe's gold band. "Give me your finger." Joe did, and Ricardo slid the ring back onto it. It settled into its broad shallow groove. There was no audible click, but all three of us felt the fit. Ricardo kissed the ring and looked up, first at Joe but then, before he spoke, at me.

"Now it STAYS there, OK?" he said.

Chapter 8
February, 2016
[flashback: 1998]

"Thanks for understanding," I said to J.J. as I bundled him out the front door. On only a couple of days' notice, Andy Ferrara had asked if he could stay over. Jimmy often slept at Kevin's apartment anyway, and there were mornings when its location was more convenient for his early classes, so I'd asked him to vacate. Still, he looked miffed as he slung his backpack over one shoulder and slouched down the street towards midtown, with barely a farewell wave.

Andy had a series of encounters with friends or clients (interchangeable terms for him) in Baltimore, which were all to be "out" – that is, at their homes or in hotel rooms paid for by them. It would be a great convenience for him to sleep at my house afterwards. Without any such suggestion from me, he proposed a very drastic discount on his normal overnight fee. "I feel comfortable with you," he texted me, "and I know you're a gentleman." He had said exactly those words at our first meeting. This gratified me, as though his repeated protestation of trust meant that at some level, in ways I could respect, he did actually like me.

After watching J.J. walk away, I drifted back into the house and tried to do a little writing while waiting for Andy. Classes had just started the week before, and I wouldn't have time to work on scholarly projects once my desk was cluttered with compositions and quizzes to mark. I drafted a few generic sentences on Calvino and Ariosto, things any intelligent graduate student might have written, and immediately deleted them. There was an interesting and original idea buzzing around the room, something tiny but new, and I wasn't catching it.

I wasn't entirely at peace about kicking J.J. out for the night. He had made a caustic little observation about who had shared my bed in the past twenty-three years: only Joe and J.J. himself; and now I was planning to admit someone J.J. called a man-whore. I was sure he had learned that term from Kevin, but Kevin would have used it as a joke, not an insult. I didn't need him explaining to me that my relationship with Joe had been important and beautiful. I didn't need his help to miss Joe desperately, every day. And I certainly didn't want him to think for an instant that he clove to a higher standard than I did. Yet I could also look in the mirror. It was extremely unlikely that a sixty-something widower would attract the loving and desirous gaze of a serious, or even a palatable candidate. A friendly, sexy, clean, skillful man-whore might well be my best option, in ways that an idealistic twenty-something couldn't understand. Jimmy had no right to judge me.

Andy was an expert on time management. Exactly on time, he was out front, waving good-bye to his Lyft driver with his lopsided, unpretentious grin. When he turned to me, his face practically lit up. One of my older neighbors happened to be walking her dog as I came down the front steps, and I could tell that, from Andy's delighted expression and quick affectionate embrace, she gathered he was a dear old friend of mine. I quickly introduced them:

"Grace: Andy, a friend visiting from the West Coast. Grace is the pride of Bolton Hill." As they shook hands and exchanged 'Hello's, Grace heard Andy's accent. She instantly asked if he was Czech. Her late husband had been in the diplomatic corps, with frequent postings to *Mittel Europa*, and she had Czech friends. He was charmed by this, and they even tossed back and forth a couple of courtesy phrases in his language. She took her leave because her little poodle was tugging obstreperously at his leash. As she walked away, she called back that she hoped to see Andy again during his stay. Something in her smile told me that she hoped he might be someone who could at least start to make up for Joe's death.

We went into the house and he glanced around him. From the front hall he could see glimpses of the double parlor to his left and of the dining room straight ahead, as well as the mahogany-railed main staircase leading up to the library, barely visible as a Pompeian red blur above.

"Nice place!" he said, with a whistle. I could see that it registered with him as expensive and classy; he had nothing more to say about it. There were no questions about family pictures, the piano, the faux finishes. Instead, he put his bag down and wrapped his arms around me. He leaned in to kiss me briefly and then said,

"Seven appointments today! I'm beat. Make me a drink?"

An hour later we were seated on the parlor sofa. I had mixed him a Manhattan and then grilled a thick filet for each of us. He won my approval by asking for his to be as rare as possible, and with a quickly thrown-together green salad and an Otterbein's Bakery cookie, that made for a fast dinner. His manners weren't bad at all, but there was something very primitive and appetitive in his remorseless sawing and chomping, with red gravy on the plate and quickly licked or blotted from his smooth lips. It felt almost homey, in a high-gloss way, to stand with him in the kitchen after we'd eaten, and even to ask him to dry a couple of dishes for me. We retreated to the parlor once the dishes were handled. Sitting closely huddled on the sofa, slack against the pillows, my right arm around his sculptural shoulder and each of us gently swooshing just a splash of a luxurious French brandy in Tiffany snifters, we probably looked exactly like a repressed, aging academic of some means and an extremely good-looking hustler doing quick sums in his head. I didn't care.

The doorbell rang about fifteen minutes into our small talk. Gene was standing at the door, and said,

"Dear heart! I saw the lights on, figured I'd try my luck, and… but *OH*, you're entertaining!" He had just seen Andy's long shapely legs through the parlor door. I laced one arm around his waist and said,

"Yes. Come in and be properly introduced! You must help me receive my guest." As we entered the parlor, Andy jumped up and extended a hand.

"Hi! I'm Andy," he said. He gave Gene an appraising once-over. I wondered if he would realize that Gene was too good-looking ever to resort to calling on his professional services. Gene, in any case, didn't miss a beat. He had stepped ahead of me to shake Andy's outstretched hand.

"I know who *you* are," he said; the gracious insinuation would have flattered anyone on earth. "Please consider me one of your greatest fans." He turned to me with a courtly smile: "And *you,* you clever minx! I am, as usual, simply awestruck."

"It's always nice to meet fans," Andy replied equably. "I have several friends in Baltimore already."

"I'll wager we have friends in common," Gene nodded. "Not even counting our beloved James here." He turned and gave me a generous smile. I took a hint.

"May I mix you something, dearest?" I asked.

"A simple beer will do… you know my plebeian tastes!" Gene laughed. I darted into the kitchen and popped a bottle for him. By the time I got back to the parlor, perhaps as much as two minutes later, I heard Gene saying, with his usual unflappable *bonhomie*,

"Turn around, handsome… turn a-ROUND!"

As I entered, Andy was turning his back to Gene, and his shorts were down around his ankles. This view of his splendid posterior was something men often paid for. Both of them were laughing, as though this were normal cocktail party banter. Gene reached forward to give Andy's butt a quick pat, and then Andy had his pants back up in one swift, graceful motion. They both turned to face me, and we sat down companionably to quaff our various beverages.

It took Gene fifteen unhurried minutes to drain his beer. Our conversation was unforced, cheerful, and easy. As he took his last slurp, he suddenly glanced at his watch and said,

"Just *look* at the time. I have intruded *far* too long on your gracious hospitality… the hospitality of *both* of you beautiful, dangerous men. I must fly." As we all stood, Andy said to him,

"Keep in touch!"

I couldn't imagine how there had been time for an exchange of contact information *and* the dropping of Andy's trou, but Gene operated always on his own uniquely swift schedule of conquest.

"Well, to be honest, dear heart," Gene temporized, "I have just started seeing someone. *No* exchange of vows as yet, but…" I was unaware of any such nascent attachment in Gene's social life, and recognized immediately that he was lying to dampen any interest or expectations Andy might be entertaining. Perhaps he didn't want to trespass on my territory. It was probably a signal Andy was unused to receiving, because he apparently didn't grasp it and just said,

"I'll see you next time I'm in town."

I walked Gene to the front door.

"Just stunned by you," he breathed, as we hugged good-night. "Your efficiency is unrivaled." He waited for me to say something mitigating. Perhaps Andy actually was an old friend of mine, through Joe's show-biz contacts, or something like that? He had to choose between believing that and acknowledging the obvious: that I had retained the services of a notorious man-whore. It was clear that he made no moral judgement about either possibility, but that he considered the less *louche* of them the more likely. Though I didn't want to lose any credit with him for the sincerity of my heartbreak or the depth of my mourning, I also was completely unwilling to have him think that legendary porn stars came to visit me only as old friends.

"Andy is a sweetheart," I said. "Just the thing for certain… *seasons* in a gentleman's life."

Gene reared back slightly to look me in the eye. His gaze for a second was ancient, primaeval: anything that spoke of erections, of embraces, of penetrations and surrenders was consecrated in his view. He was happy for me.

"Have at, I say. Literally what*ever* makes you happy, even for a night, is my devoutest wish. Gay Baltimore salutes you. And *call* me after he's gone."

By the time I returned to the parlor, Andy was supine, naked on the sofa. He stretched luxuriantly and smiled at me:

"I'm *so* tired," he yawned.

"Don't get too comfortable here," I said. "Why don't we retire upstairs? You can get in bed and I'll join you as soon as I wash up and turn out all the lights." He surged upright and somehow had his discarded clothes in his bag and its strap over his shoulder in moments.

"Lead the way," he said, smiling.

"No," I countered; "*you* lead the way." He paused at the top of the first flight and looked back at me, with sudden modesty and an appealing uncertainty.

"Which way?" he asked, seeing the guest room at some distance, straight ahead, but more stairs leading up above the ones we had just climbed. I pointed that way and was again rewarded with the sight of his rippling back and heavy muscular buttocks shifting and clenching with every step. He tossed his bag on the bedroom floor and peeled back the covers on the sleigh bed. "Which side do you want me on?" he asked. I gestured for him to take the farther side, where Joe and Jimmy had slept.

"…Unless…" It had just occurred to me that he might want to shower or brush his teeth, and I gestured vaguely towards the bathroom.

"No, thanks," he said; "I took care of all that at my last friend's hotel room. I'm good to go. Just very tired."

"Then I'll be back in just a few," I said, as he slipped under the top sheet and flicked it down so that his silken torso was fully in view.

It took me only a minute or two to rinse my mouth, wash my face, and splash on some Acqua di Parma; then quickly, and as silently as I could, I checked the lights in the back of the house. I had an absurd fear that if I took too long I might find that Andy had dematerialized in my absence. But as I flicked off the lamp by my bed and climbed in next to him, in a room now lit only by the outside streetlamps filtered through the slats of the shutters and the bare branches of the trees outside, he came quickly to my arms, in a mass of strength and entreaty. He laid his head on my shoulder confidingly, and then turned his face up to be kissed, as though we were lovers too long parted. After a moment, he murmured,

"Did you leave the tip somewhere?"

"Yes," I whispered back; "it's in my top desk drawer. If I forget in the morning, remind me."

"No," he said kindly, "I trust you."

Within twenty minutes he had accepted from me everything which he had earlier professed to find almost impossible, and wasted in my hand what must have been at least his eighth orgasm of the day. Five minutes after we had returned to bed from a quick smiling wash in the adjoining bath, he was sleeping soundly next to me, face down, one leg thrown over mine, and my arm where he had firmly put it, around his supple steely waist.

I felt very grateful to him, dazzled by his beauty, thrilled with the élite consumerist indulgence to which I had just treated myself. I was astonished at the erotic performance Andy had somehow raised me to, and awash in a kind of self-congratulatory auto-voyeurism.

I also felt old, dry, and alone.

The next morning Andy came up behind me as I was making coffee in the kitchen. He wrapped his smooth arms around me and nuzzled my neck. I had just been clearing my throat to tell him that I probably shouldn't see him again. I barely recognized the man – me – who had awakened with a flesh-and-blood love god in his arms. The instant fondness in the eyes that had opened to meet mine, though flattering, didn't assuage my sense of squalid calculation on both our parts. But –

"I have an idea," he said. "I'll probably be coming to Baltimore a few times a year now. All the gentlemen I saw yesterday liked me quite a lot." I wondered if he was including Gene in his mental tally. "I was thinking I could stay here like I did last night, but on the house." I could hear the asymmetrical smile in his voice now. "And you *know* that's not easy for me!" My mind went back irresistibly to the perfect tight squeezing caress he had mustered during our lazy slow ride at bedtime.

"But…" I stammered, completely derailed from the little farewell speech I had prepared, "I mean, you know I like you and it goes without saying that you're way beyond hot and gorgeous, but… are you suggesting something like a relationship?"

In about three seconds I had decided that I could be completely unashamed of a porn star boyfriend. I sincerely didn't judge his work, and I knew from personal experience that he could bestow real gifts on the men, of whom I couldn't possibly be the most fragile or neurotic, with whom he worked. Even with Joe himself, in our earliest days, I had noticed that his vastly greater sexual experience didn't make me think less of him, though it made me nervous of comparisons with his prior tricks and boyfriends. If Andy were proposing some kind of union, I could imagine myself explaining it to J.J. in something like those terms. I had told Andy just the bare minimum about Joe's death, and about Jimmy Jack's presence in my home and life, because he had naturally asked if I lived alone in such a large house. Now I finished with,

"I guess at some level I feel like I'd need to figure out what to say about you to my little godson." Andy smiled. I'd shown him a picture or two of Jimmy, and he knew he wasn't little. "He's just come out and he's very romantic, and for some reason he idolizes me."

I heard him think a second before he replied.

"I told you I'm not gay, right? I have a relationship with my girlfriend." I nodded, and he suddenly grinned and shook his head as though my last words had just sunk in. "And by the *way*, of course he idolizes you… But really, I'm not kidding. I think you're a very nice man, and it would save me a few bucks to stay with you instead of getting a room when I come to Baltimore. The sex you like to have with me…I could get used to it for a friend like you, and still do my job with my other friends. Let's face it, I'm not a virgin. We wouldn't be married, and I wouldn't always be 'there' for you or vice versa, but you'd know there were a couple things I saved just for you." This was all logical enough. Then his voice became almost sentimental. "The best part for me last night was sleeping with you. I felt safe." It was hard for me to believe that a muscle man like him ever felt anything *but* safe. "Do you know what it's like for a man like me to let another man inside me? To do that I have to feel like you're bigger and stronger and smarter in some way, like I can be weak and still be OK. When it's over I want to feel like I can let you hold me and do all my thinking for me till morning."

This was way more than I had planned on hearing him say. I found it fascinating as a slice of erotic psychology. I respected his candor and self-awareness. Now, finally, I turned to face him. His expression was sweet and artless.

"You say that to all the guys," I said. He laughed.

"No."

"But don't you have lots of friends who put you up when you visit other cities? Is this how it works with them?"

"*Hell* no," he said. "In other cities, I stay in hotels, or with other straight friends in porn. Remember, client-friends always want me to be a top man. When I'm done with that, I just want a guy to let me alone. If I slept with them, they'd all be pestering my cock all night, and if I let them get me off, I might be too tired for my appointments the next day." With despicable vanity, I recalled that he had come in my hand the night before, not at my suggestion or insistence. Perhaps he had no appointments till the next day and hadn't needed to bank his climaxes. What he was implying about his own sexuality and what he was offering me appealed very deeply to my basest egotism. He shrugged the terrycloth robe off and stood naked in front of me. The movement of his shoulders was meek and imploring as it released the robe and bared him to me. He stepped free of the worn cloth and came into my arms, a straight magnificence of slick skin, muscle, and submission. He was a perfect match for my least sentimental libido. My hands strayed by instinct down to his monumental rump, now on private, exclusive offer to me. He relaxed. He could tell I was yielding.

"So this would be all for me?" I asked, while nibbling his lips.

"On the house," he said. "To be honest, you're the only client who's ever asked me for sex that way, so that part is easy to promise."

"Let's keep in touch about it, then," I said. "If you're lucky, I won't remarry before you come back to Baltimore."

"Oh," he said admiringly, "you've got a little *at*-titude. I *like* that!" He broke from our hug and slipped one arm very firmly around my neck. It was not at all clear that I could have broken away from him if I'd wanted to, but he quickly released me so that I could go back to making breakfast.

An hour later, as he was calling his Lyft, he let me look over his shoulder at his phone to see what picture he used for his profile. I also saw at a glance that his real name was Ondřej Dubček. He saw that I'd seen.

"I never share my real name with anyone," he said, pocketing his phone. "See? I trust you. That's *two* things that no one else gets." We stepped outside to wait for the car.

I always assumed that anything taking place on my front steps might be noticed by any number of neighbors. When his car pulled up, he turned and gave me a great manly bear hug, and kissed me on both cheeks. "I'll call you when I'm coming back. Hope it works out."

"So do I," I said. I reached around and patted the seat of his tight pants. Suddenly I felt very powerful, and very fond of him. Joe was farther from my thoughts than he had been in months. "Safe travels, my friend."

Classes at my university were back in full swing by the time Charles Ribera came to stay for two nights. Kevin slept under my roof both those nights. It had been years since I'd seen Charles. He had had no reason to see photographs of me since we'd last met, whereas I had been able to track the decades on his face in publicity shots on CDs and in magazines. He said something generic about my looking great, which made me think he was in fact smugly cataloguing my vanished hair and softening waist. He had changed surprisingly little except that his hair was almost completely white. He also seemed shorter and more compact. He wasn't stout at all, and was probably no shorter than before, but there was a sense of heavy gravity around him, as though he were a streamlined statue of very highly polished granite. He moved with self-conscious stateliness and made constant references to his advanced age. The Boys frisked around him, taking his bag, hanging his coat. In a free moment when we were standing alone together in the front hall as they hustled his things upstairs, he said to me,

"Again, I am very sorry about Joe. I got the sense you had something real."

"Your note," I said seriously, "was lovely. Thank you. Joe was irreplaceable." I didn't want to speak sentimentally of Joe in Charles' presence; I remembered how dangerous Charles had briefly been to us. I wondered if Charles was single. "Come in and let me fix you a cocktail. Or would you rather go to your room first?"

J.J. was back with us by now, and said,

"Your bag is already up there, and the blue towels in the guest bath are for you."

"My, he's well trained!" said Charles. "And it's so *hard* to get good help these days." He knew from my e-mail invitation who Jimmy was, and I found this jibe a bit uncalled-for. Jimmy himself seemed not at all offended.

"I want to play for you after dinner," he said. "Would you sing us something?" Famous classical singers had never been a big thing in his life, though Lyric had taught him some of the wispiest repertoire. He thought Joni Mitchell was one of the greatest vocalists of all time. Kevin and he had done some studying up on Charles on YouTube. By now they were declared fans of his. Charles looked slightly hassled by this request, but said,

"If you could run through a couple of the Caplet with me that would be great." His gig the following night in Washington was to be a program of French Romantic and Impressionist *chansons*, a welcome break for him, he said, and a chance to show the warmer timbre of his mature voice. These songs, I thought, also contained no top notes to speak of, no rapid passage work, and no trills. Perhaps his warmer timbre was in fact a kind of vocal twilight. I would miss the concert because of a campus donors' dinner, but Walter and Ricardo had gotten tickets the minute it was announced and would give me an honest account.

After dinner that night, Jimmy did play two Caplet songs for Charles. Their stark harmonies appealed to Jimmy, and he played through them with a kind of excited discovery which exactly supported Charles' ardent voicing of the disjunct melodies. Charles took a moment or two to confirm some tricky pitches and rhythms, pretending to be embarrassed to ask his very distinguished collaborative pianist, with whom he was to rehearse the next day in DC, to repeat them for him. Then Jimmy asked if he knew Mozart's *Abendempfindung*. Charles made a rueful face and said,

"My dear, didn't you know Wolfgang *wrote* it for me?" Then, after a very sweet *mezza voce* run-through of perhaps my favorite song ever written, J.J. segued into some rolled chords, thunk-thunk, oddly open and evocative. Charles, visibly drawn to him, without being asked or given any further clue, stepped closer to the keyboard and suddenly sang,

"Come again! Sweet love doth now invite thy graces…"

Kevin and I sat, abandoned and forgotten, while those two gavotted their way through a heart-clutching few minutes of pure art. My old piano, unsuited to orchestral effects, seemed to blossom into its best self in evoking the lutes and dulcimers and virginals of the 16th century. Ladies in farthingales, gentlemen in lace ruffs and padded sleeves, rustled quietly into the room to listen while Charles' thick Latino voice wove its way around these plain, sumptuous songs.

It had been many years since I'd been in the room while Charles sang. His voice was completely his own, beautifully maintained over decades, the core tone instantly recognizable and still lustrous and powerful. There was no virtuosity needed for the Dowland songs, but his even registers and graceful lilting ornaments were perfect. Jimmy looked up over his shoulder as they ended, and said,

"G.J. makes 'Come again' sound sadder." I blushed, and Charles, once it occurred to him who G.J. was, looked angry. When Charles and I first knew each other, I was much more actively involved in classical vocal music circles in Baltimore and Washington, and we had shared some almost collegial conversations about schleifers and *appoggiature*. Those days were long gone. J.J. was alluding to a modest local life in which I still sang in church, for friends, for myself, or with J.J. at home of an evening.

"No," I said, "I think you're remembering 'Time stands still.'"

"'Come again,'" Jimmy insisted. "When you sing these rising fourths…" (he sketched them on the piano) "you make it sound as though the singer knew he would fail. Charles sings them as though he were already sure of getting laid." Charles, who had been hovering nearer the keyboard than necessary, gave a relenting smile at this.

"That's the energy of the rising figure," he said.

"G.J. fights the obvious," J.J. replied. "I'm not saying one is right." He started rolling chords of his own on the piano, and Kevin stirred in his seat.

"You're going to hear Boy Genius improvise," he said with a wink to Charles, who seemed almost to notice him for the first time. Kevin got up and stood to the right of Jimmy, forcing Charles to step slightly aside. Still standing, he added his own treble melodies to whatever Jimmy was outlining below. Their communication was wordless and respectful. As they gradually developed ideal universes of their own abstract aesthetic, Charles started to vocalize, jamming, humming, scatting, occasionally accessing a very high, throaty tone, with never the risk of cracking, but edgy and almost ugly. It came from some part of his musical soul not linked to his profession. There was a tendency to choose modal solutions, something Sephardic, Mozarabic, Aztec, Punic in his imagination. It was like being drunk in Sevilla at 3 am while Flamenco artists limned rhythms and tonalities so odd that you seemed to remember having heard them from your grandmother at bedtime in a forgotten life, on a two-mooned desert planet, inside a volcano.

Suddenly Charles stopped short, in mid-note. The ragged silence that fell over the keyboard, as Jimmy and Kevin realized that Charles had cut off his growling vocalizations, left the room panting. Charles looked tired, frightened, and embarrassed.

"I can't do that the day before a classical program," he said, apologetic and proud. "It's a different voice in my throat." I understood perfectly. My own throat was sore from listening. The Boys were more disappointed.

"You are amazing," said Kevin, simply, reverently. Charles didn't know him well enough to be as flattered as he should have been.

"That was... out of body," said J.J.

"But it shouldn't be coming out of *my* body," said Charles, in a sour tone I recalled from the past. "*My* body needs to sound even and smooth and *élégant* tomorrow evening. You boys are bad for my vocal health." Within a few minutes we had started our migrations upstairs.

Charles and I had breakfast together the next morning, before Jimmy and Kevin came down. I had heard him vocalizing quietly in the guest room, and I went to the kitchen quickly, intentionally banging and clinking as I started the coffee and toast so that he would know I was up. He was unexpectedly cheerful; I would have predicted some sulkiness. While I was rummaging in the refrigerator, he hummed something virtuosic, a quick flourish of tight coloratura. After a second I recognized one of the tenor arias from *La Cenerentola*.

"Oh," I asked, "are you doing Rossini now?"

"I think the window has closed on that," he said. "I'm a bit long in the tooth for those roles, and I'm too good for character parts. When I was young enough for Ramiro, my posse thought the orchestration was too heavy for me. And I was busy with the French Baroque anyway."

"Well, I don't know," I said. "You look wonderful; nothing a black wig couldn't take care of. You'd be a dream Almaviva in some ways."

"'*Some* ways'?" He gave a little scowl while doctoring his coffee. I smiled.

"I don't think of you as broadly comedic, that's all," I parried. "You'd nail the lyric yearning stuff… the passages that sound like updated Mozart." He wagged his head, slightly irritated with discussion of any limits to his artistry. "Are you a Juan Diego person?" I asked, hoping to change the subject.

"Oh please," he said; "don't tell me you've been drinking *that* Kool-Aid!" I was surprised, much as I'd been once when I learned that a friend didn't like peaches, in fact found them slimy and squishy. I remembered stammering to that friend that I thought literally *everyone* liked peaches.

"Oh dear," I said. "I love everything about him."

"His slick commercialism? The way his voice is exactly the same in everything he sings? The way he makes Mozart sound like Richard Rogers? And the whole media narrative of the humble handsome *straight* opera star graciously helping the slum kids of Lima learn to play the viola?" Though it hadn't occurred to me that Charles would dislike Flórez, this little burst of pent-up invective wasn't at all out of character for him. I wondered if Charles' sexuality had ever been an obstacle to his career. His professional circles, mostly practitioners of less-performed repertoire, certainly included many gay headliners… conductors, countertenors, rebec *virtuosi*… and a fan-base of overwrought gay purists who also collected Mucha posters and wore paisley shirts and scarves well into their seventies and eighties.

Flórez instead moved within the enormous publicity machines of major opera houses and recording companies around the world, and perhaps his personal life made him an easier sell, and a better fit for repertoire that the larger public was already pretty sure it liked. I realized, guiltily, that I preferred Juan Diego as a singer in almost every way.

"Well, there is always something a bit facile about any mega-star, I suppose," I conceded. "However, for the record, I'm a huge fan of his. His 'Una furtiva lagrima' at the Met a couple of years ago was purely spellbinding. Not just the impeccable legato and piercingly perfect intonation; also the goofy butch little personhood of Nemorino that he created out of nothings. He pulled one hand out of a pocket to rub his nose during one big phrase, and I thought it was a moment of spontaneous genius in physical characterization; then I saw a video of him doing it in Berlin back in 2007 or so, and he did the exact same nose-rub, and it still worked. Like Pasta's ornaments in 'Casta diva.' Once you've got a perfect product, keep producing it." Charles looked bored.

"Is this the only jam you have?" he asked, looking darkly at the jar of apricot preserve. "I think apricots are grossly slippery."

"This artisanal raspberry is almost nothing but pips and grit," I said, pulling it off the door of the fridge and sliding it across to him. The woody, barely sweet concoction had been a gift from a foodie friend, and was both demonstrably all-natural and not very good: what my mother would have called "earnest." "You'll love it." As he unscrewed the lid, something occurred to me. "For what it's worth, young Jimmy doesn't like Juan Diego much either. The first time he heard me playing one of his CDs, he scrunched up his nose and said, 'That voice is *huge*.' As though, 1) it *were* huge, and, 2) volume were by definition a bad thing. I think he finds all that forward focus a bit violent." The mention of J.J. lit a visible spark in Charles' eye.

"Speaking of your extremely handsome young relative," he said (he had latched on to the idea that J.J. was my nephew), "I want to say it's perfectly clear that you're in love with him. No one on earth would blame you for that." He leaned slightly forward, closed his eyes, pursed his lips, and gently shook his head. It was an original nuzzling little gesture, showing the tenderness he saw in my feelings and also his own appreciation for Jimmy's good looks.

"To be perfectly honest," I said, slightly chilled and resentful at Charles' claim to know me so well, "I'm more in love with his lover-ette Kevin. Jimmy Jack is my little boy. The whole incest taboo kicks in pretty heavily there." Charles shook his head impatiently.

"Self-knowledge," he said, implying that I had none. I was flustered for a moment.

"Charles," I said, "it's obvious that I'm in deep mourning, is it not? I am not contemplating the debauch of someone who was circumcised virtually in my arms." He did not look at all chastened, but some cloud crossed his face.

"You were happy with Joe all these years, then? You were faithful to each other?"

"Yes," I said, simplifying intentionally. "I mean, 'happy'... that seems to imply that everything was easy, which was not the case. But yes, we were a very stable couple. We were lovers up to the day he died." A wave of desolation washed over me. I knew simply to duck and hold my breath. Within a second or two, it passed. I gave a wan smile.

"And how about yourself? Have you been bedding your groupies? I'm sure you are besieged with lewd offers."

"'To be *perfectly* honest,' as you would say," he said, a little bit more mean than teasing, "yes, I have, and yes I am. It gets old. Always the oddest, most intense men. Lots and lots of young men, too, as I've gotten older, hot about politics and music history and LGBTQ+ stuff; acronyms I can't keep up with... not actually that erotic a pool for me. But never celibacy, thank Whomever."

"I would have pictured you settled with someone years ago. You were so in love with... who was your bf who did porn for a while?... Tory. I never thought he deserved for you to be so attached to him, but at least it was clear to me that you wanted to love someone, a lot."

"Yeah, Tory did kind of a number on me. I haven't made quite that mistake again." By "mistake," he seemed to mean the dream of romantic love. "We're still friends, of sorts. He's a pudgy teddy bear of a man now. Twenty years ago or so, he signed on with a steady, homely guy who still thinks of him as a hot young trick, and Tory still acts like one – demanding, jealous, bossy..." He looked thoughtful. "In a lot of ways, I'm glad we didn't end up together. I wouldn't have continued to find him interesting.

He's not interesting at all, really, now; just kind of sweet and conventional and stupid."

"I have hooked up a couple of times recently with a porn star," I said. "I've thought of you and Tory in that context. I was a bit shocked at Tory's work back then, but somehow it bothers me not at all about this guy now." He looked dishy and fascinated.

"Who?" he asked. I told him, and he whistled. "But I always pictured you as a top," he said, after quickly consulting what was evidently a precise mental file on Andy Ferrara. It had become clear to me when we first knew each other that Charles and I, too, would have faced issues of sexual compatibility.

"For some reason, following the mysterious logic of the hotly desirable, he has conceded that point to me, and he has proposed waiving all fees in future if he can sleep here when he's in town on business." That sounded a little like bragging; in fact, it *was* bragging.

"I remember that sleeping with Tory felt like getting a freebie," he said, looking rather far away. "Knowing that men all over the country were beating off looking at his videos made me feel kind of like a very lucky bargain hunter." He mused briefly. "But of course, he didn't hustle; he just did porn and had this very clingy weird infatuation with me. Well, I mean, until he suddenly didn't anymore."

"Candor requires that I tell you I met Andy on a professional basis. His first sleep-over here was very sharply discounted, which I now gather was his way of auditioning me for this new arrangement. For some reason he says he feels 'safe' with me."

"Of course he does," Charles said. "You may have a fantasy of being wicked, but a child could tell from across the room that you're a romantic. Let alone a man-whore looking for cheap lodgings." Something reminded him to be courteous; after all, he too was saving a few dollars by staying with me. "And maybe, 'to be honest,' he secretly likes to get fucked, and figured out this way to get that occasionally taken care of without having to do it completely for free. That's important more for his psychology than for yours; it lets him keep thinking that he only does it as a trade-off for a room. For all we know, he has similar arrangements all over the country." Andy, of course, had denied this, but it didn't seem worth getting into that level of detail with Charles.

"So let's call it a win-win, then. In a way, it's a dream fulfilled," I said. "Obviously he's extremely attractive, and as an erotic scenario it is almost embarrassingly perfect. But it's not love; it's not Joe, for instance. Maybe it's a little like your stalker fans. Hotness, but no future." Charles made a leap.

"It's good that you and I never got involved."

"I didn't realize you knew that was even under consideration," I said.

"Oh, I could tell what you were thinking," he answered. "You are probably not aware of how transparent you are."

"Well, you're right that there was tension between me and Joe for a while because of my celebrity crush on you. That's why I tapered off on contacting you. I realized I'd hurt Joe's feelings for something I never meant actually to pursue physically." There was a silence; he had nothing to say, and I gathered it had never been very important to him. "Still, I want you to know that I have never stopped admiring your work and have always remembered you very fondly." He glanced up, looking cautious and not especially friendly.

"Nice speech," he said. For a moment, at this dry little riposte of his, I felt a petty, superior dislike for him. 'No wonder he hasn't met anyone after all,' I thought; 'in some ways, he's really not that nice.' Then I was ashamed, thinking that he had lived a solitude which I had greatly feared and barely escaped. "I'm glad you had a Joe," he said after a moment. "I had a porn star: amazing sex for a year, what I thought was deep passion, and then a slow realization that he wasn't such a huge deal after all. And I've had affairs. It's all fine. I don't actually like people that much, anyway."

Looking at the clock, I realized it was almost time for him to start gathering his things to go to Washington. We both heard the Boys starting to stir upstairs… drowsy voices, running water, their bedroom door swinging shut. Charles glanced at me just as we heard them start down the stairs from the third floor.

"Self-knowledge," he said, waving his spoon at me.

I was in my car by myself one evening, listening to a classical music show on the radio. Joe was at home, just back from several days in LA having his picture taken to sell… what? Probably beer. Yes: it was that campaign on the beach: there were shots of Joe and an athletic young woman whose yellow hair flicked perfectly over her shoulder every time she laughed, both of them in skimpy bathing suits, flopped face down in the sand, squealing and giggling and kicking their bare feet in the air. Apparently out there in the American heartland there were heterosexuals who would look at those pictures and decide they were thirsty and should go buy beer, whereas to me the obvious reaction for anyone with a pulse would be simply to want to hop on top of Joe and never let go.

Tonight the station was playing excerpts from a new recording of *Judas Maccabaeus*. I tuned in just after the start of "Sound an Alarm," so I didn't hear the tenor's name. I was pretty sure I'd never heard this voice. There was definitely a voice there, not exactly beautiful, but thrilling. It was dark and penetrating, with a frontal resonance as if the tenor's upper sinuses were made of steel. There was no float, no faking, in his upper notes. He smacked them head-on, as though he'd used a pole to vault flat-footed onto a platform ten or twelve feet above the ground. From his middle voice you wouldn't have thought that he could go much higher, but then, with the force of a rising geyser, he ascended with a perfect match of tone to what I guessed was an A or a B-flat. He ornamented extravagantly: a lot of quick passage-work, a strange, personal, very fast trill in which the two pitches alternated with the precision of a Gatling gun, and the last exposed "Sound" with a hard *sforzando,* then taken back to nothing before swelling in a long measured crescendo that broke into a quick cascade of coloratura. His embellishments imitated the trumpet's turns inventively, they showed an amazing accuracy in bravura, and they fit the martial text. The song made me want to go sign up for an army to free some fatherland or throw off some yoke of oppression. No one else on the recording, though, seemed to be awake. The full orchestra, when it came in on the rousing fanfare at the end of the aria, sounded scratchy and dispirited. The chorus entered, brow-beaten, on "We hear, we hear," supposedly answering the tenor's call to battle. I could practically hear the swaying of the sleeves on their Indian-bedspread blouses. The poor overworked tenor had tried to set up a battle-cry, but they'd pretty much dropped the ball.

The announcer came on at the end of the chorus and named the performers. The tenor was Charles Ribera. I'd been seeing his pictures in the record store for some time. He was rather good-looking and I liked his grave smooth face. He was getting a big push from the publicists, for the expanding market of consumers who wanted to hear grown women sing like eight-year-old boys, under the baton of conductors who wore dreary hippy shirts and called the orchestra the "band." Now that I'd heard him sing, I was tempted to buy the full recording of *Judas Maccabaeus* for Ribera's sake, but I was afraid the soprano would sing "So shall the Lute and Harp awake" through her nose, and that she'd be wearing a denim blouse in her photograph. My curiosity overcame me, however. My favorite record store at the Rotunda was only a few blocks away, so I detoured on my way home.

"Oh, I know him," Joe said that evening at home. I had the refrigerator door open and turned around to see him looking at the cover picture of Charles Ribera on the CD I'd just bought. I hadn't been able to bring myself to buy the *Maccabaeus*, but I'd seen an ad in the record store window for this new solo release of Ribera's: a full recital, with harpsichord and lute and chamber orchestra as needed, of songs and arias of Dowland, Handel, and Mozart.

"No you don't," I said.

"Don't tell me I don't know him," he said. Joe always got a bit hot if he thought I was implying he had no class, but, Connie and her cherished Tebaldi recordings notwithstanding, Joe was slow to become an opera maven. He was polite about my involvement in the classical music scene in town and always came to hear me when I did solos in church or with the professional concert choir I sang with in those years. He sat next to me at the symphony and opera and hadn't once fallen asleep, but it would have been a major stretch to suggest that he'd taken to it all like a duck to water. I couldn't imagine he even knew who Charles Ribera was.

I had also been afraid that Joe might notice that I had a mild crush on Ribera's picture. Now it turned out that Joe already knew the guy. It reminded me of the time Joe tried to slip into New York for a day to see friends of ours without calling his folks: he ran into their next-door neighbor as she came out of Bendel's, and got a very peppery call from Connie that night when he got back home to Baltimore. There was basically no point in trying to keep things from an Andreoli.

"OK," I said to Joe. "You know Charles Ribera." He nodded as if he'd won a point in court. He was apparently not going to say anything else, so I gave him the satisfaction of asking him: "So how do you know Charles Ribera?"

"He used to go out with somebody I knew in LA," he said. "I think they broke up, but I'm not sure."

"Who?" I asked. At one time, Joe had known virtually every worthless bar-boy and starlet in LA. But I imagined Charles Ribera, if he was gay at all, being partnered with some grey-flannel assimilationist lawyer with glasses and a bluff manly affect – a gay activist as well, why not? who militated for gay marriage and said we were 'just like everyone else.' To my knowledge, Joe didn't know anyone like that.

"His name is Tory," he said. "You haven't met him. We were roommates for a while. We're not really all that tight."

"What kind of guy is he?" I asked. Whoever he was, I imagined that Ribera was wasted on him.

"I doubt you'd like him much. He was a... flight attendant." I made a disgusted face.

"Charles Ribera dated an air mattress?" This was one of Joe's terms for flight attendants; or "peanut whore"; or "sky slut." He gave me a funny look, the way Italians looked at me when, after all my correct subjunctives, I tossed in a word in their local dialect.

"Well," he said, "he works for USAir." This apparently proved he was really terribly respectable. "He tricked with Dennis once. We all hung some." The fact that he'd tricked with Joe's pal Dennis put this Tory in a largish class. "I mean, he's an OK guy. You'd just probably call him a bimbo." There was a pause. Joe had left something unsaid.

"So?" I asked.

"Well..." He reached into the liquor cabinet and gestured at me with the bottle of Gilbey's: Did I want a martini? I nodded, and he turned his back to me as he collected the vermouth, the shaker, the ice, and the dried mint, three or four flakes of which were his martini secret. "Dennis introduced him to some guys who cast porno. He's done a bunch of videos with Catalina now. I think he may have given up the airline."

"So he's really made something of himself," I said. "It's a real Horatio Alger story. This is a great fucking country." Joe glowered at me and I knew that politically I was completely out of line. So "Are they still together?" I asked. "Oh, you just said you don't know."

"I'll ask Dennis when I talk to him."

"You might have told me you knew Charles Ribera, you know," I said.

"How did I know you would even have heard of Charles?" Joe answered. Suddenly *I* was the one who couldn't be expected to know famous people. "He wasn't a big deal then, anyway, at least not professionally. I knew he wanted to be a star. He got some gigs, but he never seemed real psyched about them. He'd complain about the soprano or the fee or the conductor, or about having to sing in the stix... Once he said, 'Mozart in Davenport: why?'"

"Did you ever hear him?" I asked.

"Around the apartment when he was visiting Tory, yes; I never heard him perform. He sings all the time. Worse than you: he... does the dishes and he sings. 'La-la "Hey-pass-me-that-pan" la-la.'"

Charles Ribera had sung at Joe's sink, in Joe's shower, on Joe's patio. I knew Joe had met Gloria Swanson once and attended the wrap-party for one of the "Terminator" movies, but this was better.

"So what did you think?" I asked.

"Oh... he's got an OK voice, I guess."

"The man is by way of being a god of bel canto," I said.

"Whatever."

"I have to call Walter," I said. "I wonder if he's heard him yet."

"Charles and Ricardo can talk Spanish together," Joe offered.

"Charles is..." It gave me a minor but detectable thrill to call Ribera by his first name. "He's really Latino?"

"Yeah. I think he's – what do you say? English-dominant. But he's from there: East LA, I think. He's super-Hispanic."

I was curious, but I hesitated to ask Joe too much about Ribera. Being a fan always made me feel flushed and foolish, even sometimes with Joe himself, though that, at least, usually led to some kind of erotic pay-off. I looked at the cover picture on the CD Joe was holding. Ribera looked tight-coiled and nervous, sleek as a blockade-running schooner. His straight black hair was plastered rigorously back but was so thick that it stood out in a low virile pompadour. His mouth, sharply outlined in his olive face, barely tried a wary smile. His eyes were large, black, and candid. He must have been in his thirties, but the expression of his eyes had the shy guarded hopefulness of an orphan's when a kind old lady visits the home.

"What's he like?" I asked.

"Dark," Joe said after thinking a moment. "Cynical. He's kind of a drag, really. Nothing makes him happy."

"Not Tory?"

"Well, he was really into Tory, that's true. He's a glommer." Joe suspected anyone who was in love of wanting to 'glom on.' He was a Leo, and his philosophy of love included an element of freedom, a paradox because he also was extremely proud of his own capacity for commitment.

"Goddammit," I said, smacking the counter hard enough that my martini threatened to spill.

"What?" Joe asked, looking amused, as he usually did at my crankiness.

"I don't know. I just think the Torys of this world should stick to what they do best: oiling their delts and giving attitude, and dating lifeguards and bar-backs. They shouldn't get all the great guys too."

"That's probably exactly what Randy is saying this very second," Joe said. I laughed. For some reason, since I'd settled down with Joe, I had on several occasions had to fend off offers from the kinds of men who had never noticed me when I was single. Randy was a graduate student in comp lit at Hopkins, terribly smart and intense and hot as only a post-modern boy with sideburns and a chain tattoo could be. He'd met Joe and me at a party and become briefly infatuated with... me. Normally it was Joe, with his green eyes and curls and pecs, who caused the ravages among the general public, so Randy's *schwärm* had touched me in spite of myself. There had been a scene at one point: he'd demanded to know what Joe and I had in common, and whether Joe understood me or not.

Joe didn't know that there had also been an evening the winter before, while he was on the West Coast, when Randy had come by for dinner. I had fooled myself into thinking that we could simply discuss his dissertation prospectus, drink Chianti, listen to cello music, sit inches apart on the sofa in front of the fire, and behave as cordial colleagues. When Randy had thrown himself at me, I had been unable to resist reaching down his baggy jeans during his startling, insistent kiss. There were several tense moments when I would have been perfectly happy to have him right there on the coffee table. The only thing that stopped me was… no, not marital fidelity or virtue, but a quick imagined conversation with Joe. I was sure that he would have laughed good-naturedly at the story and asked me, 'So, was he good?' My only answer would have had to be, 'Yes… probably a lot better than I was.'

"Now look, Tiger." Joe came across the kitchen to me and put his arms around my waist. This was a familiar routine of his: mollifying his curmudgeonly older lover with strategic praise and flirtation. "We both know that if Charles had met you first, he never would have even looked at Tory. So relax. But then if Charles came on to you, I would have shot him, and now I'd be in jail." I laughed. It annoyed me that I had never developed even the slightest defense against this kind of patent manipulation.

Sex by then had changed for us. When we started out together it seemed simpler. The first night he slept with me in my house in Baltimore after our whirlwind ten days in Rehoboth, I told him he was a gift from God. It wouldn't have occurred to me, in that state of infatuation, to ask him to brush his teeth before kissing me. In those days, neither of us ever said 'Wait a sec' or 'You're crushing my arm,' much less 'Not tonight, honey.'

As the years went by, it seemed harder to schedule our little passionate interludes, and when one of us was up for it the other was as likely as not to be thinking of work or bills or feeding the dog. My sudden flashes of hot passion for Joe usually came when he was far away and I came across his picture in a magazine while sitting in the dentist's office. 'Oh look, everybody,' I always imagined saying, 'this incredibly humpy number is my lover. If he were here right now, I could have sex with him, and you couldn't!' There might even be some of that excitement still stored up when I picked him up at the airport a few days later, but then he would get off the plane tired and distracted, and tell me funny stories about the job on the way home, and put his bag down, wash up, and crash.

The pattern of our life together had been set by his placid, catlike enjoyment of our domesticity. He got a psychological reward from the respectability of living with and being faithful to a nice steady college professor, just in case there was still someone around who thought he was a twit and a bimbo. He loved saying, "It's not just sex between us," and

155

proving it by lying chastely in my arms. I accused him at times of believing that there would be a prize given in Heaven for every night we didn't have sex. Scenarios of hotness often seemed to offend Joe, as if I were throwing his old life up in his face. I had to flavor every approach with gestures of respect and tenderness.

"You want to put on your buddy Charles' CD?" Joe asked me. "Before we go upstairs, I mean." 'Going upstairs' was our code phrase for making out. It made him feel sophisticated to know what classical music conduced to cuddling. Poor Scarlatti and Vaughan Williams and Dvorák had gotten pressed into service pretty regularly; there had been tense moments at the Symphony when the first bars of "The Lark Ascending" made us both smile and blush and squirm.

"No," I said immediately. It embarrassed me to think of making love with Joe while Ribera sang in the background. I knew it would throw me off; it would have been as distracting as having my suitor Randy break into the room naked. There was a relatively innocent explanation for my answer, which I hoped he would fall for.

"You know how I get with singers," I said. I could barely even carry on a conversation if there was singing within earshot. Joe still laughed about a time Linda Ronstadt came on the radio just as we were getting down to it, singing "Long long time," and I glazed over, mooning over memories of my deep crush on my Italian professor in college many years before: someone I'd barely thought of since 1979. He'd finally had to get up and turn the radio off, and even so we weren't able to recapture the mood. Another time I got so wrapped up in Arlene Augér's scales and turns in *"Ach, ich liebe"* that I more or less forgot Joe was there, not something he went for as a rule.

"Right," he said, looking at me cannily. His arms were still around me and now he shook me fairly hard and smiled. "I think it's pretty lousy the way you're falling in love with Charles Ribera on me," he said. "You can't fool me, you know."

"Damn," I said. I defended myself with a frank challenge: "How's *your* high C today? You could try to banish him from my mind."

"'Try'?" he said. He leaned forward, closed his eyes, and licked my chin.

"Come on," I said. "Upstairs. The time is now."

The next day I waited till Joe was out of the house for a couple of hours and played Ribera's CD several times in a row. He didn't sound like anyone else. A few notes and you could recognize his voice. I was proud of having passed the needle-drop test at a party recently hosted by one of Baltimore's most advanced opera queens; he played one randomly chosen second of a tenor singing an "ah" vowel, and I instantly said, "Björling." When the other guests asked how I could tell, I said, "The same way you know it's your mother on the phone when you hear her say 'Hi.'" The acoustic of Ribera's voice was like that, as recognizable as handwriting. He fairly crooned in the Dowland songs, his voice hollowed out to match the deep *thoonk* of the lute, with mournfulness thrown over his tone like a veil. Though his singing on this CD was less brilliant and risk-taking than what I thought I'd heard in the car, nevertheless it was extremely accomplished. The few displays of bravura were as punctilious as the compulsory figures in Olympic skating, as metric as the dicing of celery in a French kitchen. After the third play-through I went upstairs, turned on the computer, and wrote,

"Dear Mr. Ribera,

Just a note from a new fan. I bought your recital album yesterday and am enjoying it very much. You meet my one great test of singers: what I call the 'simple song' test. Anybody can learn to sing flashily, but to make a very plain melody sound truly beautiful, as you do in 'Come again' for instance, is the mark of a real artist – like Victoria de los Angeles singing *'Ebben? Ne andrò lontana.'*

I am a professor of Italian at the state university here in Baltimore, and I coach the singers in Italian repertoire at the local conservatory. My language and literature work makes me all the more appreciative of the attention you pay to text in your interpretations.

Enough adulation. I really look forward to hearing more of you. If you are performing in the area any time soon, I would be delighted to come hear you in person. Perhaps you would let a new admirer buy you a glass of champagne.

Sincerely, etc.

P.S. My lover, Joe Andreoli, knew you slightly in Los Angeles, through mutual friends. He is not sure you would remember him. JCMcM"

The postscript was a nod to my conscience. I didn't expect an answer from Ribera and would probably never have to tell Joe I had written him, but I felt that by mentioning him I was at least keeping faith. I also knew that in my mind, I was flirting, rather seriously, with someone completely unlike Joe who attracted me in completely different ways from him. I addressed the letter to Ribera, care of the recording company, and took Ootch on a short walk to the mail box at the corner. It would be easier on my nerves if the letter were out of my hands, out of the house, before Joe got home.

Walter called that night. He was all excited because he'd just bought the *Judas Maccabaeus* CD and wondered if I'd heard of Charles Ribera. I said I had, and dazzled him with the story of how Joe knew him and his feckless ex-. "How's the rest of the recording?" I asked, keeping it casual.

"Just what you'd expect," Walter said; "just so much foo-poo." This was Walter's immemorial term for straight-tone singing. It enraged Marie's lover Clare, for whom music died with the waning of the clavecin. "But wait till you hear Charles call forth his pow'rs and dare..."

"Plus," I ventured, "he's cute, no?"

"Mmm... a little on the hydrodynamic side, I think."

"Sleek, you mean." Joe, on the other hand, was rough. I could feel fingers, not necessarily mine, slipping across Ribera's smooth cheek, none of Joe's sandpaper snags in the way.

"Whatever..." Walter's voice was dubious, and I imagined it was a little disapproving too. "He'll be at Wolf Trap in late August, in *Entführung*. The twenty-seventh, I think. Should I get us tickets?"

"Belmonte?" I asked.

"No, he's listed for Pedrillo."

"That's shoddy casting," I said. His '*Oh, wie ängstlich*' on my CD is sublime." I looked at the kitchen calendar. "Joe won't be here. He goes up to New York that weekend. Get three tickets. Boys' night out!"

Backstage, after that performance, we three met Charles. I had heard back from him, in response to my written request that he notify me of appearances in the area, and he put us on the visitors list. He

158

remembered my fan letter, especially the line about de los Angeles. He also did remember Joe, and asked me to give him his best regards.

Chapter 9
March, 2016
[flashback: 1997]

"This is a small job, sir," said Lorne, our handyman/contractor for over twenty years. A small leak had started in the ceiling of the dressing room on the third floor. Calling Lorne was the kind of thing that Joe would have handled in the past, and I had dreaded making the call and conducting the negotiations, sure that Lorne would say the entire roof needed replacing. At our old house in Charles Village, he had done major work, including building a garage from the ground up and completely gutting and renovating the kitchen and two bathrooms, but he had always also been willing to come by on short notice even for tiny jobs. He had a list of twenty or more regular clients whom he kept happy by this balance, either building an addition on the back of the house or changing the lightbulb in an elderly widow's oven. "I can just caulk around the base of the chimbley and slap on some silver roofing paint, seal it up real good. The roof itself is fine for another ten years at least."

Lorne looked as sexy as always – rangy, scruffy, cocky, friendly. He was calling me "sir" because Jimmy Jack was in the room; he had always called me or Joe "boss" or "babe" depending on his mood and the moment. He must have been around forty-five by this time, but the hard physical work he did had kept him muscular and swaggery. Blue collar guys in Baltimore as a class were used to working well with gay clients. Even thirty years earlier, I had often noticed that men who came to my house to fix the dishwasher or paint the window frames seemed unfazed by the fact that I lived there alone and had a picture of Tom Selleck in a bathing suit on my fridge. Generally they would find an excuse to mention that they had a few other clients who were 'single guys,' and they were often gently protective of me, as though they understood that I lacked certain kinds of masculine know-how. When and if they became regular presences in my home, as Lorne now had, they sometimes took on a slightly flirtatious tone. Lorne's "babe," affectionate and never disrespectful, suggested that, without him in our lives, Joe or I might have been washed out to sea by forgetting to flick a switch or turn a knob somewhere in the basement. He also often indulged in explicit homosexual banter, usually domineering on his part, with his male subordinates when he brought a team to our house. Joe and I had always taken this as a signal that he and his men were 'OK with gay stuff.' Old-school Baltimoreans like Gene and Patrick shared titillating tales of times when such men actually put out... lingered late on a job, asked if they could shower before heading home to the missus, left the bathroom door ajar to afford enticing glimpses, consented to strokings or even embraces... and then showed up for the next job as though nothing had happened.

"A lot of them hustled as teenagers," Patrick had once explained. He had worked for distinguished decades in interior design and had wrangled, apparently in every sense, with countless contractors and workmen. "Even after they're all grown up and married, they know which side their bread is buttered on." The arching of his eyebrows on this subject was nothing short of lewd. "And of course, in many cases they're simply *lovely* men."

Appetizing as Lorne was, I had been already happily married before he ever entered my – our – home. He, too, was married to, or at least living with, a woman named Misty. At the time of Joe's death, he had expressed his sympathy very touchingly in a note left under the door, written in his dreadful scrabbling hand, but surprisingly elegant and correct in diction, as though he were remembering exercises learned in grade school. Entering the house on this latest call, he had taken his baseball cap off as he crossed the threshold, and said simply,

"This house won't ever be the same without Mr. Joe. I'm sorry, boss." His rugged honest face registered real sadness. I gave him a big hug and felt sincerely fond of him. I also noticed the resilience of his flesh through his denim shirt. He had probably never been in a gym since high school, but his fine big body was toned by constant, demanding work and filled out by beer and burgers.

He was standing at the counter in the kitchen, after a trip to the roof without me. J.J. had tagged along with him, responsible and curious. He was learning new rituals of adulthood by observing the tones I used in addressing working people. I often noticed him observing and memorizing turns of phrase suitable for different kinds of interactions. It had occurred to him only recently that most adults did not address absolutely everyone identically. He was getting better at breezy and, thanks to Kevin, at gay, but I felt his attention now to my gracious and egalitarian. He had cocked his head just so a few weeks earlier, when he listened to me chatting with the cleaning lady about shenanigans at her storefront church, shaking my head and trading her verse for verse of Scripture. More than once, she rebuked the prowling Satan, who might, that day, have broken a figurine she was dusting on the parlor mantel if the Lord hadn't led her to catch it deftly on its plummet to the marble hearth.

"Oh, he *will* kill your joy," she had testified, in sad acknowledgement of the Tempter's craft and power. J.J. had followed this conversation as if watching a National Geographic documentary.

Lorne asked me for a small advance, and took out his wallet. It overflowed with old receipts, business cards, and Post-Its, and had been extensively patched with duct tape. He slid my two twenties into a very slim wad of cash. I wondered if perhaps I should buy him a new wallet for Christmas or International Handyman Day.

"I'll be here tomorrow around noon," he said.

"Jimmy, can you be home then?" I asked. "I'll be in class till two." J.J. nodded.

"Excellent," said Lorne. "I'll see you then, Mr. Jimmy." On a sudden sentimental impulse, he leaned in to hug me. "I hope you're home before I finish," he said. "I hope I get to see you."

"So do I," I said. I didn't rush to break from his hug, enjoying the unjudging affirmation. His arms didn't move, and my hands strayed up and down his strong back for a long moment. When I released him, we had a brief second of eye-contact which he broke by patting me hard on the shoulder.

"Love you, buddy," he said, bluff and busy, as he bent to pick up his tool box. Over his shoulder, I briefly caught J.J.'s warning eye. He would find some pompous way of putting words to his reservations when we were alone.

After dinner that night, we were together in the upstairs parlor. Jimmy stretched out on the long sofa, and I took the old wing chair. His little Ted Talk about the unsuitability of my flirtation with Lorne, interlarded with digressions on the necessity of shared cultural and intellectual interests between lovers (himself and Kevin providing the inevitable illustration) had come and gone, and I hadn't once slapped his smug young face.

Upright against the arm of the sofa, he looked fondly at me from under scrunched brows, as though I were his funny little boy. Though the room was chilly, he had kicked his shoes off, and the soles of his big bare feet were only a yard or two from my chair. I very seldom saw his father in him, but this evening I was reminded that Tony's strong, shapely feet had always attracted me during my decades of loving him. This new young adult Jimmy had the feet of a marble Greek athlete, all elegant ridges and arches and tendons, as neatly cut as an Ionic cornice. I knew I was slipping into what could easily become an aesthetic quicksand, looking as though at a work of erotic art at a young person I was sworn to protect and honor. I felt justified by my lack of rising desire, so unusual for me in the presence of any other appealing young man that I gave myself credit for it.

"I've decided you should marry Charles Ribera," he said, smiling and pleased with himself. "I can't get his voice out of my mind. Not his performance in DC. I mean, I liked it, but… that weird improv he did with Kevin and me, where his voice was all mystical and dark and alien."

I was startled by this whole little speech. I had been positive he would return to his denunciations of my attraction to Lorne.

"You think I should be abducted and romanced by a swart mediaeval Mediterranean assassin?" I asked. "Perhaps held captive in his bandit lair while he woos me in savage song and lays his purloined treasures coaxingly at my feet?"

"Yeah," he laughed, nodding.

Many years before, I was walking my dog Ootch in Patterson Park and ran into a young local guy who often loitered there, and who probably had mental retardation of some kind. We had spoken many times before. He was always cheerful and engaging, cracking himself up extensively as he extemporized absurd Dada scenarios on the slightest pretext. He would find his way, step by step, through complex, hilarious balderdash, and had a delighted inhaling snort, almost a "Yep," at each successive elaboration. This particular time we met at the edge of a small lake clogged with bulrushes. He said, as if picking up a conversation on-going for weeks,

"Yep, they can't control the weeds, so they're moving the lake to the top of the hill."

"Really?" I asked. "How are they going to do that?"

"With a pump," he answered promptly, and pointed at a steep rise nearby. "They're going to pump the water right up there where the Pagoda is."

"Are they going to tear down the Pagoda?" I wondered aloud.

"No, they'll put the lake around it."

"But how will they keep the water up there? Won't it just run downhill?"

"No," he said, by now completely amused by himself. "They'll plant trees in a circle to hold the water in place."

"But won't it take a long time for the tree trunks to grow into a solid wall?" I asked. He chortled.

"Yeah, but they'll put a big..." He looked furtively around for his theory, then found it: "...a big *net* between the trees until they grow together."

"So in the meantime this *net* will hold the water in a circle, above ground, around the Pagoda?" By now, I was laughing with him.

"Yep," he said, "that's just how it will work." He chuckled under his breath, knowing that he was talking total nonsense.

Jimmy's laugh now was exactly like that.

"I think if Charles can sing like that, even sometimes, he's complex enough for someone like you."

I let it go.

"Who knows?" I said, shrugging. "You may be right. He's a true artist, and in many ways a very nice man." I could tell in my marrow that I had no attraction whatever to Charles any more, and that most of me wouldn't care if I never saw him again. To my relief and surprise, J.J. turned instead to something which he had brought up occasionally over the previous couple of months.

"G.J.," he said, "tell me about Dino. You talk about him sometimes." Any further discussion of my putative attractions to a handyman or an early-music star was dismissed. Dino was a subject both dear and confusing to my heart, dating back almost thirty years. If Jimmy had detected something charged in my sporadic references to him, he wasn't wrong.

"Oh," I said, "he was my favorite of all my pet students. He was in my classes a few years before Joe and I got together, so he's pushing fifty

164

now… I don't see him often. He was at Joe's funeral; that's probably the last time we talked."

"Did I meet him there, do you think? No, you would have told me when you've mentioned him since then. What does he look like?"

"He's very Italian looking, of course. Dino Surace; he pronounces it 'sir-ACE.' Neapolitan ancestry. He's tall and broad-shouldered; he stands perfectly straight and has the most marvelous thick curly hair, nicely greying now… very sharp profile. He is one of those Neapolitans probably descended directly from Greek colonists twenty-eight hundred years ago."

"Good-looking?" Jimmy asked. "All your boys are good-looking, I think."

"Oh, very," I nodded. "And he does a lot for a pair of tight pants. He's got college-age kids now; I barely know them, but he's been pretty good about checking in every so often since he graduated. Recently divorced, unfortunately. I liked his wife; I liked the way she was loving and sentimental and supportive but also kind of mouthy with him. She's Italian-American too."

"So he kept in touch based on what kind of relationship?"

"It was always a loyalty-gratitude thing for him. Very *"Ciao, Professore,"* as though I'd saved him from a life of ignorance in the slums. But…" I drifted into silence; I couldn't quite think what I had meant to say. It was something a bit sad.

"But what?" Jimmy prompted. He was smiling patiently, as though I were prattling.

"Well, he was objectively great. He was the glue that held his cohort together. He was always the one who made the class go; he would answer the question when he could tell I needed just one right answer to get the ball rolling; he laughed at my corny jokes… But he was more than that. He was…"

"What?"

"He was the only student I've ever been absolutely sure loved me. I mean, I literally thought he might be in love with me. He gave off no gay signals at all; he looked at pretty girls in tight sweaters and made jokes in class about his crush on Cindy Crawford. But he would always wait after class to talk to me. He always wanted to be the one who walked me back to my office. He would even drop by my house sometimes. He had a way of pulling off his jacket or sweatshirt so that I'd see his torso for a second or two. Of course, I thought that meant that he was completely indifferent, unaware of any potential ambiguity, but then I also thought that none of my other students ever did that, whereas with him it was dozens of times. He loved hugging me, back when that wasn't even a thing yet. He wanted all his classmates to know he was my pet; he wouldn't let anyone else go to another classroom for me to borrow chalk during class, or carry the projector."

J.J. smiled noticeably at the mention of chalk and the projector, as though I'd mentioned doing multiplication on an abacus and writing with a quill in elementary school. I hadn't even referred to the time Dino helped me unjam the mimeograph machine in the departmental office.

"I just sometimes thought… that he wanted to try something with me. And I cared about him, quite a bit. His adoration was flattering. It wasn't exactly sexual for me; he was definitely good-looking and sexy, but… he was in some other category for me: an affectionate, smart, funny young guy who would always be next to me, helping, respecting, listening…"

"He's all grown up now, but you still talk about him as a kid." J.J. was trying to piece together the scattered elements of something quite foreign to him. Of course, he couldn't possibly understand how it felt to be older than someone. "And you thought he was handsome, right?"

"All my students are more or less good-looking to me," I said. "In fact, I usually think they're all adorable. That includes the girls, so stop looking at me like that. 99% of the 1% of me that might be considered latently heterosexual involves young women in my classes. I often wish that their peers could see them as I do. I worry that straight boys don't see how lovely my girls are, because they're smart and hard-working and modest and strong, and lots of boys don't like that. Girls or boys, it doesn't matter; I almost always like them. There's something very tender about them for me; not just my pets, not just the Dinos.

"That's the life of a teacher, no?" asked Jimmy.

"When it works, yes," I answered after a moment. "On a good day, it's worth it. They're my stake in the future, proof that my voice will last another generation or two. But on a bad day it feels like they all graduate, they outgrow me, they disappear."

"How does the word 'love' fit into this story?" he asked. "Did you 'love' Dino? I'm totally sure that he loved you. You collect young surrogate sons, G.J." he said. "It's not a sex-thing. It's a love-thing for you. Your love for what humanity can be in the future. Most of them disappear because you've taught them what they needed and then they move forward. It may hurt you in a way, but you should be very proud of it." This was a deep affirmation of aspects of my emotional and professional life which part of me had always feared might be, at their base, perverse. Jimmy saw them as lovely and wholesome. "But not all of them disappear on you."

I looked across at him. He was a savings bond reaching maturity. I had agreed to love him before he was born: adoring his father, learning to respect and love his mother despite the howling jealousies that beset me; even hoping, when the time came, that they might actually have the child whose conception I had dreaded. Then there had suddenly been this little Jimmy in the world, a bundle of limitations and brilliance, a dogged loyal hand tugging at mine. No one else on earth could have walked me through the valley of the shadow of Joe's death.

"I'm the one who stays," he said.

Jimmy and I went to DC on an art excursion the next Saturday, while Kevin stayed in Baltimore to study. Walter and Ricardo were to join us for a Piero di Cosimo exhibit at the National Gallery and a show of images of the Virgin Mary at the National Museum of Women in the Arts.

Jimmy was kind of an *enfant sauvage* in art museums. He would slouch, indifferent and unimpressed, through rooms of acknowledged masterpieces and then gaze for minutes at a time at completely uncanonical pieces whose provincial eccentricity appealed to him. He could walk past a sublime Bellini unblinking and then lose himself in the obsessive crinkles of the foliage framing the head of a Dosso Dossi nymph or the nubby melons around a frigid Crivelli Madonna. The Piero show might have been hung just for him. There were whole rooms which I sized up and dismissed in a restless moment, but there would be Jimmy mooning over the odd *pince-nez* of some attendant saint or the musical notation on the scrap of parchment left on the parapet by a hawk-faced old man with bizarre inward-folding ears. Sometimes I would hear him humming as he stood just close enough to a painting not to set off an alarm. Later, he would have no idea what a given painting looked like apart from the couple of square inches that had drawn his eye, but he might be able to recapture the aleatoric tune he had hummed on seeing it. Ricardo noticed the humming at one point, and whispered to me:

"He's going to write a piece called '*Homage à Pierre de Cosimo*,' for tape, prepared piano, and bassoon," he said, "and you are going to *hate* it."

The Mary exhibit was even more off-putting at first for J.J. He went in saying that he didn't know anything about art history and wasn't interested in Christian iconography.

"Why would you be?" I asked. "But Walter is an Episcopalian agnostic, Ricardo's a lapsed Catholic, and I'm a practicing Calvinist, so the imagery itself isn't devotional for us. I think of it as pagan and foreign but maybe strangely insightful about the human and the divine." Jimmy wandered aimlessly before suddenly going into a trance in front of Desiderio's "Panciatichi Madonna." I joined him.

"Imagine being her," I said. "You're just a nice Italian girl with no ideas about anything until suddenly the most holy thing in the universe needs your protection."

"She's Jewish," he said. "She can handle it." I looked again at the shimmering gauze of a relief in front of us. There was no question that this slip of a girl was up to the task. She was wispy and filmy and barely a quarter of an inch deep, delicate, exquisite; but she was marble, pure and hard and radiant. I smiled, remembering a Jewish woman I knew whose only son came to her, all unexpected and beyond all imagining for strangeness and specialness, and who rose to the occasion and tended to him with a grace and firmness which no one had seen in her before. J.J. couldn't possibly remember the recalibrations which I had seen his mother accomplish in his first year of life, but he knew maternal competence when he saw it, and he called it Jewish.

"I love going to museums with you," I said.

"Don't bring Lorne here," he answered. I felt put down and offended on Lorne's behalf.

"In point of fact," I said, "he might enjoy it. He would do what you're doing: look at things honestly, say what he thinks. Don't be such a snob." His eyes were shifty for a minute. Maybe he'd expected me to laugh in appreciation of his rapier wit. "And I don't... well, I *try* not to take nice people to things I don't think they'll enjoy." He looked at me sideways. He didn't look at all reprimanded or abashed.

"I know you," he said. There was no apology implied.

He suddenly turned to face me and put one arm around my neck. He looked pitying, vastly wise and powerful. He leaned down to kiss me quickly on the side of my head, stroking my neck as though I were his child, his doll. Three or four people, guards and other visitors, reacted to his gesture. It was 2016 in Washington; no one was going to call the vice squad. Nevertheless, there was a palpable coolness, something about 'Gay rights, yeah, fine… but don't rub it in my face,' 'What if there were children here?…' It was a brazen act on his part. It showed that I was certainly not what most people would have assumed I was: his father. I was not only proud of him for it, but proud of myself.

Two days later, I got home from school a bit later than was usual, maybe five pm or so. The second I came into the kitchen, I knew that Jimmy was in the house, almost as though my brain stem recognized his scent, one part in trillions. He and Kevin had dined together more and more often since the semester started, and sometimes I didn't know, till I got a text around six, whether one or both of them would show up for dinner, and where they would sleep, if together. There had been no such word that night.

There was no sound coming from anywhere in the large house, no sign of disturbance in any of the first floor rooms. The mail was on the floor of the front hall, untouched since it had been pushed through the chute by the postman. I called "J.J.?" a couple of times and then, heading back to the kitchen and tossing all the flyers and junk mail into the recycling, started up the back stairs. I pulled my tie off as I went and put down my book bag by the desk in the second-floor study; there were papers in it I would correct that night after dinner. I continued up to the third floor, flicking the lights on in the stairwell as I went because there was no light coming from upstairs.

Jimmy's door was open but his room was completely dark. I was suddenly frightened as I glanced into it from the landing at the top of the steps. The light from the hall showed a large hunched shadow outlined against the bedstead.

"You OK, buddy?" I asked, hearing the quaver in my own voice. "Mind if I turn on the light?" The room was eerily silent, and it took me a second to steel myself and flick the switch. I saw J.J., crouched like a wounded stag, squinting at the sudden brightness, and was acutely relieved that he was moving and breathing. I could see tears all over his face; his pale eyes were shrinking hard against the invading light.

"Oh, honey," I called, and jumped forward. I kneeled awkwardly on the edge of his bed and he lurched away from me for a second, then just as quickly came at me and clutched me so hard I was scared again. "What?" I put my arms around him tentatively. He was shuddering. Not a single sound had come from him yet. "I won't let anything hurt you," I said. "Nothing, nothing, nothing. It's OK. You're strong." A dreadful terror rose up in me as I remembered cradling Joe in my arms as he died. Jimmy was dying... some terrible unsuspected undiagnosed congenital weakness, my fault somehow, and I couldn't save him. There was probably a first-aid protocol I should know, but I wouldn't remember it in time. "You're my forever boy," I croaked out. "I love you forever." His shuddering stopped; so did my heart, at first, as he fell still against me.

"I'm not dying, G.J.," he whispered coldly after a moment. He was still hugging me so hard I could barely breathe.

"Oh!" I cried. I could feel myself start shaking, dry-throated as that fear drained away, and I kissed the side of his face, his curls, his ear. "Oh! Thank God. You scared me..." I shook my head, cleared the fog of terror, and remembered that I had found him frozen and rigid with grief just a minute earlier. "What is it, honey?"

"When you call me 'honey' I feel like a little boy," he said, sounding irritated.

"I'm an idiot," I said.

"Kevin dumped me today," he said.

Then, thank God, he started sobbing, squeezing me hard, rubbing his face on my chest with moans of heartbreak, moans clearly painful for him to make, agonizing for me to hear. But, 'This I can almost handle,' I thought.

Jimmy Jack was going to write an anthem, with brass and organ, for my church Choir to do on Easter at the end of that month.

He had attended church a few times during the year. With church people, he still called me "Godfather Jim," at least much of the time, to credential himself. They all knew he was Jewish, and no one thought of him as a potential member, but he was familiar and well-liked.

At one Communion service he attended, we sang my favorite Friedell anthem. He asked me closely about it after the service. I told him it was also sometimes done as a simple strophic hymn, also nice, and that the tune was called "Union Seminary." He didn't mention the words at all, but he loved the parts writing, and was fixated on some aspects of the melody which had never occurred to me.

"The first phrase is symmetrical solfège," he said: "OK, it starts on *mi*, but then it's *so-la-do-re-do-la-so*..." He sketched this out in his very focused, dark, deep voice, a bit irregular in its support and still apt to break into little squeaks, but very clear in pitch.

"Huh," I said.

"And why does that rising major triad sound so great?" He was pursuing something in his mind about tonal music. "'Thou-art-in'... were those the words?"

"Yeah, I know: simple building blocks, beautiful tune," I said.

"It seems too easy. It gives this fantastic lift to the line."

He had not written his own text for the Easter anthem, but instead had pieced together snippets from all through the New and Old Testaments. The Choir had rehearsed the new piece a few times already by the time of J.J.'s break-up with Kevin, with him conducting, elbowy, disarming, and earnest, winning the hearts of all the choristers while confusing the hell out of most of us. After a few run-throughs, the piece began to feel natural to the Choir, with crests and climaxes and drastic dynamic effects from whispers to roars on almost every page, and we were singing it quite confidently. It started to sound actually beautiful in J.J.'s extraterrestrial way. He had written a solo of several lines for me, to the text, "For love is strong as death; death hath no dominion over him." It was, for him, surprisingly melodic, chant-like and melismatic, arching up to high E's which sounded dramatic in my voice but which put me at no risk of missing them. At our first reading of it in my parlor, I had delightedly told him, "I can absolutely nail this," and he had smiled up from the keyboard like a young Bernstein and said, "I know. I wrote it for you."

On Easter morning, after our choral warm-up, I found him pacing nervously in the corridor outside the Choir Room. Everyone was sure the piece would go well, and everyone had wished him good luck. No one in the church but me knew that his heart was broken. I checked my watch.

"Show time, champ," I said, patting his shoulder. He nodded miserably. Together we entered the sanctuary. He sat with the brass upstairs; he would be conducting their prelude pieces. The other choristers and I gathered downstairs in the narthex for the processional hymns, but first I slipped out of line and into the pews to speak with Tony and Rachel. They had arrived the night before, and had come to church on their own a few minutes before the service. They sat close to the front so that they could get the full acoustic advantage of the room for Jimmy's anthem.

"Our boy's in one piece?" Tony asked me with a wary smile.

"Oh yeah," I nodded. "He's fine – very stoic. The minute the music starts, he'll be totally himself." Rachel nodded.

"The usher was a friend of yours," she said. "She was so kind when she heard we were Jimmy's parents. 'We *love* that boy,' she said. 'He's so talented... and such a *sweet*heart!'" Rachel had on a beautifully tailored grey suit and a single strand of irreproachable pearls; the only sign of the Rachel we knew was a deeply saturated crimson silk scarf. This was a very unusual look for her, a break from her trademark ethnic accessories and jewelry. It was as if a Pre-Raphaelite princess had borrowed clothes from Barbara Bush to mingle with Presbyterians.

She looked still a little shocked by J.J.'s hysterics the night before. During the ten days since Kevin's abrupt announcement, J.J. had been through cycles of wild grief and stunned, haunted silences around the house with me, while ghost-walking through his obligations at school. Watchful as I was, I knew he was doing OK. Only once had he come to my room during the night. I had lain there, quiet and apprehensive about possible melt-downs. After only a minute or two of lying on the bedspread in a mournful droop, he had sat up and said, "No, I will be fine in my room."

The arrival of his parents had triggered a minor setback. Lowering his guard, he had tried to tell them what had happened, and about halfway through the simple story, he had started howling as helplessly as a child in the grip of a tantrum. He had buried his face on Rachel's shoulder and she had rocked him, as I was sure she had many times in years past; there was something about the fit of their two bodies that looked fully habitual and comforting for both of them. As she looked up over his head, though, she caught my eye. Of course, I thought: he hasn't done this since he's been this big and strong. She knew he would be fine. The grief I saw in her eyes was that she realized this would almost have to be the last time he would come to her arms this way. She didn't enjoy it at all; it was visibly painful for her to see him so distressed. Still, she showed an almost guilty pleasure, a knowledge that most mothers would have had, ten or more years earlier, their last taste of being so desperately needed by their boys.

The music went splendidly. Jimmy's piece was note-perfect; we all seemed to have completely internalized his astral ear and found a way to bring his sounds down from the ether in joy. He was swinging his arms like a windmill too wild for Don Quixote to brave, yet somehow the complex internal rhythms were perfectly clear in his oddly cocked wrists and fingers. When my solo passage started, he gave me a mature, encouraging look. My best line was on the word "dominion," as the melody rose to a D on the second syllable and then, in a syncopation, went up another step for two beats on the high E before coming down the scale. Without looking at Jimmy, I saw him gesture for greater volume from the brass as I held the E, and I pulled off a crescendo which I'd never attempted in rehearsal. I felt a slight exhalation of admiration from the basses around me and knew that we'd scored a real effect together. Before the Choir's next entrance, I looked down and saw J.J. beaming at me. He was completely transported. By the time we reached the last page, with its steady crescendo to a majestic, suddenly major final chord, with sopranos and trumpets throwing a brilliant B-flat, his gestures were like the blades of a helicopter, higher and higher, circling. If he had actually levitated, no one would have been surprised. I thought that I had never in his entire life seen a smile of such pure joy on his face. For several minutes, he had not thought of Kevin.

The stunned, enraptured silence which followed the fade of the last notes was like an immense shared angelic smile. We were all afraid of an uncouth cough or sneeze or baby's cry from downstairs, but none came. After about ten seconds, the service continued. Jimmy Jack left his little podium and came to sit with the Choir. The men on my pew scooted over, tightly overlapping, so that he could sit next to me. He settled in with a happy little snuggling motion as Choir members reached to pat his shoulders and knees. Then he turned to me, pulling us close, rubbing his nose against mine.

"I'm so happy," he whispered. "And your solo was sublime." He faced forward again and I reached to take his hand.

"Proud of you," I said.

I could tell that the entire Choir, and even the unnecessarily butch brass players from Peabody, most of whom knew Jimmy at least by name, thought we were absolutely dear. So, as the feeling sank in, did I.

Dino rang the bell right on time. We were supposed to go out to dinner. Joe was on the West Coast for a week or more, and Dino had suggested we hang out. He and Joe liked each other quite a bit. Dino had intimated that he could look after me while Joe was away, as though I couldn't feed myself or stay out of mischief. In fact, he'd told Joe not to worry about me. There was some kind of Italo-American freemasonry between them, a secret handshake or a pledge to protect me. I had decided to make dinner that night rather than going out to the steak house on Eastern Avenue which Dino had suggested.

When I opened the door, he was looking about as good as he knew how to look. He had on a deep brown silk shirt, open at the neck to show the entrancing bony ridge between very rounded pecs dusted impeccably with black hair. Like a good Italian boy, he wore a thick gold chain and a crucifix. I had seen it countless times before, but the silk shirt with its glimpses of man-cleavage gave it a more stylish focus than usual. As usual, he was wearing tight jeans which made his agile long legs look taut and curvy. He was in his later twenties by now and had graduated a few years before. He had launched what would become a good career in accounting and had been dating a string of girls, always very pretty and almost always named Jennifer. On policy, he had always brought them by to meet me (and Joe, once there was a Joe), and I had always liked them until it turned out they were superficial and materialistic. Dino was very interested in getting married. I found it incredible that so many of these bright young women put the brakes on at a certain point, decided Dino wasn't cool enough, or got tired of his cheerful, respectful, sweet, bourgeois, smoking-hotness.

He held up a bottle of limoncello, which was still rather hard to get in Baltimore in those years. We had had it in Naples when he traveled to Italy with me the summer before Joe and I set up housekeeping, the year after he'd graduated, and he'd remembered that his grandfather made it sometimes. Dino knew a fair amount of Neapolitan from home. He had won me points in Naples with his casually dropped tags of dialect. The staff of the hotel near Santa Chiara where I always stayed were used to my correct professorial Italian, but got an immense kick out of my smart-alecky *scugnizzo* traveling companion.

"Let's put it in the freezer now," he said. "Maybe we can come back here after dinner for a nightcap."

"Nothing easier," I said. "In fact, we're not going out. I've got two T-bones ready to grill *alla fiorentina* and a simple salad to toss." The whole Florentine steak craze, too, hadn't burst yet onto the world stage the year of our visit to Italy; it was another exotic experience we'd shared. He had been a great credit to me with my snobby Florentine friends when they took us to a blue-collar eatery in Santo Spirito. The gravel-voiced waiter had roughly interrogated even the locals on whether or not they knew what they were ordering when they asked for *un po' di ciccia,* "a little meat." When a pound or two of three-inch thick, blazing red steak had been placed before each of us, and we had started quaffing the carafes of bone-dry Chianti, I had asked Dino what low-class Americans might drink with dinner... that brown, bubbly drink, I prompted... He looked vague for a moment and then, getting his cue, said, with a self-satisfied grin as wide and sunny as the Bay of Naples, *"Hoha-Hola!"* That had garnered slaps on the back from all the Florentines, topped only by their reaction when one of them asked him, *"Hai una* 'girlfriend'*?"* and he looked foxy and replied, *"'Una'?"*

He opened the freezer and slipped the bottle of limoncello onto the stacked ice trays. For no reason, and to my own surprise, I stepped close behind him and patted his butt. It looked, as it always did, very good, and was harder than I'd expected; of course, if his jeans had been any tighter, they would have exploded. Though I pretty much trusted myself not to cheat on Joe, I wasn't crazy about what that pat suggested I thought of Dino. I knew myself well enough to be aware that I had always liked looking at him, but I had never harbored any illusion that he wanted me to touch him.

"Huh," I said. "I don't know where that came from. Oops." He looked over his shoulder at me.

"I don't mind," he said. "It's like we're football players." He stood another moment with his back to me. "Do it again, but don't apologize this time. Just grab my ass." I did.

Then we started setting out the dinner things.

Dinner came out well and we had a nice rambling talk. At a certain point, there was a lull, and he filled it with a surprising,

"Jennifer broke up with me last week. She says she's decided she doesn't want to have children."

"I'm sorry to hear that," I answered. "Wait… were you actually talking about getting married, starting a family…?"

"Well," he said, "*I* was talking about it." He looked suddenly very sad. I wasn't used to seeing him sagging and sorry for himself. I remembered that all previous Jennifers had decided he wasn't cool. That's what he thought was really happening here: this latest Jennifer didn't care about children one way or the other. She thought he was old-fashioned, a good-looking Catholic boy, an uncool accountant. Hot guys had more mousse in their hair and less symmetrical black-and-red leather jackets, with big motorcycles or drug habits.

"I think she's literally the stupidest person on earth," I said. "Nothing she could say or do should make you wonder for one nanosecond if you're a fantastic guy or not. I kind of want to punch her in the nose."

He met my eye for a long instant, still looking very mournful, and then said,

"Thanks." He lifted his wine glass at me as though he were toasting me. "I love how much you like me. It means a lot."

"Just look at yourself, Dino," I said. "You're a total sweetheart, you're a perfect gentleman, you're smart and funny, you've got a good job and no bad habits, and you're super-cute. For God's sake, what do these Jennifers want?"

"Not me, I guess," he said, looking down, disappointed, tired of feeling this way. He wasn't gloomy by nature, and in less than five seconds he jerked his head back up and grinned, faking it but touching me with his valiant optimism. "Umm… do you have any limoncello?" I had to grin back.

"Funny coincidence! The greatest guy in the world just happens to have brought me a bottle a couple of hours ago," I said. "Let's see if it's chilled by now."

We sat side by side on the sofa in the living room area by the front door and started sipping the sweet frigid liquor. 'Uh-oh,' I thought, '*this* could be tomorrow's hang-over.' I held back, in fact, but he poured himself four or five of the thimble sized cordial glasses we were using. He was tall and big enough that the alcohol affected him less than me; still, his posture slackened a bit and his slouch brought him closer and closer to me, until our shoulders were touching. It was a feeling as sweet as limoncello. There was something boyish and safe in having him so close. I didn't feel any passion for him, except gratitude for his friendliness and sympathy for his sadness.

"Why did it take *you* so long to find someone?" he slurred, with a heavy-lidded glance over at me. Our faces were inches apart. "I remember it used to strike me as weird. Like why men didn't fight over you." I had a shuddering memory that Tony, many years before, had said this to me, also under the influence of sweet alcohol, just before a mortifying failed attempt to accommodate my desire for him. Dino stretched a little and settled deeper into the sofa, giving a comfortable hum or sigh, as though we were two puppies in a small soft bed. I felt almost the same way, feeling that this charged, warm closeness was exactly what I desired with Dino. "I'm glad you have Joe. I love Joe," he said, sounding suddenly vague and sleepy. "But I still want to be the one who takes care of you in your old age."

"Aww," I whispered, smiling. I was very touched. I realized after a minute that he had dozed off. I sat there in a glow, feeling strong and vigilant. I wondered what I would do if he fell asleep there, leaning against me. Could I slip out from under his weight, perhaps get his shoes off and toss a blanket over him, without his waking up? Would I kiss his forehead? I felt intensely fond of him.

A few minutes later, around 10:30 or so, the ring of the phone cut through the house like a gunshot. Dino stirred, snapping up into a responsible position in case I wanted to answer it, but I said,

"No, let the machine pick up." We heard Joe's voice on the outgoing message: "Sorry to miss your call," etc. Dino turned back to me for a moment, as though maybe to lean back against me or to say something sentimental. Then Joe's actual living voice suddenly invaded the room.

"Hey, Tiger," it said, "it's me... must be going on eleven in Baltimore. Just calling to check in. Oh, wait, isn't this the night you're having dinner with Dino? Maybe you're out now... Give him my best if so – and tell him he *can't have you!*" He chuckled a little at his own tiny witticism. Dino actually smirked a bit, too. "No, seriously, I'm glad he's keeping you company. I'll see you at home in a couple days. Call me here if you get the chance. Love you!"

The sound of Joe's voice filled me with the usual missing. I had a lover, and he and I belonged together; Dino and I both knew it. He must have felt me stiffen slightly and shift a millimeter away from him. He rubbed his eyes, stretched, and stood up.

Within ten minutes, and after the biggest bear hug at the door, Dino was gone. I couldn't wait to tell Joe about this lovely evening with Dino... not every detail, out of respect for Dino, but enough to show good faith and to share a smile.

Chapter 10
April, 2016
[flashback: 1996]

I was sleeping when J.J. came into my room. It was dark outside, and since I had gone to bed just before midnight, I was confident mumbling "Happy birthday" to him.

"Thanks," he said, nestling into his spot next to me.

"When we're both awake," I said, "I'll tell you about Petrarch and Laura. April 6."

"Deal," he said.

A few hours later, with cheerful sunlight streaming through the louvers of the inside shutters, I woke up, and within a minute or two I felt him stirring next to me.

"Happy birthday again," I said.

"You know you've mentioned Petrarch to me every birthday since I was five?" he said, grumpy and eye-rubbing.

"Sue me," I said. "I'm a professor of Italian. You were born on April 6." He rolled over to face me, trying to smile a bit, still very sleepy.

"I won't have any happy days anymore," he said. "Birthdays or otherwise. Kevin hates me."

"J.J.," I said, "wake up. This is *why* you were born on April 6." He didn't answer, but he made a funny frowning face of concentration and came a bit closer to me, as though he were five and I were his mother.

I felt all the color drain out of my already sufficiently pasty face. His nice-sized penis was standing, and through his pajama leg it was pressed, casually but palpably, against my thigh. Morning wood. Just from the pressure on my bare upper leg, I was acutely aware that it was a *very* nice member, beautiful as every part of him was, and meant to make Jimmy and someone else very happy. He seemed to have no sense that anything was unusual in his appeal for a hug from me with this pert envoy sent on ahead. My body temperature was suddenly about zero.

"Wo big boy," I said, coolly I hoped; "why don't you keep that on your side of the bed?"

"Oh," he said. "No one wants that. I forgot." He rolled over, away from me, and started to shake silently. A lot seemed to be hanging in the

179

balance, and I waited a moment before I sat up in bed and swung my legs to the floor, away from him. Then I reached and patted his trembling shoulder. He wasn't crying; he was just shaking.

"Jimmy Jack," I asked. "Let's try our favorite question again: Who do you love most in the world?" He waited a long moment before saying,

"Since Kevin dumped me… I guess you. Well, and Mommy and Daddy."

"Do you ever imagine having sex with me?" He gave a violent little tantrum of shrugging and squirming.

"No, of course not. Gross."

"Trust me on this, then," I insisted. "Your hard-on doesn't belong in my bed. It's something that can cause you a lot of joy and a lot of trouble – and not only you. A lot of people would respond to it. Under literally any other circumstances in the world, *I* would respond to it. You need to handle it with a lot of class and caution."

"I thought I was safe here," he said, almost a whimper. I was old enough to count to ten before answering.

"This is the safest place on earth for you," I said. "I need to be safe here, too."

After a moment, he turned back to face me. He pulled the loose top sheet into a shapeless, modest wad in his lap. He still looked confused and put down, almost as though he'd come on to me and been rejected, though both of us knew that that was exactly what had just *not* happened.

"Tell me why I was born on April 6," he said.

I got up and went to sit in the rocking chair a few feet away, as if I were going to read him a bedtime story instead of waking him up to face his twenty-second birthday.

"Petrarch had his first glimpse of Laura in church on April 6," I said – 'Once upon a time…' "He fell in love instantly. He loved her devotedly his whole life, even after she married someone else, had children; even many years after she'd died of plague in 1348. She never loved him; she barely knew he existed."

"Was he a creepy stalker?" he asked, the voice of the times.

"He was a literary artist. Her name reminded him of the laurel tree that Daphne turned into to escape from Apollo when he was trying to rape her. But Apollo, god of poets, to compensate for having lost her, made it his favorite tree, took its leaves as his emblem, made them the symbol of artistic achievement. By losing Laura, Petrarch got laurels: became a famous poet."

"This story implies that Petrarch is Apollo," J.J. said. It was a fair point: the artist's egotism, self-absorption, and vanity. "How much of that fame would he have traded to be her lover?"

"Probably every bit of it," I admitted. "But that wasn't an option for him. Life gave him lemons, and he made art, poetry, beauty. And he made *her* immortal. The best revenge." That sounded almost sadistic… but then, Hugues de Sade was precisely whom Laura had married, and Petrarch was merciless in his own way, too. "Without her rejection, certainly no one would ever have heard of *her* seven hundred years later, and quite possibly no one would have heard of Petrarch, either. I mean, he wrote lots of other books he thought would earn him fame, but it's his Laura poems that have created his legend." Jimmy listened to this with a concentration that reminded me of years past when he sucked his thumb. After a minute he responded.

"I'm lying here wondering what your point is."

"You're lying there thinking that no good can come of what you're feeling right now," I said. "I'm sitting here telling you that you may make some amazing art out of it." My mind went back to a master class at Peabody years before. A young soprano had burst into tears while singing *"O del mio amato ben."* Her classmates squirmed, knowing that she was thinking of her own recent break-up. I spoke directly to them; meanwhile, the pianist, a very low-affect young virtuosa, had risen from the bench to unexpected heights of empathy, and was embracing the decompensating soprano's heaving shoulders.

"If you've never felt this way," I said to the class, "you'll never be a classical singer. This is what most of our repertoire is about. Feel it; own it; memorize it. When you're feeling it for yourself, it will lacerate your vocal cords, but later, when you have some distance but remember how it felt, you can sing it. Most people spend their whole lives repressing these emotions, so when you sing a song like this – right – it's like ten years of free psychotherapy for every person in the audience." I gave Jimmy some abbreviated version of this, and I could see his eyes shifting under lowered brows as he took it in.

"Your heart was never broken," he said after a while. "You had Uncle Joe."

"*After* my heart was broken, savagely and irreparably, more than once," I said. "You *will* love again. Meanwhile you're master of an infinite space, in and of yourself."

He sat up, still sulky and sad, and leaned back against the bedstead, looking exhausted.

"Someday you'll tell me about your so-called heartbreaks," he said. "I don't believe in them. You're half of one of the world's great love stories. I'm a weird terminally uncool guy who gets dumped. But I just decided I should get up and go to school."

Running into Kevin ten times a day at Peabody was hard on Jimmy. He usually tried to talk to Kevin, and would get a deft brush-off. He didn't know if Kevin was seeing anyone else. The reason Kevin had given him for breaking up was that they were looking for different things (which I took as gay for 'I want to sleep around'), and that had led to Jimmy's ruminating extensively on what things he should want, things that Kevin would want as well. Perhaps if they talked enough, J.J. could understand what he meant, and could start changing himself into the boyfriend Kevin was looking for. "He says we'll always be friends and love each other," J.J. would tell me disconsolately. "But he won't talk to me. What kind of friends is that?"

I would sometimes try to comfort him with anecdotes from my own antediluvian record on the dating scene. Decades with Joe hadn't completely effaced the memories of how sad I'd been over disappointments by guys whose names and faces I could no longer even remember, but whose words (their 'You're sweet' or 'It's not you; it's me' or 'I think sex would ruin our friendship') were still deeply imprinted. Practically every emotion he was experiencing was familiar to me, but my sad stories from the 1980s were as personally relevant to Jimmy as the sorrows of Edward II and Piers Gaveston. The only thing that really comforted him was my saying that Kevin probably missed him more than he realized and would eventually come to his senses. In the meantime, the best thing J.J. could do, I suggested, was to stay busy and make time pass as quickly as he could.

For that reason, I was glad when he announced that he was going to Philadelphia one weekend with another friend, Jake, whom he'd never mentioned before.

"A potential new… special friend?" I asked. He winced and rolled his eyes; of course it was too soon for him to be considering new adventures. But he summoned the gumption to give a dishy response:

"No, Jake is straight. He's a… trumpeter." I laughed, startled. He was right; he was learning: I had literally never met a gay male trumpeter.

The house was huge and echoing with him gone for two days. Five minutes after getting home that Friday evening, I already couldn't believe I'd been able to survive in it alone in the early days and weeks after Joe's death. It was Joe whose absence filled the house for me now, not J.J.'s. I had a couple of quick abysmal drops, when for a minute or two my grief for Joe was as intense and agonizing as it had ever been. Then it would pass. It even occurred to me that I should start keeping a log of how often these moments came and how long they lasted. My theory was that they would be more widely spaced, and shorter, as time passed. Rooms, pieces of furniture, pictures, dishes, clothes, CDs, books: thousands of inanimate things recalled him. I could picture him everywhere. With Jimmy out of the house, I found Joe waiting for me around every corner.

That night, as I was about to turn out the last light in my room, I glanced at his picture on my bedside table. I had kept it by my bed for going on twenty-three years now. It was the first picture he had ever given me of himself, a beautiful professional print of his début shot as the Pennington Man. I had always been fascinated by it. It made him look almost unbelievably handsome, in black tie with his curls subdued into a slick glossy wave. He was glazed and waxed and filed to a perfection so splendid as to make him look conceited and impervious. I had complained at the time that the printing had normalized his eyes to an uninteresting blue, whereas in life they had always been like the view of Ireland from the air: twenty million colors, but all of them green. Yet, even with hundreds of pictures over the years that looked more like the Joe I loved, this had always been my favorite. I loved seeing his natural, unassuming good looks manipulated into a beauty which a perfect stranger would have to acknowledge, and which matched the beauty of his heart, which perhaps no one could see as I did. Almost in spite of the photographer's intentions, Joe's essential dreamy sweetness came through the honed enamel surface.

This night I looked at the picture and felt a deep ache of sorrow. It was as if someone had suggested I might get over Joe's death in time, perhaps find someone else, move on, love again, come eventually to think of Joe only once in a while with a fond nostalgic smile. Perhaps Joe could hear me considering this possibility.

"Oh Joe," I said out loud, in a whiny feeble voice I hated; "never, never, never." Then I turned the light out and lay down.

The next day I was surprised to get a text from Kevin. He asked if he could drop by. I texted back that he should come over after lunch. Even on a Saturday, I would never offer a guest a drink that early in the day, and it seemed best to keep our encounter sober and lighthearted.

When I opened the door, he was looking down the street, his hands in the pockets of his windbreaker. Spring was trying to come, but the day was still brisk and blustery. He seemed even shorter than usual out of doors, and slightly waifish, huddled as though storm-tossed. When he turned to me, though, with his smile alight and his eyes sparkling, I saw that he had no need of comfort.

It was very flattering to see how glad he was to see me.

"Godfather Jim!" I was standing on the threshold, one step higher than he was, and he reached up to hug me. His head rested below my ribs and my arms couldn't really go around him; I could only rest one hand between his shoulders and the other on his hair. Sensing even in this awkward clutch how exquisite a real embrace of his might be, I felt suddenly very, very sorry for J.J. He must miss Kevin terribly… his brash sunny company, but perhaps even more this vibrant physicality of his. Perhaps only he could have led Jimmy out of his chilly, apprehensive virginity.

"How bad is it?" he asked me once we had settled in the parlor with our steaming cups of tea. He hadn't asked me if I was mad at him; he knew without asking that I wasn't.

"We're devastated," I answered. "We cry, we think it's our fault, we think no one has ever felt this way." He smiled gently.

"We're very innocent," he murmured. "We're a child, really." Our eyes met. "It's almost an honor to be our first love." His expression became uncharacteristically tender for an instant. "God, he is so... lovely." This assessment made him sound vastly older than Jimmy himself, worldly, doting, but objective. He paused. "And so much *work*..."

"I know how lovely he is," I said quietly. "I also know he's lucky that his first love was so kind to him." I pondered the fairness of the question I wanted to ask, and then ventured it. "Are you seeing someone else?" He shook his fine head very quickly.

"No," he said. "I broke up with him for his sake. It's not that I wanted to move on; he's super-fun, and I..." (he hesitated, rightly unwilling to abuse the missing word) "... I really, really *like* him. I just didn't want him to have only one lover for his whole life." I thought of J.J.'s father, who had been faithful to Rachel almost since he started dating her as a brilliantly sexy and handsome boy of fifteen or sixteen. But Tony had been straight, and had never been even remotely spectrum-y. "And I knew he was never going to break up with me. There's probably some simple kid living on a farm somewhere, who will just get married as a virgin at seventeen and live with the same person forever. But not a composer; not a crazy dreamy guy like Jacob."

I thought of all the times I'd heard men claim to have broken someone's heart for his own sake; occasionally, that heart had been mine. Every time, I had wanted to massacre the guy who said it. The universe consisted of people who broke up with others and of those who got broken up with, and the former used this cowardly line to feel noble. Kevin's insight sprang from real affection. He shot me one canny, open-eyed look and said,

"You know, don't you?" Something in his voice made him suddenly a Grace Kelly character, or one of Henry James' forthright but tender young ladies. "You are the great love of Jacob's life."

"Of course I do," I said.

If we had been drinking, we would have toasted each other. We did something almost equivalent in the eye contact we exchanged over the rims of our teacups.

As he was leaving, I told him that I wouldn't tell Jimmy about his visit, but if Jimmy guessed, I wouldn't be able to deny it.

"Anyway," he said, breezy and sensible as always, "we'll all be friends in the long run."

Jimmy blew in the following evening. He looked big and strong and re-energized, and I could tell he had stories about Jake and their weekend with Jake's blue collar, deeply unmusical family. First, though, he stopped in the front hall, his eyes vague and fixed on nothing, his bag still looped over his shoulder.

"He was here," he said. His look to me was not at all accusing; Kevin had every right to be wherever he chose to be, and I could invite anyone I wanted.

"Yes," I said; "he texted me yesterday morning and he came over for tea in the afternoon." After a couple of beats, looking at his crestfallen face, I asked, "How did you know?" He shrugged.

"Maybe I smelled him. Something like that. I can feel him in the house." In the back of my mind, I thought that such sensitivity was proof that the attachment should not have ended. Perhaps I should text Kevin and tell him that, after all, he and Jimmy should make up; they were meant to be together. I could see in J.J.'s eyes that he was thinking the same thing. I put my arms out and we hugged. He was his shy self again, taking my hug stiffly.

"He wanted to know how you were holding up," I said. "He's extremely fond of you." He was completely immobile in my arms for one second.

"Big whoop," he said. I chuckled.

"I missed you this weekend. Welcome home," I said. When I released him, he kept one arm around my neck. I could never predict the terms of physical contact with him. I felt like one of those people who experimented with keeping panthers as pets.

Despite his evident misery about Kevin, he was excited about something. He fished a few pages out of his bag and went to the piano in the parlor. He had drafted some pages of a song cycle that weekend. It was to be six songs to poems of Petrarch. He seemed to be imagining a performance at which six singers would traipse onto the stage *seriatim*, each to perform one of his starry tunes with piano (or theorbo, or oboe…). But the third song was definitely for baritone – for me – and piano, and it was about half written.

"*Non più al suo amante/ Diana piacque,*" he had written. By Jimmy's standards, it was very tuneful; this had been happening more and more all year. Since August, he had listened to countless hours of my opera recordings, often to my running commentary, and I prided myself on his growing appreciation for tonal gestures and passages. Mozart was easy common ground for us, though he had never learned to share my love for *Rosenkavalier*, nor I his for *Lulu* and *Wozzeck*. It was enough for me that the rising scale at the climax of Ariadne's *"Es gibt ein Reich"* struck him as "perfection." In this Petrarch song, there were nods to neo-mediaevalism: open fifths, Picardy thirds, strumming syncopations, hemiolas, melismatic lines made of groups of two and three, scattered schleifers. I enjoyed the upward sweeping lines; they were flattering to my aging voice, yet gave a feeling of youthful, hopeful, not quite disenchanted love. For Diana naked and virginal at her bath, he had invented splashing, shrinking lines. The outraged frigid goddess was also the normal shy beloved, wanting to be loved, hating aggression, willing to be gently wooed under a clear sky. The poet, the intrusive hunter, violating the beloved's privacy simply by existing, stumbling into his own annihilation yet glorying in it, ready for any immolation… he had also caught Jimmy's attention. There were lines for him in the bass that were stalking and bumptious but not ungraceful. I leaned over Jimmy, my hands on his shoulders, to mark my way through a first reading of the first several lines of the song. I glanced down after a couple of minutes, and saw that there were tears on his face, soundless and unabashed.

One evening that month, Dino called me to say we should catch up. I asked him how he was doing and was surprised when he sighed a bit forlornly and said, "As well as could be expected, I guess. You understand that." I had been expecting him to ask how *I* was doing, and remembered just in time that his wife had recently left him.

"Any news?" I asked.

"Our divorce will be official in the next month or two," he said. He took a short pause and added, "I know you're getting over a lot of stuff too, these days, in a different way." We agreed on a date for dinner at my house the following week.

Jimmy was fascinated. I told him he couldn't stay for dinner: Dino had very private things to discuss with his old Italian prof. Jimmy agreed to pretend he had to go study at the library at Peabody if I let him stay for a glass of wine with Dino first.

When the doorbell rang, J.J. ran to open it. By the time I got near the front hall, I heard him saying,

"You must be Dino. I'm Jim's godson Jacob. He's told me all about you. I must have seen you at Uncle Joe's funeral." Dino looked a little disoriented. He knew who Jimmy was, but they hadn't formally met and he hadn't expected him to open the door. He found a vague reply to Jimmy's welcome, and as they shook hands, he looked over J.J.'s shoulder and seemed relieved to see me.

"Ciao, prof," he called. When we were close enough, he gave me one of his towering bear hugs.

He looked superb, with his greying hair glossy and his face burnished and shiny. His naturally athletic body exuded forcefulness through the short-sleeved business shirt and khakis he was wearing. He filled the pants very nicely, making me envy the lucky tailor who had perhaps measured him closely to make them exactly tight enough. His eyes were a bit dull, though; his divorce must be wearing him down.

We sat primly in the parlor with our glasses, a little platter of *crostini* on the coffee table before us. Dino and I were in club chairs while J.J. sprawled on the sofa with jutting knees and arms flung wide across its back.

"We were sorry to hear about your separation," J.J. said. His sympathy was a bit presumptuous, because he didn't know Dino at all, and his "we" implied something about him and me which wasn't true. Dino, guarded about showing his sadness to a stranger his son's age, nevertheless seemed to take J.J.'s words as they were meant.

"Thank you," he said, with a stiff nod. "It means a lot to get… your support." He had hesitated over "your," but his gesture included Jimmy.

"I just had a relationship end," Jimmy continued. "I know it's not easy. And of course, Jim is in mourning." I could never get control of any conversation in which J.J. took part. There was a young brontosaurus blundering through my parlor, and I could hope only to wrestle the most precious Fabergé out of its way amid the general crunching of heirlooms under foot.

"Jimmy," I attempted, "let's let Dino choose the topic. We don't need to talk about personal things if we don't all want to."

"No," Dino generously answered; "it's good to get all that out in the open. I appreciate your kind thoughts. And I'm sorry about your break-up, too, Jacob. We don't need to dwell on all that tonight." I had poured him a double shot of Jack Daniels. With these words, he tossed it back. I had been sipping on mine and was no more than a few drops into it. Without a word or look from me, J.J. got up, went to the kitchen, and brought back the bottle, replenishing Dino's shot. He was quietly humming a fast little rising scale for my benefit. It was one of his favorite opera tags: the infant Joan Sutherland sprinting up the scale in the "Bolero" from *Vespri Siciliani*, so laughingly carefree it was hard to imagine she hadn't tossed a champagne glass into the grate on the staccato high note at the top of *"in-e-e-e-e-e-e-e-e-bri-ò!"* He often sketched that scale as a way of proposing inebriations of our own: instead of saying, for instance, 'Time for a cocktail?' or 'Shall I open another bottle for the guests?' He was now helping me get Dino liquored up. I wasn't sure at what point in their seven- or eight-minute acquaintance he had decided that Dino was to be my next conquest and new love.

When he saw Dino pick up his glass again, he suddenly glanced at his iPhone and said,

"Wow, I had no idea how late it was. I have to meet my study group at the library in ten minutes, and it takes fifteen to get there." On his hurried way out the front door, after a bluff handshake with Dino, he lifted his eyebrows at me in secret encouragement.

Dino and I didn't speak of very personal things for most of the evening. I did notice that he kept his own wine glass full and seemed to be bracing himself for something. If I had worried at all about J.J.'s over-serving him, he made that scruple moot. Still, while cherishing the fact that he still nurtured an *amicizia particolare* for me after almost thirty years, I was in mourning. That may have made it easier for me to enjoy his unforced good looks. The years had softened the oddness of his high-bridged Neapolitan profile, and his recent disappointments had made him seem gentler and more introspective. He smiled tenderly when speaking of his children. I suggested that perhaps he should bring them by, so that I could get to know them better after all these years. Maybe I thought he would appreciate my help in parenting them, with their mother less in the picture. But in fact, they were grown now, out of the house and no more Dino's than hers.

"You seem to think that hanging out with their dad and his old friends is at the top of their list of fun things to do," he shrugged. I felt foolish for having proposed it.

"Well, I guess my main point is that I'm sorry that you and Kelsie have… come to the end of something. I mean, of course you'll always be a couple, in a way, dealing with the kids, and their kids, if and when, and…" My voice trailed off, and I just lifted my glass with a helpless gesture, to which he responded with a hang-dog clink of his own. "I *am* sorry," I finished, dully.

An hour or so later, we were seated on the sofa in the upstairs parlor. The deep blue walls glowed in lamplight, looking richer and sweeter than by daylight. I enjoyed being just a few feet away from Dino, both of us backed into our opposite corners, one leg up, almost facing each other. Our bent knees were far apart and our arms on the back of the sofa could not be expected to brush. Memories of seductions attempted in my pre-Joe years, sometimes prompted by a casual touch of fingertips in just this position, seemed very distant. We had small glasses of fierce white grappa in our hands, with the bottle on the table in front of us, and we were clearly on the verge of a mellow comradely talk about maturity, loss, and resilience.

"You've forgotten, probably," he suddenly said, "but I never have… that time years ago when you rubbed my ass in the kitchen of your old house…"

"If I ever forget that, may my tongue cleave to the roof of my mouth," I said. I smiled as if to suggest that it was a memory made completely chaste by the intervening years. He suddenly moved a foot or two closer, his nearer knee within inches of mine, his shoulders an easy reach for the thrown arm I still had not moved. I felt acutely inhibited, knowing that I might be a moment of two away from making an embarrassing pass. I had never consciously speculated on what Dino's broad shoulders might feel like to my hand. A scent was coming from him, a bare trace of some classy cologne he had applied hours before. He was relaxed and slack and companionable, in a heap of friendliness, close enough for anything. I could barely hear him breathing. He was evidently weighing something. To break the silence, I attempted, "So, really… how are you tracking since your separation? I'm sorry I've been selfish this year; I've lost track of other people's situations. But I *have* been thinking of you."

"I miss her," he said. "I don't like being single, and I'm not good at it. But I also have no interest in dating again." I made some kind of vague sympathetic hum.

"What do you miss most?" I asked, for all the world as though we would compare notes as recently bereft married men.

"Someone next to me in bed," he said.

"You mean the sex? I get that for sure," I replied. He chuckled but shook his head.

"No, I mean having someone there. Someone who knows me." Then he added, to be honest, "Someone I *thought* knew me, anyway; someone I *thought* I knew. When my lawyer calls me now to tell me what *her* lawyer says, I just think, 'Who is this woman? Who does she think *I* am?'"

"So it's been acrimonious," I said. "I'm sorry to hear that; I've always liked her. I hope things settle down in time. You can't be at loggerheads forever; you'll still be co-parenting…"

"Ah," he said – a sound like a quacking duck – "the kids don't need us anymore. They're grown. Yeah, Kelsie and I will see each other at holidays with them, or at their parties. Anyway it's over; it's not important."

"*You're* important, Dino," I said. "I'm sorry this hurts you. One of my friends told me recently I was lucky my lover died instead of leaving me. It's a different kind of sadness, and I think they both pretty much suck, frankly." Now it was his turn for the sympathetic nod of the head. "You'll get through this. Just keep being the greatest guy in the world. It's what you do; it's who you are."

I could have said these exact words to anyone in Dino's circumstances of whom I was fond. He could have looked like Danny de Vito's less sexy little brother and, if I'd liked him, my solidarity with his sorrow would have been identical. He hunched another inch closer to me. He sighed and then spoke; I could tell that he'd practiced what he would say.

"I was thinking we might consider… seeing a lot more of each other now. I mean, maybe private time. Do you know what I'm saying?" I nodded. "I would love to be with someone who really knows me, without all the craziness of romance and raising a family."

I reached just far enough to pat his shoulder, finally. It was soft and strong and rounded. I had been sure I was completely innocent of any seductive intention but now in an instant I was seriously considering marrying Dino. He smiled and leaned his face closer to mine.

"Men get each other," he said. "We wouldn't have all the second-guessing and weird misunderstandings. That's all that Kelsie and I fought about: Why didn't I remember her sister's birthday? or I said she looked great, but not the right way, or God knows what…" He paused. "You and I have always gotten along – no squabbles over stuff that doesn't matter; no sudden crying and stupid flare-ups. That would just feel so nice for once." Again, I nodded. But…

"You know, "Dino," I said, "there's an ancient Greek myth that after Orpheus lost his wife Euridice, he decided not to love women anymore because his heart was broken, and he turned to the love of men. I think that's what you're experiencing. Women are too much work for you; they bring up feelings that are too deep. You think being with a man would be easy."

"It would be," he said stubbornly. "Men understand each other. You and I like each other. That's all that matters."

"No," I said. I wanted to sound gentle but I was suddenly frustrated, almost angry with old fears that weren't really about Dino. "Men loving men is hard work. Two big male egos in one room. Two weirdly entitled humans duking it out."

"No, you'd always win," he said. "You're my prof. You'd tell me what's what."

"You say that, but No. Were you ever bullied in high school for being 'queer'? I was. 'Hey, McManus, queer! I'll meet you out in the *park*-ing lot!' Actually, they said, 'QUEE-uh' and '*PACK*-ing lot'… this was New England." He laughed, a bit scandalized. It was incredible to him that I had ever been spoken to with disrespect. He must have been a nice kid, innocent of that kind of brutality, and it had never obtruded on his notice. "And more than once, if the jocks or the auto shop kids cornered me and

192

taunted me that way, there would be some math teacher walking by who made eye contact with me but decided not to risk his tenuous authority to break up this Darwinian scene. Eventually I grew up to be a fancy college professor, and they can all blow *me* as far as I'm concerned, but that's my history. *That's* what gay means to me. I don't think you're there."

There was a long silence. I knew that I'd said way too much; he was probably grossed out and thrown off. Instead, he lurched suddenly to his left, twisted to face me, and fell in a swooning hug across my chest.

He was very heavy against me, a big warm bundle of confusion. I put my arms around him, amazed at how massive he was. He kept his eyes closed, too nervous to look at me. His face was turned up to me at an uncomfortable angle.

"Maybe I just want someone to hold me," he said quietly. He sounded more than a little drunk, and his words were banal, though I gave him credit for what this hug must cost him. I was deeply fond of him, deeply touched. The contours of his back, sharp to my hands, let me almost imagine what it might be like to take him to bed. He took my right hand by the wrist to guide it down his back and past his belt. "Feel familiar?" he asked, smiling slightly without opening his eyes. After twenty or so years, it actually felt a bit different from how I remembered it. His pants weren't as tight as the jeans he'd worn in his twenties, and his muscles had also softened with time. Nevertheless, it was nice to stroke him and to feel so cozy. He gave a soft sigh of contentment. I pulled his head back and kissed his forehead, the strong bridge of his nose, his closed right eye, his cheek.

As my lips approached his, he put his tongue out, just the tip, so much like a sunning cat that I almost laughed. He was a straight guy trying to imagine how to kiss another man, thinking that a little tongue might be hot, or even just polite. I felt this tip of rigid tongue barely slip between my pursed lips, and felt too the way his mouth didn't open.

I was not very disappointed, much less humiliated, by his slight recoil. Yes, for an instant when he flopped onto me, I had imagined what life might be like if, after all, Dino had been waiting in the wings for me all these years. But he would have had to want, truly, in his nerve endings, at least sometimes, to kiss me as lovers kiss, and we had just seen clearly that, in practice, he didn't.

"Dino," I said, "it is incredibly sweet that you would ask me to hold you. I will hold you anywhere, any time. I'm thinking maybe this isn't the kind of closeness we're meant to have. I don't think this is really who you are." He sighed again; this time, it was a heavy sigh, full of sober acknowledgement. I could feel him tense physically as if he were trying to sit back up, but he couldn't quite, yet. His sprawled arms reached gracelessly around me and he just mumbled,

"Give me one more hug." As I did, he continued to lie across me, savoring a last moment of hope. "No man in the world has ever given me half as much as you have. I've idolized you since I was eighteen. I guess I just thought…" His voice trailed off. Then he shook himself, rallying, and said, "Maybe I'm just afraid to date again. What woman is going to want…"

"The right one will," I said, shaking him slightly. By now, he was alert enough to bestir himself and resume the vertical. The air on my chest felt frigid with his big frame off me. "And I'm not going anywhere. You didn't want to kiss me just now…"

"No," he insisted; "I *wanted* to. I like you that much. It's just not what I'm used to."

"And to be frank," I said, "when you put my hand on your ass, you were suggesting something else I don't think you're used to, or would want to get used to…" He looked confused, not with me, but with himself.

"That's true," he nodded. "The patting feels good, but the… next steps are hard for me to picture. I just wanted to be good to you; to be close in a way that would feel real to you." He didn't sound drunk anymore. "You never know, right? Maybe we'll both feel different in six months."

"You could have found a new lady by then," I said.

"Or I could have talked you into teaching me the next steps," he answered. The flirtation involved in that sounded purely theoretical. Maybe he was relieved that nothing had come of his rough huddle into my arms. He wrapped his left arm around my shoulder. "This feels nice; this is Dino and the *prof.*"

After a gentle lull, I said, "Are you OK to drive home? You're perfectly welcome to stay here. There's a guest room, or you could crash with me. If you just need someone to hold you."

194

"I think you've held me enough for tonight, at least," he said. "This is what I needed. My head is totally clear now."

At the front door, he leaned down and gave me a little kiss on the lips, no tongue tip, no shrinking.

"This was perfect, *prof*," he said. And again, "This was what I needed." I wasn't sure if I'd had anything *I* needed, though I did feel very attached to this affectionate, confused, and hurting man. He put his hands on my shoulders and leaned back to look directly into my eyes. "I'm going to call you next week," he said; "I want us to get together a lot more often now."

As I stood on the front stoop, waving as he drove away, I noticed Jimmy rounding the far corner of the street on his walk home from Peabody. He glanced at me, and at Dino's retreating car, and shot me a quizzical look: What just happened? As he came up the steps, I smiled and said,

"It's not going to be Dino. And we love each other. Welcome home."

Yes, Joe was good at a number of things. Yes, he was famous at first for those cologne ads in the magazines. Yes, he was a very successful model, just the right amount of handsome; there had even been focus groups, apparently, to determine if both gay men and straight women would find him attractive as a spokesman or model, and he had hit the very narrow target of appealing to both those demographics without straight men finding him suspiciously good-looking. The wild pop tenor one heard at coffee houses and open-mic nights at clubs around town: yes, that was Joe – my own Linda Ronstadt, I sometimes called him, his voice dense and focused and belty like hers. There had even been that time when he dragged me onto the stage to sing a Karaoke duet with him of "More Than Words," a song I almost knew from hearing it dozens of times on his party tapes. Counting on me to feel my way into the second part while he torched the melody, he had earned me one of the most resounding ovations I had ever received in a gay bar. And of course there was his acting. Yes, Joe was a very talented guy.

But I often thought his very greatest talent was simply sleeping next to me. Sometimes I just wanted somebody there making a warm hollow in the bed, muttering occasionally in that deep touching mystical language of dreams, looking suddenly worried or sentimental for a moment, just barely smiling at a pat on his arm or a tug to his curls: Joe was great at all that. He slept more than I did. Over the years I logged a fair number of hours watching him sleep. My grandmother used to say, "I don't think young people are ever 'slept out,'" and I watched Joe with some of her tolerance for youth and its manic energies and exhaustions, though Joe was only seven years younger than me, never a kid at all, really. He was likely to accuse me of being condescending if I said he was cute: telling him he looked like a little boy when he slept provoked a butch frown and/or a punch to the upper arm. When I found myself unable to resist pulling him closer, reaching around to scratch his chest hair, licking the back of his neck, I was always careful to keep my voice low and manly. If he was near enough to the surface he would murmur "Jim" or "Tiger" and hunch back against me; otherwise, just a hum of recognition and a – hard to describe – a slight turning-up of the thermostat: his body's way of saying it had noticed my presence was just to make itself a tiny bit warmer. And where was his mind at such times? I think it was onstage somewhere, some shrill tawdry showbiz venue where the audience screamed and waved lighters in the air; or a soap opera sound stage where starlets pouted and flounced, or a fashion shoot on an island with jazzy beachwear and palms and poses across the hoods and fenders of boxy RVs. Joe's mind, while his humpy body warmed me in Baltimore, was always off somewhere being famous. Because, deep down inside, my Joe always knew he was a very big star.

He had tuned in to one of his top-40 radio stations and was amusing himself by singing along while I drove. He worked it fairly hard, putting on a little show for me, checking with smug sidelong glances to be sure that I was noticing. He rapped on the dashboard, brandished an invisible microphone, cocked his head, pointed at unseen fans and winked when they swooned and shrieked, and made odd hot motions with his arms and shoulders to sketch in the dance he would have been doing if he had room. I was in a good mood, and I smiled. Part of me would have been bitterly disappointed if these little acts ever stopped.

It was late afternoon, and the summer heat was at its thickest. We had the windows rolled up and the AC on. When we stopped at a red light, a sporty little red car pulled up next to us on the left. The driver was a young woman. She was alone; her windows were up too. She was pretty: long frizzy blond hair, a blouse with big ruffles, some flashy jewelry. She looked like one of those feisty chain-smoking girls from East Baltimore who worked as office managers, good-natured and competent enough to stand with arms akimbo and order people around and call them "Hon" and still be popular. If they ever made a TV movie about this woman's life they would have to get Reba McEntire to play her, in her classy-but-tough lady-clothes, because this woman, mind you, was a success, and she was not cheap.

She was singing along with the radio too, beating the rhythm on the steering wheel and tossing her head to flick her long hair off her face. I took a long moment to look at her before I noticed that she was nodding in time to the same song as Joe.

"Hey, Divo," I said, "look." I nodded my head at her car and he saw what I meant.

"Hey!" he said. He reached over my arm and tooted our horn. The young woman turned towards us. She was preparing to do a 'Back-off!' thing if we were clueless whistlers. Joe grinned at her and put one fist in the air, mouthing the words broadly so that she could see what he was singing. She smiled and did a big shimmy from the shoulders, arms out, in time with the song. Glancing ahead to be sure the light was still red, she sang the next line, marking the beats with big nods of the head in Joe's direction. The light turned green and she gave an unexpectedly dainty lady-like wave before pulling out with a short sharp screech of tires.

"That was fun," Joe said.

A day or two later, Joe came home from running errands. I was reading something, perched on a stool in the kitchen space at the back of the ground floor of our house.

"Hal says Hi," he said. Hal was the minister at my church.

"You saw Hal?"

"Yeah," he said. "I went by the church after the hardware store. I was in the neighborhood anyway."

"So you... just went by? To talk?" I asked.

"Yeah." I was a little unsure what my reaction to his calling on Hal was supposed to be. Joe went to church with me sometimes, and he liked my church friends for the most part, but it had usually stopped there. Maybe this sudden visit to my pastor meant that he was facing some kind of spiritual crisis; maybe I should have picked up on that. Joe was fidgeting, waiting. I was supposed to say something supportive and wise.

"Anything you want to tell me about?" I asked, touching his elbow. I hoped my smile was plain and sincere enough.

"Mmm," he said. He wasn't sure. "Maybe." He reached into the refrigerator and poured himself a glass of ice tea. I stepped out onto the patio and picked a sprig of mint. I came back into the kitchen, clapped the mint once between my palms, and put it in his glass. "Thanks," he said. He chewed a leaf for a second and then kissed me. He started walking back towards the front door, into the living room area. Pausing with his back to me, he said, "You."

I stood by myself for a moment, wondering what he meant. Then I followed him.

"You talked to Hal about me?" I said. He had just sat on the sofa. He kicked his moccasins off and put his feet up on the coffee table. He reached for a magazine, and made a face when he saw that the only one on the table was *The Nation*.

"Yeah," he said.

"'Yeah,'" I said. "'Yeah, yeah.' Stop saying 'Yeah.'" I was standing over him at the end of the sofa. Finally he looked up at me and laughed.

"OK," he said. "Come sit here." I went and sat next to him and he put his arm around my shoulder. This always made me feel as if he were older than me, because he was bigger and stronger.

"I told him I thought maybe we should get married," he said.

"What?"

"A Holy Union," he said. "Like you were talking about a while back." I'd told him about the union service for a lesbian couple that had taken place at the church one weekend he was out of town, but I'd never suggested we have one of our own. He had always been very sensitive about getting too engulfed in my life in Baltimore, having given up much of his own in Los Angeles for my sake.

"I wasn't thinking of you and me," I said. "I mean, I wasn't dropping a hint."

"You weren't?" He sounded a little put out, as if I'd said I didn't care.

"Well... the church isn't really your thing, is it? I mean, a Holy Union only makes sense if you're both really invested in the community."

"You know I like the Jensens, Mrs. Baldwin... I always like to hear what Hal has to say." I nodded. Bob and Luellen Jensen had had us over for dinner just a few weeks before, and Joe had yakked for days about how much he liked them. Every time he attended services with me he made a point of being charming to Lydia Baldwin, the flinty, tender-hearted president of the Presbyterian Women. He'd also commented several times on Hal's sermons, saying more than once that Hal spoke "good common sense," a big compliment for Joe: like saying someone was "real genuine," which, come to think of it, he'd also said about Hal. But his sudden interest in church life seemed unmotivated to me; I had a slight suspicion I was being managed.

"Don't you think we should talk about it together before you talk about it with Hal?" I asked.

"That's just what he said," Joe answered. "So we're talking." I didn't say anything for a moment. Then I ventured:

"To me, it would imply something about other parts of our lives. Like, would you want to be a church member, and go to these New Age Bible studies or serve breakfast with the homeless program..."

"That's not what you mean," he said. "I could do all that." He snapped his fingers, showing me how easily he could pick up a liberal syncretist Christian lifestyle.

"So what do I mean?" I asked submissively. When Joe decided to read beads, it was generally best just to brace myself and let the tsunami wash over me before I tried to reply. He was smiling, but his eyes were a little furtive.

"You're not sure how you feel about me," he said casually.

"Joe!" I was surprised. I thought I was very good at making him feel adored. He knew how long I'd waited for someone to come along; he'd seen me cry: the whole thing. "Those long nights of burning kisses haven't convinced you?"

It was a misfire. He waved one hand, as if to swat away a stubborn gnat. He thought I was giving him a line. Even after three years, I forgot at times that Joe didn't take men's wanting him very seriously. "That," he'd once said, "is just natural." I put my head on his shoulder. I'd never been sure how to handle this one. Joe ought to know how I felt. I'd paid a lot of dues, courting him, learning about him, being patient, opening myself up. Of course I wanted him too. Only someone with Joe's very rich past could find it insulting to have men attracted to him; personally, I never tired of it.

"I wuv you," I said. "You know that." He patted my shoulder and said,

"Yeah yeah." He took his arm off me and hunched forward to get up. I patted his back while he was still seated.

"I'm glad you talked to Hal," I said. "I'm glad you felt like you could." He looked back at me over his shoulder and made a smirk; apparently this didn't sound like affirmation to him. "And I'm excited about this Holy Union idea. It's a lot to think about." I knew what he wanted: he wanted me to scream with joy and clap my hands like a girl in a Fifties movie. He drained the tea out of his glass with a funny gulping noise.

"Yeah," he nodded. He slipped his shoes back on and snapped his fingers for the dog. "C'm'ere, Pooch," he said. *Dai, Andreuccio, cammina.*

"Actually I just took him out," I said. "Just before you got home."

"Like he gets tired of this, right?" he said. He had a point: though Ootch was getting older, he still found the energy now to do his little dance by the door, bowing and sidling and saying "Roo" as if he hadn't been out for six weeks. Joe slipped the collar over his head, and they headed out to Patterson Park a few blocks away.

They were gone quite a while. My churning thoughts read that as Joe's sulking, staying away on purpose to show that he'd noticed my tepid response to his generous suggestion.

Joe was always the spontaneous, sensually attuned one, the one who had infinite options and might leave me at any moment. I was the crabby scowling self-protective neurasthenic. I thought about what he'd said. I thought about how shy he'd been, his attempts to be casual about a conversation with Hal which had clearly been a stretch for him. He got points for that. Mostly, though, my mind stalled on one image: Joe and Ootch, killing time in the Park to let me think. They must be circling the pond and the Pagoda by now, taking an unnecessary turn down to Eastern Avenue, perhaps even visiting the construction site of the Ukrainian Catholic church, with its domes sitting on pallets like giant wooden mushrooms, waiting to be gilded and swung up into position. Ootch of course would be having a marvelous time. My mind couldn't rid itself of one idea: that Joe was taking time with my ridiculous old hound, giving him the long walk that I somehow found ways always to be too busy to give him, and surely thinking of me as he offered this gentle courtesy to a funny sentient being who was very dear to me – who, in some 'Love me, love my dog' way, *was* me. There was a decency and a faithfulness in the two of them together which shamed me.

I was one instant from grabbing my keys and running up Baltimore Street to find them when I heard the front door open again. Ootch ran up to me as soon as Joe had unfastened his leash. He was wagging and smiling, eager to tell me all the smells of the Park, the outrages committed by impervious cats, the absorbing tales of fugitive squirrels, the rancid remnants of crab feasts scattered on the grass and dating back several days, in which Joe hadn't let him wallow. Joe smiled at me tentatively without meeting my eye.

I felt tears in my own eyes without knowing quite why. I reached my arms out to him, straight in front of me, like a bad actress doing lyrical Chekov, and he let me hug him, ducking his head to my shoulder.

"I've missed you," I said. "Promise never to be gone for so long again." He looked up at me, smiling uncertainly, to be sure of what I was saying. "Yes, of course," I said. "Yes, always."

"You have never once known how happy you were, right away," he said. "You always take a while to be happy."

"I am such a drag," I admitted. "Will you marry me anyway?"

Typically, Joe liked to have the last word. Our pattern was always that I would say something overbred and over-subtle, and he would come back with some chthonic Zorba-esque rejoinder, after which we would make out, sometimes on the floor. This time, though, he said nothing. He was very tender and gentle in my arms, like an African violet or an Easter lily, something lovely and delicate which might shiver to pieces if the temperature dropped even one degree. I waited for him to phonate, but no sound came, and I realized with incredulity that he couldn't speak.

I looked down, lifted his chin to see his face. This was an unusual collapse in him that made him shorter than me for this one embrace. I saw that he was crying.

"Oh," I said, and kissed him… or he kissed me, it didn't matter which.

Hal was was proud of his standing as the most progressive Presbyterian minister in town. The AIDS epidemic and gay/lesbian rights were the issues that had defined the latter years of his pastorate, as civil rights had stamped his youth. He had guided me through the disillusionments of my search for love. When life sent me Joe, the least likely and most perfect possible partner for me, I was at first half-apologetic in describing him to Hal.

"We have almost nothing in common," I said, assuming that a straight man a generation older than me would find our union unsuitable. "He's unchurched; he's not intellectual and it's not clear what kind of career he wants or could be good at. I'm not sure what my friends will make of him."

"Jim," Hal had said, almost sternly, "none of that matters. Is he good to you? Do *you* love and respect *him*? That is all that your real friends will care about." I realized now that he had been more than prepared for Joe's unannounced visit to his office. This was why, more than once over the years, my mother had said to me, "I'm glad you've got Hal in your corner."

By the time we were actually planning our Holy Union, Mom was Joe's biggest fan. Her kidney cancer diagnosis had given urgency to her loyalties. She wanted to know that there was someone for me before she left. She knew that I'd always been afraid Joe would tire of me sooner or later. But by now, Joe had met my terms, doggedly attended adult discussion groups and exerted his irresistible charm on the doughty *grandes dames* of the congregation, and they had all ganged up on me and we were going through with it.

Mom and Connie put a fair amount of Gay Nineties energy into synchronizing their participation. The Andreolis had my family badly outnumbered: on the McManus side of the church, there would be only Mom, my sister, her husband, and their son. Connie decided that Mom should sit on the aisle in one front pew, with Connie herself directly opposite; Dominic and their clan would fill in the rest of that side of the front pew and the two behind it. The placement of the two mothers, Connie said, would allow her and Mom to reach across to hold hands if things got emotional. Fond as they were of each other, I thought it very unlikely that my mother would need this support. Mom suggested a color scheme for their dresses, maybe fearing that Connie would choose something too tropical. They were elaborately co-conspiratorial on the catering and flowers, though Joe insisted on simplicity and economy and refused to let any parents foot any bills.

Well, *that* was a service. My favorite Peabody student tenor sang Mendelssohn's "If with all your hearts" just before the processional. Then the Choir, of which I was normally a member, sang Parry's "I was glad" as Joe and I walked up the aisle, hand in hand, last in a parade that featured my sister, Tony and Rachel, the cutest of Joe's toddler nieces and nephews, and, walking just before us, Walter as my best man and Ricardo as Joe's. They were carrying our rings, purchased that summer on the Ponte Vecchio in Florence, where we also got narrow matching bands to dedicate to the Madonna of the Vow in the cathedral of Siena (we hadn't disabused the priest on duty there of his assumption that we were brothers giving thanks for a marriage in our extended family). I heard Walter hum in admiration as the sopranos in the Choir rose to a vault-filling B-flat in the final cadence of the Parry. Later, before the vows, two of Joe's show-biz friends down from New York sang a fearlessly belty duet version of "Make Our Garden Grow" from *Candide*. Then the pop soprano in her flaring sequined red-carpet gown melted everyone's hearts with a tender, introspective, still-brassy "Build My House" from *Peter Pan*. When she changed to "*our* house" on the repeat, I could feel myself get misty. She ended on a big high F for the word "love," which I would have attempted to float, but she Ethel Merman-ed it as though building a house only of love were an act of will, courage, and defiance, as was surely true.

The church was nicely full of everyone from the Presbyterian Women, austerely festive in their shoulder-padded cocktail dresses, to the Country-Western gay bar crowd, rattling with turquoise and pewter trim here and there. Hal preached something about the *Song of Songs,* David and Jonathan, Ruth and Naomi, and human love as a living image of God's love for humanity. The church had gathered in force to support us by putting on its very swankest, happiest show.

Everything was going smoothly till our vows. I had an unbidden flash-back to the TV show *Rhoda* from my college days, when the heroine was late to her own wedding and then, flustered but triumphant, through her tears, vowed to her groom Joe, "Joe... ya know?" The self-conscious originality of that line had sounded a bit off to my late-adolescent brain, but it came back to me now and interfered with the poetic vow I had written and memorized to surprise my own Joe with. Hal prompted me, and I limped through my little speech. Joe squeezed my hands and smiled. It was his turn.

"Jim," he said, "Tiger... all I can swear – all I can promise you – is... *te vojo bene assai.*" I heard Connie in the front pew let out a soft, sweet wail, and without looking I could tell that she had turned her streaming face to Dominic's shoulder. Within instants, there were audible whimpers coming from the Andreolis' three packed pews. To my breathless astonishment, I saw in my peripheral vision that Mom had sprung from her seat and crossed the aisle to put her arm around Connie as well; Connie groped with her right hand to stroke Mom's cheek.

Joe's eyes flickered but didn't turn from mine. Suddenly he was weeping. He laughed and shook his head, hating himself. I threw my arms around him and a collective "Aw" went up from the congregation. No one minded; they thought we were darling. I had hoped that the whole thing would be dignified, manly, classy, spiritual. Maybe we would show straight people how it should be done. But it became just an adorable gay mess for a few moments. People were smiling through clouded eyes, hugging strangers, laughing out loud and clapping indulgently. A few minutes later, rings in place and slippery salty kiss out of the way, we and the members of the procession turned to face the choir loft and listened to a stunning Mozart *"Alleluia"* tossed off by our Choir diva. She blew us both a kiss at the conclusion and curtseyed deeply to the people gathered below, who had burst into applause at her crowning high C. Then, to a rollicking *bourée* from the "Water Music," we all ran down the aisle, Joe and I dodging the roses pelted down on us by the Choir, and around the corner to the church hall. There, various kinds of deplorable music encouraged dancing, and incredible amounts of pizza, beer, and cheap champagne made for a very long, crowded, hilarious, diverse, un-Presbyterian evening.

No ardent virgins, kept strictly sequestered by social-climbing parents in mediaeval Tuscany till after their nuptial Mass, could possibly have had a sweeter, tenderer, wilder wedding night than Joe and I did when we eventually staggered home. The broad flat gold bands on our enlaced fingers as we settled into each other's arms were astonishingly erotic to me. Our sex life had been intense from our very first shared night at Rehoboth, but the Union had sprinkled some sort of holy water on our bed. To be with Joe that night, to be wrapped in his strong submitting arms, to supplicate at the gates of his shrine and kiss the altar in an ecstasy of gratitude on admittance, was a kind of complete Edenic mutual interpenetration which made us wonder, stammering, how we could ever have felt close before.

Chapter 11
May, 2016
[flashback: 1995]

Andy Ferrara texted me in early May to ask if he could sleep over the following week. That would be the last week of classes, and the night he was proposing was clear for me. I mentioned it to Jimmy and got the predictable eye-roll.

"You've been sleeping with someone you love for years now," he said, sententiously. "Including this past year." Apparently his own scattered nights next to me and my decades of sleeping with Joe established a pattern on which Andy had no business intruding.

He did not have the option of staying at Kevin's now. It was awkward to know he would be a hundred feet away when Andy shared my bed. He cringed at the thought of what might happen between a beauty for hire and me under a roof that felt like home to him now. I felt defiant; he had no right to judge me, and I was entitled to my own consolations. I congratulated myself on not telling him out loud to stop being an arrogant young pup.

A couple of days later, well before Andy's visit, I came down to the kitchen one morning and found him already hunched over a cup of coffee. He looked up at me and did a double-take.

"Wo," he said.

"What?" I asked, totally blank.

"I just haven't seen you wear anything that bright since…" His voice trailed off, because he meant, 'since before Joe died.' It hadn't even occurred to me as I was dressing, but he was right. It might have been just the bright spring air breathing through the house, but my hands had picked a red and white pinstripe shirt and a stiff silk tie, a bright blue with large red polka dots. My blazer was slick blue cotton. It was a change from the drab tones I'd been wearing for months, and I hadn't noticed.

"Mmm," I said. "I think I've been missing this tie; that's all." I would have to call Connie in the next few days. She would be fascinated to hear that I had put on a bright tie. We were still weeks short of her personal deadline for laying aside her mourning.

Then Jimmy Jack brought up a new distraction of his own.

"I'm all excited," he said, sounding nervous and flat at the same time.

"About what?"

"I'm meeting my new friend David to study for our exam." He stirred his coffee more firmly than necessary.

"That will be nice." I was vague and distracted as I looked for the milk in the refrigerator and then realized he already had it out.

"David is smarter than me," he added.

"David… *oh,* your new friend David," I said, snapping back into focus. "Who's David?" I realized he had mentioned him twice while I was pottering.

"Just some guy," he said. There was a blush implied in his tone of voice.

"I don't believe you," I said. He glanced up at me, all cagey innocence. Then he looked down to slurp his coffee.

"He's in my Advanced Theory class," he said. "He's about my height, I think." J.J.'s first comments about Kevin, I remembered, had been to say that he was "crazy-smart," and that he was a little guy.

"If he comes back here to study with you later," I said, "you can ask him to stay to dinner. Or any day, actually. Well, not Thursday; you know that's Choir."

"OK," he said, with studied indifference. "He may be coming over next Wednesday." That was the night Andy was penciled in for, as Jimmy knew full well. Andy's final friend *du jour* was to take him to the Prime Rib for an early supper after their session, and then he would call a Lyft to come to my place. I hoped that David, if he came, would have left by the time Andy arrived.

David did come by for dinner on Wednesday, and Andy did show up in time for dessert. David was as smart as Jimmy had warned me. He was also, as advertised, around Jimmy's height. It took me more than a moment to adjust to that visual: I had gotten used to a ginger Ewok darting around Jimmy's knees, and it was startling to see instead a stiff nerdy Marine rearing up next to him, shoulder to shoulder. Not handsome at all, he was still attractive. He was gravely respectful and had an odd ramrod posture; he projected a righteous and stolid reliability. His hair was pale blond, worn in a military buzz cut. His rumpled shirt and chinos hung loosely on a taut, lengthy frame: a harsh Calvinist pioneer. He was a young man you would trust with a rifle when menaced by a hungry bear. "Jacob thinks the world of you, you know," he had said with studied correctness, as though I might *not* know.

Jimmy didn't seem to be smitten, exactly, but his eyes followed David. David had a tendency to pontificate, to condescend. I didn't mind his pompousness for myself; he was so obviously trying to be grown up. I liked it less that he corrected J.J. on a couple of points of uninteresting objective fact. He seemed to see J.J. as cute and young and uninformed. I was fully aware of J.J.'s social limitations, but I wasn't a bit ready to cast him as the bimbo in any relationship. David's quiet curtness made me wonder if he would be a success in the classroom if he ever became a theory teacher, as would be normal with the qualifications he was acquiring. Clearly, though, he thought his career path would be to get a Congressional Medal or McArthur Grant in music theory and never have to get a job. His wide square shoulders and manly jaw made me fear he would go through life sure that he was the smartest person he knew; his imperious chin, more and more as the evening wore on, suggested to me that he considered himself wiser, manlier – better – than Jimmy. Jimmy was just enough of a fool to fall for that.

When I started to clear the table and bring out the cordial glasses and chocolates, I prompted Jimmy to play something for David. They drifted into the parlor and I heard J.J. strike a few of his lyrical dissonances. Backing through the swinging door into the kitchen, I just heard David say,

"Yes… but don't you think a B-flat? See what that does?" My piano gave up a surprising major chord, unexpected in the context of the phrase J.J. had been sketching. J.J. made a slight hum of assent. Every single knuckle of his fingers understood exactly what David was suggesting, but it was not where he had been headed. The piano and I both thought it was a step too far. Some jangling followed, which became fainter as I ran the stack of plates under warm water in the sink.

As I came back into the parlor, the doorbell rang. I didn't know how much Jimmy might have told David about Andy, but the disapproval in his own face was heavy.

Andy came through the front door and kissed me before he noticed that we weren't alone. Glancing to his left into the parlor, he saw Jimmy at the keyboard and David standing sentinel behind him.

"Hey, guys," he said, passing through the door and extending a shining hand. He looked at Jimmy, still seated before the keyboard, and said, "You must be the godson. Jim talks about you all the time." I wasn't aware of having said all that much to him about J.J., who shook his hand politely but remained cool.

"You must be the professional beauty," he said. This Cukor retort impressed me. Andy was not stung.

"Oh, 'beauty...' at *my* age..." he said, smiling modestly. David apparently thought J.J. needed rescuing.

"I'm David, a friend of Jacob's," he said, holding a hand out stiffly. There was a charged moment when they seemed to be rivals for Jimmy, mastodons about to duel. But Andy then instead came back to stand by me, and put one arm around my shoulder. So as not to seem inhospitable or antisocial, I put one of mine around his waist.

"Let's go back to the table," I suggested. "We were just about to have dessert. I've set out some fruit and chocolates. Andy, can I make you a drink?" As J.J. and David resumed their places in the dining room, Andy followed me into the kitchen and I poured him a couple of fingers of Scotch. He was bluff and friendly, standing very close to me, making quick small talk about his day. Seeing I was anxious to get back to the table, he leaned in for one moment to whisper,

"Your little godson is quite impressive, even if he hates me. David seems like kind of a jerk, no?"

"Jury's still out," I whispered back, moving towards the door. "Jimmy doesn't hate you; he thinks it's too soon for me to have new... friends." Andy reached to take my hand and pull me back gently, just long enough to give me a light kiss.

"He's right," he murmured. "But I like you enough to rush you a little." I looked for an instant into his pale hazel eyes, for a clue as to what he could possibly mean by that. He was straight, a high-class hustler, half my age, and vastly out of my league. We were just out of sight of the two in the dining room. I reached around him and pulled him in.

"You're sweet to say that," I breathed. I wasn't ready for the little nibble he took on my lower lip, and the shy giggle, full of erotic promise, with which he said,

"I've missed you."

Then he turned me around and, with a little fond jab to the small of my back, showed that we could now rejoin Jimmy and David.

As we came into the room, the two of them were exchanging whispered remarks as furtive as ours had been. I wondered if there was some dawning intimacy. David seemed to pride himself on his own politeness; his slight condescension might be meant as courtly. Andy asked Jimmy about classical music. He said he'd enjoyed hearing Jimmy improvise while he was waiting on the stoop for me to answer the doorbell, and that he'd been impressed by his "chops." I knew that whatever Andy had heard from the front steps represented about 5% of J.J.'s capacity.

"If you're lucky," I said to him, "Jimmy will play you Hoboken XVI": a flashy Haydn sonata which J.J. could knock out with absolute metronomic accuracy in a way that always quickened my pulse. Andy gave a very convincing impression of a man who had the slightest idea what I was talking about. Jimmy, however, just gave a squirming shrug.

"Actually, G.J.," he said to me, "David and I should probably head out. We have some serious studying to do and his place will be quieter." He and David exchanged a glance which was not at all passionate; then he turned back to me and said, evenly, "I've got my key. I may crash with David if it gets late." His eyes were entirely for me as he spoke. There was no sidelong promise or entreaty to David. He did not look especially happy.

"…OK," I said, a bit confused. "Or text me if…" My voice tapered off. He wouldn't need anything. He was perfectly safe and had as much access as he wanted to my house and my concern. His sulky tone implied that, by even having an overnight guest, I was expelling him from Eden. Andy looked at me across the table, as though Jimmy were our child and I, the stern, clueless father, had to be signaled to give him his space or let him make his own mistakes.

Jimmy and David were gone within five minutes. Jimmy didn't hug me good-bye; David, unexpectedly, did. I had a disoriented feeling that perhaps, even though I wasn't sure I even liked him, he and I were close allies in an unspoken pact to protect Jimmy.

"Take care of our boy here," I murmured to him during the moment our faces were close and no one could hear. As we pulled back, he resumed his rigid erectness and answered me, smiling, clarion-voiced,

"Of course I will." He might as well have posted something on Facebook about my having commissioned him to look after J.J. I could see Jimmy's embarrassed, furtive irritation as he slipped out the door. David gave me a knowing salute before following him.

My mind was completely absorbed in their departure when I turned back into the empty house – empty except for Andy – and tried to give an insouciant grin of dismissal, as though Andy and I had had to postpone our real hello until the young men left. He had his arms crossed on his superb chest, half porn star, half Zen master. He looked at me with an exasperating ancient wisdom, as though he were about to tease an enigmatic truth out of me and make me feel foolishly oblivious to my own real feelings. Though I could see kindness in his eyes, I already bridled at whatever claptrap he was about to unload on me.

"You love him so much," he said, nodding indulgently. "He's your son." I made some helpless gesture, as if I didn't want to talk about Jimmy Jack. He persisted. "But not like most sons. He's jealous of me. He hates the idea of your having sex with anyone, and especially with me."

"Jimmy hates the idea of anyone having sex with anyone," I said.

"That's not the point," he said, patiently explaining me to myself. "He doesn't want to be your boyfriend, but he wants to be your first priority, always." I felt a petty irritation that he, a near stranger, was exactly right about Jimmy and me.

He had the advantage of being compellingly attractive. One was almost forced to want him. To feel myself roused to respond to his bodily presence was like seeing a very elderly friend stand at a wedding banquet and execute a creditable tango, to the fond applause of younger relations. Once we were both undressed and under the light covers, with a cool enough breeze coming through the open windows that it was pleasant to feel each other's warmth in the bed, he came to me as Diana to Endymion, a divine beauty bestowing himself on an inert mortal. The mightiness of his embrace masked a deep, premeditated surrender: somehow, he was determined to belong to me and to seek shelter with me.

Bitter experience, as recently as my last date with Dino, had taught me that a slight shuddering recoil from kissing was the emblem of irremediable straightness, even in men who sincerely thought they might like to have sex with me. Andy somehow, by shy weak pecks and nibbles, let me know that I was to press him, to pry his mouth open, to occupy him like a conquered territory. His kiss became submissive and passionate at the same time. I had seen several of his videos, but I had never seen him take evident pleasure in another man's kiss. My role apparently was to make him accept and then, in short time, welcome this final breaching of thresholds and prohibitions. The kiss became complete and convincing.

In those long minutes of embrace in the darkened room, I wondered if this might actually be the start of an unconventional new attachment. If I began to introduce Andy to neighbors as a new partner, it would take Bolton Hill about seven minutes to be abuzz with tales of whoredom and West Hollywood and compromise. I could also tell that I liked him more than I'd thought. Every man has his price, I mechanically told myself; mine, it seemed, was a kiss.

Quite naturally I was on top of him, he on his back pulling me to him, wrapping his steely legs around me. He had the professional skill to know exactly how he should be positioned, and he managed it so that I could easily start a slow insertion. My conscious mind pointed out that I knew about his sexual practices only what he told me, and that I should not take anything about his health for granted, though in all honesty I completely trusted him on the subject.

"Just a second," I panted, and reached into a drawer on the bedside table. It was not graceful or effortless, but I managed to slip the condom on. He was able – *Ecco un artista!* – to recapture the mood of a minute before seamlessly, or if anything, more intensely. Entering him felt natural and easy and exquisitely enjoyable. His face was slightly contorted, as though with pain. The grimace made him no less handsome, and his show of strain or reluctance or resignation to altered status was hotly gratifying to me. We had a few minutes of entwined rocking, during which he stifled a few yelps by reaching up entreatingly to be kissed. Then, as from a thousand miles away, I felt his legendary cock release itself between us.

"Andy," I whimpered into his open mouth. "Ondřej."

At the sound of his own name in his own language, he clutched me suddenly tight. It was a spasm that might have been deeply intimate or might have signaled a reawakening revulsion at what we had just been doing. I did not know which of those made me suddenly explode inside him. His own orgasm was so fresh that it felt almost like a simultaneous climax. We held each other harder than ever before and some of the surrender was completely mutual. Though he had mimed some discomfort or reluctance at certain stages of our coupling, his response to my cresting passion was to laugh quietly and kindly, as though proud of a nervous teenager playing his first piano solo in public or winning a spelling bee. Gasping and red-faced, I was grateful for his approval, and after a few moments of mindlessness we collapsed into each other's arms. As before, he took the role of the adoring young partner, submitting without servility, turning to me for strength and comfort. Though taller than me, he found a graceful way to huddle down in the bed so that his heavy noble head rested naturally on my chest.

Without an instant's warning, I started to cry.

"What is it, sweetheart?" he asked. The endearment sounded completely normal but carried no implication of actual closeness. It was what he might have said to any nice man in whose arms he found himself. He was friendly and correct and humane, nothing more. He cared because he was a nice person.

"It's Joe," I said. I could feel tears spilling down my face, which was turned straight up to the ceiling. The pillow case would be uncomfortably damp for the rest of the night.

"Of course you miss him," he said. "It's not even a year yet, right?"

"Right," I nodded. "And…" My voice choked off and he had the class to wait. "I haven't had that kind of – of – "

"Orgasm?"

"Yes – since Joe. For years, they were only for him. Only with him." I was panting as I spoke, keeping my voice very low because I didn't want to sob. "Part of me thinks that this means I really like you. But we don't really know each other that well. And the other part of me thinks I'm cheating on him." Andy pulled away and lay next to me, closely touching along our arms and legs, but not embracing. He too was now looking straight up.

"I can't tell you I'm going to be your new lover," he said after a while. "I can't say I'm going to be Joe now."

"Right," I replied very quickly. "And no one *can* be. I can't lay all that on you. You won't want to meet all my friends, go to church, be publicly known as my partner…"

"You know, I could do most of that," he said equably. "I have no problem with gay guys; half the world knows I have sex with them. Having people know doesn't scare me a bit." He seemed to be studying the ceiling for cues. "Obviously I like you enough to have certain kinds of sex which aren't totally my thing. I mean that. I let you fuck me because I like you; I even learn to enjoy it." He patted my slack belly, a homely, lover-like gesture. He laughed suddenly. "Hell, I even ask you for it!" He had a gift for saying exactly the right thing, like Dante's Thais, if only I could trust it. "But you don't need to be introducing a guy like me to the kind of people you hang out with…"

At this, *I* squirmed in protest. I had already decided I could brazen that out if Andy and I were truly right for each other. People would adjust, or not, in due season.

"I like you, too," I protested. "'A guy like you'… don't make that sound like a bad thing, like my friends or I look down on guys like you. If you and I felt a certain way about each other, there's no one on earth I wouldn't introduce you to proudly. Really."

"Thanks," he said. "*'Really,'*" quoting me. "But it's not just that. I really like my girlfriend. I want women in my life. I don't see how I could keep my straight life and be really with you. And I'm not quite ready for my son to think of me as an older man's butt boy. That's crude, but it's true."

I appreciated his honesty in all of this. He could be offering me a way out of a terrible mismatch, by showing how our needs and wants were objectively incompatible. But he risked spoiling that easy exit by turning towards me again and wrapping his arms around me.

"On the other hand, I want what we just had – a lot – in the future. I would consider marrying you for the sake of…" He gently took my right hand and slid it down his back to Ground Zero. I kissed him.

"I still miss Joe," I said miserably. I pictured my gravestone: 'Knew Love; Settled for Less. What a Falling-off!' There was a Victorian draped urn and a willow tree. "You're not Joe."

"I know. Let's just go to sleep. We are not going to solve this tonight. Sweetheart…" His eyes were closed now. He snuggled into me in a way that, if it weren't for Love, would be enough.

Hours later, I awoke. It was still pitch-black outside. Andy was a warm, easy body next to mine, and I noticed in his favor that his weight on my arm had not made it numb or tingly. The house was eerily silent. I remembered that Jimmy wasn't there, unless… had he perhaps slipped in silently while Andy and I were sleeping? Or, worse, might we not have heard him if he'd come in while we were at it?

I pulled my arm out from under Andy, and he stirred enough to make a sulky hum of interrogation.

"Pit stop," I whispered, and got out of bed. I didn't really have to pee, but I wanted to check if Jimmy's door was closed, which would mean he had returned. Obviously he would not have come to my room to check in, knowing I had company whose presence he resented.

From the corridor outside my bathroom, I could see down the hall that his door was open. There was no silhouette against his bedstead. He was sleeping with, or near, tall stiff judging David; bad enough if they were still estranged over David's suggestion of the major chord, worse if they were exploring passion on the basis of David's assumption of superiority.

I trailed back to bed. Andy was still awake, as I had hoped he wouldn't be. He welcomed me with a hug and a nuzzle to my shoulder.

"Relax," he said. "He's fine. He's sleeping next to a bodyguard."

I liked his wit. I lay next to him, still stiff and nervous.

"He belongs here," I said.

I could feel him looking at me in the dark.

"You two are too much," he said after a moment. It wasn't unsympathetic, but he sounded a bit weirded out. I didn't want to lose him over my convoluted relationship with Jimmy Jack.

"It's fine," I said, not honestly, and hugged him warmly. He was not Joe, he was not Jimmy, he was not Tony; he was not Love. He was Andy, and he felt, at the very least, fine.

We were in the kitchen the next morning, having a leisurely post-coital breakfast. I was wearing my own ancient bathrobe this time. He was wrapped in a spare robe from the guest bathroom, a very baggy seersucker number. Our unglamorous attire made our talk over coffee and toast feel domestic and natural. He leaned back and stretched and said,

"You know, I don't have to be in New York till dinner time. You don't teach today; how about if I hang out here for a while? I was thinking maybe we could visit your friend… what's her name? She speaks a little Czech? Nice older lady…"

"Grace," I said, feeling slight prickles on my face.

"Yeah. She was very nice. Or whatever sounds like fun to you. If I catch the BOLT Bus at 4:30 I'll be in plenty of time for dinner."

Taking tea at Grace's house would put Andy in a new category. She had clearly seen him as a potential new partner for me. If that story got launched in the neighborhood, the scandal when some wickeder neighbor recognized him would be harsher. It might be unfair to Grace to ask her today to open her home, all unawares, to a man-whore. Of course, she might not mind a bit; she was one of those incredibly up-to-date seniors. I just wondered how I might answer if she asked how I knew Andy.

His offer to spend the day with me was touching my feelings. I might find that I was jealous of his dining in New York with a client. If we started dropping in on classy friends of mine, looking for all the world like two nice gay guys sharing a day of social calls, a certain ball would have started rolling, in my mind at least.

"What's your plan for dinner?" I asked, temporizing.

"Meeting a publisher's art director," he said. "He wants me for the covers of some romance novels. I won't be doing porn forever, but there are other ways to make money by taking my shirt off." That was so honest I laughed. I was also glad that, this time at least, it wasn't a client he was meeting. I took so long to comment that he pressed me: "So?"

"Oh," I said, shaking my head as if to clear it; "yes, that will be great." He got up from his stool at the kitchen island and came around to mine. It would have seemed rude not to put my arms around his waist; for good measure, I also untied his robe and ran my hands up and down his bare back. His throaty chuckle was one of power, of winning: he had been absolutely sure I could not resist his surrender.

"All yours till 4:30," he whispered.

Both of us jumped a bit as the doorbell clanged through the house.

"Haven't your friends heard of texting?" he asked. "They actually just come by and ring the bell?" 'Welcome to Bolton Hill,' I thought. He trailed after me to the front door.

There stood Gene, looking pert, hunky, and distinguished, a look no one else I knew could pull off. I was delighted to see him, though I knew that now any ambiguity about what Andy was doing in my house would be obliterated by Gene's visit, not only for the neighborhood but for all of gay Baltimore.

"Dear heart," Gene murmured, leaning in to hug me before glimpsing Andy over my shoulder, his innumerable charms barely concealed. "OH!" he shouted once their eyes had met. "WEL-come back to Charm City! We have all just *missed* you so." He brushed me aside and clasped Andy firmly; Andy laughed, flattered and genial. Gene turned back to face me accusingly. "YOU, you mean thing…! I thought we had agreed you would share – as you know *I* always do." The world knew that Gene never shared. He directed his attention back to Andy. "I think it's time for unveiling." He untied the cord which Andy had just re-knotted, and then brushed the robe off shoulders which Andy allowed to slope. In one second Andy went from a nobly robed citizen on the Panathenaic frieze to Phryne naked before the leering judges. I was as gratified as if Gene had praised, again, my Needles mahogany roll-top secretary.

"Well don't just stand there," said Andy, reaching out his arms. Gene embraced him, growling into his ear and presuming to bend him backwards slightly as if Andy were the Ginger to his Fred. Gene was muscular enough himself that they looked about evenly matched, except that Andy was naked, of course, and enjoying his own availability to admiration and touch. For a crazy moment I wondered if they had been in contact since Andy's last visit. Maybe this chance encounter in my front hall had actually been planned between them, and Gene's arrival meant that I might soon be superseded.

That exact second, we all heard a key in the lock of the outer front door. Because I always locked both doors, there was just time for Andy to duck and put his robe back on and tie it before Jimmy unlocked the inner door and poked his head into the hall from the vestibule. My life had suddenly become a Feydeau farce. Jimmy seemed surprised to find half of Baltimore standing inside, blushing and flustered.

"You guys just getting up?" he asked. "Oh hi, Gene." He turned to Andy and me and straightened up a bit, as if to deliver a line he'd rehearsed in his mind. "I wanted to get back in time to say good-bye to you, Andy." He must have chosen his words with the idea that they would sound decently polite to Andy, who didn't know us, and yet communicate clearly to me that he intended never to see Andy again.

"Good news," I said. This was fraudulent; I knew Jimmy wouldn't like it. "Andy's sticking around till late afternoon."

J.J. nodded quickly, as if acknowledging defeat.

"Well I have to study most of the day. Plus I'll play the piano some. Let me know if it's bothering you." He started up the front stairs without making eye contact.

"When since your birth has your playing ever bothered me for one single second?" I asked, reaching to touch his near forearm gently on his way up. He nodded again and then took the stairs two at a time. We could hear him a few seconds later blundering up to his room by the back stairs.

"He's the most adorable boy on the planet," Gene breathed to me, softly in case J.J. could hear him from the third floor. "And I mustn't stay... I just came to say – well, Paul is coming for drinks tomorrow night, and I would love to have you join us." Paul... I had forgotten that Gene nursed a hope of fixing us up. He turned to Andy with an ambassador's smile and crooned, "Just a very old friend; no one who could steal our James from all of *your* loveliness, dear beauty." He literally slipped his hand into the front of Andy's robe and gave a tug to what he found within its folds. Andy laughed and then patted Gene's face with a genuine fondness which made me like them both more.

"I'm not the jealous type," he said. He reached to put one arm around my waist. Gene looked at us like a sophisticated aunt for a moment, and then blew us a kiss on his way to the front door.

"Tomorrow night is Choir rehearsal for me," I said.

"Oh," he said, hand on the doorknob. "I sometimes forget about all your holiness. Well, I practically promised Paul you'd be there. Stop by for a nightcap at 9:30 if you can. He'll still be among us, I think. Toodles!"

As the door closed, Andy turned to hug me. His advances were still surprising to me; I couldn't keep myself from wondering what his angle was, what he could possibly want from me. Yes, perhaps, a safe and manageable way to explore one facet of unsatisfied curiosity in his extensive sexual repertoire; perhaps some fantasy of class or respectability. Yet I knew that he had many wealthy A-list admirers, who would take him to the Prime Rib as a matter of course and shower him with trophies of privilege. He had plenty of what he would call class without vamping a college professor.

In the event, our day together went very nicely. Not just the shared shower, where he was slick and warm and completely available; not just the carnal, whispering cuddle at nap time. Tea at Grace's house was a delight. Andy was either a genuinely charming and thoughtful young man or quite an accomplished actor. His behavior with a gracious, worldly-wise older lady was impeccable. They traded simple pleasantries in Czech. He told me on the short stroll home that her accent was good and her grammar delightfully correct and old-fashioned. He made me promise that I – "we" – would invite her to dinner next time he visited, which he implied would be quite soon.

When it was time for me to take him to the bus stop, he insisted on going first to the top floor with me to say good-bye to Jimmy. Jimmy would have just shaken his hand, but Andy pulled him in for a one-arm shoulder hug, and said,

"Take care of this gentleman for me."

"It's my job," J.J. answered. He gave Andy a surprisingly steely moment of eye contact, a frank challenge which I could tell Andy found hilarious.

"I know you're good at it," Andy said. "He's told me."

In our short talk on the sidewalk, standing among his fellow passengers as they waited to board, he showed subtle skill in seeming either a butch young straight friend of mine or my discreet, classy life partner. Even his light parting kiss, on the lips, might have read as European or romantic, depending on the beholder. I found that I actually missed him a bit once he was on the bus, and it pleased me childishly that he leaned over a passenger in a window seat to wave to me just before I turned to walk home.

Half an hour later, I was in the kitchen pouring myself a heavy shot of whiskey. There were final projects I should be grading on my desk upstairs, but first things first. I didn't have a plan for dinner, and I assumed Jimmy would be dining in, so soon it would be time to check the fridge and try to be creative.

Lupus in fabula, Jimmy came crashing down the stairs within a minute or two. I wondered what his mood would be and I was braced for a scolding, to which I would reply hotly and firmly. He turned the corner clumsily into the kitchen, brow furrowed, looking forlorn. Had he feared I would elope with Andy and wire him from Niagara or St. Tropez?

"You're back," he said. "I haven't given up on Dino, just so you know."

"Neither have I," I smiled. "It's probably too soon for me, either way. I even said that to Andy. I almost cried because he wasn't Joe." In fact, I *had* cried, but it felt disloyal to Andy to tell Jimmy that.

"You're close in a way," he said. He looked around and then shambled to the far side of the island, at loose ends, nothing really to do. I gestured to him to come stand by me. I put my arm around his waist once he had slouched to my side.

"I realize I haven't asked you about David," I said. He made no sound, but there was a vibration in his waist which told me I'd hit a minor nerve. After a moment he said,

"There's no David. David isn't anything."

"David's a presumptuous imbecile," I said. "I hate him."

I could feel him laugh, not from amusement, next to me.

"Less than twenty-four hours ago, you told him to take care of me. I've always thought I was some huge deal to you. Now you're telling guys you hate to take care of me."

"I will physically, with my bare hands if necessary and with not a backward glance or shadow of regret, kill anyone who hurts you," I said. He waited about fifteen seconds to reply.

"Good to know. Thanks." He was dishing me a bit; I smiled.

"So?" I asked. He stepped away and rounded the island again, to slump onto one of the stools. Without asking, I had poured him a glass of Chardonnay and slid it across to him. He looked away furtively.

"We made out last night," he said. "In his bed. Somehow it made sense to make out while he was saying we couldn't be together."

"How did you get into his bed?" I asked.

"We were studying and it got late. Then it was bedtime, so he asked me to join him and I did. It was that or the living room floor for me." He hesitated. "Plus I liked him."

In the mid-1970s, as I was spreading my own timid gay wings, that would have been a completely satisfactory explanation. My standards for J.J. were higher than my standards for myself ever had been.

"So…" I didn't know what to ask. "You were making out and he was saying you weren't really right for each other? Simultaneously?"

"I wasn't stopping him," he shrugged. "I'm not super sexy, you know. I mean, not super sex-oriented. It seemed easier just to let him get off." I said nothing, but I hated thinking of Jimmy in the arms of anyone who didn't understand his importance. "He thought he was being nice. He said I should date other guys, find my way… What he meant was I'm lame; I'm not enough. There's something missing with me, apparently."

"Did you ever feel that with Kevin?" I asked, my face a mask. I was wondering if I had a meat cleaver large enough to cleave David.

There was a flicker of pain in J.J.'s face.

"No. Kevin loved me. I knew that." I went around the island to stand by him and put my hand on his back.

"That's your default," I said. "You never, never settle for less than that." He looked sadder and sadder, and a moment later I heard him make a gulping inhaling little sound. He didn't cry, though.

"David doesn't matter," he said. I shook my head in agreement: 'No, he doesn't.' "I am still in mourning for Kevin." He leaned back on his stool enough to turn and look at me directly. "Speaking of settling for less…" For an instant I had no idea what he was talking about. I raised my eyebrows at him in question, and he chuckled. "Andy… after Uncle Joe? Instead of Dino – really?" Feeling judged, perhaps already convicted, I took the stool next to him.

"Apples and oranges," I said. "There's a good chance I'll never have another great love. Lots of people never have even one. Do you think I am entitled to another one? Or should I be celibate forever now, if I can't match that once-in-a-lifetime…?" Again, I remembered crying after my little climax with Andy. Jimmy was right in a way. I didn't want to spend my last decrepit decades having pathetic tawdry mercenary sex to try to make up for Joe's absence. It was Joe's fault, really, for dying. He was forcing me to squalid expedients. I should have told J.J. that Andy was much nicer than he realized, perhaps a plausible successor to Joe, but those words would have frozen on my lips. And really we should have been talking about Jimmy Jack himself. He was processing his first major break-up, and his godfather might be expected to say something wise.

"You know," I tried, "I did have a dating life before Joe. I'd developed a theory that I would never find anyone. Remember, I was over forty when Uncle Joe and I moved in together."

"Oh right," he nodded; "your famous heartbreaks and cynicism. You've never told me about them."

"Well," I said, "the usual unimportant flirtations and also-rans… but of course you know all about the *great* love of my life before Joe. Frustration, misery, rejection, terror, feelings of worthlessness; near misses, tantalizing brushes with carnality, scenes of jealousy, devotion, affection, renunciation…" I was speaking lightly. These memories were so distant that they seemed almost funny in retrospect. He seemed to think I was joking.

"Some silly boy?" he asked. "Some roommate or co-worker?" He was smiling, sure that I wasn't serious.

"A roommate, yes," I said, puzzled. Suddenly my face turned red and his turned white. At the exact moment I realized he didn't know, he realized what I meant. It had never crossed my mind that he didn't know this story; I'd assumed that it was part of his family's lore, or was communicated without words through some vapor hovering in the Glencoe rafters and raining periodically down into his cradle.

"Daddy?" He stood up suddenly and walked fast around the island… once, twice. His joints were stiff and his movements were flailing and spasmodic. It was a behavior he hadn't shown since he was five or six. Then he sat again next to me. His face was completely blank, expressionless.

He didn't look incredulous; he looked stupefied, shut down. The two men he loved most in the world, and associated least with sex, were smeared by the same sloppy brush of stifled, misdirected desire. His squeamish soul recoiled from every part of the images forming in his mind. He stared at me in silence while I counted to a hundred.

Then he took a slug of his ridiculous Chardonnay.

"I just decided you and I should go to Italy this summer," he said, slapping his glass down on the counter. I laughed, relieved.

"Rome, Florence, Siena, Venice… or Rome, Naples, overnight ferry to Sicily…" I said; "we'd have *such* a good time. It may be too late to get tickets for early June, though," I said. "That would be the best time to go."

"Daddy can get us tickets in business class." He was channeling his wealthy father, butch, entitled, and once the love of my life. He sounded embarrassed to say "Daddy" out loud, because he had just, for the first time, allowed across the threshold of his imagination a picture of his father as the object of my passion. He knew enough about the gay world now to frame speculations, from which he instantly withdrew, on how that passion might have been enacted. But he kept up his patter. "He says there's always room up front."

On our first visit to Florence together, Joe's eye for art intrigued me. With his actor's perspective, he often made seemingly naive comments which initially amused me and then, a moment or two later, struck me as brilliant.

He stood respectfully before Martini's "Annunciation" in the Uffizi, for instance, and then muttered,

"She looks pissed."

I was a nanosecond short of launching into a brief address on International Gothic and mediaeval standards of courtly elegance, when I realized for the first time that she actually *did* look peeved. Poor girl, she had every right. Her quiet reading had just been interrupted and her secluded life turned inside out by a crouching, obsequious, uninvited angel in a frankly fabulous plaid-lined cloak.

Later, in the Accademia, we stepped into the long corridor which climaxed at the feet of the much-trumpeted triumph of the human spirit. Joe kept his composure and dedicated real fascination to the laboring Prisoners, the twisted evangelist, the desiccated Pietà. At the moment of the requisite swoon before David, though, he became oddly detached and abstracted, showing no signs of rapture, and just commenting wryly that the other tourists referred to the statue as "him," not "it." After a minute's gazing, he squinted.

"Huh," he said. "That's amazing."

"What is?"

"If you squint, it's like you can see his belly moving when he breathes."

"I adore you," I said, after about ten seconds of silence.

In Borgo San Lorenzo we saw a shoe store with prices that were not horrifying. Joe wanted some new dress loafers, so we stepped in. The young saleswoman brought out a few of her favorites… stamped, fringed, tasseled, two-tone, punched, and crimped. Joe tried them all courteously, and then said,

"*Ma… non ce l'hanno qualcosa senza frangia, senza…?*" He didn't know the word, and made a gesture with his right hand, palm down, wriggling all five fingers: 'no fringe, no tassels…'

"*Senza nappine?*" she suggested.

"*Ecco,*" he said; "*senza niente,*" 'no nothing.'

She returned with a black pair so sleek and tight-fitting that it looked as though Joe had stepped into two shrunken lacquered race cars, mini-Batmobiles. He took a few steps and remarked on how comfortable they were.

"*Queste,*" he said, nodding curtly as he always did when sure. "*Sì, le prendo. Bellissime sono.*"

"*Sono come due sculture di Brancusi,*" I said, and was gratified at the immediate approving chuckle I got from the salesgirl.

As we walked out a few minutes later, Joe said,

"There is literally no place else on earth where a salesperson in a random shoe store would get a reference to Brancusi." He liked Florence, in other words, despite his Roman roots, despite what he called Florence's "icy soul" and the cool appraising mercantile gaze that conditioned every interaction with the locals.

I talked him into taking the bus from Florence to Siena instead of the train, even though he said the diesel fumes might give him a headache and he might get carsick.

"It's more scenic," I said.

"Oh, you and 'scenic,'" he said.

"Besides it's barely forty-five minutes," I said, "and it takes us right to the center of town. The train takes forever and leaves us at the foot of the mountain."

Then inevitably some guy on the bus got taken theatrically ill and was laid on a front seat groaning and begging for air, and all the other riders got wrapped up in loudly promoting their private theories as to what was wrong with him and how best to attend to him, and finally the driver decided to stop off in Poggibonsi to put the sick man in an ambulance, and in all the trip ended up taking over two hours. No one seemed to believe the man was seriously sick, and the moment he was handed over to the ambulance crew the bus took on a kind of carnival gaiety. But by then somehow the cramped air of the lurching crisis-laden bus had made *me* feel rather green. Joe instantly forgot that he had initially thought he might get carsick. He always got off on playing nurse, and was doing some fairly heroic window-opening and collar-loosening for me when he caught a glimpse of Monteriggioni out the bus window.

"Wo," he said.

"Oh, that," I said. By the time I'd finished telling him about the giants in the *Inferno*, my head was clear again, and it was only a few minutes more before I could point out Siena's cathedral sitting up striped and shimmering on the horizon. Beyond it was the Torre del Mangia, and I told Joe how it was sometimes called the *gran pipator di stelle*, the "big star-fucker." This was an indirect bit of flattery, because that was what Walter had called me when he first heard I was dating Joe, whose hotness was legendary among my friends long before we reconnected.

I always enjoyed showing off for Joe in Italy. The hotel landlady made it easy for me when we walked through the door. She gave me a strategic smile of welcome and said *"Professore!"* as if she'd been counting the days since my last stay there two years before, whereas in fact it had taken her a minute on the phone to remember who I was when I called from Florence to make the reservation. She was a chic woman around my age, sharp in the face, wearing a white silk blouse and black miniskirt. She looked at Joe for just a moment, and then at me.

"*E la signora?*" she asked. At my last visit I'd been travelling with Miranda, a friend from Rome, and the landlady had been apologetic that she'd had no double bed to offer us.

"*Non è potuta venire,*" I said; 'She wasn't able to come.'

"*Ma mi ha chiesto un letto matrimoniale, vero?*" she asked. She was right; I had asked on the phone for a double bed. Joe's looming, affable masculinity suddenly made sense to her.

"*Sì sì,*" I said bluffly. "*Non si preoccupi.*"

"*Per noi va bene,*" Joe said, standing almost at attention. The landlady glanced at him with new alertness, surprised by his Italian.

"*Oh signora,*" I said, "*Le presento... un mio collega.*" Joe smiled at me a bit ironically and I knew I couldn't get away with that. "*Il mio compagno,*" I amended: not just a colleague; a companion. "*Il dottor Andreoli.*"

"*Dottore,*" she said with a grave little bow. It was 1995; I was impressed by her swift adjustment to my traveling and sleeping arrangements. Had she smiled this same suave, efficient smile when the King of Bithynia checked in with the young Julius Caesar? Had she perhaps even given an extra dusting to Michelangelo's studio when she knew Tommaso de' Cavalieri was to drop by for a drawing lesson, hoping perhaps that today at last her grouchy genius tenant would be made happy in ways which she forbore to name or imagine? "*Italiano, dunque?*"

"*I miei nonni sono di Roma,*" Joe said; 'My grandparents are from Rome.' "*Io sono americano.*"

"*O voi romani!*" she said, menacing him jokingly with a few chops of her right hand. "*E l'italiano lo parla meglio di noi, proprio come il professore!*" She included him generously in the compliment she always paid to my Italian – 'better than ours!' We took our bags and she led the way to the top floor of the narrow little building, where she'd promised me a discount for the five flights of stairs and a panorama in recompense. "*Ecco,*" she said proudly; "*secondo mio padre questo doveva essere la fine della torre.*" Clearly her father was right: this would have been the top terrace of the mediaeval tower into which the hotel had been built, with craggy battlements for throwing God only knew what onto the street below during spasms of civic unrest. The room occupied almost the whole top floor, with a modern pitched beam ceiling and windows on two opposite sides, of varying widths and heights as dictated by the irregular gaps in the old fortifications. A small bathroom had been fitted into one corner. The room was something beyond charming, and the view made you want to cry, stretching over the city's tiled rooftops on one side, and out over the countryside to the Basilica dell'Onoranza on the other. I opened a window on the city side and leaned out, confirming that by craning the neck to the right one could see the *pipatore* itself in the Campo.

"What *contrada* are we in?" Joe asked, after the landlady had left us.

"Aren't you just the smartest?" I said.

"Oh... smart enough to be your colleague, you think?" Clearly I wasn't to be forgiven for that.

"Nicchio," I told him quickly. I loved the neighborhood mostly for the sake of its brilliant dark blue flag and rampant scallop shell device.

"Do I get a scarf?" he wanted to know.

"Of course you do," I said, "if you promise never to wave it till we get back to Baltimore. Outsiders get sneered at if they pretend to understand too much about Palio. And I don't like being sneered at by the Sienese."

"Who would?" Joe said. "That landlady scares me. She'd kill us for fifty *lire*."

"No she wouldn't. You saw how she dotes on me. Just don't mention Cosimo I and we'll be OK." Joe just looked politely curious, and I said, "The Medici duke of Florence who conquered Siena in 1555. We're still furious about it. We brood."

"Oh, I know him," Joe said airily, apparently still bent on being smart and good. "Cellini did him."

"Better than anyone," I said, and kissed him.

"She took it pretty well," he said.

"What?"

"Us being together. Didn't miss a beat. Well... missed one beat but not two."

"That's because you charmed her with your Roman grandparents. You're a great credit to me, you see." His eyebrows went up.

"Newsflash," he said. He started to unpack.

I looked around the room for a minute, loving the yellow light, the tile roofs glimpsed out the serried windows, the raucously chanted Palio hymn coming up from the street and promising horrors to the rival Val di Montone *contrada*. The numbing savage melody was hoarsely shouted by crowds of young Sienese whose accurate profiles would suggest poised, noble voices instead of this throaty wine-coarsened yowl. Within two days, the streets below might be convulsed by parades of delirious boys waving in victory the silken banner and silver charger on a pole, and sucking on pacifiers to celebrate their victory in the race. (*"Gli venissero storti tutti i denti!"* a friend had hissed at me once as the deplorable youth of the victorious *contrada*, the hated rival of her own, had roiled obnoxiously by: 'I hope it makes all their teeth come in crooked!') I had been awakened by this same melody one night in Florence a few years before. What were these Sienese kids doing, drunk and regrettable, in the middle of a November night, waking the Florentines with their raw song of neighborhood rivalries? Most of the youthful screaming in the over-saturated streets of Florence in those days was Simon and Garfunkel sung sloppily by unwashed German art students. Another hundred yards down the street, the Sienese singers started shouting "Montaperti!" to enrage the Florentines, defeated there on that memorable day in 1260, when they still liked to remind visitors that they'd had the opportunity to level Florence to the ground, but had decided not to.

I was wondering how much of this story I could tell Joe without boring him. He came up behind me and hugged me around the waist.

"I can tell from the other side of the room how much you love it here."

Then I realized that we were actually together, alone in a room with a double bed, in one of the places I loved most on earth.

Chapter 12
June, 2016
[flashback: 1994]

Gene brought Paul by again, for a drink, on the spur of the moment. This seemed an odd coincidence: Paul lived miles away. Perhaps Gene had called him and hissed one of his conspiratorial 'Get your ass over here!'s after noticing that there was a workman coming and going at my house and I was probably at home. Lorne was indeed there, replacing some leaky old faucets in the master bath. The simple little job entailed a few more trips than usual to his truck because none of his usual assistants had come with him that day. Lorne regularly hired his trashy high school classmates away from their lives of cousin-marrying and drug abuse (things with which he had probably flirted himself in early adulthood) and then bossed them around mercilessly. Usually their job consisted of passing him tools, running to the truck for a screwdriver, or cleaning up after Lorne had finished his work. They sometimes failed him at the last minute, as they had today; this usually made his work easier. It also made him chattier and more flirtatious.

At some point during this plumbing job, he called me to show me how stripped some of the old handles were. I nodded appreciatively, not knowing quite what I was supposed to be seeing, and at his invitation I leaned very close to him so that we could peer into the same dark pipe. I put my hand on his muscular shoulder to steady myself.

"Aw," he said, "that feels nice." Then he aimed his flashlight to explain something about washers and threading. "You're going to love these new fixtures, hon," he concluded. He was just old enough that he still used that Baltimorean term of endearment for all ages and genders. Then he straightened up and got back to what he was doing.

Not long after, I heard Gene rapping on the inner front door and was happy to let him and Paul in. It was close enough to 5 pm that I didn't mind mixing some martinis, and we sat on the back patio. Paul was as pleasant and good-looking as I'd always thought, but nothing he said stayed with me. His irritating nervous little laugh cackled out over the banter that Gene and I tried to keep up, usually after he'd said something intended as flattering or teasing, which I generally found simply dumb. Gene could see that his candidate was getting nowhere.

It was a relief when Lorne came to the kitchen door and called out to the patio that he was leaving. I bobbed up and told Gene and Paul to wait; I would pay Lorne and be right back. Lorne, when I joined him in the kitchen, seemed almost an old friend compared to Paul. I felt very fond of him for a moment, and when he mentioned a low price for the work he'd done, I got a mild thrill of bourgeois patronage from peeling an extra twenty into the small wad I handed him. He chatted companionably as we walked to the front door. He turned to smile a good-bye, and put one arm around my neck.

"I still miss Mr. Joe, Boss," he said.

"Almost a year now," I nodded. "Thanks for remembering."

"I don't forget things like that. You two were always my favorite gentlemen clients." He paused. "And if it wasn't for Mr. Joe and my missus…" I didn't quite understand the gentle vague expression on his face. "But this is how we're meant to be." It hit me then that he was referring to my arm around him upstairs earlier that afternoon, his around me just now. That made me smile.

"Yes, this is perfect. Thank you, Lorne. I am always grateful for your work, and for your… your class." It was a happy word choice; he beamed, gratified.

"And my fine Dundalk ass, right, Boss?" He gave a brazen laugh and I was forced to laugh back. He wouldn't have said that in the hearing of any of his assistants, though he had sometimes quietly dropped similar comments when one of them was in the next room. It wasn't the first time I'd wondered just how far he might have gone in his early adulthood, perhaps hustling his male clients a bit, and never losing a scrap of his masculine self-assurance by doing so.

"Always that!" I agreed, reaching around to smack it as we hugged good-bye.

As I turned back towards the kitchen, I heard Paul and Gene coming into the house. Their visit was not going to last much longer in any case; I was not falling under Paul's spell.

"Let's absolutely do this again sometime soon," I said. "Lovely to see you both." After kisses to right and left, I saw them off from the stoop. As they strolled away, whispering a post mortem, I heard Paul giggle.

When Jimmy showed up in time to start cooking with me, I told him about my near-misses of the afternoon, with both Lorne and Paul, and he laughed, harder than I had heard him laugh since Kevin left him.

"I'm still betting on Dino," he said.

At my computer a few days later, I was surprised by a ping. Randy, the Hopkins grad student who had been briefly infatuated with me years earlier, had asked to friend me on Facebook. I had lost track of his whereabouts and assumed he had gotten a tenure-track job in another city, but here he was, still in town. He hoped to discuss options for adjunct courses at my university. He expressed condolences for Joe's death, which he had only recently heard about through mutual acquaintances. I glanced at his profile. Incredibly, he was in his forties now. I saw that we had any number of friends in common, and it was strange that we hadn't run into each other over the years. I accepted the friend request, and spent a minute or two scrolling through his pictures and posts before answering his message. His profile featured rants of obscurantist belligerent literary theory, full of cold, smarty-pants political skepticism. He gave frequent voice to the libertarian know-it-all clichés of his age cohort. He had closely tracked and embodied the fluctuating culture of hipsterdom. He sported various configurations of facial hair (a few years earlier, I had sourly asked Joe, "When did fashionable young men start looking like Civil War reenactors?"), multiplying tattoos and a few piercings, immense stomping boots or the tightest possible jeans, selfies with microbrews and avocado toast. Though he usually appeared in group shots with a crowd of friends, his relationship status was "single."

He came by for a drink a few days later. He hadn't seen the Bolton Hill house, and he didn't seem to love it. This put me somewhat on the defensive; I was used to swoons of admiration.

"Aren't we grand?" he asked, trying to sound smart. He may have guessed from the parlor's stateliness that I was not going to vote for Bernie Sanders or Jill Stein. He was living in Hampden with three housemates. The summer was a lean season for him, but he hoped that the English

Department at my school was hiring for the fall. I gave him the chair's e-mail and told him he was welcome to use my name.

"Would you like a martini?" I asked. "I'm rather smug about my martinis."

"Vodka, dirty," he said.

"Oops," I said; "this is a gin-only house." He made a face and said he'd just take some white wine. I poured him some of Jimmy's Chardonnay. He'd made enough snippy comments of his own by then that I didn't mind saying,

"Vodka always makes me wonder who put the mashed potatoes in my cocktail. I always feel like I'm drinking starch."

We continued our talk perched rather primly on the sofa in the parlor. He looked good in his own way. His conversation was guarded and often snarky. He was a terrible academic name dropper, not just Peirce and Saussure and Lacan, but, worse, the famous scholars and thinkers he'd worked with at Hopkins – worse because he implied both that he knew them all very well and that he saw beyond all of their work. I wondered how many of them even remembered him or knew that he was still angling, in his mind, for their attention and admiration. Because he mentioned several fringe academic conferences which he had helped organize, I asked him politely about venues for publishing his work.

"Oh," he said dismissively, "that rat race. No, my work is too political. I mostly blog and self-publish on social media. I'm doing intersectionality; it's never going to be publishable in this corporatized academy. I guess it would have been easier if I were interested in something socially sanctioned like the Italian Renaissance."

I gave a rueful nod to avoid hurling my gin martini in his smug vodka-lover face.

As I was starting to think of ways to end our conversation, he surprised me by asking for a house tour.

"Didn't you have a big brown leather sofa?" he asked.

"Yes, it's in the upstairs parlor."

"Oh, the *upstairs* parlor?" he laughed, as though all my domestic arrangements were comically pretentious.

"Well, let's see what you would call that room once you've seen it."

Upstairs, he greeted the brown leather sofa like an old friend. It came back to me that we had been making out on it that one time when Joe's call blessedly interrupted us. Randy flopped down on it now and patted the spot next to him. I sat a bit farther away than that.

"Remember that time…?" he asked, with a small sultry flounce on the pillows.

"Yeah," I nodded, trying to look respectful of whatever he seemed to be feeling.

"I've thought of it often. One of life's 'What if?'s I guess." He looked at me with a strange vulnerability. For a moment I almost felt compassion for all his missed chances. He was a smart, good-looking young man, who might have a lot to offer the right person, if he could relax and let himself be a little less edgy and rude. There were things he wanted me to say or do that I knew I wouldn't, and that would make him even more defensive in his next encounters.

"I guess," I answered noncommittally. I didn't move any closer, and he understood.

"I *am* sorry about Joe," he said.

"Thanks." He counted to five.

"To be honest," he went on, "I never really got that relationship. You didn't seem right for each other."

"For what it's worth, you're literally the only person who has ever said that." My voice was not as chilly as I intended. "I don't think you knew us quite well enough to say it."

He was gone within ten minutes.

When Jimmy got home, I told him about Randy's visit.

"Our house has become a season of 'Gay Bachelor,'" he said. "And it's not the twenty-two-year old grad student who's starring; it's the sixty-something widower. Weird."

"I know," I shrugged. "What is this strange power I have over men?"

Tony texted me that evening and suggested we Skype each other after dinner. Jimmy and I were flying to Rome in several days, in high style thanks to some cashing-in of frequent flyer miles by Tony. When it came time to call, Jimmy perched next to me at the desk in my room. Rachel and Tony swam into view on my laptop and took a dizzying moment to align their webcam, during which J.J. lurched and yelled, "Turbulence!" His parents laughed. Rachel looked a little tired and said she would stay just long enough to check in.

"How's life in Baltimore?" she asked with a pale smile.

"Godfather Jim is beating off the suitors," J.J. said. "Apparently every man in Baltimore, gay or straight, wants to marry him." He turned and beamed at me as if this were exactly the speech I'd hoped he would make.

"Jimmy Jack!" I protested. "That's ridiculous." Rachel and Tony looked solemn. They knew my heart was in the grave.

"I'm serious," he insisted to the webcam. "I just sit here and take notes on how to bring guys to the altar. We've got a married contractor and an adult film star fighting over him... oh, plus a friend of a friend, of suitable age; a former student, recently divorced; and some pretentious junior academic. All totally smitten..." I could feel myself in danger of blushing. Tony and Rachel had always heard only the most rigorously bowdlerized version of my love life, as, for that matter, I had of theirs.

"Jimmy, behave," his mother said almost sternly. "You're being silly."

"Well," Tony offered, "we should never sell Jimbo short..." He gave me a little man-to-man smirk.

"... and meanwhile, I can't *buy* a date," Jimmy concluded. This was a line I'd heard Kevin use, speaking of a friend, a month or two before. Rachel's brows contracted just a bit.

"Are you... interested in meeting someone new, so soon?" she asked.

"He's twenty-two," Tony said. "Of course he is." But J.J. suddenly deflated.

"There will never be another Kevin," he said; his disconsolate look was almost comical.

"Aww, buddy..." Tony said.

"Anyway," J.J. said, rallying, "I should go do some writing. I love you both. Don't stay up too late, you crazy kids" – meaning his father and me. He stood and leaned down to kiss the top of my head; I barely glimpsed a little moue of weary irritation on Rachel's face. She got up too and excused herself. Watching her stand, just a trifle stiffly, I noticed for the first time that she no longer always moved like a young woman.

Tony and I exchanged a few vague comments about the weather, the upcoming trip to Italy, and the increasingly grotesque presidential campaign. Rachel was a longtime friend and supporter of Hillary Clinton, and part of her tense weariness required no explanation. Tony himself was still getting used to J.J.'s being gay, and the banter about my dating had not been quite as hilarious to him as J.J. probably intended.

"So how is our boy really doing?" he asked me. Then he spoke over the answer I was starting to give: "No, actually, how are *you* really doing? We're coming up on your *yahrzeit*. It's not an easy time. Is Jimmy right about all these guys hitting on you?" He gave a little smile of encouragement.

"Nah," I said, waving one hand dismissively. "I'm not looking for that. The *yahrzeit* is the real story. Jimmy's right that I apparently have options. None of them is Joe."

"You'll tell me if there's anyone important, won't you? You know I'll be thrilled." He looked at me rather shrewdly for a second or two, my personal Yoda/Yenta. "Or if not, not. You're fine as you are."

"I wish we were close enough for me to hug you," I said. My smile was a little tight, but I meant it. Tony knew what Joe had been, what he still was. He honored that even in what he didn't say. I knew exactly how it would feel to put my arms around him, and it would have been a deep comfort. "Tony."

He smiled, not realizing I was trying to change the subject.

"Tony," I repeated. "We should talk about something. Something embarrassing." He looked alert and fully conscious, but not sure what I could mean. "Are you alone?" He glanced over his shoulder.

"Yes," he nodded. "Rachel has gone upstairs." His face radiated butch honesty and good nature; it was a face I had loved since 1970.

"Jimmy didn't know that…" I wanted him to nod as though he knew what I meant, but he just looked earnest and willing. "… that I – loved you. I was trying to tell him that gay life isn't always easy, that our hearts can get broken, that my life hadn't always been a happy marriage with Joe, and I mentioned… well, I didn't *even* mention, I just alluded, because I guess I thought he must have always known, understood already in the womb. It just didn't even occur to me that he didn't know."

"How did he take it?" Tony had looked down as I spoke, but looked up at me now, recovered and frank.

"He regressed. He got all stiff and stalked around the room a couple of times without talking. His eyes kind of went dead. It was like he was five again. Then he changed the subject and we were back to normal. I'm only mentioning this because he may raise the subject with you. I think it's kind of haunting him."

"I would have assumed he knew as well," Tony said. "But... 'knew' – what does that even mean? What's to know? He's always known we were best friends. He's always known you were gay. We were never a couple, and he knew that too. So...?"

"Mmmm... I think that he's got some pictures in his mind now which are weird for him. He knows a little about gay sex now. Not that he's all that crazy about the details, even so... but he can imagine desire, or acts, or... I don't know. So I think he wonders..." Tony looked very serious. He himself didn't like thinking about certain details, between himself and me, or involving his son. He also didn't want to miss any chance to know his loved ones better.

"I'm glad he's living with you this year. Rachel and I wouldn't have known what to do or say if he'd come out at home."

"We're having talks parents can't have," I nodded. "But I don't think I ever tell him anything you wouldn't be comfortable with." I hoped that was true

"I wouldn't be comfortable talking to him about safe sex with men, for instance," Tony admitted. "I wouldn't have a clue what to tell him about guys he meets. This is all on you, Jimbo. God bless you." His "God bless you" was almost a joke, almost a Southernism: 'Better you than me,' or, 'You poor jerk.' It was also, about 8%, a prayer. "Does he still come to your room at night sometimes?"

"Yes," I said.

"Still just a kid in some ways. He's still depressed about Kevin?"

"Yes," I said. "He's adjusting and moving forward, but Kevin is always hovering in the back of his mind."

"I'm glad he's got you in his corner this year. I mean, close by." He paused. "He's not like other kids. And he's got a safe place in Baltimore for those oddball late-night conversations he likes to have. Needs to have."

I gave Tony credit in my mind for the distance he had traveled since Thanksgiving, when knowing that J.J. came to my room at night made him nervous. I should have been grateful. But...

"The Neuberg Boys always know they can trust me in the dark. I'm totally safe." This awkward remark had come out of some dark corner of my mind which I didn't know existed. It sounded bitter and frustrated, as though part of me felt emasculated by their trust in me. I would have loved to boink Tony; that had been a familiar thought for decades. Now I seemed to imply that the attraction extended to his son, a shocking profanation. I stammered, suddenly mortified, rushing to add some extenuation; if I'd been able, I might have said, 'I mean...,' or, 'Where did *that* come from?...,' or, 'No, forget I said that...'

Tony looked at me steadily, with a knowing patient smile as ambiguous as any Greek kouros.

"The Neuberg Boys always know you love us. That's all. And we love you for it... maybe not as much as you love us, which might not even be possible. Everything else is bullshit."

There was something beautifully passive and puppyish about him and Jimmy. They both were willing to accept as much of my foolish love as I could bring them. It was a gift in a way. Tony gratefully letting me love him through his marriage, which at one time many years before had broken my heart; Jimmy sleeping next to me in peace, knowing himself completely safe, when his own first love went smash on the rocks of life: they had given me the great gift of taking my love as a given. I didn't know I was crying until I felt the cool tears on my face.

"You miss Joe, don't you?" he prompted me.

"Yes," I said, a moment later; "and I love you."

Two days later, Dino called out of the blue and asked if he could come by for a drink that evening. He was going to be in the neighborhood on an accounting assignment and would break free at quitting time. There was nothing on my calendar and I suggested he stay to dinner. He showed up around 5:30, with a bottle of Brunello under his arm.

"Marry me?" I asked when he showed it to me.

He was sitting on a stool in the kitchen, sipping a martini and watching me slice and flour some chicken cutlets, when Jimmy blundered in from his summer job at the Peabody music library. His face lit up when he saw Dino, and he jogged left around the island to give him an awkward hug.

"The Wedgwood?" he asked me officiously. He meant that he was going to set the table, and he suggested the good dishes, my mother's wedding pattern as he knew. I nodded and smiled. Jimmy looked at Dino and added, "We always use the Tiffany silver, of course, so that doesn't mean we're trying to impress you."

"I'm impressed anyway," Dino laughed. I wondered if Dino had ever even noticed the sterling pattern which I had started collecting piece by piece when I turned forty, long enough ago that I had probably already had two place settings when he first came to dinner at my house. Either way, he had always registered and seemed to appreciate a certain formality at my table. He would probably always think of me as classy in those ways.

"So..." he asked over the *pasta al frantoio* half an hour later. "Where are you going in Italy?"

"Just Rome," said J.J. "This time, anyway."

"Staying with Miranda?" Dino asked me, eyebrows up.

"No, she's teaching in London this summer and her niece from Subiaco is using her apartment. She offered to let us stay there, too, but I don't want to horn in on Sabrina's adventure in the city."

"Well tell her I said 'Hi' the next time you talk to her." He turned to J.J. "You are so lucky to be seeing Rome with this guy. Now promise me you'll keep a list of your 'Holy shit!' moments." He turned back to me with an in-joke smile. When we had been in Rome together, years before, he had been the perfect fall-guy for some of my favorite surprise reveals, like making him walk along the wall of a certain building in via delle Muratte so that, with one step and without any visual warning, he was suddenly facing the entire Fontana di Trevi. He'd had a charming rube way of standing, goggle-eyed, before whatever monument I'd set up for him this way, and then hissing, "Holy shit!" before turning to me and looking thrilled. It always had the ring of truth, though he was also following the only rule I'd given him: "When I show you something I think is amazing, if you don't particularly get off on it – fake it!"

"So what was your favorite?" J.J. asked. Dino twirled his glass by the stem.

"Apart from the food? Probably... I guess the Pantheon?" This was a diplomatic choice. I was touched that he remembered it from so long ago. "Just thinking that something so perfect was built so long ago, and it's still standing there like new, blowing your mind." He fingered the big gold cross on his chest. "It's not really a church... well, actually, I guess technically it *is*... but to me it's the most spiritual building in the world. It's like it spins around this pillar of light; it's cosmic." Even though Dino was significantly bigger than I was, I wanted to take him onto my lap and hug and kiss him for an hour, based on the look on his face as he delivered this memory. He'd validated my entire teaching career in fifteen seconds. Then his expression changed. "But the food... oh my *God*. And I can't tell anyone in my family this; they're all *Napuletan*... but I even liked the pizza in Rome better."

All through dinner, Jimmy prompted Dino's memories, asked his opinions, and encouraged him to talk about his career and family, as though I needed help drawing him out. He leapt up between courses so that Dino and I could continue talking while he took care of things in the kitchen. He even deglazed the chicken Marsala on his own, having watched me do it a couple of times during the year, and then brought me the salad to toss at the table. He was bustling around like an Old World matchmaker, on the brink of referring to Dino and me fondly as 'young people,' much as he'd called his father and me "you crazy kids."

After dinner we all hand-washed the silver and loaded the dishwasher, and then J.J. excused himself to go check his e-mails, a technology I knew he barely ever used. Dino, who had a son in college, must have understood, and looked at him cannily as he said good-night.

"Great to be with you, Jimmy," he said, letting himself be clumsily hugged. Then, left alone, he and I looked at each other and smiled.

"Upstairs," I said, grabbing a chilled amaro out of the fridge.

In the second floor parlor, without hesitation Dino sat in the middle of the long leather sofa so that, wherever I sat, we would be very close. I sat to his left, and after I'd poured us each a decent slug of amaro, we clinked our glasses. He immediately put his long left arm around my shoulder.

"That kid loves you like a son," he said. "It's beautiful to see. Does he get along with his dad?"

239

"Oh yes," I said. His question had implied that perhaps J.J. had found in me a good substitute for a negligent or abusive father. I felt so close to Dino in some ways that I was surprised that he knew next to nothing about my decades of friendship with J.J.'s parents, let alone my passionate long-ago love for Tony. "We're all very close. I hope you get to know Tony and Rachel much better."

"Now that you and I are going to see each other more often, right?" He toasted me again.

I nodded.

"My relationship with Jimmy Jack is different than a father's. It's a very, very long story."

"We have plenty of time," he said. "We may both be doing some co-parenting in the future." He seemed to be light years ahead of me, on some path where he and I already shared responsibility for Jimmy's growth and happiness. I gave him a confused little smile and he explained. "I just mean, I'm enjoying getting to know Jacob, and I want you to know my kids better in the future. So you can have that kind of relationship with them, too."

His children were generic Italian-American kids, extremely good-looking, easily sociable and completely without shyness, much more fashionable and cool than he'd ever been. His name was Antonio, but hers, like her mother's, was something American and of its time... Madison or Brittney, spelled some odd way, maybe. I didn't remember finding them especially interesting. It was hard for me to imagine they would ever want to sit at my knee to learn life's mysteries. At best, and more likely, they would be impersonally, breezily polite in ministering to my fusty needs in my long decline into old age.

He leaned his head down to my shoulder. I felt a deep affection for him; I was quite used to that, though I could sense it shifting inside me, trying some boundaries. With my left hand, I reached around to stroke his face, and then gently pinched his cheek a couple of times. He smiled; I could feel his facial muscles lift between my fingers.

"You did that once to me in class. Do you remember?" It would have been absolutely against my policy to do any such thing; it would have revealed my soft spot for him to the whole class, and to him. Suddenly, though, the memory came back from decades before, perfectly distinct. I had been passing out graded papers which they had turned in only two days before, and one of the students had complained that I had been so prompt, as though she would have preferred to postpone any disappointment about her grade. Dino, who always sat near the back of the class, said, in English, "Hey, don't you mean, *'Grazie, professore,'* for getting our work back to us so quickly?'" The whole class swiveled around to laugh at him, acting as though he were shamelessly sucking up to me, and I had indeed chucked his cheek satirically, to indicate that he had said exactly the right thing and that they should all strive to be more like him. He had smugly bridled and simpered, playing along, and it was funny because he was generally quite solemn and stiff, never cocky or presumptuous, and not cool, as he always said.

"How could I *not* do it?" I said now. "You were just so damn cute." I paused. "Have you been dating at all, Dino?"

"No, I think I'm in real live single mode now." He sounded a little constrained. "So *prof...* Jim..." His voice was nervous; I didn't recall his ever having called me by my name. It was a noticeable step for both of us. I had been resting my left hand on his chest, but I reached up again to stroke his cheek. "I want to try something again."

Very slowly, very gently, he straightened up a little and leaned over to kiss me. I was completely willing to try. He was authentically dear to me, more than nice to look at, brave to be saying what he was saying. He was palpably taller and squarer than Joe. Embracing him was a new feeling, but it was comforting to have my hands on his broad back. I worried at what might seem to him a sagging, wrinkled, elderly body beside his; I could not imagine how he would go from a lifetime of Cindy Crawford and Jennifers to me.

We did kiss. I liked tasting the amaro on his lips and was relieved to think that, thanks to the same bottle, I too presumably tasted OK to him. I sensed again his lack of exultation at the contact of our mouths, but he was intent on trying, and he stayed with me. After a couple of seconds, it was better. I liked feeling our breaths mingle. He murmured something I didn't understand. It was a murmur of indistinct contentment or liking. Then I wasn't sure which one of us was murmuring, and realized it was both. I could feel his tongue not retreat when mine touched it. He was definitely game to try, and within the minute or so that our kiss lasted, I knew he had traveled a great distance. When he pulled away and our eyes met, he didn't look turned on or emboldened, or repelled. He looked relieved. It had been a success for him, proof that he could do it. He knew he could be with me, however that was to be defined and perhaps whatever it entailed.

"Dino," I asked, "what would it mean to you to be with me?" His eyes were soft and honest.

"It would mean being safe with someone I love," he said. "It would mean getting out of this whole rat race of dating ladies at my age… greedy bimbos or lightweights or divorced women desperate to settle down with any decent-looking guy who's got a job."

"Think of the trophy wife you could get, though. You could find a smokin' hot 23-year-old for sure." He didn't smile. I realized that was a real possibility in his life, and he'd probably already considered it.

"Nah," he said. "I couldn't introduce anyone like that to my daughter."

"Well… how would you introduce *me* to your daughter, your son?" He looked puzzled. "Obviously, I've known them since they were born, but I mean, what would I be to them? Are you ready to tell them I'm your lover? Is that part of what you mean about co-parenting?" He hesitated. "And… are you going to be gay now? There's a whole culture and identity there. Parties to go to, jokes to laugh at, marches on Washington… politics, rituals…it's not just whether you and I like each other or not. I can have affairs, or cuddle with an old friend, or have a monogamous love, or pretty much anything in between, but whoever is with me is with a gay man, and that means something about him, too." He scanned my face with curiosity and concern. I could tell that he was questioning himself, not one bit sure of where he would come down.

"Let's lay down," he said.

"'Lie' down," I said, and he smiled and nodded. We kicked off our shoes and he lay with his back against the back of the sofa. For me not to fall off, he needed to hold me around the waist. Our crotches were pressed together without embarrassment, though I didn't feel any immediate stirring from either of us. Our faces were so close that we were almost kissing just by talking.

"That's a lot for me to think about," he went on. "I was thinking more of telling my kids you were… my special friend, my mentor, someone

I've loved since before I met their mother." His free use of the English word "love" was new, but it was no more than he had said to me for years in his dialect, something that sounded to me like *"Ti vo' toto bo,'"* a Neapolitan version of Joe's Roman *Te vojo bene assai.* "But I'd honestly have to think about the rest. Yeah, like you say: am I going to be your boyfriend now? Your... 'lover'?" The word clearly was difficult for him. "Do I tell people who've known me forever that I'm a gay guy now...? I guess we'll have to figure that out. But if I'm sure you're with me, like, on my side..." He smiled, a brave, determined smile, making up his mind to face all these things.

"Well at least," I ventured, "you definitely have significant teddy bear skills. This feels very nice."

"Yeah. It's what I meant about mostly just missing having someone next to me at night. Someone to hold."

He was so sweet in so many ways that I half-agreed with him. And since I wasn't in love with him, and didn't think he was with me, he might be right: companionship, trust, shared habits, holding someone nice; they might be enough. He had ardently chased a bevy of Jennifers who baffled, delighted, fascinated, and wounded him, and finally found just the right wife... but then she, too, after decades, had turned to ice, and now treated him as an enemy, a stranger. I had had twenty-odd years of a deep, passionate, challenging relationship, and I had just survived a harrowing year of grief. The love of my life had died too soon, and the world owed me some consolation. Did I really require public stances and policy statements, "I am what I am," stamped gay ID cards? Might it work simply for two men to be friends, to sleep side by side, to screw casually from time to time, with a masculine shrug of the shoulders when it came to feelings and labels and principles and declarations?

As a gay activist in my twenties, I had heaped mental scorn on guys who got married, 'not knowing' yet that they were gay; I was firmly in the 'Oh, I always knew' camp. I looked down on guys who went into church and promised a lot of things that they knew weren't true, and begat children who would then have to seek counseling for decades, and broke the hearts of women who had married them in good faith. Then, when these hypocrites (as I saw them) did come out, they instantly snapped up all the available single gay guys, who found their straight pasts a sexy proof of real manhood. Guys like me, the Drama Club alumni and Judy Garland fans, couldn't compete with the recently-outs... their ex-wives and the frustrated bonds they boasted of with their children. But... how could a man love another man without having lain awake nights in his teens with a hard-on, remembering a breezy chat with the kid next to him in the tenor section of the Glee Club? How could he love anyone who hadn't been weirdly fascinated by Mary Queen of Scots from the very first second he heard her name at age seven? I didn't see where Dino fit on that continuum.

There was something else, urgent and primal. An almost-divorced father of two was in my arms and claiming that something about me was more important to him than some pretty girl's tight sweater. I needed some promises. I needed him to let me in – into himself, into his world. I did have an offer on the table, from Andy, and, without any of the peripherals, it promised me one form of assurance which I realized was essential.

"There would be something else to think about, though," I pressed. "You know what I'm going to say; we've discussed it before. There are things that should happen in bed between partners, things which might not be second nature to you. I'm old, but I'm not dead. Of course, time might be on your side. I may slow down a bit at some point in the next few years... but for now I'm kind of a selfish bastard about some things." He gave a solemn little nod.

"I haven't forgotten about that." I respected his honesty, his not pretending not to understand and his not ducking an awkward topic. "I think it might feel natural to me in a way. It's how I would imagine a lot of being your...special friend or whatever. I'm used to looking up to you, to thinking of you as the teacher or the... the boss, I guess." I shook my head, frowning. He was a man, a grown-up, a citizen, my equal in every way; I realized that I hadn't gotten my real point across to him.

"You know..." I started. I had a tingling in my face which meant I was going for broke. "You know, when I was a teenager... even through my twenties... guys like you thought – well, *you* probably didn't, because you're a nice guy, but – the world seemed to think that straight boys like you were better than gay boys like me. That we weren't even boys at all. Like, if jocks beat me up, it was my fault because I wasn't a real boy, and maybe the way I'd looked at them made them *uncomfortable*..."

Dino bridled at this.

"You've talked about that before. Don't blame me for that b.s. I wasn't that straight boy. I mean, I was a *straight* boy, but I wasn't *cool*, remember? I never fit in. I didn't push other kids around."

"You know I'd be looking for monogamy, right?" I insisted. "I wouldn't want you sleeping with me but then leaving your number – *our* number! – for waitresses at diners."

"God, you hate straight people!" he said. "Who do you think I am? I have never cheated on anyone I was with. You even *know* that! But you've got to make some speech."

He was right and I was embarrassed. Vulnerabilities from fifty-odd years before were resurfacing in me, and I was subjecting him to rants that weren't in any way about him. He was trying to wrap his mind around what it would take to be the lover of my old age; my response was to accuse him of complicity in atrocities committed by clueless jocks in New England years before his birth. He would have had every right to stomp out on me that second.

"You're right, and I'm sorry," I said quietly. "But if we do this thing, you've got to make the leap. You've got to be my lover; you've got to share this life that I have." There was a long silence, during which he studied my eyes intently. "Joe and I were married. Legally only for a few years, but we had a Holy Union in church long before that. I'm talking about physical intimacy, but what I really mean is: Could you imagine marrying me? Literally in front of God and everybody?"

Miraculously, I felt him soften at this.

"Now you're talking my language," he said. I was slightly ashamed to have been the one using sex as my line in the sand. "But marriage to a man… that's a whole new idea for me. Marriage is what I've always wanted; what I've always thought was normal. And you might just be my favorite person now. But…" He didn't finish the sentence. He was seriously, honestly torn. It was starting to dawn on him that the cozy, low-stress, undefined companionship he'd been suggesting wasn't a real option. "The sex isn't what throws me off. You've taught me harder things than that. I know you'd never put me down or hurt me. We could just try it sometime and see how it goes." For an appealing moment I imagined *that* trying, after the major progress we'd just made on the kiss. He wanted to prepare me for the reality that this might be a bridge too far. "We might both just burst out laughing."

"Or it might turn out to be your favorite thing ever," I said. "You might decide you need it every night." This startled him, and he laughed. For the first time, I noticed that his closeness was turning me on. I couldn't tell if he felt it or not.

"You are *such* a horn dog. I *love* that about you." His smile at me was half weary and half admiring. I recalled how, so many years before in Italy, he had noticed every time I was secretly (I thought) ogling a good-looking guy, and how he teased me about it even as his own eye checked out all the pretty girls. But now his eyes were darting around the room; his mind was covering some new territory. He looked back at me. "Marrying the *prof*... Would I be your husband? Your... wife? You will definitely have to put a *ring* on it, man!" He laughed, to himself. He was half-way there already. I remembered Joe's odd intensity in proposing to me. 'God, these Italian guys,' I thought; 'so stubborn and devoted, and *so* conventional.' From simple force of habit, I glanced at my wedding ring. It was hard to imagine what it would take for me to wear another one, or what I would do with this one if a time came when I might want to change it. Dino's eyes followed mine, and the flirtatious mood was instantly gone.

He sat up, so I sat up. It was not completely graceful. The stiff leather seat cushions slid out from under us and we had to stand half-way to reposition then. By the time we sat back down, arms around each other's shoulders, the mood had changed. We were both wide awake and upright, and it was quite late. He shook me hard.

"And... I guess we'll also have to figure out how I get *my* rocks off." He yawned and stretched, taking his arm off me. His shift from conditional to future hovered between us. I pictured his cock for the first time; there was nothing distasteful in the picture. He sat up straight and leaned forward as if about to stand, smiling back at me over his shoulder. "So this conversation isn't nearly over. And now it's time for me to go. I'm going to call you the minute you're back from Rome."

"Here's my concept," I said. "When I get back, you and I go out to dinner and then spend the night somewhere. Here, your place, even a hotel if we want. Just to have some hours in the dark together and see how that feels. No need to rush anything physical."

He leaned over and kissed me on the cheek.

"I like your concept. A lot."

After he left, I felt a little let down and at loose ends. Scarlett: "Aren't you going to kiss me good-bye?" Luckily Jimmy, who apparently had been doing a chaperon eavesdrop, drifted downstairs a minute later.

"So?" he asked, eyebrows way up.

"We'll see."

He smiled and put his arms stiffly around me.

"What am I going to do with you?"

He drifted into my room sometime in the wee hours and fell asleep without a word. I took a moment to flick the sheet over him as though I were tucking him in. Then I fell back asleep myself and dreamed of Joe.

I often had vague, companionable dreams of him from which I would awake and think simply, 'Joe was here.' But this dream was one a person would remember in detail and could transcribe into a journal a month later if asked. Joe and I were dancing – slow, ballroom – on a stone terrace overlooking a formal garden lit by blazing stars and torchères. The trees surrounding the garden were immense, looming over us with weird emerald highlights twinkling amid their rustling midnight heights. We were in some kind of movie, and he was dancing with me because his co-star had canceled, failed to appear, been fired. I didn't know the dance, but Joe knew how to make it a success, back-leading expertly, making me look good, tossing his head from time to time in a Dionysiac luxuriance, then doing a half-spin to come to my arms with his back to my chest. His apple scent was unmistakable, aphrodisiac. His pine-green eyes sparkled as he looked back at me over his shoulder, and there was a perfect suppleness in the way we moved together. I felt the admiration of the other actors and the crew, all standing just outside camera range, breath bated, hoping that the shoot would work; so much depended on it, because the entire film project could be bankrupted by a bad take. Joe was a great actor, a poised and balanced dancer, a generous partner in every way. Every time I felt nervous, about to slip up, make a clumsy step and ruin everything, I relaxed into his trust and confidence, knowing everything would be all right. At our last spin, as I realized we had made it to the end of the routine, it was not the other people who cheered us. It was the towering, approving trees, green beyond greenness, their branches making a silky agitating roar.

I awoke in the dark with Jimmy Jack's arms around me tightly. He was the person I loved most in the world now, and my disappointment at finding him next to me in bed was so deep that I started to sob silently. Joe's body which had so perfectly filled my arms a moment before had slipped away forever and I felt a terrible loneliness.

J.J. woke up almost immediately. Perhaps my slight shuddering had awakened him. I was glad that my cries were silent and that he couldn't see the tears on my face. It wasn't his fault that he was a needy child and not the love of my life. He too recoiled just perceptibly with surprise, and relaxed his clutching arms.

"I was dreaming that I was slow-dancing with Kevin," he mumbled, sounding heartbroken.

"Aww honey," I said, "I'm sorry." He rolled away from me and looked up at the ceiling. "Maybe you should call him before we go to Rome. It might be the right time to have a talk as real friends." Naturally I thought that his dream, coming at exactly the same time as mine, meant that Kevin was his Joe in some way. I ruled out coincidence. The alternative explanation, that he was psychically attuned to my thoughts and had subconsciously translated my dream into the terms of his own story, seemed no less a sign from above.

He thought about my suggestion briefly and then said,

"I think you should get a puppy." He had heard stories, and seen pictures, of Ootch, and knew that it had been years since Joe and I had had a dog in our lives.

"I have you."

"You think I'm your pet?" There wasn't a shadow of amusement or resentment in the question.

"You know how sometimes I growl when I hug you? I used to do that with Ootch."

"Yeah, what is that?"

"It's that there aren't words for how wonderful you are," I said. "It's primal and doesn't have a name or a taxonomy or a technical lexicon."

He squirmed for a moment, as though the sheet were wrapped awkwardly around him. Then he suddenly rolled over half way to face me.

He spoke urgently; perhaps he too was grateful for the shadows on our faces.

"What did you want from Daddy?" he asked. "When you were in love with him?"

He sounded so uncomfortable already that I thought a blunt question couldn't make it any worse.

"Did you have sex with Kevin when you were together?"

"Yes."

"And you were in love with him?"

"Totally."

"So you understand. That's what I wanted: that whole combo. I only got the feelings-and-friendship part."

"But that wasn't enough?" This worried the ethereal, disembodied part of him.

"You know it was enough," I said. "My life would be unimaginable without your father. He's my rock." Some of his nerves ebbed. "I'm a person with hormones, though, and I would have liked the other, too. There are things I love to do with the person I love."

"But how could you look at Daddy and..." He stopped. He was imagining me imagining fucking Tony. I waited to answer.

"It was always love. You know how handsome your dad is, how magnetic and lovable. Of course I noticed that and responded to it. But I loved him enough to... accept what was possible." I had almost said, 'to settle for less.'

"He loves you, too," he said. "I'm sure he always has."

"Of course he has. I have never doubted that for one second. We've always been best friends. Well, Walter and I too, I guess." He knew that my intimate friendship with Walter had no erotic ambiguity. I could feel him start to relax. "And that even dates back to before he gave me the very best gift ever."

"What was that?" I heard the little smile in his voice. He knew.

"That was when he and Rachel made you."

A moment later, he scooted close enough to kiss the top of my head.

"I'll see you in the morning. Love you." He stood and stretched and headed down the hall to his room.

Ten days later, he and I were walking together down via Sistina in Rome, towards Piazza di Spagna, and we passed the Hotel Hassler Villa Medici. Our modest three-star was on the upper stories of a building a couple of blocks closer to via del Tritone. It was a radiant morning, not yet hot, and I thought we could start our day's explorations by going down the curvilinear Spanish staircase. On our way down, we would salute Keats, and then feign interest in the Armani windows at the bottom on our way to the Ara Pacis. As we approached the little obelisk (I had stopped a moment to tell him about Hadrian and Antinous, commemorated on the faux-Pharaonic shaft) a limousine pulled up to the hotel. As the swathed and luggaged passengers stepped out, a doorman said, "Welcome to Hotel Hassler." J.J. looked at me, eyebrows akimbo, amused at his own worldliness, and said, "'Hotel Hustler?'"

He had already commented, several days earlier, on his theory that the staff at our hotel thought he was my kept boy. I had poo-pooed the idea, hating anything that cheapened him, though I secretly admitted that he was probably right. Our room had a double bed, and he wasn't my son: we had different family names, as they'd noticed in taking our passports.

"Oh," I laughed, "I have *such* a story to tell you... remind me tonight when the Sambuca flows." Sambuca was a new passion of Jimmy's. In the early 1970s, on study abroad in Rome, it had made me feel like a sophisticated wastrel, Mastroianni in a white linen suit; now, though I still enjoyed the taste, it gave me a headache. Knowing this, when I ordered a grappa or amaro after dinner, Jimmy would grandly offer me just one sip from his glass of Sambuca, crowned with its three floating coffee beans.

Much later that day, though still too early for dinner, I made J.J. stop with me at a caffè in front of the Pantheon. Their Negroni cost E.11, a *salasso,* or "blood-letting," as a Roman friend of mine called the price. It was worth it to me for the view. We had probably been inside the Pantheon three or four times already on this visit, but it wasn't something one grew tired of. I had stood for a few moments one day in the shaft of slanting light, closed my eyes, and imagined that Hadrian himself came to speak to me. This was a fantasy I had indulged many times over the years: I would wait to see what this commanding gentleman, always wrapped in a sumptuous gold-embroidered purple toga and handsomer than his portraits, might say to me. This time the imperial connoisseur had smiled and said, "He's adorable." It was etymological: J.J. was 'worthy of worship,' a divinity of sorts, like Antinous himself.

Jimmy took a sip of his Negroni and made a face I knew by now. He found it too bitter and would not finish it, and by pouring about half of his into my drained glass twenty minutes later, he would provide me the perfect dose. But the sour alcoholic slap gave him the courage for a question he must have been pondering for a while.

"Hadrian and Antinous," he started… having heard me speak of them before: "does that imply anything about you and Daddy?"

"Meaning, did I ever think of him as… my youth beloved?"

J.J. had seen past the simple love story which I liked to tell about an emperor and a shepherd lad, and deconstructed some political tensions about men more, or less, powerful, about "consent" between partners placed at near-opposite ends of entrenched hierarchies. I wasn't sure how he could possibly imagine that such discrepancies in power had ever existed between Tony and me: young Tony on his way to wealth, fully empowered by his straightness, by whatever it was that made his penis rigid; and young me destined for a poorly-compensated academic career and whatever stigma went with being gay in my generation.

Suddenly, in a rush, with the world's most sublime dome floating superb and ponderous before us, and a squalid pantomime of flirtatious waiters and plodding, bored, underdressed tourists unfolding between, I felt a stab of compassion. J.J. wondered what I felt about *him*, his father's son. There were possibilities of perverse transferred desire, making up for past chances lost, which would have been troubling to anyone, let alone a spectrum-y gay boy already freaked out by the mere facts of attraction and arousal. Jimmy knew that it was unconventional for him to come sometimes to my bed to talk, but he felt safe there. Was he really safe, after all? Perhaps I was nursing fantasies of revenge or of replacement; perhaps Jimmy was to make up for what his father had never been. And I, the gay roué, the professor adored by unsuspecting straight boys for decades, was perhaps just the one to even the score by taking advantage of the son of someone who had spurned me.

I lifted my glass for a moment and he took my hint, clinking his against it in a wordless toast.

"Do you think your father ever thinks about having sex with you?" I asked. It was a cruel, ugly question, a rhetorical gamble on my part. He was an adult and I could ask.

"No," he said, not shrugging or making any faces of disgust.

"I don't think so, either," I said, "even though in some ways you look very much like your mother, to whom he's been strongly sexually attracted for almost fifty years." He took this in. People had always told him he looked like Rachel, even when he was a misassembled homely boy and she a universally recognized beauty. Even now, as his looks settled into their adult form, all he really had of Tony was his pale polar blue eyes.

I was suddenly irritated at both his parents.

"I still can't believe you didn't know that I loved him," I said.

"Mommy always said he was 'very special' to you," he said. "But I knew that. You were best friends. You loved each other. 'Very special' sounded right to me. I liked thinking that boys could feel that way." He looked up at the weather-beaten façade over his shoulder: M-AGRIPPA-L-F-COS-TERTIVM-FECIT. I wondered if Hadrian had kept that inscription because he thought Agrippa and Augustus had been 'very special' to each other.

"Anyway, I don't want to talk to you in detail about me and your father, except to point out the obvious: the desire was all on my side. What *he* wanted was for me to be his best friend and to love him and believe in him, and all that turned out as he wished. To discuss sexual fantasies of mine would make one or both of us look ridiculous or grotesque to you, and we don't deserve that. Adults are able to draw a chaste veil over the image of their close friends and family having sex. I'm going to bet that you don't like to picture your parents in bed, for instance." Here he did shake his head, hard, not with the burlesque revulsion of most kids his age, but promptly, somberly, scientifically. "So there is such a thing as the incest taboo. There is such a thing as respecting generational boundaries."

I leaned forward into the caffè umbrella's shadow; the slanting sun had suddenly slipped down to where it hit my face. I tapped his glass again with mine, at which he smiled and performed the ritual pour, giving me the half he hadn't been able to choke down

"You're as sacred to me as you are to your father," I said.

Someone in a richly embroidered purple toga stood next to me. Fully responsive to J.J.'s allure, he also supported something altruistic in me, something kind, dedicated to the holiness of future generations. For a moment I understood what the wistful, trusting, beautiful young man in the Bithynian camp might have meant to him... perhaps too what the overwhelming, dazzling emperor might have been to the predestinated shepherd.

Jimmy looked up at me.

"I know that," he said.

In Piazza di Pietra, relatively empty at that hour, the intact colonnade of the Temple of the Divine Hadrian loomed up, dramatically lit from below. I told J.J. how Hadrian's adopted son Antoninus had fought the Senate to have him declared a god, and had then built this temple in his honor. Opposite it, in a store window, was a model showing the original appearance of the temple and its vanished precinct, so detailed that we were able to see which of the non-matching cornices that now crowned the building was original. We noticed a young Roman family in the echoing piazza. The toddler son was sitting on the ground near the store, digging between the large granite cobble stones with the plastic spoon he had kept from his gelato. His parents were lounging yards away, against the iron rail of the temple's podium. Suddenly the child's mother glanced over at him and noticed him playing in the dirt. She called out,

"Massimiliano! Ma cosa stai facendo? Quelle manine, lì? No, stupidino, smettila..." This neatly proved one of my pet theories: that the smaller and more winsome the Roman child, the more likely he or she was to have a pompous Latin name. Maximilian's mamma rushed towards him, fishing a wipe out of her purse, and started energetically on his offending little hands.

"Ma sto facendo dei lavori!" he cried, insulted; *"sto facendo dei lavori!"* Carrying out excavations was a sanctioned activity in his city, and he knew it. He felt completely justified, and glanced up at me, embarrassed to be treated like a child while doing something so grown up, and perhaps hoping that as a reasonable stranger I might defend him to his mother. His eyes caught the light reflected from the shop window. For an instant they met mine, and I smiled at him and then at his inexorable, loving parents.

They were aware of how extremely cute he was, and rightfully unwilling for him to rub his baby hands on the stones over which thousands of tourists had walked, littered, or spat all day long. During the instant our eyes met, I registered physical shock at the familiar green of his eyes. It wasn't at all that most Romans had green eyes, but just that this child's eyes and Joe's clearly came from the same gene pool. I was walking streets which many, many Andreolis must have walked for centuries.

Jimmy and I smiled again at the parents as they whisked their protesting little archaeologist upright and started back towards home in Testaccio or Monti. A couple of steps later, J.J. reached to take my arm and pull me closer. He could see tears on my face.

"I know what you're thinking," he said. "Poor little godfather."

"I'm fine," I said, grateful for his sympathy. He nodded.

"I miss him, too," he said, "every day. It just sucks."

We were in our room, starting to wind down the evening, J.J.'s shoes kicked off, my jacket tossed over a chair back. A car stopped in front of a building nearby and the music of its radio reached our floor. It was some film score, neo-Romantic, softly rhythmic and lyrical. J.J. pulled me onto the only patch of open floor in the room, at the foot of the bed. Without words, he hunched his face down and forward in a slow chicken-neck motion as though he were dancing alone. I knew I was supposed to dance with him. I reached my arms around his waist and he joined his hands in the air behind my neck, his elbows resting on my shoulders. It was no surprise that he was an awkward, shambling dancer, but he understood the beat by instinct, and his tall taut body marked it with subtle subdivided lurches of his hips and shoulders. It was a passionless little *paso doble* we improvised, filled with suppressed chuckles. I wasn't sure what had made him grab me that way… perhaps our moment of shared grief for Joe on the walk back. Our comic shuffle around the cramped bedroom was nothing like my dream-dance with Joe, a Hollywood turn with a debonair and lissome beloved. There was something babyish about how Jimmy dipped his head to my shoulder, something sweetly under-socialized about the wordless way he had pulled me into our dance.

He moved more and more slowly, till he stopped.

"I miss Kevin," he murmured to my neck. I nodded; there was nothing to say. They were going to get together when we were home in Baltimore in a few days. Apparently their phone call, just before we left for Rome, had been pleasant.

He sighed now, a pensive sigh, but not an especially sad one.

"I think I should get my own place for my second year in Baltimore," he said quietly. I was very surprised, but I nodded again. "Super close to your house, I promise." I had a small proud happiness in knowing that he felt strong enough to move forward. I also appreciated his promise. He could move to New York or Milan or Shangri La if need be, when the time came and he was rich and famous, but for now I needed him close. I knew he felt this too, as we stood there in our loose dancers' embrace, the car radio silent now and our dance finished.

"My godfather is all grown up now," he said after a minute. "He can take care of himself."

Joe and I got off the 61 bus in Piazza Barberini and strolled up via Sistina towards the Spanish Steps. He had been in Rome years before, on tour with his singing group at Yale. We were here now on a first-anniversary trip. Miranda, who had always put me up in Rome since my grad school days and had insisted on hosting us on this Roman *luna di miele,* clearly preferred him to me now, and showed it by always giving him tips on how to protect himself from ruthless Romans like her. She had taken me aside that morning and suggested that I try to get us up to the terrace of the Hassler Villa Medici near sundown for an aperitivo before dinner. She wanted to be sure I was romancing Joe as he deserved. She warned me it would take some smooth talking, since we weren't staying at the hotel.

We walked into the lobby, all *Belle Époque,* choked with potted palms and heavy with gilding and smoked mirrors. Joe, with his tight designer jeans, blazer with sleeves shoved up to the elbow, and open collar showing perfect chest hair, was a walking fashion plate. I, podgy in my cotton sport coat and wearing my one expensive tie, flashed what I hoped was a convincing entitled smile at the frigid *concierge.*

"*Vorremmo prendere un bicchiere sulla terrazza, se è possibile,*" I offered.

"Ospiti nostri?" he asked. Joe's chest had registered with him; he had sized us up.

"Questa volta no," I admitted. *"Una mia amica romana ci ha consigliato il vostro panorama. Spero che possa trovarci un tavolo."* I had two L.10.000 bills in my right jacket pocket and wondered at what point I should brandish them, or if the going rate was perhaps higher.

"Everything is possible," he said, nodding. "Follow me." His accent was atrocious, and I knew my Italian was vastly better than his English, but I nodded submissively.

He led the way to the elevator, speaking briefly to the blindingly handsome young man who operated it.

"I due signori al terrazzo," he hissed.

"Subito." He appraised us at a glance, and nodded. I reached into my pocket and took the two neatly folded bills between my index and middle fingers, then reached out to shake the *concierge's* hand as we stepped into the brass cage.

"Thanks for your help," I said, our eyes resolutely meeting. Though the cash disappeared into his hand as though it had never existed, his face showed no expression at all. As our beautiful lift attendant closed the sliding door, I wondered: might or should I have stepped in with just a toss of my head? Or on our descent would I be stopped at the door with a bill for a *supplemento*?

The other clients on the terrace were largely wealthy men with unnatural tans, heavy gold rings, and blonde trophy wives, but at two or three other tables the portly millionaires had attractive young men sulking and bridling next to them. There was nothing tawdry about the view. To the right, the dome of Saint Peter's shimmered in raking light, with twilit birds swirling in the middle distance. Via Condotti angled to the left below us, and farther in the same direction we could see great swaths of the Roman skyline soaked in the yellow glow. We spent a few minutes trying to identify the various domes and pinnacles while waiting for our Negronis to come. Joe was loving this. It suited his sense of his own stardom. On impulse, feeling that I had safely paid off the world, I took his hand and kissed it.

"Divo," I said.

He nodded. The waiter came and deposited our two brimming red glasses, and a bowl of peanuts. The little scrap of *scontrino* under the bowl showed a figure approaching $40. Joe and I toasted, and then he took his first sip and leaned back in his chair, relishing the view and the setting. Two tables away from us, a young man much less good-looking than Joe was sending something back to the kitchen, while his harassed and complaisant older friend simply nodded wearily at the waiter. Joe noticed it and smiled.

"What do they call this place again?" he asked. "The 'Hustler Medici'?"

Our times together had seldom been so glamorous and upscale. The sunset was photogenic and suffused the terrace with a cinematic golden glow. Looking across the tiny table at Joe, I saw all of his magnetism and charm in sharp relief. He grinned over at me from time to time with a stealthy promise of passion and with genial good nature. It all felt like a scene from one of those cheesy films about uptight Anglos finding their sensuality and spontaneity in Italy. The expensive Negroni had the virtue of delivering a genuine boozy punch. After half an hour or so of devouring him with my eyes, I stole a sideways glance and convinced myself that no one in particular was paying attention to us. I leaned over for an instant and kissed him, mouth to mouth.

"What was that?" he asked, amused, as I settled back into my wrought iron chair. I did notice, too late, that one of the young men on the terrace was smiling at us, condescending and comradely at the same time.

"Just the inevitable and natural reaction to your loveliness," I said.

"Would you say I'm of a hallucinating beauty?" Miranda had told us at breakfast a couple of days before not to miss the San Zeno chapel in Santa Prassede, because it was of *"una bellezza allucinante."* Joe had fallen in love with the phrase and applied it to everything we saw from then on: a banana gelato, the Colosseum, the Menfis style toilet brush in our bathroom at Miranda's.

"I think I'm hallucinating right now," I nodded.

Some time later, we took the elevator back to the lobby to start on our evening prowl. The dazzling operator was still on duty. He smiled at us conspiratorially, wishing us well. He had apparently decided we were less unappetizing than the couples he routinely ferried to the roof.

"Buona serata, signori," he said, respectfully, kindly almost, as we stepped out of the lift. His perfect face betrayed no flirtation of any kind, but his courtly attention was a benediction.

"A Lei," we replied in unison. Buoyed by his approval, we swept past the *concierge* in the lobby. He ignored us, and I wasted a moment trying to interpret his indifference: had I tipped too little? too much? Or did the elevator operator count for more in some inscrutable hierarchy of hotel staff, because of his beautiful face and discreet manner, and had he perhaps, in some imperious wordless way, let the *concierge* know that we were the right sort? Moments later, we were through the revolving door with the evening air caressing our faces.

"That," said Joe, "was hallucinating beauty. That elevator guy should be a model."

"One look at you and he despaired," I said. He smiled, and on impulse, I put my arm around his shoulder. I knew how to flatter Joe, and I knew that the pay-off was worth it. "Have you been good?" This was how I had often prepared him for delightful unexpected sights on this trip. He nodded, eyebrows up, and I steered him down a street to our left, to see the house whose door looked like the maw of a leering monster, a baroque fantasy useful to Roman mothers, who for centuries had terrified their children into good behavior by threatening to hurl them into it.

We were leaving my favorite trattoria in via di Monte Giordano after lunch a few days later, and part way down via del Corallo we saw that some workers had opened a large hole in the street to address some plumbing issue. They were all dressed in the blue overall *tuta* of Italian laborers, formless and liberally smeared with various kinds of grime. They were sweating heavily, some of them with handkerchiefs tied around their temples, and it would have been hard to aestheticize or eroticize them. Their voices were raucous and they had harsh *romanaccio* accents. One of the younger ones was standing on the pavement leaning on a shovel, perhaps about to jump back down into the pit, but first he stepped aside courteously for us, balancing gamely on its edge with his back to his colleagues, so that we could pass safely by flattening ourselves against the wall of a building. It was a tight enough squeeze that all three of us had to acknowledge the awkwardness by friendly smiles.

"Prego," he said politely as he let us by. As he raised his head a bit, he and Joe made sudden eye contact. Though Joe was, as usual when traveling, dressed up a bit and looking very glossy and swanky, and the young Roman worker was a filthy mess, there was a resemblance between them too obvious to ignore. They might easily have been brothers: a similar build, identical coloring, matching curls, the general cast of features quite alike, even the squinty regular-guy eyes… the other man's a pale hazel, very nice eyes, really, though without any of Joe's emerald enamel tones.

Joe asked him, almost stammering,

"Ma come si chiama di cognome?" As usual, he was perfectly courteous, addressing the working man formally while asking his family name.

"Antonelli – perché?"

"Ah," said Joe; *"io Andreoli. I miei si sono conosciuti a Brooklyn, ma tutti e due sono di discendenza romana."*

"Wow! Mia mamma si chiamava Andreoli." All three of us laughed at the coincidence.

"La mia si chiamava Piattelli," Joe answered, *"ma da quando si è sposata usa il nome di mio padre."*

"Piattelli? Davvero? No, ma… anche alcuni dei miei si chiamano Piattelli… saremo cugini! Lei è proprio 'romano de Roma'!" The Roman worker's mother had been an Andreoli, and he had relatives with Connie's maiden name.

I noticed young Antonelli staring at Joe for a moment as their pleasantries tapered off, as if thinking about how his own life might have gone: fashionable clothes, trips abroad, lording it over the other Romans a bit on his visits home. Joe quickly took out his *taccuino* and a pen, and gave his putative long-lost cousin our address and phone number in Baltimore. Neither of us had e-mail at home in those days, and it was unimaginable that a blue-collar Roman would. He also might have been embarrassed about where he lived, or not have wanted to let globe-trotting sophisticates like Joe and me see his writing. At any rate, he promised us he would ask his extended family if they remembered any of Joe's grandparents, and be in touch if so. He might even come visit his American family someday! Friendly laughter, a handshake deferred with some embarrassment because his hands were so dirty, waves and nods of good will... then Joe and I walked on and he hopped down onto the hole and got back to work.

Joe was always cocky with me about that chance meeting. We never did hear from his Roman cousin, and hadn't even gotten his first name; Joe would certainly have looked him up on line years later if we had.

Connie's maiden name was indeed Piattelli, though of course her family in Brooklyn spelled it with one -t-. She always refused to believe me that it was spelled with two in Rome; she even implied that I thought so only because I spoke hoity-toity Italian and didn't know the real people's language. As we were packing to come home from this first trip of ours to Italy, I threatened Joe that I would bring a Rome phone book home with us to prove I was right, but he smiled protectively and said,

"That would break her heart."

Miranda had gone down to the street to signal to the taxi she had just called for us. Our bags were zipped and I was shouldering mine to follow her, but Joe stopped me.

"One last look," he said. Miranda's balcony commanded a nice view of the neighborhood: post-Unification apartment villas, none more than five stories high, with the towering trees of Villa Torlonia punctuating the horizon a few blocks away. The sky was a clear morning blue, still cool, though the sun promised a blazing day. Joe slipped one arm around my waist. Below us roared the traffic of a major artery which ran past Miranda's courtyard building. Despite the loud urban symphony of the awakening capital, there was something still and majestic about the view. Without a single important bit of architecture in sight, the harmonizing earth tones of the stucco and the gritty white of the travertine trim were lovely as they gave back the hot light of a Roman sun.

"I can't wait to get home," Joe said, "but I also can't stand to leave here."

"I know," I said. "Same." He turned to me and gave me a small sentimental kiss.

"Eternal," he murmured. "Rome; you, me."

"Yeah," I nodded. We smiled, a smile I would never forget, simple and frank and comradely. We stepped inside, grabbed our bags, and almost ran down the stairs to meet our cab and kiss Miranda good-bye.

I had always envied Italian the word *psicolabile,* psychologically unstable, or showing a tendency to "slip" mentally. During the last few weeks running up to the anniversary of Joe's death, *psicolabile* was what I saw in the mirror. I was distracted, cold inside for weird moments, giddy at times, bored, tired, weepy without warning and when least expected, irritable (mostly with myself), forgetful, detached and obsessively engaged by turns. Yes, I had gotten used to Joe's absence. By this point, I never forgot that he was dead; I never thought, 'Oh, I should tell Joe…' I was moving forward; I was even considering seriously the possibility of launching a new relationship, probably with Dino, just maybe with Andy Ferrara, conceivably even with Lorne… not any kind of substitute for Joe, of course, but a twilight romance of muted fondness and tapering passions. There should be someone, for instance, with whom to savor J.J.'s growth in the coming ten or fifteen years… someone other than that kind, wispy, pallid Joe who sometimes fluttered close enough to be heard over my shoulder.

The oddest things made me cry in those weeks. Stories or songs of loyalty, of survival, of attachment, of enduring devotion that standard cliché couldn't describe, moved me almost unbearably. Once, Jimmy and I watched a YouTube clip someone had recommended to us, of Audra McDonald singing "I Won't Mind," and it was so completely my story with J.J. himself that I started sniffling half way through and grabbed his hand. Hymns in church were a minefield: "Abide With Me," or "All Through the Night." One Sunday we sang "For the beauty of the earth," and at the line, "friends on earth and friends above," my larynx stopped in mid-phrase and I had to sit down in the middle of the Choir till the song was over, thinking of Joe and how nothing but song still connected us.

One day, Gene and Carl from next door were over for a beer, and I was telling them a story from J.J.'s childhood. J.J. himself was there, and knew the story by heart, so he had stepped into the kitchen to refill a bowl of peanuts. Joe and I were visiting Glencoe when Jimmy was three or four. Joe reminded me to check about some logistical detail of our travel plans, and I snapped, "Can we talk about this *later*? My nerves are *shot* right now!" Tiny J.J. rounded on Joe like a bantam shop steward and yelled, "His nerves are *shot* right now!" For some reason, this little anecdote threw Gene and Carl into gales of laughter, and as Jimmy joined us in the parlor just in time to overhear and roll his eyes at the familiar punchline, it struck me suddenly as completely hilarious as well. I started laughing out of control. To laugh that way seemed a new experience physiologically. There were muscles in my face and around my diaphragm that engaged crankily, as if they'd been lying there clogged with rust and mildew. For several seconds, I forgot everything except the almost forgotten pleasure of laughter. Then in an instant it became piercingly painful: it was obscene for me to feel such delight in a world without Joe. I started crying in a loopy, snorting, gaspy, unbecoming way, which hurt me physically around the midriff and in my throat. None of the three friends in the room seemed at all surprised or thrown off. Gene and Carl made sympathetic clucking noises, but deferred to Jimmy, who moved quickly to stand behind my chair and clamped his hands on my shoulders as though I might otherwise shoot up out of my chair and injure my head on the plaster moldings of the high ceiling.

That night, I awoke shortly after midnight and wasted two or three hours in restless futile attempts to interpret the stripes of light which the slatted shutters cast on the ceiling. Did they spell something? Were their patterns like railroad ties, pointing in some direction? I was miserably lonely. I looked at my hands and forearms in the raking streaks of light: they looked strangely wrinkled and sagging, irregularly spotted, the hands of an old man. I remembered recently putting my hands into a powerful air dryer in the men's room at work; the flesh of my busy strong hands streamed in veiny gelatinous ribbons in the hot blast of compressed air, as if my skin might peel off completely. I felt like a Nazi in an Indiana Jones movie whose face disintegrated at the sight of a mystery; my whole being might be reduced to a mere moment of grotesque special effects.

I was sixty-four, a widower, and alone for life. There was no point in praying about it. My prayers for years before Joe had been selfish repetitive petitions for love; then, once we were together, for continuance in joy. Since Joe's death, they had dried up. Basically, it seemed to me, the universe had tricked me with a sense of false security in my happy marriage, and now that I'd seen through its cynicism and cruelty, I was too proud to bow

262

and scrape for favors, groveling to authorities who had proven their caprice and unreliability. On the off chance that the world was run by someone actually nice, whoever that was would be perfectly justified in reminding me that I'd severed ties a year before, burned bridges, encamped in a lonely desert of my own creation. There was no point in adopting pious pretense. I had lost respect for whoever was in charge: *Signor, perché me ne rimuneri così?*

Suddenly I remembered that I wasn't lonely. I got up and walked in silence down the hall.

"Jimmy Jack?" I called softly into the dark back room. I heard his steady breathing, just on the verge of a snore, a youthful version of the stertorous racket I had been accused of by Joe, and occasionally by Jimmy himself. Then I heard him make a confused waking-up humming noise. "Can you come to my room for a while?"

"I don't think even Daddy and Mommy ever actually asked me that," he mumbled. Within a couple of seconds, though, he was standing upright, with the street light from the back alley outlining his unruly curls and showing the crab print on his baggy silky pajamas. He followed me to the front of the house, barely opening his eyes.

In my room, he flopped down next to me and pulled the covers up to his chin. He was asleep again within seconds. I counted to thirty. Then he threw the sheet down to around his waist and rolled over to face me.

"Oh, wait," he said. "You wanted to talk to me."

"I'm too told to be worrying about, 'Will I be alone?'" I said. I didn't bother with any preamble. "I've been in love; I should be content and just sing 'Hello, young lovers' to everybody I see, and count my blessings and cherish my memories."

"It's natural you wonder about the future. You miss Uncle Joe. You want someone next to you."

"Not 'someone,'" I said, sounding whiny even to myself. 'Someone next to me': that was what Dino said he wanted: a relaxation, comfort and habit in place of love. "I want Joe back."

"Pretty sure he won't come back," he said. There was almost a teasing smile in his voice, not at all unkind. "Also pretty sure he'll never really be gone. You may find someone to be with, but he'll never be Uncle Joe, and he'll never take his place." He waited a minute, and then asked,

"Do you think he'd want you to find someone else? Would he have, if you'd died first?"

"Well, the second question is easy. Yes. He wasn't always faithful to me even when he was alive."

"That's not fair," J.J. said quickly. "You told me about that. He was sorry; he ended it and he shielded you from it." He was right, though I had felt a moment's serious attraction to my own anger and hurt feelings. "I'm sure he would want you to be happy. Maybe in a relationship; maybe on your own. He'd support you either way. Maybe you can be happy with just the memories of your life together. But that's not what I'm getting from you right now." I thought a minute.

"He saved me from years of thinking no one wanted me. Then he died and left me. I'm back again to thinking no one wants me. I'm stuck. I'm in this stupid loop from 1990. I'm an old man who has learned nothing – not from sadness; not from happiness."

"You're the textbook definition of a man who needs nothing," J.J. said quietly. "You don't need a boyfriend to make you whole." His father had recently told me more or less the same thing. "And by the way, you've got more irons in the fire right now than anyone we know."

"The last time I was single, everyone told me I was fine with or without, and it didn't help then, either." That wasn't quite right. Twenty-two years with Joe maybe hadn't taught me anything, but they had certainly aged me. Before I fell in love with Joe, I was having a midlife crisis about aloneness in the desert of gay dating in the age of AIDS. Now, I was a man entering old age and looking at the end. I didn't particularly care about having a man in my life. I cared about being old, about dying, about my life being basically over. Less than a year before, someone younger and much healthier than me had died in my arms. I could die, too, shockingly soon, unready, an unaccompanied soul in a grey void – *nec ut soles dabis iocos...* Even as I thought this, and felt the dread with cold clarity, I knew I was being ridiculous and self-pitying.

"Well, did you think you'd die together in a plane crash? Otherwise, one of you was going to be alone at the end, whatever happened." Jimmy Jack was too young to teach me anything about end-of life imponderables, except that he just had.

"No, but… Joe was younger," I tried. "I would die first and he would have to deal with being a widower. This was supposed to be his problem."

"But he was wiser."

"Oh, thanks," I said, actually stung. He went on, not confounded.

"He was *much* wiser. He already knew you would be together forever. He already knew about existential truth. You're the one who needed this life lesson."

"So he died to teach me a lesson. Swell. Great fucking way to run a world." He paused; he seemed almost shocked.

"It's weird to hear you curse," he said after a moment, in a guarded voice. I thought of myself as using bad language fairly often, but realized that I probably self-censored when he was around. "His death was his death. It wasn't about you. You shared it with him: you were a hero in his last few minutes." To be honest, I thought, I had been a frozen tin man with good manners. "Whether you decide to be with someone else in the future is your decision, not his." I bristled, impatiently, as though he were speaking cynical cant.

"He's gone," I said. "We'll never hold each other again; he won't get on my nerves or say anything dumb or sweet, or make me crazy or cheer me up." I could feel the tears forming in my eyes and I was mad at someone.

"But you've told me you dream about him and then know he's been here. You've told me you hear him speak to you sometimes." His voice was patient, condescending to a child on a crying jag. Instantly my fury was with him. His squeamishness about physicality made it easy for him to imagine that love could subsist without touch or exchange of fluids; in fact, in a desert-saint ascetic way, he probably preferred that. As he was repelled to think that I had once had carnal designs on his father, he now might feel a grim preachy satisfaction in telling me that I shouldn't miss the physical presence of the man who had been my lover since before his birth.

"Oh Jimmy," I said, "you don't know how much physical things count for. You think we're all starlight and cobwebs and diaphanous translucence. Dreams and auditory hallucinations don't take the place of a flesh-and-blood lover."

"You make me sound like an idiot," he said. "Which I'm not. But I know you. You don't *have* hallucinations. You're not schizophrenic. Sometimes Uncle Joe is here with you; that's a simple fact and you know it. It just can't be in a form that comforts you completely."

My anger puffed up for a second or two. 'Arrogant whippersnapper,' I thought; 'how dare you…?' Then, just as quickly, it deflated. He was right that I'd spoken down to him. His response was so gentle and forbearing that I was ashamed.

"Yes," I said. My voice sounded squeaky and pinched. "But this whole system of mortality is just so deeply *flawed*…!" I said. "I reject it; I am not resigned to it. I hate it. It's stupid and it has to be rethought."

Jimmy waited a second and then burst out laughing.

"Hear, hear!" he said. "Time to reorganize the universe! You tell 'em, G.J.!" I lay there briefly in resentful silence, until I suddenly laughed myself.

"God*damm*it!" I yelled. "GodDAMMit!" We were silent for a while. Then…

"You're OK now," he said. "I'm going back to my room."

I nodded. Miraculously, I felt fine.

"I'm OK now. You are the single most wonderful thing in the world since the beginning of time."

"Except Uncle Joe," he said, sitting up.

"Except Uncle Joe," I said, and reached to pat his shoulder before he left the room.

I checked the step counter on my iPhone: nine hundred fifty since we had left my front door. Jimmy Jack and I had a list of apartments to look at that Saturday, and this was our first stop. It wasn't an apartment, really. It was a tiny two-story house down a narrow brick walk leading back from Park Avenue along the flank of a small row house. The row house had a back door onto a patio perhaps as much as nine feet square, and the miniature place we were to see had windows on each floor facing onto that patio, as well as on its other two exposed sides. It was basically square in plan, a foot or two wider than the row house; the corner where the walkway ended was sheared off on the ground floor and the entrance was on that angled wall. The realtor had given us the key and we went up one step into the first-floor room. It was paneled, simply but strikingly, in vertical grooved slats of faded teak. There was a miniscule kitchenette, as efficient as a sailboat's, with a fold-down table that might seat four in a pinch. The main space was mostly occupied by a built-in two-sided sofa and matching coffee table, facing an iron wood-burning stove in the corner opposite the door. There was a built-in desk under the far window. All of these were trimmed with the same wood as the walls. An iron spiral staircase led up to a bedroom exactly the same size as the lower space except that it was a full square, without the sliced-off corner for the front door. The area corresponding to the kitchenette was occupied by a bath. It had a sliding door and a drain in the middle of the floor, and it was obvious that to take a shower one would first have to remove anything that couldn't get wet – towel, toilet paper, underwear – and toss it all on the floor outside. There was a queen-sized Murphy bed and a built-in armoire and chest of drawers. The whole place was sparkling clean and sanely designed. There was something Japanese about its unpretentious, inventive refinement. I imagined an entire parallel universe in which I might live off the grid, grow my own vegetables, get back into yoga, and possess only one perfect celadon vase, one Armani jacket, and a Vermeer.

"If we were in mediaeval Japan," I said, "this would be the Emperor's hunting lodge." It would be ideal for someone like Jimmy, who owned basically nothing. Just to prove we weren't vaporing dreamers, we measured with our hands to be sure there was room for his keyboard; it would fit easily on top of the dresser upstairs or the dining table or desk below. From my basement surplus, I could supply one club chair, some folding dining chairs, and more than enough dishes and linens to get by on. I made Jimmy run up and down the stairs a couple of times. I imagined he might bump his head on the iron steps, but the ergonomics were faultless, and there was plenty of room for his flailing elbows and ankles.

I called the realtor, and she said it was still available. We hurried back to her office to surrender the key for the time being. As we retraced our nine hundred fifty steps home, elated, I suddenly felt a little sad. J.J. didn't need to be told.

"I'm keeping my keys to your house," he said, as though we'd been arguing about it. "I'm coming for dinner at least once a week. You are not allowed to climb a single ladder to change a single light bulb. You'll come to my place sometimes and teach me how to cook."

"You'll practice on my piano."

"Yeah," he said. A few silent steps later, he added, "I'll still miss you."

Kevin and Jimmy had made dinner plans for a couple of nights later. This would be their first long talk alone in months. Jimmy and I were standing in the kitchen when the doorbell rang around 5:30 that evening, and he visibly took care not to react too much.

"Deep breath," I counseled. He took one, nodded curtly, and then lunged down the hall to open the front door. Whatever happened there wasn't mine to see, but it took only moments for them to drift back to the kitchen. Kevin was beaming. J.J. loomed over his shoulder, showing pure delight and adoration, and they looked as lovely together as they ever had, but Kevin's glow, at least at that moment, was for me.

"I've missed all your fabulosity," he said. "Our glamorous legendary godfather…"

"Get over here, you hilarious pipsqueak," I said. He twined his arms around my waist, and I did something I'd wanted to since the first time we met: I leaned down and kissed the top of his precious head. Having the Boys reunited under my roof, even for half an hour, was bliss to me. The three of us talked in the parlor for a while before they headed out for pizza or sushi or tacos. Kevin treated Jimmy with regal, cordial fondness and just enough flirtatiousness to honor the romance they had shared without in any way seeming to want to rekindle it. J.J. couldn't stop smiling, but I felt his disappointment grow with each breath. He understood that, at least for the time being, they were not going to have a relaunch.

They were gone for a couple of hours. When they came back, they rang the doorbell. I ran down from my third-floor study, wondering if J.J. had forgotten his key, something he had never done. I opened the front doors and found them sitting on the marble steps as comfortably as a couple of country boys swinging their bare feet from a bridge and chatting or sharing the silence while they fished. Jimmy looked up over his shoulder and smiled at me.

"Kevin can't come in," he said, "but he insisted on coming back to hug you good-bye."

"I would have taken to my bed in grief if he hadn't," I said. The red elf stood and turned to face me.

"Definitely *au revoir* and not *adieu*," he said. "Jacob and I have decided we'll be hanging out a lot more in the future, now that we know where we are."

"Well then, I'll remain an unshifting feature in your variegated young life," I said. Jimmy's simple smile didn't seem forced. I knew that he was capable of sobbing over Kevin, so if he could look happy through all this, perhaps all he really needed was a maintenance dose of his small pal's company. After Kevin and I had exchanged our farewells, I stepped back into the house and let them take whatever parting suited them. It was only a few seconds later that, looking out the parlor windows, I saw Kevin saunter away, head thrown back and shoulders squared as always, with his unique aura of success and confidence radiating from him. I was slightly apprehensive about how J.J. would look when he trailed in.

He stood in the front hall for a moment, head down.

"Did you have fun, honey?" I asked tentatively. He looked up at me quickly, as if he'd forgotten I was there, and smiled.

"We'll always love each other, he says."

"That makes me happy," I nodded.

"Me too. But he thinks we're not meant to be lovers." I watched him closely, trying to see if it hurt him to say this or to have heard Kevin say it. He waited to go on, while I did my best to maintain a wise gentle understanding smile. Then he took in a sudden deep breath. "So… I guess I have to look elsewhere for crazy sex now." I must have cackled slightly in surprise at this remark, because he gave me a crooked smile, apparently meant to be wicked.

"Who are you and what have you done with Jimmy Jack?"

"I'm the new model," he said. "Try to keep up." He looked and sounded distinctly proud of himself.

"OMG," I said. "There's a dangerous predator loose in town: Jimmy on the prowl. Lock up your sons and husbands, y'all." We looked at each other directly for a quiet moment. His energy was low; he seemed neither sad nor exultant. He was simply making a realistic adjustment, an acceptance both of things that wouldn't be and of his own need for erotic contact. Kevin had given him a great gift.

"There's a horn player who works in the library with me who's kind of sexy," he said. "Jasper, if you can believe it. I think I'll see if he wants to have lunch with me."

"Anyone named Jasper has got to be intriguing," I allowed. "At least, if he's not actively hideous."

"That he is certainly not."

For the first time ever, Jimmy and I were actually dishing. I felt about twenty-five, and I liked it.

Joe had died on a Saturday; the first anniversary of his death fell on a Monday. Connie and I planned to talk the next day, when she would put aside her mourning for the first time. We spoke on the phone fairly often, but usually reserved Skype for special occasions. She was always a bit shy about the technology; she thought the cam made her look puffy and elderly. She had a bit of, and was probably in fact the source of, Joe's touchy vanity. Without being in any way conceited about their appearance, they had both always disliked anything which distorted or mischaracterized the image they intended to present. The weird angles and bleaching light of the webcam were embarrassing to Connie, and frankly did nothing for me, either. Still, we both enjoyed being able to see each other, even *"au naturel,"* as she liked to say (she pronounced it 'Oh natcher-AL'). We already had made another Skype appointment for Joe's birthday a couple of weeks later.

As the anniversary approached I was finding myself more and more back to normal in my choice of clothes. I still put some thought into dressing for my talk with Connie. I knew she wouldn't go garish her first day out, and I didn't want to seem frivolous. I opted for a candy-stripe blue and white shirt with a triangle of grey T-shirt showing at the neck. When I called her, we could hear each other before her cam clicked on, and she apparently could see me in the meantime, because I heard a smile in her voice as she said,

"Ma che bella camicia!" Then my own slightly wavering image shrank suddenly into a corner of the screen and the whole monitor glowed with her pale face.

She was smiling shyly, as though she had just stepped out of a dressing room in a fancy women's shop, hoping for my approval. She lifted her head, perhaps to minimize the wrinkles at her neck, perhaps to mask her own astonishment at the unfamiliar picture she saw reflected now. She was wearing a beautiful satin blouse, with a large floral pattern in white, grey, and pink, and she wore an untied shot silk scarf draped loosely over her shoulders, shifting pink and grey.

"Well hello GOR-geous!" I said. She did look wonderful, and surprising. Without realizing, I had gotten used to seeing her in all black.

The night before had worn me out. I wanted to hold on to every blazing, shocking detail I could recall of my last five minutes with Joe. It would be disloyal not to keep them fresh forever. That night, though, I noticed that many details were now gone. It required intentional concentration for me to feel the abyss of grief that had been my every breath for months. When had that started to fade? Getting up this morning after a fitful unhappy night, I sensed that something was lighter. I looked forward to talking with Connie, and to seeing her out of black, and here she was. 'There's real wisdom in this culture of mourning,' I thought: 'we honor grief, we observe the year, and then life goes on.'

"Hi, *caro*. How are you?" Her voice sounded so kind that I suddenly felt tears in my eyes. It was obvious why we were talking, what we were remembering. I shook my head and smiled; she could tell that my voice was blocked for a moment.

Jimmy, in his room just down the hall, had heard us, and as if on cue he came lumbering in.

"*Ciao, Mamma Constanzia,*" he said cheerfully. He got a kick out of calling her that, especially after our trip to Rome. "You look especially magnificent today. I know it's not a super easy day for you."

"Sweet boy," she said. "I'm OK. Do you really like this blouse? I didn't want to go overboard, but I'll be honest: I was happy to put away the black blouses and dresses this morning. I'm not saying I won't wear them again some days, but..."

"We'll wear exactly what we want to wear," I nodded. "Every day. Is that blouse new? It's perfect. It doesn't hurt my eyes but it definitely says 'We're still here.'"

"Little Caterina took me out shopping last week." Cathy was Connie's senior daughter-in-law, more or less my age, and little only in Connie's loyal memory; she had apparently been a slip of a girl when she married Joe's oldest brother Carmine. Because they had set up housekeeping just down the street from the senior Andreolis' house, Connie had conscripted her as her vice-regent in the clan. They scrapped at times, enacting Mediterranean tropes of in-law friction, but Cathy had mastered the gentle art of knuckling under to the imperious matriarch when she had no alternative, and over the decades it had become obvious to the family that the mantel would fall on her shoulders in due time. She was doggedly devoted when trials came, defending both Connie and the prerogatives of the reigning female Andreoli. Naturally it had fallen to her to take Connie shopping for this make-over. I could picture them: Connie still a raven of ill omen in appearance, but starting to peek out curiously at colors of renewal, and Cathy, barrel-shaped, brisk, critical, whispering the backstory to the shop girls, and raising her voice to call out, *"Oh, mamma, yes!"* or "Not that one, sweetie… it'll wash you out."

Jimmy excused himself after trading a few sentences.

"What a nice boy," Connie said when he was gone. "He has been a lifesaver for you this year."

"Not always easy," I said, "but indispensable. And I've had to remember not to take him for granted as a source of comfort; he's been grieving Joe in his own right."

"Joe loved him, and he knew it," she agreed. "He was like your child in some ways… yours and Joe's, together." She paused. "Joe loved everyone, I think. He was just so *good.*" Now the seal was broken on her self-control, and she cried a little, without embarrassment to either of us. My throat was tight, but I could hum my sympathy and fellow-feeling. "Oh, Jim. I still have mornings when I wonder why I keep waking up; why I should even bother getting up." That wasn't quite true of me, but I could feel and see that my own face was red now. Her sadness meant that I had been right to spend my adult life loving Joe. Nice strong sensible people like her had loved him. Maybe that meant that I was nice and strong and sensible as well.

"He was just so *good,*" I repeated.

272

"I wish my arms could reach right through this machine and hug you, *caro*. What a year you must have had. Do you *know* how much my boy loved you? Have I told you that often enough?"

"I know. No one could tell me often enough, but I know. I just miss him so – I don't need to tell you about that, I know." There was nothing either of us could say. We looked at each other in glum, sweet silence for a moment.

"Wait, I don't think you know this," I remembered out of nowhere. "Jimmy is moving out at the end of this month." She looked stricken.

"No! Why? What are you going to do?"

"He should have his own place for his second year in grad school. He wants to start dating, I think. We've found him the most adorable little house just a few blocks from here. We'll be in and out of each other's places. I'm committed to teaching him how to cook, for one thing." I had a sudden inspiration. "His parents are coming to help him move out, the last three days of the month. Why don't you come, too? We'd all love to see you, and…" She didn't look convinced, and suddenly I very much wanted her to come. I resorted to a shameful manipulation. "You could cook for us while we're packing." She smiled, very gratified.

"It will take you four minutes to pack that boy's stuff," she said, pretending to dismiss my idea.

"Four exhausting minutes, after which we'll all be clamoring for *cannelloni*. Please, Connie." She laughed.

"I'll think about it and let you know."

"OK." I knew she would probably come. "Meanwhile don't let Mr. Mattucci see you in that new blouse… not unless you want him to propose." Mattucci was a widower who ran an old deli down the street from her house, and his crush on Connie had been a family joke since long before Dominic's death. She waved one hand.

"That old fool," she said.

A couple of days before the end of the month, Tony and Rachel came to visit, ostensibly to help Jimmy move. As Connie had implied, that would amount more or less to packing a large suitcase and slipping his keyboard into its canvas bag, but there were ceremonial niceties to be observed; we wanted to mark this new season in his life. Connie herself had agreed to come down, too, which led to some adjustments in the accommodations. The official guest room was hers by right. Tony and Rachel would rough it in Jimmy's room, and he would crash with me for his last two nights under my roof. Rachel had categorically refused my suggestion that they take my room and I camp with Jimmy in his. I was also throwing a party his last night in the house. Walter and Ricardo were motoring up from Washington, bringing Marie; Gene and Carl were coming; Kevin had said he wouldn't miss it; and at J.J.'s insistence, I invited Dino.

Tony and Rachel got a rental car at the airport and texted when they were just a few blocks away. Jimmy and I stepped out to the stoop and were there to wave them into a parking spot in front of the house. Rachel jumped out as soon as Tony switched the engine off and got immediately wrapped up in Jimmy's long arms. He still had his way of seeming stiff and awkward, even with her, and I noticed how much bigger he suddenly seemed, or rather, how much smaller Rachel did. She wasn't actually shrinking, but because I had always seen her as monumental and commanding, I hadn't gotten used to how much shorter she now was than her little boy. She leaned back to scan his expression. It had been a couple of months since they had been together in person.

"My sweet son," she murmured. Her voice sounded both kind and principled, as if she would never give him an affirmation that wasn't utterly sincere.

"Mommy," he answered.

Tony by this time had stepped out of the car, popped the trunk, and fished out a couple of small summer bags. He was starting to shoulder them when Jimmy called out,

"No, Dad, let me help you."

Tony's face registered a tiny shock, instantly covered. Rachel and I too exchanged a nanosecond's look of surprise. I think all three of us grown-ups were pleased at this epochal monosyllable, but I also felt an ounce of sorrow. When J.J. first learned to talk, he went through about a year of saying "jale" for "ginger ale," and it had always felt like Eden to me to hear him say it. The first time I heard him casually say "ginger ale," with a little wriggle of complacency at mastering an adult word, I had all but fled the room in tears. Now, suddenly and without warning, Tony was "Dad." Rachel silently clutched the recent "Mommy" to her heart for a moment and, I guessed, prayed that the dreadful day of 'Mom' might be postponed a while yet. Tony raised one eyebrow almost ironically, but with a barely suppressed beam of approval, and said,

"Well listen to *you,* Jacob. Thanks." He gestured for J.J. to come take some of the luggage. J.J. went to hug him as well, and Tony, maybe just a bit smug about his quick promotion, got both arms around him and kissed him loudly on the cheek. Then he looped the shoulder straps of the two larger bags over Jimmy's neck and took two small duffels by their handles for himself.

Connie wasn't to come till the day of the party, and she would stay for a couple of days after Jimmy moved out. Meanwhile, he couldn't wait to show the tiny house to his parents. He and I had taken to calling it "950." He basked in their 'Ooh's and 'Ah's as if he had built the place with his own hands. Rachel whisked him to the Giant to lay in some basic groceries and cleaning supplies. It was true that, keeping house for himself for the first time, he might well have bought only matzo, ground beef, dried cranberries, Fabreze, and Chardonnay. I was gratified to hear that he had told her my catch-phrase, "Replace the back-up," one of my core principles of gracious living: always keep the larder stocked with one unopened container of every absolute staple, and add that item to the shopping list when the time came to open the reserve.

The day before the party, she and I were alone in the kitchen. She had inventive ideas for the menu and was starting the catering early. As she started to orchestrate some *crudités* and cold cuts, and roll out the crusts for some exquisite summer fruit pies, I was content to perch on a stool and hand her whatever she asked for. I hadn't watched her cook since Thanksgiving, and then I had been too recently bereaved to focus. I had forgotten that she normally took off her wedding ring when she was kneading, rinsing, slicing… something my mother had always done, too, to my great fascination when I was a child. Rachel's finger showed a pale stripe when her wide antique rose gold ring came off. There was nothing conventional or stodgy about her, except that her long marriage had literally marked the flesh of her hand.

She seemed dashing, almost reckless, as she tossed berries and sugar in a large bowl and squeezed a half lemon from at least two feet above, squirting with festive abandon and laughing at her own messiness. A strand of her lovely silver hair had pulled free and trailed in front of her eyes as she looked down. The gesture with which she smoothed it back with the side of her wet right hand was charming, as though she were a coltish Old World country girl just learning her way around the kitchen. For the first time, I wondered if J.J. got some of his goofiness from her. I was overwhelmed with a wave of nostalgia, both for the hip, funny young Rachel I remembered from the first years of our friendship, and for the deeply beloved boy she had brought into the world and who was about to leave my home.

"I will miss our Jimmy Jack," I suddenly said. She smiled privately before looking up at me.

"He told me yesterday how much he'll miss you," she said. "I almost wonder why he's so determined to move out. He would have been leaving in a year anyway."

"I guess I've been kind of *in loco parentis* this year. He may feel that he needs to spread his wings."

"No," she smiled; "never *parentis*. He told me you were his Auntie Mame. He definitely sees you as *much* cooler than his parents." I fished a couple of berries out of her mixing bowl.

"We can't have watched that movie more than six or seven times this year," I said. "His lips move now when we see the hunting scene. 'MUH-thuh of Jeff-uh-son DA-vuss... she's passed the *fox!*' I guess something stuck." I waited before going on; she might not completely love what I had to say next. "He implied to me recently that he might want to date more freely than he's done here. Maybe he feels a little embarrassed or inhibited about bringing someone here if he's not sure it's serious." Her face turned slightly somber. "He was sure with Kevin," I finished.

"How do you really feel about Kevin?" she asked me, without meeting my eye. She and Tony, amazingly enough, had never actually met the little guy; they'd been called on to admire his pictures, and they had sat gamely through dozens of infatuate anecdotes, but had never gotten to assess his real in-person delightfulness.

"Oh," I said, taking a stab at casual, "I like him a lot. I've known thousands of smart young gay guys, and he's definitely one of the nicest. He has been scrupulously kind to Jimmy, but I think he knew from the beginning that their relationship meant something more to Jimmy than it did to him. Or... not more, but something different. When Party A is experiencing first love and Party B has been around the block a few times already, it's never quite fifty-fifty. Based on what I've gathered of their most recent conversations, their attachment is not going to be reborn as a romance... maybe, if we're all very lucky, as a tender, durable friendship. Kevin is a very good influence in J.J.'s life. He's sophisticated and experienced, but he's taken the time to introduce Jimmy very gently to some aspects of... of incarnation which were challenging for him. He genuinely cares for him, I think."

Rachel listened to this little sermon with one eyebrow lifted and just a trace of skepticism.

"I'm glad Jimmy has been here this year," she said after sorting her thoughts for a moment. "Anton and I couldn't have advised him on any of these details." Tony had said more or less the same thing on cam a few weeks earlier; their marriage was a union of equals. "And you've been vigilant to see that he was treated kindly and with respect."

"It's been very much a two-way street," I said. "He is shockingly honest; he's not self-filtering enough to hold back. He has set me straight on any number of occasions when I threatened to vapor myself into embarrassing tizzies."

"However," Rachel pressed, not acknowledging what I'd just said, "I would say he'd *already* experienced his first love. Her name is Lyric." I knew that Lyric had not been love. She was confusion, adolescent striving for answers, even well-intended pretense and, on her side, some manipulation of a befuddled, tractable, desirable boy. This wasn't something to argue or debate with Rachel, though. I paused and chose my words.

"I know this isn't exactly your dream for how his life would turn out. But I need you to know that his presence here this year has literally saved my life. I don't think I can ever thank you enough for that. No one else could have done what he has, and I truly consider him the dearest, most wonderful human on earth. His coming out was never a prerequisite for my cherishing him that way."

"No," she said, shrugging and letting herself smile wanly. "I know that. He's been a life force for you in a year of mourning. Youth and becoming and emerging..." She looked out the window and her voice caught. "For a moment when I first learned I was pregnant, I thought he might be a girl. I remember you asked me what we would call her…"

"'Sarah, or something starting with an S,'" I quoted. I remembered perfectly. There had been a happy moment when Rachel and I considered that possibility; her mother's recently deceased sister Sarah would have had the honor of the little girl's being named for her. But even as we discussed it, Rachel said that she knew that she would have a boy, and that Tony had already decided that they would name him for me. "You and I both loved him before he had a gender or a name or a sexuality. It didn't matter then, and it still doesn't."

Rachel reached out one arm to hug me.

"He's a baffling…" (her short hesitation made me think for a moment she was choking on a slice of radish she'd just nibbled) "…*young man.*" I realized she had stopped herself, just in time, from saying, *'boy.'* Then a spark came into her eye, and she lifted her head with that heavy, proud tilt I had always liked. "But very magnetic; truly one-of-a-kind." I nodded. Her arm around my waist was suddenly very strong. "You see him as we do. As *I* do. The way he has grown this year… gotten so brave and big and *symmetrical…* that means he's leading the right life."

I loved her "*symmetrical.*" She was right that, for over twenty years, he had been askew, strung slightly awry, but was now, in a matter of several months, a cantering, eager-eyed yearling. She was incapable of saying what she really meant: that J.J. had become handsome under my roof. That would have been like boasting of her own good looks, something that was foreign to every ganglion and corpuscle in her. "What a gift you've been to my family this year… *dear* Jim."

My self-centeredness since Joe's death had clouded my memories of who Rachel really was. As we stood side by side in my kitchen, I now remembered how she had sponsored the launch of my love for Joe so many years before, not entirely selflessly, granted, but with patient counsel and gentle promptings, hospitalities, and discretions. I choked up. It would have been nice to say something gracious, about the gift she and Tony had been to me, to *my* family, but all I could do was pull my left arm off her shoulder and point at my wedding ring. Our eyes met and we both smiled.

I had had some idea that Connie's role at the party would be to sit in the big wing chair in the parlor and receive the other guests like Queen Mum, but I was forgetting, as I often had, that she didn't think of herself as either grand or old. She was taking her assigned tasks very seriously, and had swept into the kitchen bare moments after unpacking and started preparing, in my largest available pan, her legendary *pasta al forno*. For a few minutes she acted as though she might be teaching Jimmy her methods, since he was moving out and would need to start cooking for himself, but very quickly that fiction was abandoned. She had never even let Joe or me in on her trade secrets, and we were both considered good cooks. Instead, she enlisted Rachel in a tight *ad hoc* alliance to arrange food service, and Tony and Jimmy and I were relegated to setting out drinks and carrying platters to the exact spots they specified in the dining room and parlor.

Half an hour before guests were expected, Connie suddenly glanced at her watch, gave a little gasp at the late hour, and then, blushing slightly, asked Rachel to help her dress upstairs. They were gone only a few minutes, and I saw when they came back down that Connie had needed someone to zip up the back of her crisp blue and white seersucker sun dress. The dress was cut just low enough, and flared just enough from the waist, to flatter her vigorous figure. She was fully out of mourning, yes, her face marked and worn, and forgetting nothing, but still glad to be with us, looking forward to a party. Rachel hovered behind her, smiling with admiration.

"Have you ever seen anyone so lovely?" she asked the room.

"Says Miss America here," said Connie, pointing over her shoulder at Rachel, who looked, as usual, splendid in the perfect way. They had been upstairs barely ten minutes, and a few of those must have been given to Connie's zipper, so the fact that Rachel's hair was pinned up afresh, that she had slipped into just the right loose, rustling summer caftan of seafoam green, and that the Lalique was suddenly in evidence, meant that she had done wonders in mere moments.

"We just had a girl-talk moment and Constanzia let me try her Charlie," she said with a smile.

"No competing fragrances," Connie explained.

"We're not savages," I said. "I think you're both extraordinary." I glanced at Jimmy. "Speaking of which," I said, "you, upstairs: comb, jeans without holes, patchouli, and maybe that orange shirt with the green palm fronds? Oh, and shoes."

Rachel caught my eye with an ironic lift of a brow. I remembered that when Jimmy was a hard-to-manage toddler, she adopted a precept from an expert on the radio, that small children could process only three words: "Coat; scarf; outside!" I wasn't even aware that I had barked orders at Jimmy just now, and she in any case had never authorized me to expand the number to five. He was already on his way upstairs to comply.

At the party itself, I felt a funny loss of control, like a man floundering comically after being pushed into a swimming pool in white tie. Walter and Ricardo showed up right on time, with Marie. I was touched to see her, and my first impression was that she was doing much better, coming out of her grief of abandonment, taking an active interest in others' lives. Her eye contact was frank and affectionate in a way I hadn't seen since Clare left her, and some of her vampy girlishness was back at last. As they entered the house, she had her hand threaded through Ricardo's elbow confidingly, and she rested her head on my shoulder for a moment after we hugged. Ricardo leaned over her and whispered to me, so that she could hear,

"Jimmy says we need to decide about Dino." This was confusing. J.J. hadn't spoken to them yet this evening, so they must have spoken on the phone, something I didn't know they ever did. Clearly they were now secret allies in managing my life.

"You know, BooBoo," Marie added (she apparently had heard previews of the Dino question in the ride up from DC), "I envy you your Jimmy. He has been fabulous for you this year. I know how much you're going to miss him." I squeezed her shoulder a moment.

"We've counted the steps between his new place and here," I said bravely. "Under a thousand. I'm not letting him off easy."

Gene stepped through the front door soon after. Beside him was a good-looking young preppy guy, whom he introduced as Carter, a junior colleague/protégé of his from the insurance agency. Carter, in addition to having the usual blue eyes and sandy blond hair, was tweedy and courteous. He had an attentive smile ready for anything I said, and was full of compliments for the house and thanks for having been allowed to come. The only surprise was that, when I patted his shoulder and pointed him to the bar, my hand met strong shapely curves which his baggy Oxford cloth shirt had not prepared me for.

As he stepped away, I brought Gene close with an arm-lock around his shoulder.

"Isn't Carter just the most *comme il faut* youth in town?" I said. "How am I ever to thank you?"

"I've given *up* on finding someone for *you,* you fast piece," he whispered. "This one is for our young J.J.. Recently single and seriously ready to rumble."

"Not so fast," I said. "Who's to say he's not meant to be mine, all mine?" My hand was still registering that muscular shoulder.

"As you weigh the hunky contractor against the international film star?" he asked. I realized that Gene knew nothing yet of Dino. "I have resigned myself to watching from the sidelines, *slack*-jawed with admiration, while you work your magic. And taking copious notes for my own instruction." Gene needed instruction about meeting men the way I needed instruction on the seven forms of the Italian definite article.

By then Carter was working his way towards Jimmy from the bar, Corona in hand. Jimmy himself, kempt and festive, the inescapable cynosure of all eyes, was chatting with neighbor Carl, who must have come in through the kitchen door. Carter was suave enough to introduce himself without help from Gene or me.

Just then, I glanced at the front door and saw small Kevin strut in. I went to meet him. The way he seemed to melt into my arms during our brief embrace made him feel almost like a fond ex-lover of my own. I could see J.J. from where we were standing; he had seen Kevin's entrance. His vague stare showed a tiny wistfulness, but he didn't step away from Carter. Rather, he turned to him, clear-eyed, and touched his elbow, inviting him to walk with him. Together they came into the parlor, and joined Kevin and me. After a moment that felt awkward only because I was there, I left the three of them chatting quite familiarly.

Rachel and Walter and I happened to be clustered in the parlor when Dino stepped over the threshold and looked around. He seemed larger than usual, tense with energy. He had on a satiny shirt of deep purple which made his eyes look black and sparkling. When he saw me, he unleashed a radiant smile that struck me mid-chest. I had never seen or imagined him so overwhelmingly handsome. I felt like a shy innocent bride in a Rousseauean idyll, happily, helplessly swooning before an eruptive masculine force of nature. He loped up to me like a powerful but friendly big cat, and without waiting to be introduced to anyone he wrapped a long arm around my neck and kissed me. He struck a perfect note between masterful and adoring. He didn't care who saw us kiss – in fact, he wanted everyone to see it – yet he was somehow also a supplicant, angling for my approval.

"*Finalmente,*" he murmured. "It's been way too long."

Rachel and Walter were gaping at each other with a wild surmise. Walter recovered faster.

"Let me venture a guess," he said, extending his right hand like an ambassador. "Dino?" He at least had heard of Dino; I hadn't mentioned him to Tony and Rachel. Dino turned to Walter knowingly and shook his hand:

"And I'm going to say... Walter?" It was hard to say which of them seemed more suave and in control. Then he turned to me, politely indicating Rachel with a raised eyebrow. "And who is the most beautiful lady in the world?" he asked.

"This is our wonderful Rachel Fleischer-Neuberg," I said. "J.J.'s mother, and one of my favorite people on the planet. Dino Surace – " (I pronounced it in Italian) " – a student of mine from years ago, and... a very good friend."

"Oh," said Dino with a kind of reverence, recognizing her name, "I guess I should thank you right off for making Jacob. I don't know what our man Jim here would do without him. Anyone else who loves Jim needs to just take a number when Jacob is in the mix."

"Yes," Rachel nodded, fully recovered. "They met when Jimmy was two days old, and they've been singing duets ever since."

"I was always Jim's favorite and *best* student," Dino said: "wasn't I?" The rhetorical question was aimed straight at me, with a large sidelong glance. "And the best-looking, of course."

"No one here questions any of that, even for the briefest moment," said Walter.

"Maybe he told you about our trip to Italy years ago," Dino went on. "Rome and Tuscany. He completely blew my mind. The Pantheon,

David, Palio, Cortona... My new plan is to take him back there with my kids someday soon. They're around the same age I was then, and they're smart enough to enjoy it. I was kind of jealous of Jimmy for getting to go this summer."

"You're right that my son is very lucky," Rachel answered, when Dino's spate of affability subsided. "Luckily for him, he knows it. Yes, now that you remind me, I do remember tales of your trip with Jim, and how you charmed his Italian friends, one and all. Let me introduce you to my husband."

"Tony," said Dino. I glanced around. Tony was nowhere visible. "Wait, let me get ready mentally. I'm meeting royalty tonight and I want Jim to be proud of me. Let's stop at the bar on our way." There was so much fiancé subtext in Dino's words and manner that I wondered if I'd missed an announcement somewhere. At any rate, Rachel seemed quite on board. She gave me a small conspiring smile as she and Dino started to walk away together.

"*Well...!*" she said softly to me, as if impressed.

"I'll be back," he said over his shoulder.

Walter turned back to me, looking stern.

"We should never have let you stray south of Florence," he said. "One night of passion in the sand years ago with a humpy Roman and you embark on a decades-long marriage. And now you are falling into the artless snares of a strapping *scugnizzo*..."

"But you loved Joe, didn't you?" I asked. For a moment, I wasn't even sure. Perhaps all these past years Walter had simply made the best of some downwardly-mobile attraction of mine. He straightened up in an instant.

"Joe was your Ricardo," he said. "I loved him with my whole heart, for me as much as for you." Ricardo himself was strolling towards us, nodding to left and to right, and Walter waited till he had joined us to continue. "Now that that's settled," he went on, "let's consult a higher power." He turned expectantly to Ricardo.

"I was just talking to Dino," Ricardo said. He apparently needed no prompting to know what we were talking about or what he was to say. "He's nuts about you, Jim. I think we can kiss the porn star good-bye now."

"You realize we've never so much as taken our shirts off," I said. I felt a dim disappointment at the idea that Andy Ferrara might never sleep next to me again.

"He told me he's 'patient,'" Ricardo said, nodding as grandly and stiffly as if he'd been wearing a *pouf* three feet high, decked with flowers and plumes, and a model frigate or Temple of Love, why not? "He's made his mind up. He's like Joe: stubborn." I blushed; Dino was actively politicking for my friends' approval. Ricardo's face softened as he sensed my embarrassment. "Honey, you're fine, either way. We all know that. I'm just warning you: Dino has a plan."

Somehow their kindness and teasing unmanned me for a minute and I felt my chin start to shake.

"I miss Joe," I said. They each had one arm around me in an instant.

"And you will never settle for less than Joe," Ricardo crooned, directly into my ear. I thought hard, then spoke:

"Is Dino 'less'?" I wasn't sure, and the silence which followed showed that they weren't, either.

"We'll see, Jimbo," Walter said after a pause. "All in good time."

At some point, my neighbor Grace dropped by, seeing the parlor lights blazing, and tossed her shawl to me after asking Carl to bring her a glass of Prosecco. It was a diaphanous cotton weave that exhaled a slight fragrance of… Carl met my eye. He had long claimed that the older ladies of Bolton Hill were regularly stoned. Perhaps Grace's shawl smelled only of incense, which, come to think of it, she had sometimes had burning when I visited her house.

"How is your handsome Czech friend doing?" she asked me. "I hope he visits again *soon.*" Her generous smile showed that she hoped this for my sake. "He's such a nice young man… so polite and so well-spoken. And *not* hard to look at." I looked around nervously for Dino; if he overheard this banter, he might think the worst. He might also see it as a frank challenge, though. Something told me he was the competitive type.

Later, I saw him chatting affably with Tony; Rachel had turned away to refill a glass, but was clearly part of the conversation. Jimmy drifted up to me, flanked by Carter and Kevin. Looking anything but sad, Kevin touched my elbow and breathed,

"ACD."

"Hmm…?" I asked, eyebrows arching.

"All the Cuteness of Dino," he said. The other two boys chuckled. I didn't know that Kevin had ever been let in on J.J.'s and my private joke about him (ACK, 'All the Cuteness of Kevin'), but here he was, cheerfully troping on it.

"I think my dad is going to be voting for Dino," J.J. said to me, sipping a Corona, casting his eye over to where Dino and Tony were chatting.

As the party was starting to break up, Dino signaled me that he was leaving. I hurried to the front door and he gestured for me to step outside with him. Being alone together for a minute, on a public street, seemed charged. I liked him enough to think that anything was possible, and I sensed that he liked me perhaps even more than that. When silence fell between us, his car keys already in his hand, he suddenly leaned forward. His free arm went around my waist; his other fist, half-closed around the keys, made an awkward wad on the back of my neck.

When I realized we were going to kiss, my mind started racing. The whole thing seemed implausible, but I could feel consent rising from every part of me. I knew how deep my mourning had been and still was. I knew that nothing would ever replace or supplant what I had lived. Still, the strongest voice inside me was a sincere, 'Well, let it be.'

As kisses go, it was well above average. Dino had clearly steeled himself for some time to this, and he let his mouth feel soft and engaged. We must have spent twenty or so seconds at it, and as we pulled apart he seemed diffident, apologetic, as though he had been both presumptuous and unskilled. His big strong face was shy and uncertain. I could feel myself rushing forward to assure him that I was willing, grateful. I didn't want him to feel inadequate in what he had offered me.

"OK," I said, "our first night together has to be soon." He nodded, his eyes confused and hopeful, and we traded nonsensical, almost loving words as we parted. He walked quickly to his car, and I turned back towards the house.

Standing just a few feet away inside, looking out one of the front parlor windows and adjusting the curtain, was Connie. As I stepped back into the house, she came into the front hall to meet me. I must have stammered something. She put a hand up to my mouth.

"You're always my son-in-law," she said. "Dino is a very nice young man and he likes you. He understands what you've been through. He told me it was an honor to meet Joe's mother. It was sweet; he sounded like a little boy who'd learned his lines for a school play. He's a gentle, respectful man." I could feel my face fall. I was aware of being exhaustingly sad. Dino *was* a very nice man; he was not Joe Andreoli. It felt disloyal to Joe even to have allowed Dino to kiss me, let alone to have encouraged and enjoyed it. Before I could say anything, Connie spoke again. "Years ago, Joey told me he'd almost ruined your marriage. He said you didn't even know it, but he 'hadn't been very nice' to you. I told him not to be silly; I knew how much you loved each other, and I knew you'd forgive him if you had to. But he thought he didn't deserve for you to love him anymore. He said that you'd been more loyal to him than he'd been to you."

'Barry,' I thought; 'Oh, Joe…' Truly, truly that didn't matter now.

Connie's eyes scanned mine closely.

"You *do* know what he meant, don't you?" she asked me. I nodded my head, afraid I might start crying with the house still half-full of witnesses. More than anything, I felt tired of tears. That year was over. "So I was right in what I told Joe. You and I both know what a beautiful life you two made together. You protected each other. You forgave each other… for things I don't even know about." She placed her hands on my shoulders. "You're one of my boys. Always, period. If Dino is going to make you happy, that will make *me* happy."

Connie hated cheap sentimentality of any kind, and she wasn't satisfied with the solemn tone she'd just struck. She saw my hesitancy in reacting.

"If you promise me to give Dino a chance, I promise *you* I'll let Mattucci buy me a glass of wine when I get back to Brooklyn." I laughed incredulously, slightly scandalized. She waited, and then smiled and nodded at me. I hadn't said 'No.' "OK, then. You're always my son-in-law." She arched an eyebrow at me, claiming every scrap of matriarchal entitlement she knew she could get away with. "You're stuck with me, *caro*," she concluded. Then she took my arm and we walked together back into the thinning group of guests.

Later that evening, I talked at some length with Tony on the back steps, where the garden air was warm and redolent. Then Kevin's laughing departure took me and Jimmy to the front door. When Carter left quite a while later, only J.J. walked him out. I got a bluff hug from Carl and an air-kiss in the vestibule from Gene. He breathed a high, throbbing *"Dino...!"* as he hugged me, and though I couldn't remember any interactions between them, I was flattered by the envy Gene pretended to feel at Dino's hotness. Grace swept her shawl back around her shoulders before starting on her fifty-yard walk home, and its wafting scent reminded me to discuss it with Carl the next day. At the very end, we all stood side by side on the sidewalk for a long farewell with Walter, Ricardo, and Marie, as we sent them off on their drive home to DC.

The five of us who would sleep in the house that night lingered in the kitchen quite a while after the clean-up was complete, chatting aimlessly and happily, until it occurred to me that we would be exhausted in the morning if we didn't turn in soon. Our little procession up the broad front stairs was like the ritual of the bedroom candles distributed to guests in a stately country home in a James novel. Tony was squiring Connie, and Rachel put her hand in the crook of my arm and gathered up the skirt of her stiff whispering caftan as if it were a House of Worth gown seven feet wide. Jimmy brought up the rear and switched off lights here and there. There was a ceremonial good-night to Connie as she peeled off, and then the rest of us wended our way up the twisting back stairs to the third floor.

Shortly after, with a quick casual smooch of dismissal to his parents, J.J. followed me to the front of the house. Within a minute or two he flopped down on my bed next to me in his boxers and t-shirt. Were we just going to drift off to sleep, or talk first?

"Carter..." he said at length, eyes on the ceiling.

"ACC – 'All the Cuteness of Carter'? Something there?"

"Something." Then he was still for a minute. "There's only one Kevin." I nodded and didn't speak. He sighed. "But that's not going to happen. So we're moving on to Carter." There was a self-conscious sophistication in his tone.

"Well, in fairness," I prompted him after another silence, "Carter is a young man of interest and substance. And right dashing, in his muted Jos. A. Banks way."

Jimmy suddenly rolled onto his side to face me.

"I just decided how you feel about Dino. Or even the porn star. It's the Uncle Joe Factor. There will never be another Uncle Joe." He met my eyes nervously as he spoke. He may have been afraid this hadn't occurred to me, and he didn't want to hurt me. "There will never be another Kevin for me."

"Joe was my *Love*," I said after a Zen moment. "But not my first love. Kevin was your first love. We don't know yet who your *Love* will be."

"Chiasmus," said J.J. a few seconds later. I wanted to hug him hard. If I had had a son, I would have wanted him to be precisely like J.J. in every way. It didn't seem fair that I was getting the child I wanted even more than Tony and Rachel had. I smiled and nodded, and rolled over to face him directly.

"I'll miss you, little boy," I said.

He leaned forward so that our foreheads were barely touching. He had never once shown any resentment of my diminutive epithets, even as he sprouted and burgeoned into the superb young man he was becoming.

"It doesn't make sense for us to miss each other," he said. "I'm always wherever you are, G.J." He had said much the same thing at the airport at Christmas time. Something welled up in me: the fat bourgeois inspiration I always felt when I heard "You are not alone," even though to the depths of my soul I was not a Sondheim person and disapproved of the way he always seemed to postpone the evening's one memorable melody until a show had run its pretentious, arty course and there were no gimmicky profundities left to deploy. Jimmy started humming. "What's your *'mi-so-la-do-re-do-la-so'* song again?" He sang the syllables on pitches, in his sleepy basso register; he was completely committed, as a matter of principle, to movable Do.

"'Draw us in the Spirit's tether,'" I murmured. Sondheim and my snobbery faded away.

"So I'm moving nine hundred fifty steps away," he said. "And Uncle Joe has moved… we don't know where, but somewhere accessible. We're all tethered."

Even if J.J. had been my son, it would have been strange for us to lie side by side, foreheads touching, to discuss things like grief and survival. I realized that, for twenty-odd years, I had never spoken of such things in such intimacy with anyone except Joe. And if what needed processing was Joe's death, who was there for me to talk to? Only Jimmy, apparently; and apparently, he was enough.

"Do you ever feel scared about what comes next?" I asked him. "After Kevin; in your new place; maybe starting to date again? Even job hunting, a year from now?" I was allowed to ask him that because my own life was a tissue of terrors: encroaching old age, infirmity, loneliness, death… he knew all this. He closed his eyes and sighed.

"Yeah." Several seconds later, he opened his eyes and looked urgently into mine. "Oh, but you…" He had just realized I had been speaking to him out of my own fear. A chasm of years instantly plummeted between us. What he witnessed in my life now would be a distant memory for him in his own sixties and seventies, and I was helping to lay the foundations for the wisdom he might someday pass on to his own much younger loved ones. What would Jimmy be like as an old man? Surely beautiful, gentle, and beloved. "We know about you," he now said, beautifully and gently. "Uncle Joe told you: You can do this. And I tell you: you're not afraid of anything."

"I'm the world's premier coward," I said. "Everything terrifies me."

"No. You're not afraid of anything. You'll live to be a brave funny wise old man. Plus you'll have All the Cuteness of Dino…"

"No, he'll be old by then, too."

"But never as old as you." He pressed his forehead tighter to mine and then released me. "Oh, little godfather o' mine." When had he taken on that cooing tone? For months now, he had spoken to me more and more as if I were the most cunning koala bear on a Qantas poster. "You can do this. And because you can do it, so can I."

In an instant, I felt fear drain out of parts of me where I hadn't even noticed it: joints and sinews suddenly relaxing, almost stinging and glowing with refreshment, as though a citrony disinfectant had been pumped through me, or bleaching sunlight. I wanted to run down the stairs and wake Connie to tell her that I'd decided to live.

"'Who is Jimmy,'" I sang, barely breathing, "'what is he?'"

He smiled; he'd played the song for me more than once… both of them, actually, the Schubert and the Quilter.

"Where are my damn garlands?" he asked, bridling. I wanted to look over my shoulder and make Joe join me in exclaiming over how big our boy was, how the purple little raisin we had cradled was now the support of our old age and a source of joy and laughter. I missed Joe desperately. Jimmy's smile faded as he watched me, and his eyes were imploring, as if I were the strong one.

"Because you can, so can I," he repeated.

I woke up to the sound of Joe downstairs talking to my cat Griselda while preparing her breakfast. He and I had returned to Baltimore together from Rehoboth only two days before. We had this one week together in my tiny house to see how we got along, before he flew back to LA, perhaps to consider moving in with me permanently. Small as it was, the house was still twice the size of the studio at the beach where we'd spent our first ten days together. There was a luxurious spaciousness in lolling abed while my new love spoke to my pet from as far away as a hundred feet. The dog Ootch was still curled up on the bed with me. He was content to have me back on the job after my two weeks away, and he had welcomed Joe with his usual willingness to make a new friend. As usual, too, he was stretching enough in his sleep at times that I thought I might have to get up to give him more room.

"Who is that who's meowing so?" I heard Joe chanting. "It is not Brigitte Bardot..." There was a moment's pause while he thought of a rhyme. I had already gotten used to this poetic form of his invention which I was already calling Annoying Quatrains for Kitty, with seven-syllable lines and an AAAA rhyme scheme, featuring the same rhyme word in verses one and four. I was pretty sure that the fourth line that morning would be something like, "It's our cat who's meowing so." After less than forty-eight hours in my home, Joe knew that I would be riveted with curiosity about the unfolding of the improvisation, with the third line being the point of maximum suspense: what could rhyme with "so" and "Bardot"? He waited several seconds while I listened to the clink of the fork stirring hot water into the food in Griselda's bowl. I was afraid to breathe and miss it. "It is not *le Père Goriot*..."

"Oh, for God's sake!" I called out, swinging my feet to the floor and getting ready to run down the stairs and kiss him. Ootch leapt down from the bed and did his best downward-dog stretch before wagging his tail so hard that he wobbled from stem to stern. He was suddenly reminded of Joe's existence and clearly couldn't wait to see him. I knew the day was coming, soon, when he would trot downstairs adoringly with Joe every morning and leave me alone in bed.

"Your mom left a message," Joe said after we'd hugged, for all the world as if we hadn't seen each other for weeks, whereas in fact we'd been making love barely an hour before. "She says she can't wait to meet me."

His smile was complacent but not entirely confident. He knew that most people liked him, but he was apprehensive about meeting my mother. Despite reassurances from Walter, Ricardo, and Marie, he had formed an image of her as a country club snob, and was afraid that she would think he was low-class. He had wondered aloud if she knew anyone else from Brooklyn, and if I thought she was "ready" for him. For that matter, he was also nervous about whether Dominic and Connie would "get" me. He worried that we were too different, that our worlds might not mingle. Mom was a WASP for sure, with perfect taste – or at least, taste which I considered perfect because she had passed it on to me intact – and a long list of genteel prohibitions, things one did and did not do, and things not to be discussed at the dinner table. She also prided herself on being a bit kooky, though, and she was very independent in her widowhood, one of the most open-minded people I knew. Joe and I were scheduled to go down to dinner at her house in suburban Virginia the following night. Joe took some courage from knowing that Walter and Ricardo and Marie would be there as well, though Marie had warned him that he had to be on his best behavior with Mom. Marie loved her, and the two of them often formed a female voting bloc of two in my social circle.

Mom's and Joe's entire future relationship was set within ten minutes of our arrival. Her constitutional discretion had kept her from ever verbalizing what she must have known about my deep love for Tony, who was her undisputed favorite among my friends from our freshman year. She did know, however, and had said more than once (gently, in the earliest years, because even without words she understood how I felt for him) that he was destined to be with Rachel, in every sense, for life. She had fretted that that might leave no one for me. There was a vibrant gay erotic energy about Joe that I thought she might find unnerving, but what she picked up on was the Nice Italian Boy. I could also feel him relaxing. Face to face, he found her honest, funny, and endearing, as all my friends had from childhood on. He was polite to the brink of gallantry with her, deferring to her, zealous for her comfort, treating her like someone famous and important. It was a bit like his crush on Rachel. In years to come, I would hear him tell his friends and co-workers, or strangers on airplanes for that matter, that his mother-in-law had been "all class" and "a very great lady"; once, I even overheard him telling someone that she was "a saint." At this first meeting, she had him sit to her right at dinner. She patted his forearm, leaned in to listen to his tales of life in LA, exclaimed over his hot-off-the-presses ad as the Pennington Man, made him the main audience of her zany anecdotes about her work in social services, and giggled at his jokes.

About the third time he mentioned his mother, Mom said,

"If your parents ever visit you in Baltimore..." (and then she hesitated, realizing that we didn't even know yet if Joe and I would stay together long enough for that to happen) "...I hope you'll find a way to bring them down here. They sound enchanting."

"I think all Andreolis must be enchanting," said Ricardo. "You know we're all in love with Joe already." Mom smiled at him. "I told Walter that we'll keep Joe, whatever Jim decides." He turned to Walter for corroboration; Walter, as he always did, nodded.

"Basically Jim gets no vote in this," Marie chimed in.

Joe was smiling shyly under the barrage of affirmation. Mom caught my eye now and gave me one of the subtle smiles by which she communicated her most important secret messages. There was one that could stop any child in mid-utterance, another to remind us to hold back on seconds until guests had been served, and one – this one – that said we had just done exactly the right thing but that she was too much of a lady to brag about us in front of company.

As we were leaving, she gave Joe her hand, but he suddenly pulled her in and hugged her.

"I am *so* happy to meet you," she said. "I hope to see you again... soon, often, often..." She added this last tag on the spur of the moment;

it was her verbal equivalent of the hug he had just given her. Then, as she hugged me, harder than usual, she whispered, "Oh, I *like* him. A most... *amiable* young man!" She smiled at her own archaism, finding it perhaps still a bit awkward to frame words of approval for her son's male lover. Her tone recalled something of the praise she had lavished on Tony after the first time I introduced them. I knew things with Joe would be OK, at least as far as Mom was concerned.

On the drive home up I-95, Joe and I talked about my trip to LA, not yet scheduled but supposed to take place within the month. I had been there before, to interview for a teaching job at USC, and I had some satirical points to score.

"They were trying to woo me as a hoity-toity East Coast snob, so they drove me around on a tour of cool old architecture. There was a 50s hot dog stand shaped like a giant concrete hot dog, and a 40s record store shaped like a giant concrete record player, and I think a beauty parlor shaped like a giant concrete hair dryer... Thank God there wasn't an old Hollywood sex shop; I mean, would it have been maybe a giant concrete...?"

Joe chuckled but didn't sound especially amused. I had to remind myself that he loved LA and would be sorry to leave it, if it came to that. He looked out his window.

"You think I'm flim-flam," he said a minute later. "You think I'm some plastic bimbo." I glanced over at him. He didn't look actually distressed.

"No," I said. "You live in the land of plastic bimbos, that's all. You need more Beaux Arts in your life. More Victorian Gothic. More Italianate brownstones."

"More Italianate professors, really; that's what I need in my life." He leaned over and kissed my cheek. Instantly my hands on the wheel felt slightly slick. I wanted to reach over and grab him.

"Wait till we get home. Really." It felt almost dangerous to be driving while feeling the assault of desire and affection. The twenty miles of highway left before us seemed an impossible, endless postponement of what I – we – needed that second.

Hours later, Joe was sleeping next to me. Our foreheads barely touched, and with every murmuring inhalation of his I could feel an exquisite increase in the pressure there. His eyes flickered under his closed lids. The windows were open to the balmy summer air, and the buzzes and chirrups of the Baltimore night made a soft lullaby. There was enough light coming from the street that the planes of Joe's face were in sharp relief. He was smiling in his sleep. In that moment he was something I seldom thought him, before or after: simply the most beautiful man I had ever seen. His face, relaxed, serene, yet still taut, was exactly right in every possible way. Goodness, gentleness, wisdom, power, and plain humble humanity radiated from him. I could feel my throat tighten with love and gratitude. It was an undeserved gift to me that he consented to be next to me in such trust and modesty. I didn't see how I was to wait till daybreak for him to open his magical green eyes again, and the need to see them was almost irresistible. I could have justified waking him up just for that, and I knew he would have laughed indulgently if I had. But I also felt the strong duty to protect him, to watch over his rest, as if I had taken a sacred vow to shield this demigod, this angel, this child. It was my life's work to stave off all the harms that clustered and prowled around us. I barely recognized the person I was in that moment. I could feel wellsprings of kindness and generosity in myself, a capacity for sacrifice, a wish to be good and noble, a belief that I might be. I wanted to meet Joe's mother that instant, to tell her what I was feeling, to promise her that I would be that person for him.

When the sun was high enough that I got up to close the shutters, Joe rolled over and opened his eyes. I lay back down beside him, and looked at him, stammering, and he smiled and hooked an arm around my neck. Once my head was on his shoulder I saw that no words from me were needed.

"Funny dream I had," he mumbled. I wondered if it was the dream I'd watched him having. "Something about a road." He stretched and then relaxed back against me. "Yeah… we were in this weird little sports car driving through the desert." I nodded. "No, sometimes it was two cars, side by side. Like little bumper cars in an amusement park. Then they'd be just one car again for a while." I could picture it exactly; surely this had been the dream which pressed us closer together each time he breathed.

"I love the image of us traveling together," I said. He made a little hum of agreement. He pulled back for a moment, just long enough for our eyes to meet. In the dim, cool room, fragrant with summer, his eyes were like green marble, dark, ancient, precious. They were the kindest eyes in the world. He knew me and loved me. I felt my life pause, then take its place, fixed and unshakeable, a rock. My mouth was as dry as the desert we were driving through.

"Jimmy," he whispered, with a tiny, shamanic smile, "this is going to work."

FINIS

Also by John C. McLucas:

Dialogues on the Beach, BrickHouse Books, 2017